THEY IS US

Also by Tama Janowitz:

Area Code 212 (non-fiction)
Peyton Amberg
A Certain Age
Hear That? (for children; illustrated by Tracy Dockray)
By the Shores of Gitchee Gumee
The Male Cross-dresser Support Group
A Cannibal in Manhattan
Slaves of New York
American Dad

THEY IS US

A cautionary horror story

Tama Janowitz

*Including special supplementary material
'Lonely Bob' by Willow Hunt*

The Friday Project
An imprint of HarperCollins *Publishers*
77–85 Fulham Palace Road
Hammersmith, London W6 8JB
www.thefridayproject.co.uk
www.harpercollins.co.uk

Limited edition hardback first published by The Friday Project in 2008
This paperback edition published by The Friday Project in 2009

A catalogue record for this book
is available from the British Library

ISBN 978-1-906321-30-7

Typeset by Mac Style, Beverley, East Yorkshire

Printed and bound in Great Britain by
Clays Ltd, St Ives plc

To Fay Weldon and Nick Fox

"We have met the enemy and he is us."

Walt Kelly, poster caption for World Earth Day, 1973

The Small Loaf of an Artist in Society

Two chihuahuas have tiny pillowcases
pulled over their heads with holes
cut out for eyes and noses.
Are they members of the Ku Klux Klan?

We do not know. Only, they must be
itchy in this warm dampness,
this summer sprinkled with peppery
flies over the ash can of our lives.

What has blighted the stout cart-
puller, the homebody, the watch cur,
Beware of the Dog, a sign
leading to reticence in strangers.

All is changed, deranged and gone,
even slouches have a political
roll to fill. This is not a country
for old schnauzers or dull doubters

who muddle and fiddle and refuse
to remember the name of the street
they live on simply because they've
changed address once too often

and their furniture grows
molds and fungi in a warehouse
in Walla-Walla Washington. Changes!
Get used to them! Some young rabble

rouser keeps yelling in the parking
lot on Twenty-Third street, where
the organ grinder used to play
O sole Mio just beneath the windows

of our mansion and his monkey tipped
his hat in mock thanks for the penny
that we threw him, although he cavorted
on hollyhocks and crushed petunias in

our Moorish garden, but it's too late
for giving an artist advice, who
having taken on the guise (gorge
and hackles) of a purebred dalmatian,
is polymorphous perverse now, indeed
always has been.

Phyllis Janowitz

1

Years pass. There are still thimbles and Unitarians. The world is the same as it has always been, maybe a little worse. It's a beautiful summer day, kind of, although violent electrical storms are predicted for later – if not that day, then sometime. And the news, too, is much the same: 40 percent of people can't sleep; a type of bustard believed to be extinct has been found; war continues.

Slawa is still out there, painting the driveway with black glop. Why did he have to wear his white high-heels? The fool, he's going to ruin them. Now he's using his knife to open a second gallon of the stuff. Murielle could easily run him over, but he moves out of the way. She is taking Julie to look for a summer job.

Julie wants to help at the old age home her mother manages, but Murielle says no. Her mother prefers her older sister, Tahnee. Tahnee is fourteen. Tahnee is too lazy to work. Murielle doesn't seem to mind this, even though she is determined that Julie, who is only thirteen, should do something. First she tells Julie to look up the job listings, but there's nothing Julie is qualified for except maybe at the Blue Booby Club as a cocktail waitress or stripper if she lies about her age.

Murielle drives Julie and tells her to go in by herself. Julie is scared. It is dark after the bright outside, the gloom of mid-afternoon in a strip club that reeks of beer with a fainter odor of bleach. At first the manager seems interested. "Show me your tits," he says, but Julie doesn't move. "How old are you, hon, anyway?"

Her mother has said she should lie, but Julie is nervous. She forgets. She looks away.

"What about any interesting deformities?"

"No," says Julie. What if he wants to hire her? "I'm only thirteen."

If she had extra breasts – or was a hermaphrodite, or at least a young boy – but these days, times are tough, who wants to watch a normal girl?

"Come back in a few years," he says. "Or, if you want, we got a wet t-shirt contest once a month, top prizes in the juvenile category."

She is so relieved she could cry. Her life is going to go on and on, frightening her. She does not want to be frightened by her own life, but there it is, lounging ominously before her, one paw tapping its sharp claws on the pavement just ahead. She goes back to the car and tells her mother there was no work for her.

"How old did you say you were?" her mother asks.

"Um... I said I was seventeen?"

"Julie, it's not just that you're plain; it's your attitude. Nobody would want to hire someone who seems sulky. You could have made some good money this summer," says Murielle. "At least you're not flat-chested like your sister. That's one thing you have going for you." She feels cruel as she says this but with a kid like Julie it's better to be blunt.

Julie thinks she will never find work. But at last Murielle gets her a job in a lab, thanks to her friend Dyllis. "Julie, make sure you do whatever Dyllis tells you," her mother says as she drops off Julie in front of the Bermese Pythion building. "I'll be back at four-fifteen to pick you up."

Her mother leaves her at the far end of the parking lot. Julie is sweltering by the time she gets to the main door. In the lobby of the vast complex the security guard sweeps an electronic brush over her before she is allowed in. Once she is scanned, her microchip will be altered and she won't have to do this again, the guard says. Her mom's friend Dyllis is waiting for her beyond the gates, buck-toothed, attractive. Even though she has always known Dyllis, Julie is still frightened at the idea of starting work.

"Ai, eet's so hot today, you know what I mean?" Dyllis has a high-pitched voice and slightly buggy, wild eyes. "Sometimes, I jes' look around and I think, what I am doing here? In Vieques, yes, it's hot, but we have trees, palm trees, you got your coconut trees, when it's a nice day you go to the beach... Here, you got no trees, everything dead. Tell me, when was the last time you saw a bird or any living creature?"

Dyllis grew up just around the block from Murielle, but two years on Vieques – the small island that was part of Puerto Rico where she worked for a government laboratory – has left her with a strong Puerto Rican accent.

"How is your mother doing, you tell her let's get together this weekend, okay?" she says as they walk down the long, windowless corridor. The black granite walls and floors are flecked with embedded chips resembling glittery stars; the only light is from the artificial ones above. Murielle has told Julie that Dyllis was able to get a good job back in the States as a lab technician with Bermese Python only because she smuggled genetic material out of the lab when she left Puerto Rico.

There appears to be no one else around. The hall is lined on both sides with many doors of different colors. "You see, each color is for a different security level. You going to be working level three, that's pretty important level. Later I got to make you sign a confidentiality form. And these are my labs."

Dyllis is in charge of six or eight of the laboratories, each housing a different experiment in progress. Canary mice: they can sing like little birds, which is a problem if they escape and breed; they sing all night. Black-and-yellow striped fish hang from the ceiling on invisible threads. "These are clownfish-cross-spider, we call them spiderfish. You see, they don't need no water, they spin a thread and they catch the flies, you want me to show you?"

She opens a box and releases four fist-sized flies, seemingly too large to get off the ground, but they hover in the air. "I call these SloMoFlies."

"Yuck. They look like flying raisins." The flies are creepy. And the fish, too, are somehow wrong. In formation, as a school, the fish on the threads lunge for the flies, then weave longer threads to lower themselves as the flies circle. When the flies go up, so do the fish, pulling in their threads.

"You see, I gotta do some more testing first, but if they interbred with regular flies, a lot of people going to buy them, they going to know after a while all the flies going to be real slow. Plus, they supposed to eat clothes that are out of style. But right now, nothing is going well. These flies, when you kill one, it makes a terrible mess."

A web of words: **J a N u A r y y y Y y y** or **J u u u uuuu u u ly** linger in the room, blocking the windows and doors; there is no escape. Dyllis is a talker, the words never seem to stop. Trails of letters spin constantly through the air around her head, forming a virtual wall.

Dyllis stops to take a breath, it is almost as if she has to fight to clear a space for herself in the middle of all these words.

"What?" Julie is confused.

"Now, over here, this is something cute, right?" Dyllis points to a cage containing feathered rabbits. The feathers are downy, pink and blue. "Later on, I'll give you one."

What Julie doesn't say is that she already has a feather-covered rabbit at home. Years before, she had come exploring with her sister. At that time the vast grounds where the labs are located weren't yet fenced in. There were still trees back then. That was when they found their dog Breakfast and the rabbit; they had been tossed out with the garbage and managed to escape. Both were almost dead and had to be nursed back to health – surely that couldn't have been stealing?

"Anyway," she says, looking at the fluffy bunny, "won't you get in trouble?"

"I'm jes' gonna tell them, it die, a lot of these animals die, and they know that. But don't tell no one, hokay? I put him in your backpack, just before you go home."

Julie doesn't know what to say. She can't accept stolen property, even if it means the animal will be killed or tortured… or can she? She has never had to contend with this degree of ethics. Of course she will take the bunny home, even though her mother has said, No More Pets! She supposes she can sneak it in.

"Lemme show you something." Dyllis takes Julie down the hall to the Women's Room. A window – the only exterior one Julie has seen – looks out into a dumpster surrounded by a tall cinderblock wall. The refuse bin is filled with animals, either dead or dying. Even through the closed window the stench is terrible, and a few things down there are still wriggling.

"Oh, this is awful. What can we do, aren't some of them still alive?"

4

"If you don't take Mister Bunny… that's where he gonna end up. Oh, sheet!" Dyllis lets out a shriek. "Look at this, somebody tossed out my experiment, can you believe that?" Over by the sink is a pot of dry dirt containing a plant with only two leaves covered with what appears to be human skin; beneath the skin Julie can see veins and arteries. "This plant disappeared, like, two weeks ago, I thought maybe my boss, he took it to decorate his office. I no want to say nothing. But now I am thinking someone took it to kill it. Jes' look."

"Is it dead?" Julie says.

"I dunno. Needs water, anyway." Dyllis shakes her head in disgust. "I mean, who would have done this, I had the plant in my window!"

Tenderly Julie strokes the leaves of the dying **common house plant** and places it under the trickling tap; the veins – if that's what they are – flush and weakly pulse. The plant is slurping up water, she can sense its gratitude. To hurt anything – some nights she can't sleep, thinking of how wretched it must be to be an ant, with people around who actually like to crush them.

"Let's go back in – I'll show you the rest of the animals and their food."

"Um… okay. Sure! Great. So, um, Dyllis, you invented all this stuff?"

"Oh, jes, and if I had my own lab I could have made a fortune. But I work for the company, which is not so bad – they give me good health insurance. So come on, let me show you the kitchen area. Here's where you have to prepare the different kinds of food." Dyllis opens a refrigerator. "To keep everybody happy, put the different things on each little plate. But some days you can chop everything and mix it, whatever, just so it looks attractive. Now, we gonna go feed some toads." She puts the plates on a wheeled cart and off they go.

The room is very hot and dry, so dry that for a moment Julie's lungs feel seared. "This room, we gotta keep it like a desert." Dyllis points to a row of glass tanks. "Don't ever touch the animals in them, they are puffball toad, a cross of puffball mushroom and toad. When they get scared, poof, they let out a cloud of spores, get you right in the face. I heard we going to try to get in the anthrax gene next, so when they puff out, they blow out anthrax spores. It's interesting, no?" Dyllis opens the tops to each tank and carefully lowers the plates to the sandy floor. Julie thinks she will never be able to arrange the food so beautifully, topped with parsley and the wriggling mealworms in a circle around the edge. "They eat the compost, too, that's because they have the mushroom gene."

When Julie was little she helped her father in his shop on Saturdays. There was always the rich smell of leather, or leather cleaner, of glue and something fecund. Maybe he had a mushroom gene, unbeknownst to her. She has been ignoring her father for so long, years, really, maybe since she turned ten or eleven, wrinkling her nose at his beery stench and cleaning-fluid breath. Poor Daddy with his winky bald spot and big proud belly; where is he now? Anything she dislikes about him is forgotten; how she misses him. Why doesn't she spend more time with him? She will be nicer to him from now on.

In Room 1829.wTd are animals that are sort of... pigs. But they are like no pictures of pigs Julie has ever seen, with human arms and legs, some too fat to be supported by such slender appendages who lie on their sides delicately putting biscuits in their mouths with their... Yuck, they look like big thumbs? Hands with nothing but thumbs? No, it is just that their fingers are half-trotters. The pigs have rilled snouts, small eyes fringed with pale white lashes, pink gigantic torsos; what is wrong with them? Julie doesn't want to ask but Dyllis tells her anyway. "You see, these pigs, they got human parts, so we can transplant what we need."

"But how many human parts do they have?"

"It's not so much as a number, these are only first generation, so it's fifty-fifty. In other words, we mix the pig sperm with the woman egg and implant in the sow."

Some pigs look as if they have worked out, done sit-ups, pull-ups and developed muscular biceps, legs with toned calves, ripped thighs. Even so, human arms are not strong enough to support the weight of a full-grown boar. Supine and languorous, unable to stand, occasionally feeding themselves with those odd hands, the pigs lie in the heat, yawning, bored. "These little piggies love to get a manicure!" says Dyllis when Julie stares, slightly alarmed at a pig's red fingernails. "If you want, when you have extra time, I got some extra polish in my desk, they so cute when they see the polish and make their little squeals!"

A boar – overweight, grayish with bristles – is gently fondling himself. He has a corkscrew-shaped penis. He looks up at Julie and starts to rub faster. Julie doesn't like the way he looks at her with a smirking leer while he plays with himself. She averts her gaze. Julie wishes now she had lied about her age to get the job in the strip club; by comparison this is much worse.

"Hey, cut that out!" Dyllis says to the pig. "We working now on how to transplant the male organ. Some guy going to be mighty lucky, if we can figure out how to avoid rejection."

Apart from the job, summer passes slowly. Here there isn't much for kids to do: in her neighborhood is the petrochemical swamp, and the local nuclear plant and the waste disposal system of Bermese Python Technologies. Here there are building materials determined to be hazardous to one's health, deposits (man-made) of chemicals or radioactive substances with a half-life of a hundred thousand years.

Somehow everyone who lives in this neighborhood or grew up here has something wrong. They blame the chemical swamp and the crematorium, the high-voltage power lines overhead and the airport nearby. Then there is the pollution from the highway, carbon monoxide, the hulks of cars leaking oil and gas and transmission fluid.

Even at the lab, mostly, the work Julie is given is depressing, not only because she doesn't know the purpose of any of the experiments (which all seem pointless) but also because of the pervasive misery. Some of her job is cleaning cages, feeding the animals, and one day, going into the pig stall with a platter of bananas (some of the pigs have been listless, not eating, and it is hoped this will tempt their appetites, which is a bit rough on Julie since she herself has never eaten a real banana, only reproductions) by accident the door to the pen swings open and the big boar, leering, comes after her. She screams and runs to the door and out into the hall but the pig is after her and gets out of the room. He is slow but has mean little tusks and gets her backed into a corner when her screams are finally overheard.

A security guard with a cattle prod scurries down the hall and jabs her a couple of times with the electrified device before he finally gets the pig subdued; the pig has both arms around her neck and whether he is about to strangle her or kiss her she never has a chance to learn.

The security guard is yelling at her in Spanish when Dyllis comes running down the hall. Julie is crying with humiliation. "I'm sorry," she says. Frightened, embarrassed, scared at having been the subject of the pig's sexual interest.

"What's he saying?" she asks Dyllis when the guard, still blabbing angrily, leads away the pig.

"What?" says Dyllis.

"What's he saying? I never learned Spanish."

"Ah, I'm not sure. He is angry, though, I theenk!"

"I know, but..." It occurs to Julie: Dyllis doesn't actually speak or understand Spanish. All she has is a Spanish accent.

After this incident she is told not to go into the room with the pigs anymore. Instead she is given a lot of agar plates into which she has to pipette exact quantities of substances she has been told must never get into her mouth. Sometimes she stains slides, or counts various living organisms under a microscope. Even though the organisms are infinitely small, they do not, mostly, appear very nice – most of them spend their whole lives destroying, or trying to destroy, others.

And yet there are creatures, such as the spiderfish, she loves. When she comes into the room they all swoop down to her eagerly and twirl around her head as if they are carousel animals.

What if her whole life continues this way – the animals, always hungry, for food, for light, for air – nothing could help any of them, herself included, to escape. Here are these animals, these animals that are wrong – herself as well. Just wrong, and they know it and suffer, with their extra body parts or human limbs that were never meant to blend. And she is guilty of not being able to feel compassion for them, but only disgust, despite how sorrowfully they regard her and plead with their terrible saucer eyes.

Toward the end of summer, one afternoon her dad comes to pick her up. She is surprised to see him. Somehow their paths haven't crossed in months, he is up and out before she is awake and gets back when she is already asleep. Usually she meets her mom outside in front; she can't figure out how her dad has gotten past security. "Dad! What are you doing here? How did you get in?"

"What you mean? I walked in, it took long time to find you."

Then she realizes he got in because he looks like one of the workers – a janitor or electrician, whatever – and she hopes she hasn't hurt his feelings. Even though he has lived in this country for a long long time, he still doesn't really get it. Why couldn't she have had the sort of father who wore a suit and did something respectable, instead of a shoe repair shop? He is so proud it's his own, doesn't he see how sad that is? Just thinking about it, her eyes fill with tears.

"So, Yulenka, show me around, I want to see what you have been doing all summer."

As if things aren't bad enough, her father is even more tenderhearted than she. The flies, the ones that Dyllis calls SloMoFlies, Julie has moved into an unused glass tank the size of a closet; it is her job to clean the tank each day without letting any of them escape. Every few days she puts rank slabs of old meat and dirty clothes into the tank. This is so disgusting, each time she thinks she is going to barf. The flies fly slowly – and they are so big! The air in the tank is stale and hot – and she hates the strange sound they make, a kind of gleeful buzzing hiss! They land all over her, it feels as if they are stinging, even though she knows they can't, and afterwards she can't help but scratch and scratch.

But her dad takes to them right away, and it really is peculiar how the whole swarm flies over to the side of the glass in unison and stare at him. Some have green eyes and some have blue, eyes the size of thumbnails. Her father has a puzzled expression. "What you do with these?" he asks.

"Um, not much. I'm in charge of cleaning up their tank and feeding them; it really creeps me out, Dad, the smell is so bad and they look at me kind of mean –"

"Cage is dirty. I clean for you."

"Thanks, Daddy, but I don't actually have to do it until tomorrow." Her father is usually so gruff, this is all surprising.

"Is nothing. I will do it." He opens the door and goes in. The flies land on his head and shoulders, she can't help but think they are licking him. On second look she sees they are wiping themselves on him, cat-like, at least so it appears, and her dad has a kind of blissful look on his face, what Miss Fletsum in school calls "the find-your-bliss look".

There are still a few on him when he comes out of the tank. He opens his jacket pocket and gestures. "Moushkas, come, my little moushkas." More promptly than trained dogs, the flies, five or six of them, go in. "Yu-Yu, they are telling me, they want fruits and a little fish. They are not meat-eating flies but mostly fruit flies. And some of them they say are becoming wery sick."

"Whatever, Dad. They're just flies. And I have to do what I'm told, it's, like, a special diet or something."

"All living creatures –"

"I know, I know. I love animals, too, Dad, it's just that, I dunno."

"What?"

"Something about them – they like you, they don't like me. Besides, I think Dyllis said they were engineered with some kind of cold virus or something, some marker so they could spread disease? I can't remember what she says. Anyway it looks like you're covered with snot. I mean, look!"

Her father glances down at the slimy trails that have been left by the flies, and shrugs.

"Anyway, if you say so, Daddy, I'll try to sneak some fruit in there once in a while. But the ones in your jacket – you're going to put them back in the tank, right?"

"No, no, don't vorry. These flies, they say, they come with me, and tomorrow, more are born, ends up same number." He is the only person who could treasure flies. Her poor father, who is there who treasures him?

"Oh, Daddy, I do love you so much," says Julie, and clasps her father around his stomach, while overhead the flies circle in their stately, slow procession.

2

Murielle stands at the window staring at Slawa with hatred. How long has she been standing there? She has no idea. Sometimes, glancing at her watch, she finds ten hours have elapsed, when it seems twenty minutes; conversely, it feels like ninety minutes have passed but the reality is only a quarter of an hour has gone by. She sees now she should have been taking out her anger on Slawa, not on poor Julie, even though the kid does drive her nuts.

Tahnee switches stations from the kitchen keyboard. She has been using the computer. There is no way to switch off the big screen entirely, or they would have to call the company to be reconnected. It's easier just to leave it on all the time. "Ma, can I go look for my dad this weekend?" she says. "I think I might have a clue."

"You can just forget that," Murielle says bitterly and then adds, in a gentler tone, "I don't know why you would ever want to find your father, he's never sent a dime for you. Anyway, I already told you, we have to go to Grandpa's, I need your help."

Tahnee shrugs. "But Mommy dear, you have Julie to help. Besides, this time it's a genuine lead."

Another time she might have been more lenient, but right now everything is irritating Murielle. "So what do you think will happen if you do find Terry? He'll probably try and convince you to sell his Diamond-C dust to your schoolmates. I know him. He's no good, Tahnee. I told you, forget it, you can go look maybe when you're older."

"I don't want to go to Grandpa's, Mom. It is so boring. Can I at least stay here?"

"Alone? Yeah, right. Forget it." Now Tahnee is looking sullen, Murielle feels a bit frightened. "If you come with me to help at Grandpa's, I'll take you shopping after. If you stay for the day."

A car pulls up at the end of the driveway – the mother of Julie's rinky-dink girlfriend, who is going to take the two girls and her own kids to the public pool for the day.

"Moommm! Mom!" A shriek the pitch of which must date to early hominid: "Maaaa!" Tahnee yells, a sour Acadian howl. "Mom! I can't find my merkin – and I need it for the pool!"

Julie comes up from the basement. She hopes her mother won't go down while she is gone. Her mother doesn't know just how many pets she has there. She has been fussing with her pets, trying to move them to different cages, but she is running out of space. All summer all her animals have been reproducing.

Even during her days off, all she does is clean cages and it is her own fault, kind of. The pink rabbit she brought home from work mated with the blue rabbit she already owned and now there are six feathered babies, cute, though one has three ears, only two of which are normal size.

Finally the lost merkin is found, or another substituted, and the kids depart. "Bye-bye, Mom!" says Tahnee, grabbing her towel.

"Byeeee!" says Julie, swathed head to toe in her thick ultra-protective V-ray-stopper swimming costume. "See ya later!"

"Bye!" Murielle yells back. She is just about to step on a cockroach when she realizes it has a red dot. "Oh, hi, Greg," she says. "Sorry about that." She doesn't know if the roach waves one leg at her, or just in general. Either way, it's hard to care! Murielle can't imagine why Tahnee is still anxious to find her father. She has told her older daughter for years how miserable Terry was to her. Terry is not Julie's father. Just after Tahnee was born, Terry left and it wasn't long before she met Slawa.

When Slawa and Murielle first met, Slawa was a limo driver – car service, actually – exotic, kind, of a spiritual nature – who gave her a ride from Newark. It turned out that Slawa's wife Alga, who was much older than he and suffered from reeTVO.9, was a resident of the nursing home that Murielle managed.

The coincidence seemed remarkable: fate. After Alga died, they married. But somewhere along the line Slawa had changed from a man who rescued her, a single woman with a kid, into a fat Russian slob who worked in a shoe repair shop.

Murielle slams the screen door. When she was married to Terry, Tahnee's father, and Terry wanted to make Diamond-C dust in the bathroom to sell, she wouldn't let him, which was one reason why they split up; now in retrospect she thinks, but at least he didn't drink.

Of course, if Terry had been caught by the law for selling Diamond-C dust, all of their property would have been confiscated, even the things that were in her name. Tahnee would have been sent into foster care. Murielle's struggles to survive, her desertion by Terry just after Tahnee was born; it means nothing to Tahnee. Tahnee would end up doing what she wanted. There has to be a way, some way, to keep Tahnee with her for a while longer. She loves that kid so much. Who would have thought her own daughter would have ended up being the love of her life?

Even so, Murielle knows there is something wrong with Tahnee. Her dead, pale eyes, white hair, white skin; but that isn't it. Other people are mesmerized by her, but not really in a positive way. They become nervous, upset. Frightened? Murielle has never figured out what it is, exactly. Tahnee has a certain cat-like indifference to people and things.

Despite this, she loves Tahnee much more than Julie, whom she almost always wants to slap. It takes major control not to. Julie's eager, earnest face, plain and scared – how is she going to get through the rest of her life unless she toughens up?

"Make sure you put on plenty of sunscreen!" she calls, hoping the girls can still hear. "Otherwise you're going to fry!" It isn't that the sun is particularly bright – there is a reddish haze in the sky – but Tahnee is so fair, virtually albino and at fourteen years old almost five eleven, all endless insect leg-and-arm stalks which only burn. Julie has brown hair, more normal color, but prone to prickly heat, rashes, asthma. The kids have never been all that healthy but it is probably from growing up around this polluted marshland.

From the window where she stands, Murielle can see the bald spot on Slawa's head. He is *still* painting the drive. How long could it take? And, how stupid to wear a swirly yellow MUU-MUU. Yellow has never been his colour, he looks sallow.

Murielle has taken to making him sleep in a tent in the yard, the flies around him are so constant and offensive. When she goes after them with a fly swatter, he shouts at her, saying to leave them alone. That is so warped. If she ignores him, and actually smashes one, it is so huge that fly intestines – or whatever it is inside them – splatter everywhere and are almost impossible to wipe off, more like paint than guts.

Now Slawa is on his knees, facing the house and looks as if he's about to topple over. It is a hot, airless day and the smell of car exhaust, burnt rubber, an ashiness that might be from the power plant – sour uranium? Bug poison? The crematorium? – blows over the marsh and through the screen door next to Murielle.

Beyond Slawa, across the road, is another house just like theirs: a white one and a half story ranch house with attached garage, a plate glass window next to the front door.

In this neighborhood no one ever uses their front doors, even though each house has a concrete walkway leading to two or three steps, planted on either side with plastic trees. What is the point of the front entrance, as if – someday – someone grand and important will arrive, who must enter through the main door and not the servant's entryway?

It's ridiculous, the development is nearly sixty years old but no one important has ever come to pay a visit, there are no front parlors, there is no life inside or out.

Two or three blocks down is the marsh, what is left of it. The chemical seepage can be smelled – more or less – round the clock. It stings the eyes. Slawa has an empty beer bottle next to the metal pail of driveway blacking, or whatever the stuff is. In a minute he will be in to get a fresh bottle. He is stout, with a big gut. He looks older than his years, although she's not quite sure how old he is; he has never bothered with the skin treatments and injections even little kids know about from school. How could he let himself go like this? He used to be cute!

He comes up the stairs holding his empty beer bottle. "Any more?" he says.

"How should I know? Look in the fridge."

"All the time like this, Murielle. Why you so angry all the time?"

"Go," she says. "I think you should go before the girls get back."

"What?"

"You heard me. I've had it. I want you to move out."

"But... I don't understand."

"What is there not to understand? I can't stay married to you any more! We're over! Finished! D-I-V-O-R –"

"What will you tell the girls?" he says. "Anyway, at least I want to finish the driveway first."

"Just forget the driveway. The way this dump looks, that's the least of it. I'll tell them... you had to go away for a while, on business. Shoe business. You can call them tonight if you want."

"Hey," he says. He is breathing heavily now and for a second she thinks he is going to hit her with the bottle. The big gut swings heavily. He's practically pregnant. His legs and arms are scrawny, though. He has an alcoholic's jug belly, under that flowing MUU-MUU. He must think the MUU-MUU hides his tummy. "Do you mind if I shower and change first?"

She guesses he is trying to sound sarcastic. "Can't you do that when you check into a motel?"

"I'm paying the fucking mortgage on this place, I can sleep here if I want. Why don't you get out and take Tahnee with you and I'll stay here with Julie?"

"We've been through this a million times, Slawa. Let's not have another scene. Take a shower if you must. Just don't leave your towels on the floor."

He goes muttering up the stairs. "I'm supposed to paint the driveway and then move out covered with tar to check into a Motel 99." He curses in Russian. Once she might have found this sexy. Now she knows he is saying that he wants to kill her. When his murderous rages strike,

Slawa is like an elephant in musth, blood-eyed, uncontrollable. Then, in English, he adds, "Stupid cow, what makes you think I have to go to a motel? There are other places I can go. You think you are the only woman out there? Many womens say to me, Slawa, you are handsome, you are so kind."

She doesn't bother to answer. It is true that to some he might still be attractive, if you are into tiger-eyed, slap-you-around, rough-trade, peasant-type Slavs.

There is only one bathroom in the house. Good luck to him, thinks Murielle. There hasn't been any real water, any decent water, in months. It is all that instant sanitizer glop coming out of the showerhead these days, stuff that leaves you stickier than when you went in. Even so, it will be nice to have one less person using the bathroom. The girls' rooms are across the hall from the bigger bedroom, one on the side of the house looking out to the neighbors and the other facing the street, neither of them large enough to hold much more than a bed: pink for Julie, pale lilac for Tahnee.

When she first moved in – Tahnee was little more than a year, Julie just about to be born – Slawa had been living alone for some time. The place was a mess. In his enthusiasm at her arrival, Slawa attempted to do some re-decorating. He bought floor-to-ceiling hologramovisions at a nearby discount supply house so each room could have hologramovisions on each wall.

But the sets were of such inferior quality that half the time the color was lousy, and then some of them stopped working; when the men came to bring in new ones, Slawa didn't want to pay the exorbitant fees for removal of the old, so he simply had the new ones installed on top. And then when those broke, he did the same thing. Now each room, in terms of square footage, is diminished by half.

With much delight he installed new light fixtures, ceiling fans, a garbage dehydrator, MereTwelve-operated self-generating devices, top of the line Siebmosh communicators – but half the time touching the light switch gave you a shock, or caused a fuse to blow. Clapping on or off worked sometimes, but often things would go on or off in the middle of the night. And no amount of scrubbing could clean the vintage vinyl flooring, which, a realtor had once told them, could make the house more valuable to the right buyer, if they were to someday sell.

When Terry had left, right after Tahnee was born, saying he was sick of being around someone who was so cheerful all the time, she hadn't thought of herself as cheerful, though it was true she was taking *Chamionalus*, but it did stop her hirsutism; that made her cheerful. Terry had grown up in the same neighborhood as she, though she hadn't known him; he was a fireman and just about the only guy she had ever met who wasn't working in a factory of one kind or another.

After they were married they moved in with her father. She worked at **La Galleria Senior Mall and Residence Home for the Young at Heart**, in Administration. It was a job with a future, especially compared to what others their age had found for jobs, working in the meat products factories; it was amazing, that two kids from their area hadn't ended up like everyone else/

Until she got pregnant when they realized both their salaries combined weren't going to be enough to enable them to buy their own place, or even rent; Terry was obsessed with making the Diamond-C dust in the bathroom, and she began to realize… that pervasive smell of an addict: violet soap, Brussels sprouts and bleach. He already had a dust problem, a problem big enough that they made him take an unpaid leave-of-absence at work. Then he decided he wanted to go to the West Coast and write screenplays, although as far as she could see he had shown no ability to stick to anything at all.

What skills did Terry have? He couldn't even write, he could only use a dictation program on the computer so what came out was pages of, "Um, so Joe goes, like fuck, um what um kind of um shit is um this." She had to admit that making Diamond-C dust was not easy, the few times he had made it before she put a stop to him the quality had been amazing, and what he didn't do himself he was able to sell for thousands of dollars a gram; of course the ingredients were expensive, the special lights needed, the hydroponics equipment, growing the crystals, inseminating the blossoms, harvesting and so on.

She had been too stupid to know, at first, that was how innocently she had been brought up! She thought he was just growing some kind of mineralized food-product for them, gorgeously fragrant; as if Terry would ever have been the kind of guy who had a nice little hobby.

Thinking of living at home reminds her she has to call her father to let him know they are coming the next day. She dials and the phone rings and rings but there is no answer… He is such a strange old man, he refuses to move into the house with them, he insists he wants to go to a nursing home. Now that she is Managing Administrative Director, he says, she could get him a discount, and she would be able to see him every day, if she wanted! It doesn't seem to matter that she has told him, over and over, the Senior Mall is the last place she would put him in.

If she doesn't remind him about their visit he will booby-trap the place; once Julie knocked on the door only to have a carton of F'eggs fall on her head, or when they went up the front path and all the sprinklers came on, spewing them with that water-substitute. Each time he denies doing anything deliberately.

Why can't he admit he's no longer up to functioning on his own? He is so antiquated he insists on using a rotary phone. The last person on the planet who really can say he has "dialed" a number. He won't have an answering machine – let alone voice mail, or a mobile unit to take with him, so she can't even leave a message.

No wonder she is such a freak. Her upbringing had been like someone from a hundred and fifty years ago! Her father with his obsessive collecting of paper goods and his letter writing – letter writing when there wasn't even a postal system any more, it all had to go Docu-Express or something!

She dials again. Where could he have gone? Maybe just out for a walk around the block, she'll try back later.

Her father never liked Slawa; Dad griped all the time how Slawa was a foreigner, and kept muttering Slawa was an old man, older than himself. At the time she just thought he was crazy, Slawa *was* older than Terry, and he was foreign, but he was so different from that cocky braggart, her first husband; he was so good with Tahnee, he never

18

treated her differently after his own, Julie, was born. She thought her father was angry, perhaps, that Slawa had a nice house for them to live in, she wasn't dependent on Dad any more.

Now she is beginning to wonder if her father hadn't been right. Just how old is Slawa, actually? And how could she have ever found him attractive? True he wasn't handsome the way Terry was; Terry was gorgeous, blond, a tight firm bottom and sassy grin. But Slawa had seemed appealing in a comforting kind of way, solid. Authentic. Now Slawa smells, she guesses because he drinks. Or maybe it is just some strange biochemistry. How stupid could he have been putting all his money into buying that shoe repair business – which is a major failure.

And his stories change all the time, she has long since given up believing anything he said. Slawa claimed to have a degree in science, a Ph.D. from Russia. But he couldn't get a science job; no one around would hire him, he said, doing the kind of work that he did, which was something – very limited, an obscure area – only in practice over there. Did that make any sense?

He couldn't even tell the truth about his age! Sometimes he had a memory of things that had taken place when he was a kid, things that she later realized, when she checked out the details, would have had to occur a hundred and twenty years ago. Stuff that had happened in Soviet, Communist times; if she pressed him, he would say something had happened and he was sent to some kind of Moscow long-term-care facility.

And when he was finally allowed to leave, all the old people had disappeared. He came home, his grandmother was gone… Nobody noticed, nobody cared, they said, yes, the old people were taken on a vacation, they all went quite happily… No more babushkas! There were shops and restaurants and bars, which hadn't been there before.

Why has it taken her so long to wonder if he really has a **graduate degree**? Now she is realizing, maybe nothing at all is the truth.

3

In the background the endless blare, no way to turn it off without
shutting down the whole Homeland Home System, "It's Maya turn
– for fun!" and then Mady Hus In Autoset Meier is on the program;
they have had the number one hit in the country for more than six
months now, after which the President's and First Man's Wedding
Registry and Wish List items are going to be shown.

Then Mady Hus In Autoset Meier come back for an encore and are
joined by none other than the Fairy Princess, it is really the Fairy
Princess herself and nobody can believe it! She has to be pushing sixty,
but she still has the touch, not much in the way of singing ability, not
much in the way of looks, but still, fantastic! And anybody watching has
the chance to *Win a Backstage Pass* simply by dialing the magic number
on the remote! The studio audience – or maybe it's just a soundtrack –
goes wild and even the President grabs his guitar to play along, "*Got
Dree? Take Harmony. Dree: it's twice as good with Harmony.*" And then
Scott, the President's fiancé, says, "President Wesley, I have to add
something at this point if you don't mind. For all you sufferers out there
– and I am one of them – when your Drena won't quit, take Dora. It
comes with its own inserter!"

"That's right, Scott," says the President, "You know, we've been
together a long time and I had no idea what it meant to be a Drena
sufferer. Since you've been on Dora, tension in our relationship has been
greatly eased. And I must say, I've enjoyed helping you by using the
inserter!"

"Oh, I know, Mister President," Scott says coyly. "But I should add,
do not take Dora if you have or ever plan to have children. Be prepared
to perform an emergency tracheotomy. If you are unable to keep both
feet in a bowl of ice water for an hour or stand on one leg, Dora may
not be right for you. Side effects may include enlarged heart, liver

failure, constipation, dandruff, ortlan and pillbox. For those of you with remaining eyelashes or a significant other, Dora may not be recommended. See your doctor if…"

Could she stand on one leg, Murielle wonders, for one hour? No, definitely not. She would have to go to the bathroom, or the dog would want to go out. She's about to make a cup of coffee when she sees she has already done so. It's evening, how can that be? The days roil out from under her, a nest of snakes gliding quickly from beneath a rock and disappearing into… where? If only it were possible to put her foot down fast, trap one underfoot, she might be able to remember Real Time.

Lifting the mug with the tepid coffee to her lips she is startled, momentarily, to find, there on the bottom, a large eye, unblinking. Then realizing it is her own, pale green, the color of an unripe olive, staring back at her reflected off the ceramic. She dials her father again. Still no answer. "Slawa!" she shouts, hearing him get out of the shower. "I am not kidding! I want you out tonight!"

"I am a little bit tired of being constantly picked on!" says Slawa. "All the time I am working and you sit there watching that stupid President, my God how can you stand it, the man is lousy idiot!"

Murielle goes past him and slams the bedroom door. Three days, four, who knows how long she will be in there sulking, it is impossible to say; brief forays to use the toilet or take some crust of food back to their room, attracting even more bugs and the bed always with crumbs.

In the meantime he is supposed to sleep on the sofa, baffled, bewildered and then, slowly, irritated, at having to beg her forgiveness for… for what? Even she would not be able to remember. This time, Slawa thinks, it is going to be different. He actually will leave, he can live in the shoe repair shop. The only person left who is important to him here is Julie, and he can arrange to visit her. His cats are scattered all over the house and even though they are responsive, they can do tricks, he

Breakfast

works with them daily, it still takes an age to round them up and coax them into their cages. Breakfast, the dog, stands watching by the door. "You go?" he says in a plaintive voice. Slawa nods. "When back?"

"I don't know," Slawa says. He is full of sorrow. "You want to come with me?"

The dog shakes his head. "No," he says. Slawa knows the dog is scared of anything new. Breakfast likes his routine. "When you come back, Poppy?"

"I don't know." There are six cages of cats; he carries them out two at a time. They are heavier than he remembers. How much could a cat weigh, twenty pounds? They resemble small mountain lions, or bobcats. He doesn't remember ever having cats like these before. Each trip he makes, Breakfast follows him to the car and back in again.

"Why you leave, Poppy?" Breakfast asks. "Where you going?"

"I don't know, Breakfast. I don't know." But still the dog asks, "Why?" again and again.

Murielle hears Slawa's car. Is he really gone? For the moment the house is peaceful, apart from the scream of the dysfunctional air-conditioning unit and the thump of the Patel boys next door playing Flosh Express in their driveway. She has begged them not to because the ball keeps hitting her wall; they continue.

At a distance the ceaseless surf pounds, not waves but cars on the thirty-lane highway that has recently opened alongside the abandoned twenty-lane highway.

She will go crazy if she doesn't get out of here, she thinks. But where can she go? Anyway, the girls will be back soon, she will have to give them something for dinner and it is too hot to move. Maybe a cold shower will make her less irritable. There is always a chance the faucets will gush real water instead of Sanitizing Gelatin.

Sure enough Slawa has left three towels, wet, on the floor – who needed to use up three towels, just for one wash? – and hasn't opened the window afterward so the whole place is still steamy, which he has been told not to do one million times. Half the tiles are coming off the walls and the plaster moldering, the floor is crooked, too. Slawa was right about the place; soon the whole foundation is going to collapse.

Last night had been the last straw, to hear him crashing around and wake up to find he had pissed again in the hall, so drunk he thought he was in the toilet. What if one of the girls saw him? And in the morning the urine stank so bad, even a dog knew better than to piss in the house!

Once she had been fond of him, he had seemed to come out of nowhere like a gentle... not a giant, he wasn't that tall... but a gentle something, maybe one of the seven dwarves, which had always seemed a bit kinky to her, what was that virgin princess Snow White doing with the seven filthy little men – not that dwarves in general were filthy, but at least in the movie Snow White had to go in there and clean the whole place – the dwarves weren't infants, they had beards, though that one – Sleepy? Dopey? – seemed microcephalic, with a tiny pointed head and huge ears –

Slawa had rescued her from that horrible apartment, one room with the two of them, she and Tahnee who was only one at the time – it was part of her salary as night-manager, but to live in the old-age home was relentlessly depressing, the smell of the old people and overheated, steamy smell of bland food; it had never seemed like a place to bring up a kid, and besides, how would she ever meet anybody there, everyone was sick and dying and/or a hundred and ten years old.

Somehow, she wasn't certain, she kept buying stuff, probably out of depression, from catalogs, or would go to the mall which you could practically walk to, when she had free time – and the debts mounting up month after month so the leased furniture was taken away; night after night of boxed macaroni and cheese dinner and canned peas and soda that wasn't even Coca-Cola but the **store brand**; she would never get out from the mess, and every damn box or bottle had its own singing or talking microchip and some were light-sensitive and others were activated on vibration so that each time opening the cabinet a whole Disneyworld chorus, though atonal, would burst out in conflagration: "*Yankee-Doodle went to town, riding on a pony, stuck a feather in his cap and called it Kraft-Ebbing Macaroni!*" at the same time as "*All around the* *kitchenette, come and get your Peases, we are good – and good for you! – Pop! Goes a Zippety pea!"* And then the deeper bass voice, *"**A product of Zippety Doo-Dah Corporation, a registered trademark. Zippety – Mom's best friend for over a generation!**"*

Terry's mother lived nearby then and helped out, babysitting, though she couldn't stand it; Lorraine smoked, even though it was illegal, and had once burned Tahnee when she was holding her, as an infant, and couldn't even put down the cigarette for long enough to hold the baby.

So when she met Slawa – and he was so kind, seemingly, he wasn't drinking so much then, or hardly at all, and he visited his wife, Alga, almost every day and then would come by to say hi to her, and play with Tahnee, and take her out to dinner – she was grateful, more than grateful and his house was nearby, less than a half-hour away, with a yard for Tahnee, etc. etc.

Car doors slam. Surely he isn't coming back? But no, it's just the kids, returning from the pool. "Didn't LaBenyce's mom want to come in? How was the swimming?"

"No water."

"I thought they were going to start using that gloppy stuff, the water-substitute?"

"They did, but we were only allowed to get in for, like, twenty minutes, then all of a sudden some girl started screaming and she was having an allergic reaction and so they decided to drain the pool in case it was poisonous or something."

They are damp and cheery, reeking of chemicals, white mulberry skin puckered from their day in the… whatever it was. Tahnee really is a beauty, with that ash-blonde hair and tippy nose, thin, wispy; Julie is chubby and will never be so pretty; her smile is pretty, though, but she has the pleading look of a beaten dog while Tahnee – there is that imperious, snotty expression, and she is always batting her eyelashes at men. You can see she is going to be a real heartbreaker. She never smiles but there is already something frightening about her. Though she is not even fifteen, totally pre-pubescent and flat-chested, there is something about her… an insect queen.

"We're starving, Mom," says Tahnee.

"Yeah, Mom, what's for dinner?"

"I'm not going to tell you to go and hang up your towels."

"Why not?"

"Because I expect you to do so without being told." It's six o'clock, dinner time for normal people. There is nothing in the cabinets or in the freezer that the girls will eat. Why not? Everything is the same, pads or stacks or cubes of texturized cultured processed food-product, grown hydroponically in sterilized growth medium in factories; flavored with emollients, sauces, herbs, spices as well as artificial flavorings and preservatives. The food contains no by-products, all of it is pure and organic. Next week she'll go see a lawyer.

"Where's Dad?" says Julie.

It was probably better to get the whole thing over with sooner rather than later.

"Listen, kids," she says, "things didn't work out between me and Slawa."

Julie's face opens in a howl.

"Why?" says Tahnee. "Slawa's not coming back?"

"He wasn't your daddy anyway, Tahnee, so I don't want to hear anything from you. I don't want anybody making a fuss, either of you!"

Julie is weeping. "I always knew that was going to happen!" Julie will never get anywhere in this world; she has low self-esteem, Murielle thinks, and is, according to Doctor Ray-Oh-Tee, whose show is on at four, overly case-sensitive.

"You'll get used to it, now we can have lots of fun without any big beer belly grunting and bitching and slapping his way around the place."

"Daddy was nice when he wasn't drunk," Julie says.

"Right, but he was almost always drunk. One husband a Diamond-C dust dope head and one alcoholic, that's enough for anybody."

"Nooooo –"

"You don't know anything, he didn't let you see but there was never a single second when he didn't have a beer in his hand and he went through a six-pack a night easily. That is why he was always in front of the TV in a catatonic stupor and plus he kept a bottle of bourbon going on the side – look, he wasn't the worst guy in the world and I know you're going to miss him –"

"I'm not," says Tahnee, "I don't even remember him already. It was like having a stuffed pig –"

"Okay, that's enough. Anyway, we're all going to have to be tough and strong. I'm thinking, we're going to get out of this dump and travel and have an interesting life."

"But I like it here," says Julie. "My friends are here."

"Not me," says Tahnee, "let's get out of this dump. Anyway, you don't have any friends, remember, Julie?"

"What do you mean?"

"That's what you said, you don't have any friends, remember? When was that, Saturday?"

"Yeah, but –"

"All right, stop it you two. Tahnee. I tell you what. As a celebration, I'm going to order us a pizza, how do you like that?"

"Yeah, yeah! Pizza. I want mrango," says Julie.

"I'm gonna have to borrow some credit from you kids. Who has money left on their micro-chips? I'll pay you back, I'll have cred tomorrow. My chip is over the limit."

"I hate mrango," says Tahnee. The two girls begin to squabble. Apparently they have already forgotten about Slawa's absence. But whether that is due to indifference, or some type of brain damage, Murielle can't determine.

Around midnight Murielle wakes with a start. Someone has come into the house. "Slawa," Murielle says, "Is that you?"

There is no answer. She doesn't even have the money to have the locks changed, with twenty-four credit chips maxed out and she can't keep up with the monthly interest as it is, even if they let her have more credit. In the morning she will have to figure out how to get another chip, people do that all the time. They can't go without groceries, can they? She should have asked Slawa for his set of keys, but that would have been awkward, he was in a rage when he drove off.

Murielle looks out the window, maybe it's someone outside? But there's no one there. All she can see is the almost full moon, with its sneering face – a Happy Face gone wrong. Long ago a conceptual artist had a grant from a non-profit arts foundation to go up there to make a face out of richly hued pigments (influenced by Anish Kapoor); only, after dumping two mile-wide circles to form the eyes, and almost completing the mouth, an explosion blew up the shuttle – and the artist – and turned that happy smile into the snarl of today's moon.

She remembers Slawa keeps a baseball bat under the bed and now she fumbles around and, holding it in one hand, a flashlight in the other, goes down the stairs. Her hands are sweating, so slippery she can barely hold the bat. If a burglar has broken in, she really doesn't see herself hitting him over the head. What can a burglar take, anyway? Nothing that would be missed.

She flicks on the light in the living room. Tahnee is lying on the couch, without panties, her legs spread and with the Patel boy from next door – the older one, Locu – and then Tahnee stares at her, with those cat-eyes, dilated, not even startled. For a second Murielle is about to say, "Oh, excuse me," and turn off the light.

Her daughter has an expression on her face of pure... contempt, irritation, that someone is disturbing her and the boy. How old is that

little punk Locu, anyway? He is kneeling on the couch in front of Tahnee's parted legs, he turns and looks at Murielle with a sopping face like a dog feeding on a carcass, about to have rocks flung at him. "Pontius fucking Pilatés," she says, dropping the bat, "what are you doing, get the hell out of here, Locu, I'm going to call your parents –"

Tahnee sits, her eyes huge, sleepy but cold, without guilt. "Oh, don't call his parents, Mom."

Eyes without guilt

"You're only fourteen years old, you filthy little bitch," she says. "I'm going to call the police!"

Locu, in his pajamas, bolts out the door.

Lazily Tahnee pulls up her panties. It is hot and her thin nighty, printed with a pixyish, mop-headed cartoon tot, only comes to the top of her legs, baby-doll style. Murielle grabs her daughter by the arm and slaps her across the face. Tahnee barely winces. "I'm almost fifteen, Ma. Don't do dat shit."

There is a reek of aerosol, or spray paint, in the air, sickly as glue. Something was knocked over? Or more of the weird polluted marsh fumes. "I'm going to puke," Tahnee says and runs to the toilet.

"What am I supposed to do with you, how long has this been going on?" Murielle shouts at the bathroom door.

On the other side Tahnee is gagging, then vomiting, so loudly she can't imagine what it is her daughter has taken. Or done.

4

Shoe repair is something he knows from childhood, he had worked in a shop – his mother's brother? He can't remember. Maybe it was because he had joined the **Tsar's Club Kids Party** and they had gotten him the job? Has he even been telling the truth, about his PhD in physics? More and more is coming back to him, but it is fragmented and torn.

He had been so happy to have his own stupid business – shoe repair, for crying out loud! – and totally surprised when, a short time later, the PADTHAI-NY train entrance closed for repairs and the casual pedestrian traffic he was counting on utterly vanished. There has never been any sign of work about to commence and years have passed.

His head smells: stale dander, scurf; beer comes out of his pores, sour yeast and hops, like the floor of a bar after closing. God, what a loser; is it something genetic? His fault? But no, it had been his first wife's family who owned the swampy marsh – two, three hundred years ago, maybe, back then it was apple trees, or potatoes – and let it be used for chemical dumping.

After this the property was sold for this cheap-o housing estate, and his wife's family were then promptly sued for clean-up costs, and stripped to nothing. All he had ended up with was the tiny house. And now he didn't even have that, only kept the hybrid petro-sucremalt fuel car. He punches in his destination and sits back to watch TV while he waits for traffic to move.

"The Amazing Hair-A-Ticks! This breakthrough in medical science is a genetically engineered hair grown by a tiny tick. The tick attaches easily to your head, it burrows under the scalp while numbing and sucking teeny amounts of blood. Totally natural, these hairs will grow more profusely than that which with you were born! Never fear, these tiny ticks are more the size of mites! Side effects may include a slight itching no worse than an ordinary

case of dandruff. If side effects intensify, see your doctor at once. A product of Bermese Pythion."

Slawa scratches his head. There is something familiar about this, maybe Julie had mentioned it over the summer. He changes channels. *"This week learn about the lives of some of the most important figures in American history: Delta Burke, Merv Griffin, John Denver, John Ritter, Dinah Shore! Larry Gagosian and Tiffany-Amber Thyssen!"*

Yes, yes, that would be something he should watch, he needed to learn about the people who had made this country America. He must try to hang on to the here and now. His cats – two Persians stippled red and white; one shorthair tortoiseshell; the fourth a Russian Blue; a Japanese bobtail; and the last a lilac-point Siamese, yowl in their crates. Kapiton, Barsik, Murka, Nureyev, Rasputin and Yuri Gagarin.

He had wanted to take Breakfast with him, but Breakfast was scared and didn't want to go, not even when Slawa told him he could sleep in the same bed with him when they got there.

After a few hours he's gotten nowhere. By some piece of luck, a neon sign is flashing that there's a space available in the parking lot! Expensive, yes, but what the heck. He shoves the cats into a couple of crates and carries the whole yowling unhappy tribe to the PADTHAI-NY subway, only a few blocks away. The cats are heavy and there's virtually no room to stand; thousands continue to swarm onto the platform to wait for a city-bound train that never keeps to any schedule. When it arrives it is so packed with people he has to barrel his way on, something he hates to do but… Whatever.

As usual, people move out of his way with that odd look, noses wrinkled; flies circle around him or ride his shoulders, but is it his fault? He has already been traveling for nearly four hours, to what should have been a destination perhaps twenty minutes away. Of that he is certain.

He'll sleep in the shoe store, just for a few nights; soon Murielle will see, it is not so easy living without a man! He is sick of not being appreciated.

He can't even tell if the train is moving; if it is, it is going more slowly than a person could walk. It's awful being trapped this way, the hologramovisions are broken, stray arms and parts of an elephant move at random, and the sound garbled. He has nothing to do but think, something he doesn't want to do. Fourteen years of marriage and then, just like that, get out.

It makes no sense. He was willing to work things out; he was ready to do whatever it took. If Murielle had said to him, Slawa, fix this or our marriage is over, he would have. He fixed everything anyway. He resoled the children's shoes, when anybody else would have thrown them out – the kids, they were American, they wanted new shoes every few weeks anyway. None of them knew what it was like to grow up rummaging in garbage pails and eating food that was literally rotten.

Slimy cabbage leaves, spoiled fish. Nobody here even knew what it was like to finally get money and go into the store, the only one that was located in the area of bleak concrete towers a good hour outside the downtown streets and inhale the screech of rotten food, the frozen fish that even frozen was obviously putrid. And what good did a frozen fish do him, unless he could wheedle or borrow cooking oil, a frying pan, a stove?

Most of the time the elevators didn't work, up nineteen flights, his father passed out on the sofa. His mother, his aunt, his sisters, all at some slave labor position in factories that made media diodes for arm implantation or organ labs, and waiting on line for hours after work to get some bread. Five kopeks to take the subway into the city. Drinking vodka at age ten just to keep warm on the Moscow streets.

You had to have a Tsarist Party Club Card or at least the Tsar's Club Kids Party Card to buy anything halfway decent. And even then, what would he have done with a raw beet? Once he had found in the rubble of a building, an old ring. Cabuchon, ruby, gold, valuable. He could have sold it, but he had not. Years later there it appeared in a drawer and he had given it to Julie. Did she even appreciate it? No!

He could live in his shoe repair store. That did not trouble him. He paid his rent, how could the landlord prove he was living there? All he had to do at night was pull the metal gates down over the doors. Or maybe he would stay open and become the only all-night twenty-four-hour shoe repair in New York.

A gray sucking descent through the long wind tunnel and the arrival, into a sort of sack; hot ash, dust, an intricate network of old hairs, half-crumbled vitamins, toast, flakes of paint. Darkness, mostly, except for a few holes in the grating overhead. No, no, he can make no sense, not of what is happening to him nor what has happened in the past. A general shredding of some space-time continuum, perhaps.

At last, his stop. He is shoved, up and out, into a massive crossroads of skyscrapers covered with blinking signs, endless streamers of electronic text proclaiming the latest news ("*Dee Jay Mark Ronstad-Ronson to Wed Lionel-John Barrymore!*", "*Sixty thousand Dead in Maltagascar*", "*NEW OUTBREAK OF PRAIZLY-WEERS IN POSH HAMPTON*", "*Polish Mike Hammer Killed in Plane Crash!*", "*Humphrey Bogart and Peter Sellers in THE MALTESE PANTHER is a hit!*" – this last due of course to new computer innovations that made it possible to reconstitute the deceased stars on the screen).

Advertisements everywhere: "*No more suffering with the Britny Chumbles... Arpeggio at last!*" And a picture of a naked woman on the beach, her row of extra breasts shrinking miraculously, and then the words "*Side effects may include constipation, diarrhea, anxiety, nausea, Formantera fungus, vradnoid spits...*" digital screens displaying acres of youthful flesh, poreless, perfect, clad in string bikinis which served as marginal containers for pert breasts and styptopygic buttocks. "*When your Drena won't Quit, take Dora! Comes with its own Inserter!*"

The largest display features eight three-dimensional holographic, disembodied, dancing penises dressed in cute historic costumes – Elvis Presley, Margot Fonteyn, Richard Branson, and everybody's favorite – the little guy, Napoleon. They are each enlarged to be ten stories high on the screen, though the real men are much shorter; the actors unzip their flies so they can emerge to perform on the quarter-hour from a giant cuckoo clock emblazoned with the Bermese Pythion corporate logo, though it's hard to discern what product is being advertised. "*It's Maya turn – For Fun! Now Available with Individual sub-cutaneous Poppers!*"

The streets are full of workers in dresses and skirts – not kilts, but the pleated knee-length wear that is the latest city street trend of men. Meanwhile a man shoves a talking pamphlet chip into his free hand, the one that isn't holding the crate of cats. "*GOT A HEADACHE?*" it says in a shrill high chirp, "*TAKE NEW HARMONY! NOW AVAILABLE AT DISCOUNT PRICES. ASK YOUR PHARMACIST. SIDE EFFECTS MAY INCLUDE PSYCHOTIC BREAK, UNCONTROLLABLE BLEEDING AND LIVER DAMAGE...*"

He crushes the chip in his hand. A banner, words floating in space, is strung out over the avenue: "*UNTIED WE STAND. Join the Marines Today!*" From all sides the distributors press in, handing out chips there's one with a deep booming voice, "*Lose one hundred pounds in thirty days. That's right, only thirty days!*" Not a bad idea, actually, he'd be down to what, a hundred and fifty? A hundred twenty?

But Slawa has heard it isn't safe. A lot of people kept losing weight until they just disappeared and there is nothing you could do to stop it.

There's a man handing out samples – it's a copy of the President's fiancé's memoirs – it's called a **book**, a present to the American people. Scott has had it privately printed, enough copies for each and every citizen, free, a wee square of papers, with a red and gold cover. And it's free! Slawa shoves it in his pocket.

To get into his shoe store he now has a circuitous underground route for nearly two blocks, and finally exits into the area that says EXIT CLOSED. This is worse than on his last visit. He pulls up the heavy gates that covered the front. It's untouched, no break-ins. Everything as he left it. He is relieved, relieved and happy; this is his home, his office, after all.

He puts down the crate with the cats and opens the door. Poor things will want water, food. With gassy hisses of contempt the cats come tumbling out, running in circles as if they have been over-wound. They resemble molecules bouncing off the floor and walls. He watches, amused, until one, the Siamese, Murka, finds what must be a hole in the wall, darts in and is gone.

Moments later a scream, hideous, from what sounds miles away. He goes to the hole, a wind is blowing out, as if there is an underground chamber or tomb far below. He hears Yuri Gagarin yowling, now more plaintively and then abruptly ceases… Has he broken his back, perhaps, or a leg? From the hole a strange odor wafts, musty, vaguely stale, almost familiar. He can't get enough of an angle to see the secret room – if that is what it is. He will have to make the hole bigger so he can go in.

"Here kitty kitty," he calls, knocking through what he sees now is only feeble fiberboard, so old it is rotten. No sound at first and then a faint meow. "Here kitty kitty." Even if he hangs over the edge it must be more than a twelve-foot drop. A wind is blowing up from below. Something he could put down there to jump onto? The cushions from a sofa he once found on the street and hauled in so customers could sit? Though how he will get back, he doesn't know. Anyway, for tonight, it is too late, all he can do for now is go to sleep.

In the morning he heads around the corner to Chez Gagni Kota. Mornings, the restaurant is empty; Bocar is almost always there before his aunt and uncle, sometimes he even spends the night there. The two of them can sit and drink sweet tea, have a chat.

Throughout the day Slawa will be back to eat.

Health food, it isn't that. Slawa isn't sure how much longer he can eat the stuff, tomato-curried rancid fish and artificial potato flakes, spinach leaves that are probably something else, processed paper maybe, everything heavy on the dendé oil which is not even dendé but… strained tallow? and too salty.

The meats are halal – so they say, though it is unlikely it is halal, let alone meat – nowadays everything comes from the manufacturer's, where piles of meat cells are coaxed into reproducing themselves until they have formed vast living slabs. Bocar says the food is authentic, because in his country the people had been starving for so many years and the famine was so dire they had long since developed national dishes based solely on donated American supplies.

He goes there, actually, just to see Bocar and make sure the kid is okay. It is no way to live, not that Slawa has to eat lunch and dinner six days a week at Chez Gagni Pota, but it is the only place where he has a friend.

What now is left? Once, on first meeting, he had even thought Bocar was a girl. If not a girl, a neuter entity, with beautiful black coils of hair decorated with feathers, ribbons, glitter. But, male or female, he was an extraordinarily beautiful creature.

Bocar was an illegal. The family had sold him to someone – some rich American – to do their military duty – and though it was frowned upon, somehow he had gotten two weeks before training camp to spend in New Jersey. He had come to stay with his aunt and uncle and cousins and his uncle had promised to send him to two-year college, after his military service was complete.

Even Slawa could have told him this was a complete lie; after military service – in the unlikely event he was still alive – he would be sent back immediately; somebody, probably the uncle, must have made so much money off of him they felt guilty – but then the uncle's partner in the business had run away with the money and at first Bocar's uncle said the vacation was over, he was needed at the restaurant, off the books.

Of course all this took a while to learn: the kid could speak English but he had learned it from books, he put emphasis on the wrong syllable of each sentence, which was how English looked on the page to one who hadn't heard it – and the truth was, Bocar was practically deaf.

He had fought with the rebels, back home, making bombs and one had gone off when he was ten or twelve, he wasn't exactly certain of his age. It had not been by choice, his village of tin and cardboard was raided by the rebels, he was taken away to join them. This year's rebels had been in power ten years before.

Now Bocar's country was ruled by an evil despot. It took Slawa a while to figure out what this meant, Bocar kept saying the words 'ev-ill de-spot' though finally he figured it out. The children – Bocar and the other kids – were told that the ruler, who had previously been a rebel and a good guy, had become one of the bad guys, and it was up to the children to assassinate the evil despot and restore the country. Restore it to what, Bocar often wondered; his country had never been any different than the way it was now. But maybe there could be change. Then he still had optimism.

35

On the other hand there were the various factions at war even among the rebels, and then the tribes – the Lala Veuves Clickot, who wanted to see the Rolo Greys eradicated. It didn't matter who took him to fight with them: Bocar's parents had died of Hepatitis P. or Srednoi gas, or slow Ebola X; he no longer knew what had happened to his brother, his older sister had been killed in front of his eyes.

When there had been food it had been flung from the sky by the airplanes: macaroni-and-cheese (there was no water with which to cook), ketchup, pigeon peas, Frosted Flakes. Anchovy filets in tins without keys, for those in a country where everyone was thirsty all the time. Jars of cocktail olives. Gummy worms, Cremora, Nutela and jars of peanut butter pre-mixed – and inseparable from – grape jelly. Bags of crispy pork rinds for a Moslem country.

It was a country where it rained every other year, if they were lucky; but it had not rained since before Bocar was born. Dry, parched, the lands continuously churned up by heavy machinery searching for… oil, or diamonds, no one was quite sure what… and when it did rain, it was no relief, it only meant that thousands drowned; the tin and cardboard villages were washed away.

The weather had not always been this way, it was said, but no one remembered if the past had been better – or worse.

Bocar hoped that his uncle, who promised to send him to school, would let him train in the field of **Massage Therapy Techniques** using **External Devices**.

But Uncle, he is slowly realizing, has no intention of ever doing so. Only when Bocar's high heels had holes in their soles did he finally manage to get a few bucks out of auntie, who sent him to Slawa's shop.

For the first time in years Slawa tidies the store. There are so few customers though, since the entrance subway has been closed, whether he is open or shut scarcely makes a difference. And the cats hate being here. At first he is so busy, cleaning, painting, he keeps thinking his cats will reappear but after a day he realizes he will have to go after them, down in the windy spot. But surely there is an easier way to get down there?

Against the wall in a back corner, behind some boxes, he finds a place where the paper is peeling; behind it is a little door.

He pulls it loose and puts his head through. Inside is blackness and cool air and a musty smell. "What?" he mumbles to himself. The flies that circle him are growing agitated. "Something back here... Cannot see... Is maybe –"

Grunting, he stands and fetches his flashlight. Then he stoops once again and waves the light. Steps lead down to pink squares, turquoise diamonds, beige and gold rectangles. Tiles of some sort. A mound of... some kind of stuffing. From an old sofa? He really can't tell. The stairs descend, curving steeply, maybe twenty feet. One of the missing cats might be down there. Then from the depths – fifty, eighty feet below? – a faint mewling, a thin yowling, and a gurgling rush, perhaps of water, perhaps a million electronic devices receiving only static and mottled signals.

5

Each night Murielle drifts off but wakes at three or four in the morning and can't go back to sleep. And she is hungry. It seems to her that she never eats, at least she can't remember doing so. She is always hungry and she never eats and yet she grows and grows.

Refrigerator

Sometimes, late at night, she wakes to find herself in front of the refrigerator. Staring blankly at first then... lo and behold, a slice of Swiss cheese in one hand, a bottle of soda in the other! Breakfast at her feet prodding her ankle with a paw until she tosses him bits of the food. Only his whimpers of "More! Please, more," rouse her from her comatose state. Does the damn dog have to have a Russky accent too?

"No more."

"But why? Why, Mama?" says the dog.

She wants to say she's not the dog's mother but she knows the dog would cry. "Because in this lifetime I'm the person and you're the dog! And, for your own health, I say so." This doesn't sound quite right. "So, if you don't like it, come back in your next life as a human being! And my recommendation is, preferably male." Lip curled, Breakfast slinks out of the kitchen with an expression simultaneously hurt and contemptuous.

How has she gotten here? Where has the food come from? She has no memory of buying the Swiss cheese, or the ham, or the puffy white flavorless Parker House Rolls.

Or whatever it is she finds in her hand, almost in her mouth. The combination lox-and-cream-cheese on a garlic-bagel, the Benny-

Goodman-and-Jerry-Lee-Lewis-Nuts-Bolts-and-Berries-ice cream – let alone how or when she ever got out of bed and made her way to the refrigerator.

Murielle wonders what is wrong with her, that she can't keep the place even remotely clean? She looks around the kitchen: implements – spatulas, knives, spoons, a blender, crumbs, dirty sponges, almost empty milk cartons – cover the green vintage Dormica counter. It gives her the skeeves, the sheen of gray grease rimming each area around the cabinet doors. In the sink strainer is a hummock of partially rotten food – bits of pasta, carrot cubes from canned soup, coffee grinds.

Bugs are in the walls, roaches and ants, a number of different varieties, fire, grease and sugar ants, the big black wood-eating ants, a strange mutated variety of leaf-cutter ants, or rather linoleum-cutter ants, at least, that is what they like to chew.

There are moths – the kind that live in food; hair-eating moths (attracted by the odor of urine), earwigs and flies. Tiny white flies that live on the children's house plants (some plants in particular have bad infestations); fruit flies, houseflies, ichneumon flies as big as a chihuahua. The news has said that soon there will be a new kind of fly, beneficial, to eat old fibers and fabric, but slow enough to be killed easily.

The scene is one of chaos from which no order is possible. Tipping out the refuse from the sink strainer does not completely empty it, bits are still enmeshed in the trap; now Mister Garbage Dehydrator with grease dripping down the sides of the plastic trash bag liner should be cleaned! The disembodied voice says, "*Who's doing the dishes!*" with a nasty, perky giggle, it's part of the hologramovision system or the computer, then a man comes over the speakers, "*Sey Vramos!*" he yells, some kind of Spanish?

The forks and whisks lying around are rinsed, stuffed into drawers, counters wiped with paper towel – nevertheless nothing about the kitchen looks cleaner. It's a kind of mental imbalance on her part, Murielle thinks. Other people have come into the room, gotten out the dustpan and broom, sprayed spritzer, wiped and tidied and polished and within minutes the place has appeared clean if not new.

But no matter how or what she does, objects seem only to be shuffled from one area to another; her attempts at cleaning only stir up more crumbs, grease, dust that emerges shyly, gaily, from secret nests and now expands in its own kind of reproductive frenzy.

From chaos it is not possible for her to create order, only an alternate chaos. Even with the friendly robototron whirling on its endless round of vacuuming and steam and plugging itself back in if it needs a charge, she is not lucky – all it does is strew dirt. Sometimes she finds it banging endlessly against the wall – which it is not supposed to – shouting, "*Will somebody please help me. Help me. Time to change my bag!*" and then, with greater panic, "*Help me! Please! I'm gonna bust my bag!*"

Still, that is not what is really the matter at all.

She has let the kids take over the living room with their house plants. It had seemed harmless enough, even positive, their hobby. They acquired clippings from neighbors – Christmas cactus stubs, rubbery succulents, the offspring of spider plants; dead and dying discards.

There isn't a single thing that perishes after the kids acquire it, no matter that it appeared completely dead it is now growing at a frightening speed, Caladium and kumquat, Dieffenbachia and Norfolk pine needing to be moved practically weekly into bigger and bigger pots. When it's time to water them, the two kids fight: "You're over-watering! It doesn't need that much!" – "Yes it does, can't you see how dry it is?" – water overflowing, spilling onto the floor, making rings under each pot.

A moist jungle humidity permeates the house: the living room windows can't be opened and roots have begun to crawl, fingerlike, into floorboards or along the walls, the tendrils of ivy and a kind of Philodendron that had air-roots waving white, obscene stumps that several times a year gave birth to a single, phallic-shaped stinking flower which was able to move to a new pot, slowly and painfully, by air-roots.

Two dwarf banana trees eight feet tall with great stalks of ripening bananas – that neither child would permit the other to pick – are so tall they hit the ceiling, the flies have merrily swarmed on the rotting fruit. Apart from the sofa, the plants – the jungle – take up the entire living room and the floor is buckled and rotted from the moisture.

The kids collect animals, too. She is passive in the face of their gargantuan demands, two giantesses – or so they appear to her – two giant daughters with gaping maws waiting to be filled with worms that she has no energy to collect. Long before Julie's internship at Bermese Pythion the kids had managed to acquire a number of animals – post-experimentation – others had actually been thrown out, scarcely alive – and Murielle couldn't help but believe these animals were products of genetic tampering of some sort – anyway, she has never seen creatures like these.

The girls, or at least Julie, keep a lot of them in cages in the basement. Mice with hair so long it can be braided. Guinea pigs with incredibly long legs, little tusks, and nasty dispositions. And the family pet? Something the kids said was a type of dog called a Muskwith who wanted – according to them and Slawa – to be called Breakfast.

Only, if it is a dog, what kind of dog jumps on the table to eat apples and using its claws climbs the curtains to the point that they are completely shredded? The kids say that a Muskwith is a modern canine combined with some genetic material from an aardwolf – who knows, though. She has to admit she is fond of the animal, though she had totally objected to it at first, a fluffy little thing with tufts of white fur and great bald patches, runny black eyes, short-legged and a long pink snout lined with sharp, pointy teeth more feline than canine.

The dog (it is apparently a hermaphrodite; at least that's what the vet says) feels alone and isolated. Breakfast often disappears for days on end down some hiding hole, or at the neighbors'; it knows everyone in the vicinity and, digging its way under the fence in the back when in a sulky mood, has other homes to visit.

All the neighbors are fond of it, fortunately, and report new words it can speak or how it affectionately likes to rest its sharp, pointed chin on whoever is around. It loves *bananas, chopped liver and the glue on the backs of stamps or envelopes.* When at home, it has a terrible habit of taking hold of one end of the toilet paper roll and running through the house; or will think of ways to deliberately hurt her, if she doesn't pay it enough attention – climbs on her lap and smacks her, forcefully, with its paw, or lifts things from her pockets, so stealthily she doesn't know until hours later that the dog has taken a whole packet of chewing gum, peeled each stick and eaten it.

Breakfast isn't like any dog she has ever known. It is cute, in its own way, and can even say a few words – "Mama" and "Breakfast" and "I'm hungry"; occasionally says "out" or "cold" – not in a human voice, but painfully, sounds coaxed under duress not dissimilar to that of a child being tortured.

Sometimes it will talk when promised a treat of chicken liver; other times in its sleep, a bad dream, she hears whimpers and "no, no," or, more astonishingly, "no hurt, no hurt." But ultimately, in time, it doesn't seem all that odd – it isn't like the dog is putting together whole sentences or anything.

Still, it isn't what a dog is supposed to be. Nothing in Murielle's life is the way it is supposed to be. Not her marriage, not even her own kids – willful, uncontrollable, sexed-up – ! Even being alive wasn't what she had thought it was going to be. But then she actually had no clue as to what it should have been like, either.

In the morning she has a Health-Nut muffin, the type that heats itself in a little bag if you pull the string, containing *ZERO CALORIES and One Hundred Percent of Daily Requirements of Vitamin C, sugar and salt.* The kids don't eat breakfast. When Slawa had still lived here he ate various health foods, yogurt with fresh fruit and nuts, wholewheat cereal with bran or thin slices of heavy dark stuff gritty with sunflower seeds that was supposed to be bread but was a closer relative of paper, hand-made from newsprint or dryer lint.

Her baking. If she had time she would have made regular meals, but why bother? The kids prefer pre-made growth products in different textures and flavors: frozen burritos heated in the microwave, pizza, everything nowadays comes from one of the factories. Slawa is a vegetarian – if you want to call it that, vegetables are expensive but probably also made out of the same stuff – and he usually ate before he came home.

Even when she tried to bake muffins with wholegrain-enriched flour, he said that anything she cooked had hairs in it, or wasn't sanitary – and it was true, the flour, no matter how recently purchased, was swarming with meal worms, moths flew out of the cabinets, jars of spices swarmed with heaving larvae of one sort or another and even the refrigerator had roaches which thrived on the cold and darkness and the spills of syrup and ketchup or ancient crusts that oozed from the walls. "It's probably healthy, to eat bugs," Murielle says. "Protein. I never get sick. Look at you, you have a cold all the time."

"It's not a cold, I am having reaction to the shoe repair chemicals," he says. "And I am telling you – you kids!" he shouts upstairs as the girls scramble, perpetually late, to get dressed. "The best thing you can do for yourself is to eat a healthy breakfast and have a regular bowel movement!"

"Ew, gross!" Their groans of contempt could be heard up the narrow six-step flight of stairs.

"Yeah, you kids with the laughing, to sneer, wait until you are in a place of work wishing you didn't have to take a big crap in the middle of the day with all your co-workers wanting to kill you for stinking up the toilet, or like me, gotta find a public toilet and getting some filthy on your shoes! You gonna be sorry you didn't listen to me then."

"Wow," yells Tahnee, "you really give me a lot to look forward to, why don't I just kill myself now?"

It is true everyone but Slawa is constipated, even the dog, Breakfast, who squats, a tortured U-shape in the backyard, slowly stumbling around for hours until finally one hard pellet drops. You might as well throw loaves to the fishes, Slawa thinks, what's the point, how could they not be constipated when they never eat vegetables nor fiber, and besides, as soon as you poop, those things, whatever they are, no one is ever quite sure, come scrambling up the pipeline to eat the... shit. These nasty primordial-looking little creatures will, with nothing but a mouthful of teeth, leave you with a buttock full of pinholes if you don't jump off the pot immediately. Whatever they are, you could pour bleach down the drains and it would kill the ones who are there but afterwards their brethren would be back, more furious than ever and could even on occasion hop out onto the floor, surfaced all the way up from the sewers.

A sourness permeated Slawa's existence that hadn't been vanquished by **Volthrapeâ**. Now that he was coming off the stuff he was like a rutting elephant seal swimming back up to the surface. How had he been able to live this long in such a mess? He ran around shouting until finally she had no choice but to throw him out. "It was the Dora mixed with Volthrapeâ that made me... not apathetic, but indifferent. Accepting. It was only thanks to the Dora that I have been able to accept my entire existence. I see that now!"

"Who cares, Slawa! Come home once in a while and help me clean up if you don't like to live this way! You were the one who wanted a shoe repair place, now you have it!"

"It was something I did for you! You and the children! The dark shoe repair shop, reeking of leather cleaning fluids! What can I care about the kids steeting gluf and pait when basically I have been stoned out of my mind for the past years?"

"So? And you think everyone else isn't?"

Anyway at least now he is gone. But... every morning – although he is not there stumping around, in his black sulk – it is still always the same thing, one thing substituted by another almost the same. "Kids! Are you up and dressed? You're gonna miss the bus!"

"Tahnee's already left, Ma! She went running!"

"Great." That meant she hadn't eaten; the child seemed to live on slivers of watermylon, baskets of those strange hairy sprouts. She would jog to school in her tiny shorts and track shoes and get a bagel at the convenience store nearby, from which she would pick out the center dough and consume only the crust. Anorexia, bulimia, Tahnee swore it wasn't true; anyway, what could Murielle do about it at this minute? "Julie, did you see a stack of bills I left on the table?"

"No. Ma, can you do something about Sue Ellen? She is getting worse and worse, she's really bothering me."

Sue Ellen is Julie's imaginary friend, a sort of unpleasant companion who Julie uses as an excuse for when things go wrong. "No, I have not seen her." Murielle turns on the HGMTV. Some kind of infectious kidney virus… the anchorwoman is saying it's an epidemic. There aren't enough dialysis machines in the country.

Now the weatherman comes on. "Excuse me for interrupting," he announces gleefully, and goes on, thrilled beyond belief, to announce "*a hailstorm is coming, the hailstones will possibly be the size of tennis balls! Tennis balls, great destruction, no electricity for the dialysis, limited though the quantities may be!*" What the heck is going on? Where has she been?

Bills. Vaguely a memory of a bill. Eight thousand and ninety-five dollars? From who? And where is it? There is no use in looking, she knows that by now. It was due, when, a couple of days ago? She had meant to search for it the night before, now she had to get to work and make sure the kids got on the bus, there is no time to look; nevertheless she begins rummaging through a heap.

"Everybody at school has them, Ma. Jommy Wakowski had one last week that started coming out of his nose and he got the whole thing but the teacher actually threw up! What the hell are they, Ma?"

She hasn't been paying attention. "I don't know. Some kind of worm, a tapeworm, I guess, that's vermicide-resistant. If you'd wash your hands… Is this something of yours, Julie?"

Julie grabs the paper. "Oh, great! My homework! I was looking for that. See, I told you – Sue Ellen takes stuff, all the time, and hides it!"

Draw a map of the United States
– Name the relevant details
– Outline the former landmasses in a different color.

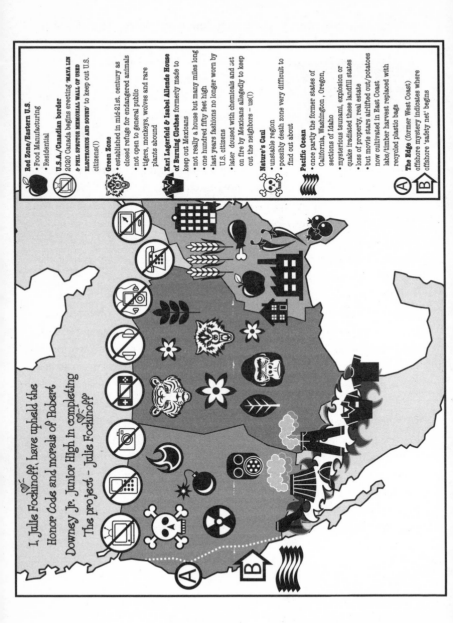

"Why can't you get organized the night before?" Murielle looks at the homework.

"Julie, did you do this?"

"Yeah, why, what's wrong?"

"Um, nothing... What's the wall of burning clothes?"

"Oh, that's to keep out the Mexicans, you know, where all the clothes get sent and formed into a wall that they soak in dirty oil and stuff, it's on fire?"

"I didn't even know about that! You really did this all by yourself? You didn't copy?"

"No."

"I'm surprised, that's all."

Her mother always thinks she is stupid! But Julie doesn't say this, she knows it would only make her mother mad. "Can I have fifty dollars for lunch? Hurry up, Ma."

"Oh God. Hang on just a second," Murielle says.

"Ma, I'm gonna miss the bus. What?"

"It's, you know, the worm thing. What the hell is it with these things, why can't the doctor give you some kind of medicine that works?"

"The bus is coming! Are you going to drive me?" Julie involuntarily sticks her little finger in her nostril.

"No, don't, don't touch or it'll retreat." Murielle takes some tweezers and grabs the worm head. The face with dark eyes and no chin is unpleasant. Then with the head of the worm in the tweezers she begins to pull, slowly winding the thin white body around the nearest thing to hand, a broomstick, which she twirls. When she has wound almost twelve feet of worm, the end breaks off and falls to the floor where, though missing the head, twitches across the room toward the gap under the cabinets. Being snapped in two doesn't seem to have killed the worm.

"I've definitely missed the bus."

"That's all I could get," Murielle says. She carries the broomstick and the tweezers over to the sink. The two of them look at the partial worm. As soon as Murielle releases the tweezers the other half of the worm uncoils itself from the broomstick and slithers down the drain, turning around once to look at them – or so it seems – with a contemptuous sneer. "Come on, I'll give you a lift."

"Gross," says Julie. "Turn the hot water on or something. Boil it. You should have flushed it down the toilet. I'm now officially late! How could it live when I could feel it snapped in two?" She sticks her finger in her nose. "I can't feel any of it in there, but I know you didn't get the whole thing."

6

Intelligent Design – Short Version

Somewhere in the universe a child is crying, "Maaaa! I'm bored!"

"Well, Adam," says his mother who is very tired and trying to get something accomplished. "Why don't you go play with your chemistry set?"

"Look, Ma!" yells Adam, a short time later. "You gotta see what I made!"

"Not right this minute."

"Come now!"

Adam's mother wearily goes to look. "Oh, Adam, that's terrific! What is it?"

"Can't you tell? Maaa, it's a new planet!" says the child with a satisfied smile. "And now I'm gonna give it the spark of life."

"No, no," shouts his mother. "Not the spark of life, honey! Remember what happened the last time! I don't want to have to clean up another of your messes!"

6

(Regular version)

The girls are open-mouthed, watching the President's boyfriend on HGMTV and eating biodegradable baked crunch poklets. "Gee, Scott, you look fabulous!" a reporter is saying. "Who designed your outfit?"

Scott is dressed in high black boots and jodhpurs, and carries a little crop. Under his other arm is a Cunard saddle, a birthday gift from Cunard – which, says the caption on hologramovision, *has been given to Scott in return for promotional considerations*. "It's all Cunard," Scott says. "Couture by Steve McQueen for the Cunard luxury line; do you know what the saddle alone would cost if I had to buy it retail?" He looks around. "Where is that stable boy? Manuel!"

Manuel is Argentinean, a shock of black hair, gumboots, short but blackly handsome. He takes the saddle from Scott.

The two men pose for the hologramovision cameras momentarily as they stare at the horse. "Christ, Manuel, he's just too darn long in the back for this saddle," Scott says at last. "You were the one who took the measurements, it's a custom-made fuckin' saddle, now what am I supposed to do?"

Manuel turns to the camera. "Let's find out, after this quick break for an important commercial announcement!"

"Come on, this guy's really starting to bug me," Tahnee says finally. "I'm bored, what do ya wanna do?"

"I dunno, what do you wanna do?"

"I wanna go to the shack."

"By ourselves or ya meeting someone?"

"Just us."

Julie is happy. Just them, this is a relief, to be alone with her sister – and even better not to have to wait outside the shack, standing guard, while Tahnee and Locu did whatever it was they did inside.

"Where's Locu?" Julie says.

"Dunno," says Tahnee. "Don't care." Julie is surprised. Tahnee loves Locu so much. She can spend hours with him, doing nothing but sleeping or half-sleeping, limbs entwined. She is happy. His brown skin, soft and hairless, his amber eyes thickly fringed with long black lashes. How Tahnee loves the smell of Locu, a mix of cinnamon, cumin, cardamom, turmeric. She knows these are the names of the smells because she has gone next door, often, to watch Locu's mother cook. Rima still does things the old-fashioned way. She opens different packets and cans and cooks them on the stove. Tahnee could almost lick him up, his warm, sweet-scented sweat. Even if he takes showers and doesn't eat Indian food for days, it is still embedded, somehow, in his skin.

Mostly they don't talk, they don't need to, it is enough to simply lie this way, felines in the sun, stroking the skin on the inside of each other's elbows or necks or gently scratching fingernails on the other's back: when they are together they need nothing else.

"You guys have a fight or something?" Julie hurries to keep up with her sister. "Is it because he wouldn't take that bubble bath with you when you wanted? Because I was reading how Hindu people don't take baths, they don't want to just sit there in their own wet dirt."

"Nope," says Tahnee, and Julie knows that is all Tahnee is going to say.

The heat gets to them quickly. Tahnee's pace slows to a trudge as they walk down the block. Some days out here when the temperature approaches a hundred and twenty, the asphalt melts. The houses are close together, no grass or trees grow and many of the front yards have been concreted over – everyone knows what the development has been built upon, that is why no one can ever sell their house; though one or two have been abandoned by the occupants; these are boarded up.

There is no sidewalk in this neighborhood but at the end of the dead-end street is a large field, bigger than a football field, with short dead grass and a large sign that says, COMMUNITY PLAYING FIELD COURTESY BERMESE PYTHION TECH. The field is divided in the center by a narrow trough, pencil wide, filled with an oozing black substance that makes any organized sport impossible; sooner or later some kid always gets a foot caught in that... stuff, which can melt a sneaker in a minute and a half. It's leakage from the swamp. Beyond the field is the marshland.

The kids have built a pathway: you leap from the door of a dishwasher to the hood from a car, to a sinking tire onto an old board. In the bubbly pitch in between, the garbage belches and viscous material, the consistency and color of melted bubblegum, rises and sinks. A quarter of a mile out beyond the field, a half a mile or less from the eight-lane highway, behind some ten-foot tall weeds, is the clubhouse-shack.

Julie doesn't particularly like steeting. She was eight when Tahnee first commanded her to inhale from a jar of **Blixsteetgluf**. The battery-acid coolness of the initial inhalation, the sensation of brain-matter plunged into dry ice; the lingering taste of... fermented milk and something blue and chemical... but then there are the two or three minutes that are – if not fantastic, the way Tahnee seems to find it – at least a sort of temporary delicate explosion: gigantic butterfly wings made of glass appear from nowhere and break.

What she hates is the way her tongue gets fat – this happens to everybody – and so she has to say "da" instead of "the", you can't say "th" which means that everybody knows what you've been doing – and the after, that horrible stench that lingers for hours on her skin and in her mouth, and the sense that she can't hear. Also, she almost always gets the skeeves, real bad.

If she had a choice, Julie wouldn't do it at all.

Oh boy, though, it is fun for Tahnee! She can just feel that icy stuff hit the brain and la-di-da-di-dim, that big gray ball of scrambled eggs up there just starting to... curdle around the edges; think of Little Miss Muffet screaming and pissing on that tuffet, think of eggs hitting the sidewalk, think of wham! A cleaver cutting right through the top of the head, everything kinda tumbling: who needs brains anyway, who was going to put them to any use?

Tahnee can always look up whatever she wants on the computer: let's say she has to know about a pop star having sex with, say, a movie star, how they went about it, doggy fashion or… she can look it up online and see it there, right in front of her!

And it is more fun to watch if her cortex is a little bit frazzled, blast the mushy stuff right out of existence, life is short! Tahnee knows she is going places, she is going right to the top, though she doesn't know yet exactly how; and later, perhaps – if she hasn't outgrown him – she'll collect Locu and have him as her little slave, that is, if she hasn't gotten tired of him. For the moment, he has to be punished; it was his idea to come by the other night and now not only is she in trouble with Mom, Locu is grounded.

While Tahnee inhales, Julie is just coming out of that initial polar land into a place that is even nastier, with her edges thawing like a plate of frozen cottage cheese in the microwave. She hears something behind the shack. Someone is out there.

Over the years the shack (or shak) has gotten more tilted; it's listing on its own petard, askew. The place is jammed with discarded mattresses, a greasy grill atop a charred hibachi where sometimes a kid will barbecue a **Tundertube Pop** made from that *extruded tasty paste that is never so good as when it is cooked outdoors.* "Did you hear dat?" says Julie who is now in the state they call trapped-in-ice. "I'm scared, get a stick, Tahnee!"

"I don't know," Tahnee says. "I didn't hear anyding, Julie."

"You didn't hear dat?"

"Maybe. You getting da skeeves again, Julie." More noise. Now she's got the skeeves coming on, too. "Locu, is dat you? Cut it out, you've pulled dat stupid trick too many times. It's not funny."

Locu has a way of hiding in some cubbyhole or up on the platform where there is another mattress and jumping out to scare them. "Please Tahnee. I'm scared."

"Whatever." Red-eyed, frozen-custard head, Tahnee goes out to look. Around the back someone (it had to have been Mason, the local Daply's

Urge kid) has wiped his ass with an old t-shirt and left the used rag next to the piled coil. "Watch where you step," someone says. "What a dump!"

Weird man, Tahnee thinks; he has the most peculiar skin, translucent, almost greenish beads of sweat on an oddly flat nose yet all in all not unattractive – those slightly bulging eyes, luminous and darkly pellucid. Too bad about the stupid hair, kind of greenish algae-colored – what the heck had he been thinking? He has a strange ominous presence, kind of cool, even cold. Maybe he'd been in jail? It's only when she's high that Tahnee has such complicated thoughts. "Who you?" Tahnee says, bleary-eyed.

"Sorry, didn't mean to scare you, nackets," he says. "I'm not dangerous." He grins.

Tahnee grins back – he's mesmerizing! – then curls her lip. Nackets? Who talks that way any more? This guy must be ancient, forty years old or something! "What are you, some kind a poncidee?"

"I came out to do a little target practice." He has some kind of gun, she doesn't know anything about guns; a big plastic gun.

"Keko desu," says Tahnee to Julie as she peeks out from the shack. "Ck, as bu?"

"Who's that?"

"Aw, dat's Sissy."

"Yeah? Sissy want to try it?"

Julie is scared. Julie has been warned against rapists, serial killers, pimps and strangers. But when she looks at him and he looks back at her she is overcome with a shyness unlike any other she has experienced. Oh! The air starts to vibrate. She can't stop staring at him. He doesn't move. Tahnee starts to giggle loudly. They resemble cartoon characters complete with lights and bells going off all around them. Julie is still frightened but she says, "Yes, I would like to try!" surprising herself. At school that is the one physical activity she is good at, in **Homeland Security Defense**, **Self-Defense**, **WEM** and **Product Testing**, she has amazing aim, it is practically the only thing that had saved her from flunking out of gym. She has never seen this type of weapon before, but

Julie bets she will surprise the hell out of him, like a character in a movie, bam bam bam.

"Neat," Julie says, trembling slightly. "What do we shoot at?"

"Come outside and I'll show you. What's your name, sister?"

"Julie."

"I'm Cliffort Manwaring-Troutwig. Old baseball family. Unfortunately, I wasn't cut out for the game, not with these hands. Worse than a foghorn for reminding me."

He holds up his hands. It is true, there are webs between each finger, connecting thumb to index finger, index to middle and so on. Julie winces. "You kids live around here?" he asks.

Manwaring-Troutwig

"Yeah, down de block. Dis is our clubhouse."

"I was wondering. I stayed here last night. I'm trying to get to New York City, I ran out of food and money. Fell asleep in my van at a rest stop and was robbed. Ran out of sugar-petromalt, can't find any for sale because of the shortages and I haven't eaten for two days."

"Oh, dat's terrible. I guess. Tahnee, do we have some food we could bring him from de house?" It may not be love at first sight, but at least it is an Awakening of Desire. Or something. Indeed their love may date back to a previous incarnation, judging from the shy stares and nervous trembling shimmering the air. Perhaps one was once Gertrude Stein and the other Alice B. Toklas; Clark Gable and Carol Lombard; Wallace Simpson and the Duke of Windsor, a binding love so strong it endures through many lifetimes, until the two involved are sick of the whole thing.

"I don't know." Tahnee shrugs. "I guess. Here, you wanna steet?" She throws the jar in Cliffort's direction. Julie winces again. Tahnee knows the stuff can explode if it hits the ground the wrong way. "It definitely takes away your appetite."

"Naw, I don't like that stuff. I'm going out to shoot this thing with your little friend –"

"My sister –"

"Your sister? You two don't look alike –"

"We have different dads."

"Is that right? And what's your name?"

"Tahnee."

"Tahnee, come out when you're ready to try out this Michiko Kamikaze. You gals ever shoot a Kamikaze before? It's not very accurate and it's pretty stupid but that's what makes it entertaining. Julie, think you can handle it?"

"How loud?"

"For a minute you can't hear anything. And it's not like what you see in movies, you know. This Kamikaze is made of extrudo, not metal, but even so there's a kickback on it. I want you to hold it with both hands – you want to watch me first?"

"I guess so."

On the far side of the dead grass, a football field length away, Cliffort has set up a paper target. When he shoots the Kamikaze it is so loud Julie nearly has a change of heart. "It sounds like a bomb or a rocket launcher or something!" Cliffort misses the paper target completely; he shoots too low and the bullet explodes into the marsh, spewing a twelve-foot high cloud of grass, dirt and marshland muck.

"You see, it's not so easy. Now you gonna try?"

"I don't know."

"Come on, you gotta try or you'll never be good at it."

Tahnee shrugs and winks at Julie; she knows how good she is. "Come on, Julie, like Dad always says, It'll be like throwing loaves to the fishes!" Julie is surprised that Tahnee is calling Slawa "Dad", something she has rarely done.

A huge plane is almost overhead. The planes fly over in the morning, and in the afternoon and into the night. All the time, planes are coming in overhead or taking off. The housing development is directly under the flight path to the airport. Cliffort stands behind her and puts his arms around her from behind to show her how to hold the Kamikaze. His hands are moist. "Right. Remember what I said, use both hands because when you pull the trigger it's going to come back at you so don't be scared."

Julie isn't prepared for Cliffort to actually push her fingers down on the trigger. Or does he? Certainly it seems like something is squeezing her hand and pulling the weapon up at the same time. Maybe there's a gyroscope inside. The force of the explosion propels her backward and the noise is so loud for a minute she thinks she is not just deafened but blinded.

When she looks up, about to chastise Cliffort, she sees he is nowhere near. High above, a glinting light coming off the airplane catches her eye. "Holy Shi'ite!" says Cliffort. "You got a hit!" It is true. What she thinks at first is merely sunlight glancing on the plane is actually a fire, spreading rapidly.

Within seconds there is another explosion as the fuel tanks go up, and then a vast black cloud, followed by things falling out of the sky: sheets of metal and twisting bits of melting plastic, glass and foam and trays and electrical wiring; suitcases are hitting the ground now and exploding as they hit into flowers of underwear and umbrellas, shoes like seed pods, clouds of talcum powder pollen.

It's all happening slowly – or perhaps quickly – a rain of hot blood and mucous; teeth and iceberg lettuce; plastic trays of hot creamy chicken and green beans mixed with entrails and chocolate-vanilla ice cream, the kind that comes in little paper tubes with an attached imbibing device. The fire is huge. Not as much falls as Julie might have thought – had she ever thought of such a thing happening – black handkerchiefs are waving everywhere until Julie realizes these are charred… things on fire, or just burning out, maybe newspaper, safety instructions, foam seat cushions or plastic toilet seats.

Drifts of blackened skin still attached to hairs waft across the sky, dander reduced to pepper falling from a grinder. They are immobile, paralyzed by the sight. Something wallops Julie on the head. "Hey, look!" Tahnee yells, darting down to pick it up. Something glints, gold and ruby-red. "A finger! Wid de ring still attached!"

"Are you crazy?" shouts Cliffort Manwaring-Troutwig, "Run! Get out of here! Run for your lives!"

7

B y the time school starts, Julie is quite ill. She may have made
herself *sick with worry*, or it may be *physical*. Her hands have
swollen to twice their normal size, blistering from within as if
they have been in a microwave oven. She still works in the lab after
school; at least this way there is no time to brood about the tragic
accident and how she has only herself to blame. But how can she not
think about it? My gosh, hundreds of people died, nine houses were
destroyed, should she confess and tell the police? She can't believe it: she
alone is responsible for the tragedy, children now without parents,
parents without children, insurance companies who were supposed to
provide for the widows and orphans going under.

She is evil, and probably evil incarnate, evil personified, even though
she had no intention of ever doing anything wrong. Her head hurts all
the time, she has inhaled the terrible fumes and now her hands are
blistered and getting blacker almost like she has frostbite or gangrene.
She has cried so much her eyes are permanently swollen.

On the other hand this year is the big Eighth Grade Test and she
should be spending her after-school hours studying. She likes her
English teacher, Miss Fletsum, but Miss Fletsum isn't the easiest teacher;
she's had her before, she's one of the tough ones. "Pay attention class!
We must do more preparation before the day of the big test! Name three
hits by Rogers and Hammerstein and two by Rogers and Hart." No one
raises a hand. "This test can affect your entire life! So, think children,
think!" Miss Fletsum strikes herself dramatically on the side of her head.
"Ow, sorry, head!" The children laugh and no one pays any attention for
the rest of the period.

Miss Fletsum is funny. Of course Miss Fletsum is also a little strange
and sometimes, often, actually, she announces to the kids that her head
isn't really hers. Once, during a minor breakdown (she had to take a

couple weeks off, afterward) she had actually gone over to Mystique and tried to pull off Mystique's head, insisting that somehow Mystique had taken what was rightfully hers.

At least now she is on different meds. "Children! The United States is lagging far behind the rest of the globe and that is no small laughing matter! Who starred in *Now Voyager*? Name five rules for owning a successful fast-food franchise! You're going to have to know these things to pass the test! Essay: what it must be like to live in Nature's Caul. Who are the sort of people who get to live there? Compare and contrast."

The class sighs and whines.

"Remember your topic sentence, guys!"

All the kids are drugged because they are hyperactive with saudiautistic tendencies and/or saudiautism. And if not openly saudiautistic then they have Sasporger's Motif, Wharf Planchette, Florie's Palsy, ADDA or vitamin deficiency caused by petrochemical solvents causing depression.

A depressed child is not a happy child. A depressed child cannot focus. "Focus, children. Fluorescent lighting," Miss Fletsum says. "Spelled f-l-u-o-r-e-s-c-e-n-t."

"Miss Fletsum, that's not what our spell check says."

"What?"

"It spells it flourescent."

"But – but –" Miss Fletsum is spluttering. "That's absurd! That's wrong!"

Miss Fletsum likes to make sure the kids know and can use clichés and idioms, as well as famous quotations. She has told the children more than once that she is an accident. She is given to statements such as, "If the shoe fits, wear it – but it will be uncomfortable outside the store," and "Still waters run deep, unless it's a puddle."

Julie knows she is lucky to have Miss Fletsum as her teacher. All the kids like her, apart from her wacko thing about her head not being the right one. Those lapses can be dangerous. But then, she is old, and something might have started to go wrong for a long time.

Miss Fletsum is so old she started teaching in the days before there was mandatory retirement; Miss Fletsum is one of the last members of the Teachers Union; Miss Fletsum lost all of her savings in the Walbuck's scandal. Miss Fletsum says, when she was growing up, people could actually read, whereas nowadays they are all spoiled because the computers are able to put everything – books, articles, whatever was formerly printed – into wide-screen high-definition hologram format.

"I will never be able to stop teaching!" Miss Fletsum says dramatically, and once more she tries to get Julie's class to learn to read. "'In the great green room,'" begins Miss Fletsum once again, "'there was a telephone, and a red balloon, and a –'"

The class groans. "We can't do it, Miss Fletsum," says Daqoyt, "our eyes don't work that way! How many times do we have to tell you?"

"And besides," mutters Cryhten, who sits next to Julie, "why should we, there are no books any more."

At least Julie is going to get extra school credit for working as an intern. It is still lonely, though. Dyllis is nice, but she is mostly working in a different lab these days, and when she is around, Dyllis spends most of her time trying to find dates on the computer.

She likes women who are muscular, with large clitori, an interest in restoring antique yachts and an appreciation of classical music such as Bartók, Aaron Copland and Stevie Nicks.

How will Dyllis ever meet anyone? She is so so lonely. She misses her friends in Vieques so much. There, in the cool evenings, everyone gathers in the central square; they can never go far because of all the undetonated shells that litter the whole island, but it is enough to walk, hand in hand, with a friend, around the *zocala*, or sit at a café and eat a dish of fried plantains or roasted pepnuts. Here, during the day, she is alone in an air-conditioned mausoleum, and at night she drives three hours back to her grim apartment, where she has to keep the doors locked and the windows shut at all times.

Dyllis knows she talks too much, but there is no way to stop herself. Even when she tells herself, most firmly, to be quiet, still the words pour out in a never-ending river until she is trapped, helpless, behind the waterfall, unable to emerge. Even when she is alone the words keep coming, though, fortunately, if she is walking down the street, everyone assumes she is plugged in to her site.

Julie never sees anyone else in the building.

For security reasons, Bermese Python has some kind of policy about employees never interacting. If Julie stays late, dinner is delivered into the lab through a slot in the door, on a tray with a menu to describe the contents. It might be poached quail eggs with strawberries and edamame, served with a haunch of civet cat in a nut crust. Or chilled candy-corn soup with blue *aji* dulce peppers and quinoa grits. Once there was a glacé encompassing *uni*, eel and snake, accompanied by multi-textured tofu strands with a sauce of *mirin* and raw squid-ink foam. The labs at Bermese Python are known for serving fine cuisine. Other people come in at night, or in the evenings – at least three shifts per experiment, people whose paths never cross.

Sometimes animals, like the adorable kitten with eyes so huge they took up most of its face, mysteriously vanish. Or in the morning things are dead in their cage. Or worse, hooked up to electrodes or blossoming with strange growths.

The fall passes slowly. Each day Julie listens to the news, wondering if today will be the day the authorities discover it is she who killed all those people on **Flight 21894**. Now she is at the mercy of her sister, who has got her doing all her chores, her homework, and threatens to blab if she doesn't obey her. Her dad is gone; her mother hates her.

Anything is better than being at home. Why wouldn't she prefer to spend all her time at the lab? The lab is kept cold and she takes a sweater with her, though outside it's usually blistering by six in the morning. It's hard to believe that when she leaves for the day she will not be able to breath in the searing heat. The temperature has been between a hundred and a hundred-and-twenty farenheit for months.

According to scientific records there *has never been* such a long, hot Indian summer since record-keeping began. The newscasters say *previous estimates regarding global warming are incorrect*: unless there is a sudden ice age, the warming of the planet will be far faster than the rate of seven degrees a century. Home air-conditioning isn't really possible.

Nobody around these parts can afford current electrical rates. Anyway, there are power blackouts almost every day, for hours at a time.

In the lab it is cold and, with no windows, always illuminated by artificial yet natural means, lighting that replaces and provides the same wavelengths as the sun. The animals are never going to be able to see anything more than the metal cage walls that surround them. It isn't right. She wishes she could save them all, even the horrid ones.

There are plenty of animals she can't deal with. The pigs continue to frighten her, though she tries to look on them with compassion. It is something in their expression, a look both human and malevolent, and the big boar is still there, more lascivious, more craven. He has masturbated himself until he is bleeding. Fortunately the pigs are too large for her to even think about taking, and how could she possibly have kept one? Each, daily, produces hundreds of pounds of steaming excrement.

Insects: **Hair-A-Ticks**, which are ticks engineered to lay their eggs in a person's scalp. And each egg hatches into a tick that grows a hair. The hair pushes its way up through the scalp. The tick lives its life beneath. When the tick dies, so does the hair that it has grown; then the females emerge to lay more eggs. The problems thus far, though, apart from the unpredictability of what color the hairs would be – red, blond, black, white or often a combination of all of them – is that some of the head ticks begin to migrate beneath the skin, so that over the years hairs can grow on the nose, arms, the palms of hands, the chest, the neck, the back and buttocks.

A person just interested in getting hair on their head might end up completely hairy, like a gorilla. According to Dyllis, a topical hair-removal ointment could be applied, though rather unsuccessfully. And if a tick came from under the person's skin while it was still alive and growing the hairs, it could implant on someone else if, say, that person was the next to sit in the same seat on a bus or a couch.

Naturally she wouldn't want these: but, as the weeks pass, though she knows it is wrong, she smuggles out more animals, small ones, caterpillars that will become moths with a five-foot wingspan, or a galaxy-nosed mole.

One of the lab technicians must have begun to notice: a sign went up on the wall, saying that whoever is taking things out of the lab is going to be caught and punished unless he or she returns the various creatures that had been taken.

Is she going to have to go to prison? This isn't out of the question. She hasn't seen another human being, apart from Dyllis; even when she cuts down on smuggling out the animals, new signs are posted each morning, with more threats.

"Don't worry about it," said Dyllis. "You got a lot of thiefs around here. Somebody took my skin-plant, ju remember?" Dyllis has covered her tracks. It's awful, the animals mewing or crying, in a state of permanent bewilderment, unable to reconcile having, say, the temperament and body design of a duck – but without a beak and webbed feet.

Marsupials without pouches that spit venom, blood-sucking lamprey-puppies – she is always getting in trouble for giving them the wrong food. Or she gets bitten. Each day Julie is more profoundly depressed. Nothing she does turns out right.

"You know, Julie," Tahnee tells her, "I could really use a recommendation from the lab where you work."

"What?" says Julie, who has bicycled home, though it is really too hot, and now as usual is preparing dinner. "But... you don't work there."

"So what?" says Tahnee. "I'll come in for a couple of days while you're there, then I can write up whatever you do and submit it for credit and get Mom's friend to give me a report."

Julie would do anything for her sister, she always has, and says, "Of course, if you think it will be fair."

"Aw, give me a break. It's not fair that you blew up a hundred and eighty-nine people, is it?"

"It was an accident. It was Cliffort."

"By the way," says Tahnee, "I've been spending some time with Cliffort trying to convince him he should keep his mouth shut for your sake. I mean, I explained, even though you're a minor, they would still put you in jail. Reform school first, then prison. I mean, if you listen to the news, the President is looking for somebody to punish. I mean, like, his ratings are going down, you know what I mean?"

Julie can't speak. Wet feathers jam her throat or perhaps tufts of rabbit fur and lard. Whatever it is, she is choked up. For weeks she has been trying to convince herself the plane crash didn't really happen; she hasn't watched the news. High from steet, the plane dropping from the sky, the stench of jet fuel, the body parts, did not seem so different from a video arcade game or a program on HGMTV. Only shreds of that afternoon occasionally tear loose, then she shoves them back into her head, where what's left of her brain, a gray pillow, has a hole that keeps letting out the stuffing.

"You're a good little sis," says Tahnee. "If I can get the credit, that'll be one less course I have to take before I graduate. Maybe you can even write up the report, and I'll just tag along for a few days, like I said, so in case I'm questioned I'll have some idea."

Tahnee spends the afternoon perched on a lab chair watching Julie work. "Come on, Tahnee, don't you want to help me? These animals really crave human touch, and they need the cages cleaned! There are so many, I usually can't get to everyone."

Tahnee shrugs. Just then the door to the lab opens. There is a tiny man, perhaps not abnormally small, but shrimp-like. He is very pink and his motions are darting, somehow backward, as if self-propelled in the wrong direction.

He's got a rumpled look: he's wearing very shabby clothing of a style so old-fashioned it must date from, gosh, the 1970s? Something like a patchwork quilt jacket – madras, maybe – and white pumps. Tahnee and Julie have almost never seen a man in a suit, not in this area, not in their world. Next to him is a taller man normally dressed in a gown, who by comparison, almost blends into the walls.

"So," the pink man is saying, "in this lab we can see some of the newer projects and how they're coming a…" Then he notices Tahnee and Julie. "Hi there, girls," he says. "You must be the school interns! I bet you're surprised the company president knows about you, but I make it my habit to know everything. Although, I didn't realize there were two of you now! How are you enjoying everything so far? I'm A. Jesse March Bishrop, president and CEO of Bermese Pythion. And this is Mr Salamonder, from the Stuyvesant Technics, who has come to look at what we're –"

Mr Bishrop is sort of... too eager. Or maybe it's not eagerness, exactly; it's as if he's translucent, or the rest of the world doesn't exist to him. Maybe it's just the way zillionaire geniuses are, almost slightly saudiautistic. He's just a little... off, with his daffy glasses, his enthusiasm and flappy arms; he's walking on tippy toes, the man is intense.

"Oh my gosh, Mr Bishrop! C.k., as bu?" says Julie. "I am so happy to see you, I never thought you'd actually be here in person, you know all those suggestions in the suggestion box? I'm the one who –"

Julie realizes A. Jesse March Bishrop isn't listening. He looks stymied. Stymied, is that the right word? It is as if all of his energy has been expelled at once. He can't seem to stop staring at Tahnee. And Tahnee is kind of smirking. What the heck is going on? Not much, as far as Julie is concerned: whenever Tahnee goes anywhere, this is what happens. Julie has watched drivers get into accidents when she walks alongside her sister. Once there was even an eighteen-car pile-up. In supermarkets men have knocked down stands of fruit with their carts. Even on the hottest days, wearing nothing but tiny shorts and a little halter-top, Tahnee does not attract jeers or hoots or whistles. Rather, something odd happens to any man she is near, and quite often women: an expression comes over them like they have been punched in the stomach. Now A. Jesse March too.

"I should have stopped in before, to see how you girls were getting along this summer. Summer, and now fall." He is half-muttering but doesn't take his eyes off Tahnee. "Are you planning to keep working over the winter? You're high school girls?"

"I probably am going to have to look for a paying job," Tahnee says languidly. She doesn't look at A. Jesse when she says this.

"I guess you girls will be getting paid to work here pretty soon! Soon. I should have made sure of that ages ago, but you know, I'm hardly ever here, my place is out in Nature's Caul."

"I guess if the pay was decent, I could keep working here," Tahnee says. "The main thing is for me to get school credit, I gotta get a recommendation."

"How would you like it if you had a personal recommendation from me?" A. Jesse glances at the lab. "Would that help? I can see you've done a good job this summer and believe me, I have seen some of the other labs and it is not easy. Anyway, I'll be happy to say so in a letter and I'll look into getting you started on a paycheck very soon – it won't be much to start, but –"

A. Jesse is in his late forties and something is happening to him. For the first time he is falling in love, although it might be something else? Never having been in love he doesn't know, exactly. It is not something he can figure out with a formula, but, like lysis, an explosion from within.

He has had four wives and is already planning to divorce the fourth. One was a lawyer, one was a stay-at-home mom, one was a stripper and… he has gosh, six kids? Or is it seven?

There is Lonald, age twenty and Cheslea, fifteen, and then… there are others, that is for certain. He can't remember the others, not at this moment, and it is A. Jesse's belief that the fabric of the universe has gotten so thin in places that it has become as translucent as cheesecloth, or theatrical scrim. But this is something strangely different.

"You know," A. Jesse mutters, backing up, "I've just thought of something. If there are a hundred people and a hundred slices of suffering, one person is going to get, like, sixty of those slices. Like, you know how one person has breast cancer and then a child who dies in an accident and then a fire?"

"Oh, I get it!" Julie says, as always trying to be amenable. But he is not looking at Julie, he is staring, still, at Tahnee.

"You do?" he says, "Let's say one person ends up with sixty percent of the suffering-pie slice, some get ten percent, five percent, one percent, well, there is one person who doesn't get any slices at all!" A. Jesse can't believe it, it is the first thought he has had that is not about science or business. He is so pleased and delighted with himself, for this idea. An idea about people! "I always thought, you see, that I was that person, the one who didn't have to have a slice. And I want to keep things that way!" He crosses the room and without paying attention begins to stroke the leaves of what appears to be the **common house plant** Julie helped Dyllis to revive.

Dyllis is standing behind him, unnoticed, at the door. "Oh, Mister Bishrop!" she says. "You know, I couldn't help but overhear you jes' now, and you are so right! No wonder you having such thoughts, you are even more brilliant than the peoples say, I guess that ees why you are a zillionaire and I am not! And how blessed – would that be the right word? – we are to have you visiting us here today in the laboratory! Maybe not the word blessed but, jes' plain fortunate? Or lucky? Or, let us praise the Intelligent Designer? Anyway, I hope these girls, they being nice to you and showing you around! If I had only known you would be here, I would have made sure I was in the lab!" Why can't she stop herself blabbing, she thinks, but it is impossible.

But A. Jesse is gone, grinning nervously, with Mr Salamonder left behind, perplexed, and Dyllis still rattling on and Tahnee, both girls, really, thinking A. Jesse is old and weird. But rich, whatever that means.

And now, a digression:

The common house plant that Julie had nursed back to health that Dyllis had found dying in the women's toilet has the soft silky skin of a young girl, each juicy leaf is alive, downy with hope and dewy expectation. Oh silent plant, if only you had been engineered to have a nice tight pussy as well! And taut, nubile breasts tipped with tremulous pink budded-nipples! Brainless, undemanding, to wrap your tender, admiring leaves around some old geezer and vibrate in harmonious orgasm. Oh stamen, oh pistil and nectar-rich orifice within petals, my God, I (the manly author) would so love to grab you by the stem and bury my nose in such cunning delight.

No. 5 Common House Plant

Thus endeth the digression.

"I guess A. Jesse thinks you girls have done a good job!" says Mr Salamonder at last. "We are already late for our next meeting, so… Nice to meet you both!" He follows A. Jesse into the hall.

Dyllis is impressed that the founder of the company actually knows who she is, kind of. "That guy has zillions," she says. "Billions of zillions. I saw him on HGMTV once with the President. I feel kind of sorry for him, though."

"Why?" Tahnee rolls her eyes.

"I don't know, he seem so nervous, and that patchy skin and he's so pink. Plus, I always think how terrible it must be when a man loses his hair like that, don't you? I guess that's why he invented the Hair-A-Ticks, ju know? So he could grow hair again."

Julie's eyes are stinging, she thinks of her own dad's winky bald spot. Life can be terrible.

"Yuck, I thought he was creepy, he was, you know, kind of boiled? What does he do with all that money, anyway?"

"My English teacher, Miss Fletsum, says he collects thimbles – ancient Unitarian thimbles? – something like that. And he breeds and shows hyenas? He's like, one of the richest men in the world and he dropped out of college to start this business," says Julie. "Gee, wouldn't that be great, if we start to get paid?"

"I guess," says Tahnee with a shrug.

"Believe me," says Dyllis, "you girls are really lucky. What if he takes a stronger feeling toward you, and invites you to Nature's Caul? Oh my God. All my life, I only hear about thees place. And, you know thees was years ago, I took a trip to see it. Of course, your normal people, they can't go in. They got the big walls all around and the security. I went with your mother, did she ever tell you? So, we were just out of high school. We were hoping and hoping, maybe some men who live inside see us, he fall in love and, who knows? But you never go in."

"You don't go in?"

"No. You take a bus, it goes all around the outside, the man, he tell you all about the homes that are inside, and who lives there. Some of the houses, you could even see from the road, and they got the green grass and the swimming pools with real water! At night, we stay in a motel, we went to the bar, but there was no one from the inside there, just the regular outside type people. Nature's Caul. I think it must be the mos' beautiful place in the world."

For a moment Dyllis is silent. Even Tahnee and Julie can't
help
      but
           be
                impressed.

7B

IN	OUT
Aureole enhancement	Labia stretch
Prince Michael Jackson Five with Quattro Formagio	Iglesias Family Dynasty
The Bono Kids and Monkey Big Saturday Show!	Dr. Sugar Apricot Heavenly Fluff Hutchinson x-cess News Round-up
Four-legged vehicles	Mady Husin Autostat Meir

8

If Slawa had time – in happier times – he did squats, push-ups and fifty sit-ups before going out; lifted weights. He showered when he could, on days when there was enough water, which wasn't so often, and when there was water it was filled with gray lumps and that greasy stuff. Their district was so low on the list they got the worst of the purified water. But even if he scrubs, that greasy feeling and the odor of waterproofing fluid clings to him, his breath smells of the stuff.

He no longer worries what is wrong with him. He knows. It is somewhere inside him, his belly maybe, a huge bubble with a tough skin. He is not certain what it is, it reeks of egg and plastic and bubbles up his throat, making it difficult to breathe. All he knows now, is he wants to get out of the house.

For years the house – and his family – meant everything to him. He would leave for work before dawn to beat the rush hour. Not that rush hour ever stops, but if he left early it could make the difference between two and a half hours and three and a half; and as soon as he locks up at night he heads for home.

He is so good at fixing things: plumbing, electrical, painting. He cleans, he cooks. It takes Slawa a long time to realize that as soon as one thing is fixed something else breaks down; he has even seen a hologramovision program about it, something to do with the weakening of the earth's electrical fields and the fact that the earth's orbit is tilting, little by little.

This may have something to do with the thin hole that was drilled, just for fun, through the entire core of the earth. Why was this done, when everyone already knew that on the other side all they will find is China? Nevertheless, now he is evolved enough to be indifferent to material possessions, she can keep the house for all he cares.

He goes around the corner to Chez Gagna Koti to see if it is still open. But it is already shut for the night and though he bangs on the door Bocar is not there. The boy is seventeen and works at his uncle's Ethiosenegalpian restaurant. Slawa never would have guessed, Slawa, that at his age, at this time of life, he would make such a good friend, especially with someone from such a different culture and generation.

They met when Bocar came to get his shoes re-soled. That was unusual in itself since most men would rather go out to get a new pair of high heels than bother to have the out-of-date ones repaired; and since Slawa's shop is located at the bottom of the first flight of steps leading down to the subway, people rarely wandered in off the street. Usually his business was by accident, someone on their way to work who broke a heel and had no time to shop for new shoes. And when one day without warning a metal grate was placed just beyond his store, and a sign on the street stated **Entrance Closed Temporarily** there were no more customers at all.

The landlord wouldn't reduce the rent, what was he to do now? He tried handing out fliers on the street, offering special discounts, he even put a poster for his business over the 'Closed' sign. But nothing made any difference.

If had he been friendlier, he wonders, might he have had steady clients? But day in and day out, crouched animalistically in those dark quarters, without ventilation, roasting hot in summer, freezing in winter, he had become like... who was it, that ancient Greek guy who hammered all the time in mythology: Vulcan?... surly, scowling and the dark hairy body banded with sweat.

So it was a surprise when Bocar first came in, coatless, shivering, taking off his sopping red pumps even before he had sat down.

"My friend, I am wondering, I have many times passed by the sign announcing Shoe Repair, and I never knew such a thing could be done. But look – !" He waved a sheaf of bills. "Auntie has given me money for you to do so." Of course what came out – shouted – was "mi fry-end, I am won-DER-ing, I hay-ve man-Y time-as pas-sed this show store —" etc.

It took Slawa ages to figure out what he was saying, and because Bocar was so deaf and he himself had a strong Russian accented English, he was not sure that what he was finally able to teach Bocar was any improvement.

No one had ever looked at Slawa in such a kindly, sympathetic way before... Or maybe the reason he was so smitten was simply a chemical response? Who knows what cinched the deal – was it that sudden look of alarm on Bocar's face, so that Slawa thought the kid was going to flee?

But before Slawa could ask what was wrong or try to stop him, Bocar asked, loudly, "My friend, which way is east?" And knelt on the floor, clutching prayer beads and muttering under his breath.

It was two o'clock and Bocar did not finish his prayers for nearly half an hour. "I must pray to Allah five times a day," he said, in an apologetic tone when he was finished. "This business of praying! Sometimes in this country it is not so easy. I am finding myself kneeling in foul circumstances, because all the time I am running, running for my uncle to the warehouses to provide the vegetables needed for his dishes, or to go for my Auntie Adamna who treats me as if I was her personal slave."

"Please, whenever you need a place to pray that is quiet, you will come to me," said Slawa. "As you can judge, I have no customers and I can clear a better place for you. I too am a religious man though not in the sense of an organized religion, but from within. Did you know, for example, that here in my shop there are seventeen ley lines, which converge? Yes, here, in this place, my shop, and there is no other place like this where such a confluence occurs except where the Trade Towers were located! You have heard of the Towers of World Trade and the troubles?" But the boy had not.

Slawa wakes with a start. He must have dozed, exhausted. His breath is sour and the flies stir, groggy, reluctant to leave the warm drowsy places on him they have selected to sleep. The cats... the hole. Still, when for a split-second he sees the eyes of one of them, the cat Murka, illuminated by his torch, he realizes he has to go down to get her. He crawls through the door and takes a step, then another, when the whole structure crashes out from under him, the whole twenty-foot-tall curving steps, totally rotten. He jumps and lands obliquely, with a thud, on something reasonably soft. Inelegant Designer, he silently curses, what can it be? A pile of cigarette butts six feet deep.

Thousands upon thousands, still stinking, one end nice and crusty from where he guesses the tobacco has begun to burn the plastic or whatever it is the filter is made from.

He climbs out. Geez, it looks like no one's been down here since Judge Crater was found.

It's an entire room, a club, a restaurant? A padded, tufted corridor past a coat check room, and most curiously there is a large painting: Christ with the New Testament in his left hand, blessing with the right – involuntarily he crosses himself; he wasn't even aware he knew how to. What is this place, a church?

"Winston tastes good, like a cigarette should!"

He jumps. Someone else is here? But no – an ancient tune blares from hidden speakers, set off by his movement; some kind of projector throws grainy pictures onto a screen. *"You're never alone with a Strand"*. *"To A Smoker, It's a Kent!"*

This joint, this tomb, is long abandoned. A mouse-gnawed ottoman, Empire sofa in royal blue velvet, mirrored walls, floor tiled in pink and gold, turquoise, beige, the place had apparently been sealed up, untouched, as if the club-goers had abruptly fled.

He can't find the cats, he can't find his way around. The light from the projector, spitting its pictures of square-dancing cigarettes, illuminates bits and pieces: ashtrays embossed 'The Pink Pantokrator Club' stuffed with butts.

Oh, he realizes, it's a Smoke-Easy, from the time when – though you could still buy cigarettes in the U.S. – you were not allowed to smoke them and the Phillips-Maurice Anti-Smoking Homeland Police Squad had patrolled the streets and were allowed without a warrant to enter citizens' homes.

Drinking glasses with the contents long since congealed or evaporated, some still with stirrer. A woman's handbag, left behind perhaps during a raid. Signs that mice or rats had once provisionally made some of the banquettes their birthing centers and sleeping quarters, though it doesn't appear there are any around here now. Nor the cats.

In the distance he hears the rumbling of the subway train, not too far away, then once it has passed he hears mewing and goes in the direction of the sound. There is a little wooden dance floor, badly warped, and a stage with a moldy gold velvet curtain; above his head a chandelier and below a heap of bird droppings. At some point the pigeons had set up residence, though they too are long gone.

Off to one side of the stage is the bar where the waiters must have served drinks. A few smashed bottles on the floor, a cigarette girl's case of cigarettes that could be harnessed around her neck and displayed in front. The Smoke-Easy must date to the mid twenty-first century before smokers started dying off after the poisoned cigarettes scandal or whatever it was, he can't remember.

It seems as if the mewing is coming from inside a cabinet and when he opens it two cats emerge, dusty and glaring, as if he is somehow responsible. Within, unopened (though no doubt stale), arranged on dark green baize as if precious gems: packs of **Marlboros, True's, Camels, Virginia Slims. Vantage, Viceroy, American Spirit, Chesterfields, Newport, Parliament. Soubranie, Rothman, Carlton, Tarleton. Kent, Winston, Silk Cut, Old Gold, Pall Mall, Gauloise**.

Kools.

So many different kinds, how did people ever know back then what type best suited them? If these cigarettes weren't stale they would be worth millions on the black market!

It's a mystery why or how the place has been boarded up, alcohol bottles intact but contents mostly evaporated.

There's a button on the wall and he presses it then jumps, startled, as large slabs of cinderblocks that looked immobile slide open and right onto... the subway platform. Quickly he pushes the button again. This must have once been the secret entrance. Fortunately it doesn't seem as if anyone on the platform has noticed, all intent on looking down the tracks.

He rests for a moment on the couch. It is more comfortable than going back upstairs, though a bit chilly; maybe the kitties will come to him in the night for warmth. Something lumpy in his pocket; oh, the little book. He turns on his flashlight to read for a minute; the whole country is reading the President's fiancé's memoirs; it's required reading! Most people – well, lots, anyway, have never read a book, not in the sense of a physical object with pages. But this book is *tastefully done* with a red cover and collaged images (torn photos, documents, ticket stubs. Sleepily he begins to leaf through the pages.

"I was born in the Caucasus. My father, an American-Negro, was traveling on holiday in the Caucasian mountains, when he met my mother. To this day I am uncertain whether she was a hundred percent Caucasian; I have been told she might have had some Circassian blood. In any event, it matters not: when I was but four months of age I was adopted by Big M'bell Glorious Mohammed Taneesqua, the pop singer. At that time she weighed four hundred pounds. She had already adopted eight other children by the time I came along, but alas would not live to see most of us grown up.

But believe me the other kids were extraordinarily beautiful! The most beautiful girls from Somalidan, Rajapakisthan, Afuzbekistan. The boys from the Sudan, Senegal! Praise be to the Intelligent Designer, is all I can say, that Mr President, our very own National Dinge Queen (no dissin' intended, just a little joke!) didn't get a look at one of my bros! He never would have taken a second glance at me!

As for Momma: diabetes and heart attack led to her demise at age fifty. Originally I wanted to call my autobiography Whites in Hot Water, because Momma always made us kids do a lot of chores. Even though she was rich, we did not get a free ride.

Most of you will remember me from my years on the global news network, where I moved up from weatherman to chief correspondent and then nightly prime time anchor.

Slawa nods off over the book and jolts awake with a start. He is having such an odd sensation. It is some kind of memory, of how as a kid, when he was homeless, the cops? What were they called? The KGB. The KGB had taken him away to some kind of institution, where he was injected. No, surely this couldn't be possible. And there... Who did he have a chat with, Beriya, yes, once there was Beriya the great, and the mental institution, electric shocks and insulin comas; oh, how many years went by, sitting day after day in a room of the sick, the sweating, the unwashed, the room full of smoke and vitriol.

Once, he remembers, somehow someone had something called a mail order catalog. How had it made its way not only into Soviet Russia during the... he guesses it was the cold war – how and not only into Soviet Union but from there to the hospital, institution, what have you. No one could believe it, it was better than pornography, it was unbelievable, what was it called, something like **Stalinberry Farms**, said one guy who could read a couple words in English, though then they all realized it must be Stalin and Beriya's farm, page after page of *cakes*, *salamis*, *dried fruits*, *petits fours*, *cheeses* and *hams*...

Was it even possible such a world existed? To them it was science fiction, even outside the prison walls they would never have had such things, and here the diet, the burnt groats, the grits, some rank cabbage or rarely a gristly bit of fat. The bread alone was occasionally authentic, though only rarely, mostly it was a cinderblock of gray, textureless and tasteless foam. When it wasn't stale.

He shivers. Better not to think. What's going on, the temperature must be close to freezing, his breath is visible in front of him, the weather is insane! He hasn't brought any warm things with him... Should he make a fire out of whatever wood he can find? He paces, restlessly, rubbing his hands together.

So his wife has thrown him out – of his own house! His daughter whom he loves so much, she feels sorry for him, a bald fat old man! What will he do, living here? He will definitely have to get a hologramovision, having those new HDHC sets, it's like having real people around, maybe even better, but of course the hologramovision won't work without cable.

In the electronic store the President is having a press conference, which means that all one thousand channels, all are receiving the same thing: the President, saying, "And these are the countries we've helped to become Safe Democratic Homelands and these –" he points to the board on the right "– are the countries who are still waiting for us to liberate them. And now I am going to ask the American people to call in on our hotline, at ten dollars a call, to help decide: which country do you think we should pick next? The money we as Americans spend will be used to repair the chosen land after we have fought and liberated them."

Slawa finally gets some kid wearing a name tag that reads 'Deen' to help him and he picks out the five-foot screen, not totally up to date: it will only receive a few channels in the Hologram-Definition mode, but at the moment he is going to try not to spend so much.

"That's the floor model, I can give you a discount," the kid says, and when Slawa nods he unclips the screen and rolls it up. "Let me see if I can find the container for it, and I'll meet you by the checkout. Give me five minutes." It's only a month or so before the equipment becomes obsolete.

Slawa wanders around the store. Here are the latest things, those flying saucers that elevate a few feet off the pavement; rare-earth boots that let you climb partway up the sides of buildings; the computer brain you can buy for your car so you can tell it where to go; the virtual reality holographic shopping game where you can also fight bad guys!

He heads for the register. Deen is busy scratching his rear end with the register gun. Slawa waits and waits; Deen is obviously high on something, but who can blame him? He clicks the register gun at the credit stud in Slawa's right ear-lobe and then he looks at the read-out, disbelieving. "You almost don't have enough credit left, you can barely get this model… You better get your credit refinanced soon. Ya want me to check again? Some times these chips get, kind of infected or something, it can help if you use an alcohol swab, you should keep them in your pockets."

"No. How am I supposed to pay – ?"

"Gee, I don't know," Deen says. He has an oily nervous energy. It occurs to Slawa that Deen might be a girl, or at least one of those neuters, so many kids are born that way these days and psychological testing shows it is better not to make gender assignation until the person is old enough to decide for him, her or itself – if that is what it chooses.

Deen lowers his voice to a whisper. "I tell you what, if you want, I can come by when I get out of work and hook ya up."

Suddenly Slawa is desperate to talk. If he goes home he will be alone. "Yes, yes," he mutters. "You see, my chip is empty on purpose. If they steal my identity then with it is going my self-esteem. I do not have much self-esteem to begin, you know. I am not caring much about who I am, it is how I am feeling about myself, you know?"

Dean shakes his head. "What?"

"Never mind."

Unbelievably, he finds the last remaining public phone. It must be an accident, really, that it works; it's just outside the men's room in the Smoke-Easy. He is lucky: he has hundreds of quarters to feed into the coin slot, funny how he was once entertained by collecting coins; the operator, a mechanized voice, keeps explaining, "*If you'd like to make a call, please deposit thirty-five dollars.*"

"Daddy?" Julie, thank goodness, the only one he wants to speak to, but she sounds despairing.

"My love, how are you, my little shapka?"

"Dad, some men were here, they wanted to know if some guy was with you, Bocar?"

"I don't understand."

"The President was on HGMTV, on the news, saying how anybody harboring a fugitive conscript is going to be prosecuted. The men said you have some kid from someplace who signed the papers to serve in the military, he was replacing some rich kid from Minneapolis? And then he escaped, or he didn't go to boot camp when he was supposed to… Daddy, are you really okay?"

"What?" He isn't paying attention. How clever they had been. After all, you can do nothing, make no transaction on credit, no phone call, without being immediately identifiable or at least traceable via microchip; the citizens give away their own identities, down to the last item, hemorrhoid ointment, toothpaste brand, dialing up *Gone With the Wind* at three a.m. If he leaves there are cameras everywhere. They could see him, at the bank, in the markets, in the subways. Even if he *could* take out all his money from the bank in cash without being seen, what good would it do – gas, food, clothes, you can't buy anything, not even stay in a cheap motel, without a credit chip. It is too difficult to think through. Everyone always gets caught. They can broadcast your face all over the country, everyone has long ago provided samples of DNA, hoping to receive an inheritance or family tree DATING BACK UP TO EIGHT THOUSAND YEARS! FIND OUT WHO YOUR ANCESTORS WERE!!!! ORDER NOW! AS SEEN ONLY ON HGMTV!!!! He will have to get Bocar and stay trapped below ground in the old Smoke-Easy.

"Dad, are you still there? I miss you. My feet really hurt, they feel like they're burning up, and my head, too, kind of like on my scalp? It feels really hot? Daddy, I wish you were here –"

"Yes, my love. I will try to come to see you soon." Abruptly he hangs up.

9

This semester is the most difficult: twentieth century literature, why did Julie have to take the academic college track? What could she have been thinking? The reading list: *Pat the Bunny, Hop on Pop, One Fish Two Fish, Curious George* and *The Velveteen Rabbit*, but these are like, for a PhD student or something, they are way too difficult. Classical Song Lyrics as Poetry: Busta Rhymes, Jackson Browne, Tony Orlando, Missy Elliott – she doesn't have a clue what they are about and she has never liked classical music!

"Yes it is work, but I believe you will find the texts to be worth it," says Miss Fletsum, "You may recollect from political history a President of long ago got the nation to read *The Very Hungry Caterpillar* by recommending it as his favorite book. In this course we will discuss cosign as physical commodity as well as parallel instigation; and the nonexistence of the text except as validified by the critic of historical neutrality and revisionism. I do understand that many of you find the written word extremely difficult, but I believe I have made allowances in that you will find a great deal of supportive material, both in song and film. Let's get back to business at hand, shall we? Tonto!"

"Miss Fletsum?" A student raises her hand. "When we talk about *One Fish, Two Fish, Red Fish, Blue Fish*, in what way are we able to reassess context according to the interpretation of the concrete, in a non-revisionist assessment?"

"Anyone want to respond to that? Sprue?"

"In my opinion," Sprue says, "any particular ideology is nearly impossible to extricate from the body of the work. To look at the Object in a sustainable, revisionist way, without negating sign, let alone the obliteration of demerit is, gosh; I don't think it's possible."

"Wrong!" says Miss Fletsum. "A bird in the hand can peck you a lot easier than two in the bush. I would have thought by now you would certainly know how to paradeduct from what we have studied so far. In viewing obtuse comprehensive equations, we can see that –"

Julie's mind wanders. The school offers a lot of vocational courses; is it to late to change? Until the plane crash, she always thought of herself as not only an expert marksman, plus she got all As in Munitions Tech. The teacher even said she should maybe think about going into Military Marketing.

She is surprised to find Cliffort and Tahnee waiting outside the school for her. She hasn't seen Cliffort since the day of the airplane crash. The only way she can not think about the crash is by taking larger and larger doses of Clear Wipe, which you can only get from a doctor but which she was able to buy from one of the kids at school. "What are you doing here?" she says.

"Didn't you know?" Tahnee says snidely, "Cliffort's applying for a job here as a teaching assistant aide now at Downey."

Tahnee spoke snidely to her sister

"In what subject?"

"Hair. He's going to drive us home."

Julie is not so happy to see Cliffort. In silence they walk to his van; Cliffort stops to pick up things from time to time and he's putting them in his mouth, yuck, stones or… whatever, maybe it's just sunflower seeds and he's picking up litter. Once again the plane crash replays through her head, except that it is now all happening in slow

motion. The front end
of the plane begins
going down, at first far
away, then closer.

What type of plane is it?

Now, picturing it, she thinks it was a **Cronan-Boeting 894 Air Luxury Liner**, with extra-wide seats and a history of bad disasters in Kazakachina.

She remembers how she kept waiting, somehow, for the plane to get back on course but it continued to descend and then, still unexpectedly, hit the swamp, and burst into flames. Maybe the chemical products in the water made it burn faster? And didn't she inhale a cloud of ash, maybe it was human remains; since that time she has never felt very good. The intense blast of heat and the hail of objects around them; a volcanic eruption turned wrongly around, so that the opposite of magma was spewing down.

Things blowing so high and fast, stuff goes all the way to the playing field, burning jet fuel, boomeranging bits of metal. The flimsy boards of the shack falling into splintery pieces and a plastic tray table had struck nearby on which partially read:

UPRI HT POSIT   DURI G AKE-OFF A D LA DING

And then being hit by that finger, she didn't know what had hit her until she saw it, on the ground, a finger with a large gold ring set with a cabochon ruby. The ring has gouged a dent in the side of her temple that, at first, she thought was her own blood but in fact later revealed itself to be nothing more than a sodden mess of tissue from the severed digit. Now she remembers, Tahnee ran over and picked it up. What has happened to it since then? Does she even want to know? The firey corpse of the plane, what's left, blazes a half a football field away; most of the explosion occurred in the air, a variety of wreckage had cascaded down either before or just after, so the field was littered with objects. In the distance people yelling, screaming, but who?

"Everything okay there?" says Cliffort. "You seem awfully quiet. What are you thinking?"

"Nothing."

"How about a return to the scene of the crime," says Cliffort, pulling up beside the field where the crash took place. "As the actress said to the bishop!" Julie doesn't know where Cliffort has been since the day he handed her the Kamikaze, but he has some super gluf, extra styff that he says even Julie will like.

"No thanks," she says. "I don't like steet any more, all it does is give me the skeeves."

"This is different," Cliffort insists.

She stares at her feet.

"Come on, Julie," says Tahnee.

"Come on, just have a bit, you steet with me and maybe I won't remember who pulled the trigger."

"What?" says Julie. When Cliffort passes it to her, she inhales. He is frightening as he takes her hand to walk through the field. "No one has returned to clean up," Julie says. "It's been weeks!"

"What?" Tahnee and Cliffort both burst out laughing, that kind of laugh that teenage boys make when they want to sound sardonic. "What are you talking about! It was, like, yesterday, simp!"

"It was weeks ago! Remember de initial **covert rescue** operation? With all dose people? In de white outfits and stuff?"

Cliffort and Tahnee shake their heads. Clearly Julie is unwell.

The high from the fumes doesn't last long and Julie realizes her sister is clutching the ring, still attached to the finger that had hit her on the head. "Ew, dat's a scunner," she says.

"What?" says Tahnee.

"Dat you're still carrying dat finger around, wid de ring."

"What?" When Julie looks again, she realizes there is nothing in Tahnee's hand at all. They tramp through the field. Almost everything they pass is charred lumps. Here and there are recognizable objects: the back of a seat cushion, a handle from a suitcase, a shoe. Coins litter the ground, stuck between blades of dull brown grass, some of which, in sections, is engulfed in cheerful gassy little flames that appear to be everlasting, like those on some cemetery memorial.

Julie picks up a wallet, virtually intact: it contains a driver's license, credit cards, four ten-thousand dollar bills. "Look," she says to her sister.

In the distance the sound of sirens can be heard.

"Gimme," says Tahnee, taking the wallet. She snatches the money, which she pockets.

A few people have gathered at the far end of the field. "Are you kids all right? Get out of there!"

"Yeah, yeah, we're coming."

"Maybe it's, you know, biochemical! Hurry up! You don't know if there's going to be more stuff exploding. Even the **Homeland Housekeeping Mission** won't touch this!"

"No kidding," says Tahnee. She starts running across the field, but somehow her shoes are gone and she is now unable to walk on the grass that is not only flaming in spots but contains extremely sharp stickers.

The neighborhood is known for these – a renegade from elsewhere. Can pierce clothing, even shoes, boring its way into flesh; caused the death of a local child, who, on autopsy, was found to have burr seeds rooted in liver and lungs. "I can't walk. De prickers!" Tahnee yells. Now that the steet has worn off, the thorns really hurt.

"Where are your shoes?" Cliffort has come up behind her.

"I don't know." Tahnee retraces her steps. A pair of blue jeans droops from a busted suitcase and she yanks out a couple of pairs of men's underwear, which she wraps around her feet.

More of the neighborhood – whoever is home at the time – has begun to gather at the edge of the field. "What are you kids doing in there!" yells Mr Patel, the father of Locu. "Didn't anybody tell you, that area is contaminated? I have the word of The Authorities it's on fire below ground, it's going to go up any minute."

It's true, the air is filling with dense smoke and the thick stench from the disturbed swamp water. But Julie can't help herself and goes on rummaging through the suitcase; a man's shaving kit, a camera, she is oblivious to how smoky the air has become. "That's that… nuthin' we can do at the moment," Cliffort says as he drags her from the suitcase and across the field. The whole place begins to burn. "I'm so fafa hungry. That darn steet wore off already, the guy told me it was the new one-hour version. Oh, hang on – it has been an hour, hch-hee. Got anything to eat with you?"

The two girls look at each other. "No," say Julie slowly. "But… we've probably got something at home, why don't you come in with us?"

The back door is unlocked. In the heat the dog is too lethargic to get up.

"So is anybody home?" says Cliffort. "Mother or dad?"

"No," says Julie. "Mom should be home soon, though."

"And is she going to be upset? At finding me here?"

"I dunno," says Julie. "I don't see why. We can have friends over. Besides, you teach at the school, right?"

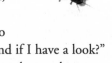

"At the moment, temporary substitute. Not to stand on ceremony but I'm starving. Ravenous. Mind if I have a look?" Cliffort opens the door of the refrigerator. A large bowl, stored on top, suddenly leaps into the air and falls to the floor where it smashes.

"Oh, Shi'ite," Cliffort says. "Sorry about that. Got a mop?" He stands in front of the open refrigerator door.

"Just forget it, I'll clean up," says Julie.

"Will you? You're very kind." Cliffort stares at her in a way that makes her uncomfortable.

Tahnee has been in a daze but now she steps forward. "Don't just stand there wid' da door – the door open," she snaps, in a voice that sounds like Murielle. "I'll tell you what's in there, because I already know!" She pushes past him. An American cockroach ambles out of the drawer marked "MEAT" and walks toward Cliffort.

"It can't be easy being a cockroach!" Cliffort says, as he steps on it. "One minute just walking around, the next wham! You're squished." With one finger he swipes up the fatty white, studying it pensively.

"We have peanut butter," says Julie. Tears have come into her eyes. *I hate him*, she thinks, *he's so cold – callous.*

"Ugh, peanut butter flavor. Can't stand the stuff."

"There's, um, some leftover macaroni and cheese. And eggs. And, um some leftover cartons of Chinese food."

"Hmm, Chinese food. That might be interesting. Mind if I have a look?" His hand writhes around Tahnee and into the refrigerator where, seemingly unconnected to his body, as if it has its own eyes, the hand picks up a carton of Chinese food and takes it from the fridge. Then he opens it, and, looking inside, sniffs. "Mmm," he says. "I think I'll try. Nice patina. How old is it?"

"It has some age. Do you want it heated?"

The young people are still woozy from the drug, the high makes everything slow, thick treacle, except when it is ice-cold and bitsy. "Nah, this way is fine. Got any ketchup?" He peers into the carton and, looking inside, sniffs. "Is it supposed to be moving around?"

"I don't think so," says Tahnee. "Maybe you shouldn't."

"That's okay. I'm interested in trying out this new live-food diet everybody is talking about."

"So am I!" says Julie.

"Oh, Julie, you are not," says her sister. "You wouldn't hurt anything that crawls, walks or flies."

"Speaking of flying…" Cliffort says, opening cabinets and drawers. "Why don't we just not mention that Julie brought down the plane?"

Julie doesn't know what to say. Was she the one who made it crash? She knows she must come forward and tell the authorities what occurred; no doubt her punishment will be life in prison, which she definitely deserves. "Sure," says Tahnee. "You want a plate or something?"

"Just a fork. Anything to drink?"

"There's soda. Or, um, want me to see if there's a 24-Projectiler?"

"No, the soda should do nicely." He takes the fork and begins to stab in the box.

There is a sound – it's Murielle, unlocking the front door. Cliffort tenses, fork poised, ready to flee. He resembles a secondary scavenger at carrion where the original killer is about to return.

"Mom!" Tahnee calls.

"Hi, I'm home!" From the other room they hear her putting down her things, bags and keys, breathing heavily in the heat.

"We, um, have a friend with us."

"Oh? They are saying that the big plane crash at the marsh might create some kind of big explosion. I was worried you kids might be playing over there." Murielle is flushed, she has spent the day trying to stop a massive escape at the Senior Mall. Some of the folks decided they were going to break out, and head for Nature's Caul. Don't they realize that even if they did make it that far, Nature's Caul is only for the rich? They would never be allowed in.

"Mom, this is Cliffort. Cliffort, this is our mother."

"Hello, Mother!" Cliffort lunges, his chair topples over and one of the legs falls off. On his fork is a cockroach, skewered on a tine.

"Sorry," says Murielle, "I'm afraid we really should get new chairs, these are on their last legs."

"Perhaps I could have a look at them, when I'm done, and see if I can fix that one. Excuse me for raiding your kitchen. I'm Cliffort Manwaring-Troutwig, old baseball family."

"Take another chair, finish your food, I can't believe you can eat that stuff cold."

"Very tasty. I was totally starving, but your girls were kind enough to offer me a snack."

Julie can't stop staring at him. Even though she is in pain – both physical and mental – and feels wretched, it is swirled together with something else. She has never had this feeling before, except when she watches Humphrey Bogart in his latest film with Zahara Jolie, even though people say these days Bogart is kind of limited. Cliffort has such pasty skin, it is fascinating, and his ears stick out, but why this is so sexy to her, she doesn't know. His eyes are huge, merciless and erotic; a dark algae smudge above his lip can scarcely be called a mustache. A rare creature has come to their home.

"You are... where are you from?" Murielle says. She guesses he is in his mid-twenties, harmless enough in a too-handsome way: emerald eyes, pale skin, intense.

"I'm from West Islap, near the United Laboratory tragedy? Born and grew up there before they made everybody move out."

"I thought so!" Murielle says. "So how do you – what are you –"

"We met him in the park, Ma," says Julie.

"We were just having a little chat. When that plane went down, a little while ago. My car conked out. Van, actually. I was trying to see if I could maybe repair it myself – I hope you don't mind, that the girls took me in –"

"You look to be quite a bit older than them, you must be –"

"I'm twenty-three."

"No, I was only asking because I'm going to fix myself a drink, I don't want to offer you one if you're not old enough, or you're going to be driving –"

He seems relieved. "No, thank you very much, unless you have some mescal... you know, the type with the worm... Perhaps I could fix one for you?"

"Sorry... no mescal... I can do us my version of a Bloody Mary. Here, I'll show you. I take Spicy W-3 juice, and then..." She gets a gallon container of vodka out from a cabinet.

"It's the most disgusting thing you've ever seen, Cliffort, you won't believe it," Tahnee says as Cliffort abruptly licks the table.

"...I measure the vodka..." Murielle begins to rummage in a pile of dishes stacked beside the sink. "Where's my measuring thingy?"

"I don't know, Ma, nobody touched it!"

"Anyway, so tell me, Cliffort, what are you doing in New Jersey?"

"I was on my way to apply for a position at – believe it or not – the girls' school, in the styling production department. My van started to break down so I stopped at the park here to see if I could fix it. And that's where I met the girls and ended up here, with what appears to be a fucked transmission, Mom, excuse my language."

"Yes," Murielle is feeling daring. "I really would prefer you not call me Mom. It makes me feel like I'll never get laid. Oh, here's my jigger." She fills and refills the jigger, until each glass is half-full of vodka.

"But I've always had the hots for my mother, and I can't help it, you remind me of her except more attractive, and with that stunning strawberry hair and zaftig figure. I hope you don't think I'm being too personal, but do you color it yourself?"

"Oh, no, I don't color it. It's the way it is."

"I don't believe it!" Cliffort licks the fork before he puts it down and touches Murielle's head. "It's absolutely ravishing. Never change it."

"Oh, please, my hair's a mess! In this weather it always gets so frizzy, and it's thinning so much, on the top."

"No, no, you mustn't think that. The only thing I would say, speaking as a professional, is –" He fluffs her hair on both sides and cocks his head.

"Mmm – ?"

"If you'd let me… I could marcel it for you." He begins to play with her hair, pushing it in different directions until it sticks up.

"That feels heavenly."

"Oh Mom, that looks so pretty!"

"And that must be where your darling little daughter got her coloring from, too."

Murielle looks at Tahnee. "But hers is almost white. Platinum." Cliffort, though, is looking at Julie. "Oh, you mean Julie! Haha! Yes, I guess her hair is the same color as mine – funny, I never really observed that." Murielle admires Cliffort, he really has a touch.

A stench wafts into the kitchen. The wind has changed. Cliffort wrinkles his nose but the others are used to sour odors coming in off the swamp, now mixed with the odor of burning rubber and hair and barbecuing meats. Murielle notices tears are streaming down Julie's face. "What the feces is wrong with you?" she says.

"Oh God, all those people! It was terrible! And it's all my fault."

"What?"

Beneath the table Cliffort pinches Julie on the leg. "What do you think, Mom, a marcel and what about… frosted highlights?"

"You always think everything is your fault; what did you have to do with a plane crashing?" Murielle is irritated. "You, you, you."

Tahnee nudges Cliffort. "Julie's got the skeeves."

"No whispering in front of other people," Murielle says. "It's rude. If you have something to say, say it to everyone. My God, Julie, what's happened to your hands?"

Julie's fingers have bloated, blistering without any sign of a fire or boiling oil.

"Ow."

"Tahnee, do we have anything to put on her hands? I don't know what that is, I've never seen anything like it before."

Julie's hands roast, white marshmallows turning gold, very slowly, although there is no visible fire beneath them. Cliffort jumps up. "I always keep first-aid supplies in the van in case of a hair disaster. I'll go back and get my salve and unguents before it gets dark," he says. "Then I can get the marcelling equipment and the hair-frosting kit at the same time. Julie, come with me, before you gets worse."

For the first time in two weeks Murielle begins to wash the dishes that are stacked haphazardly beside the sink. "He seems like a nice boy," she says. "Do you think I should let him do my hair?"

"I think it would be fabulous."

"He can stay here, if he needs somewhere to sleep. I think he's real cute, kind of. A little wet behind the ears, but cute."

"Mom! Keep your hands off him, I think Julie likes him."

"Julie? Has it come to this, then, that I have to compete with my own daughter? I still have my reproductive organs intact!"

"Please, you gotta promise you'll keep it in your pants."

"Oh, all right. You can be such a party pooper sometimes, Tahnee. So – Dyllis told me the CEO of Bermese Pythion stopped in to see you girls! Tahnee, I didn't realize you were helping Sis, that is so lovely! I love to learn that you girls are so close to one another. Why can't you share these things with me?"

"That CEO guy? He's a creepy shrimper."

"Don't talk that way! Dyllis says it was really exciting that the CEO was in the lab. He could help your girls, you know. He's one of the richest men on the planet."

"I guess." Tahnee fingers the ring that fell on Julie's head at the plane crash site. It's still in her pocket. She had forgotten about it. In her hand the ring feels greasy and when she looks down she sees someone else's hairs are wound around the ring and the stem of the hardened blue finger, in which rigor mortis has long since set.

10

Nobody in the area is exactly healthy. Certain houses, the kids all have terrible cases: of warts, wens, wheals, pustules and pimples. Dewlaps, scabies, nevis and nervous tics, boils, bunions, bad breath and bursitis, as well as *low self-esteem*.

And their mothers, too.

The worst thing going around is neo-epileprosy. People twitch and convulse and body parts fall off. But there are plenty of other things, so graphic they must remain unmentioned.

Around here, jobs are few: junior administration, personal assistant to the comptroller, machine setup supervisor. Forklift operator; sheet metalworker; marketing; customer service department – entry-level position. Minimum-wage employment can be found in the food processing plants – although most products end up getting shipped to Asia – growing cookies, grape capsules, great sheets of flesh and vats of milk, twelve generations removed from any cow! Then there is Bermese Python Technologies, but there are so rarely any Opportunity Positions advertised as available, apart from Publicist, Quality Control Associate, and Groundskeeper. Who knows what really goes on in that place, anyway?

The options are limitless, but the opportunities are all the same.

President Wesley is on HGMTV. Of course he's always on HGMTV, Murielle thinks, but when does he have time to tape it, or sleep, when he is in everyone's homes (on the PRESIDENTIAL Network Channel) twenty-four hours a day? "Folks, I wonder how many of you believe in the *Power of Prayer*," he is saying. "Look at how I was able to get the Intelligent Interior Designer Bill passed in our schools – it was thanks to you, the American people, and the marvelous Power of Prayer. And what a difference it has made, praying to the Intelligent Designer's Modality! Today, for a limited time only, in four easy payments of –"

She goes for the remote control but the President knows. "Hang on, Murielle!" he says. "Just a minute, I'm not finished!" Fuck you, she thinks, and switches the channel anyway. Probably her credit rating will go down a notch because of this, but she simply can't stand his voice any more and turns instead to a floor-to-ceiling three-dimensional scene of snow-covered mountains. In the distance an elk, or maybe a reindeer, lifts his head from where he has been grazing on grass beneath the snow. Apart from the gentle rush of the wind in the mountains, the house is quiet. It's bliss, for Murielle, that Slawa is gone. The guy was so low-class, she thinks, he was the only one in it.

Then the realization: she has no clue as to what may come next. How will she survive?

Was he really that bad, Murielle wonders, but it was a question of getting him out, killing him, or being killed. There have been times when she thought he was going to kill her: one look in his eyes was all it took to see that nobody was home! He was elsewhere. What was left was a curdled tub of rage. Now, looking through the mail, she realizes Slawa hasn't paid the mortgage in ages, this latest bill is for the past three months, the enclosed letter mentions foreclosure. How could she have simply relied on him and trusted him when she handed him the bills each month?

He hadn't wanted her to work, but she hadn't listened and kept her job at the nursing home even though initially she didn't even make enough for what she had to pay in after-school child care and a newer car, let alone the monthly installments on the automatic equipment updates; but somehow over the years she had worked her way up and even without his salary they would be fine. Marginally fine. Kind of.

The girls are old enough now not to need a sitter after school; when she doesn't get home until late there's a big **Mega Mart Family Station** a few blocks from the house, where the kids can go to buy an ice pop. And Mega Mart Family Station has some wonderful, unannounced bargains! Like the time the girls came back with a complete **Enchanted Forest Outer Space Virtual Play Realm**, even though it did turn out to be factory reconditioned and ended up doing some minor kind of brain damage to them.

Anyway if she could do it over again she wouldn't have married Terry – let alone Slawa – nor had children right away. She is still a good-looking woman, though, blue eyes, hair frosted and styled – thanks to Cliffort – in the latest manner. Maybe she has gained too much weight – but men have always loved her little Irish mutt face.

She flips channels; the President notices immediately. "Welcome back, Murielle!" But before he can commence again she turns to the news, and the anchor woman is saying, "In our headlines this evening, an undisclosed source has told foreign affairs reporter Deiter Mandel that Gloria Polykovna and Amos bin Kaba have split. Calls to the couple's Nature's Caul mansion have not been returned. A spokesperson for the couple says the rumors are unfounded and that the couple has made no plans for a separation. In other news, more than twelve thousand were killed at a Brazilian soccer match just outside of Rio. When we come back, this week's Mega Globe lottery is up to two billion dollars."

She puts the hologramovision back to a Wallpaper station, this one of stingrays under water. Who are Gloria and Amos? Is she losing her marbles? How sad they split up, and why?

Murielle isn't able to keep up with herself, let alone all the other stuff. Maybe she has an imbalance. She dreams about eating and wakes in front of the refrigerator, spooning mayonnaise into her mouth.

At first she thought it was Slawa, until she woke at just that moment and realized it was she who had been eating all the grease. She has to admit it, she is no longer plump. She is actually fat. They live in the designated biotech production region that grows the Homeland Nation food; raised in giant airplane hangers, a sort of cellulose mash that is flavored and textured, turned into different shapes – corn on the cob,

95

turkey breast, but thank God now it's no longer necessary to harm any animals. She knows people who work there, each floor has a separate name: Chile, which grows 'grapes' or Washington for 'apples'. 'Asparagus' and 'strawberries' come from 'California'. The airplane hangers are here and there, New Jersey is lucky to have gotten the contract for so many, producing everything sweet and succulent and tasty with beautiful labels on all the crates, saying **Chilean Grapes**, *a product of* **New Jersey**. Each grape is as big as a tennis ball, seedless, a sack of skin containing gelatinous liquid, always in season, each with twenty percent more calcium than a five-ounce glass of milk and a hundred percent of the daily recommended amount of sugar! Now a Muslim could eat pork, a Jew, lobster, a vegetarian might dine on meat and a vegan dairy and eggs – because none of it was anything other than mock tissue.

And then it comes over her, one of those true anxiety attacks. There must be some pill she can take, the full weight and realization her husband is gone, she is alone, what the hell was she thinking and what the hell is she going to do now? She lets out a yell, "Help! Help!" She is panic-stricken, heart pounding, unable to get air, my God what is going to become of her?

The house is silent, except for her mewling, until one of the kids shouts from upstairs, "Aw, Ma, would you knock it off?"

Maybe she can catch her breath if she goes outside. She stands on the front step. There are no street lamps but at a distance the glare from the highway on the far side of the marsh lights up the sky and in each house, through the windows, the flickering epilepsy of hologramovision screens can be seen. A smell of barbecuing meats wafts, hot fats and flesh intermingled with a sweet sewagey smell.

Maybe she shouldn't have thrown Slawa out, things are worse now, he actually did fix stuff and now already windows don't shut, doors squeak, lights no longer work – on the other hand, since he hadn't been paying the bills, apparently, how much worse could things be?

Murielle is restless and it isn't even like there's a bar anywhere nearby that she can go to and at least look at other people. The bucket of asphalt is still at the foot of the drive where Slawa left it the night she threw him out. His first wife, Alga, had, years ago, planted flowers in a concrete well in front of the lower floor window but everything had long since dried up; the heat had turned it into a bed of sand. A figure moves past the blind in the house next door. A rap on the glass upstairs in Tahnee's room. She knows the two kids are working out signals of some sort, probably waiting for her to go to sleep so they can sneak out and meet. She could call the Patel boy's parents, but what's the point? Anil might be sympathetic, probably ground Locu, whatever – but Rima is crazy, she will no doubt blame Tahnee. Why stay in this hellish dump anyway, especially when there is – how much back-mortgage to pay? And quite frankly they scarcely have any equity in the place since taking out the second mortgage. Which had been Slawa's idea, to take the money and buy that stupid hybrid car, for what, so they could afford to take a trip when now the fuel for the hybrid was more than a regular car? And the traffic virtually unmoving?

How pleased she had been to finally have her own house when she had first moved in with Slawa, and it was only an hour or so from her father; there were even buses one could take – not that, in the end, she went there very often. She loved her house, until one day for the first time, she went into the backyard and found the old garbage, great heaps of old bread, crusts and moldy English muffins and then... baked beans, plops of canned baked beans. The food had not petrified, exactly, but it hadn't rotted, either, stuff these days was filled with too much artificial preservatives and chemicals to do that. Instead it had taken on a heaving, living quality – intact, perfectly formed, bubbling. A sort of tar pit of cheese doodles and pickles. Slawa said it was food for the birds. What kind of idiot would put baked beans out for birds; there aren't even any birds in the area.

And the bugs! The whole neighborhood has them. Some kind of mutation from the benign poisons industries. You could put out traps, spray, boric acid; you could get a professional exterminator in to bomb the whole house (you had to go away for forty-eight hours) and it is true that when you come back there will be a layer of carapaces on every surface: but it still doesn't kill 'em.

They feed off hair, flakes of dander, the stuff in the mattress. Crumbs, a spot of bacon grease. You can take the garbage outside but they gnaw through the plastic bags, squeeze themselves into minute crevices in what appears to be a solid metal garbage pail; dine, and come back into the house where they lay their crunchy egg sacs, from which a thousand infants emerge. They are inside the refrigerator when she opens the door, where invariably she – or one of the kids – has spilled a little milk or hasn't fully properly sealed a plastic bag full of chicken thighs. There are roaches frozen into ice cubes, and the worst part is, she knows that on an individual basis, they have personalities and full, rich lives that she is putting an end to.

Not only does nothing kill them, but some bio-genetic-industrial-plastic-engineer had the great idea to make 'em glow-in-the dark and love music. At night they gather glowing and swaying softly in corners – one species can even make little humming sounds of its own – and you are supposed to crush these things! The happy, glowing dancers! They are everywhere, in the electric fan, emerging from the light sockets, behind the mirror on the closet door.

There are times when she knows why Julie hates it when she kills them and would never do so herself. Some are actually kind of cute! Curious! Peeping out from the edge of the kitchen counter, antennae waving, what idiot had thought to introduce the music-loving gene into their DNA, you get the feeling, sometimes, they might also be dancing, lined up according to size, little ones in the front row... Nothing too loud, mind you, old-fashioned novelty songs about monkeys and coconuts.

There is one roach with a red dot or bump on one side of his back who isn't afraid of them; Tahnee was about to squish him when she realized he was looking up at her, and decided to befriend him. They named him Greg and he comes when they call him, and in order for him not to eat the poison, they have a tank for him to live in with food scraps and a roof over it if he wants protection.

Something vitreous and fringed fills the wall, gently throbbing. Involuntarily Murielle lets out a scream. What the heck? An invasion?

Oh, she realizes, an eye, someone is playing a joke, putting his or her eye up to the camera… One of the kids? A prank call? "Hello?" she says.

"What? Who is this?" The huge eye, eight feet tall, eight feet wide, blinks and trembles.

"It's me, Dad. Step back from the camera, you're too close!" Now she is looking up his nostril. A picture, a video, of feet, feet in mismatched shoes, white mock croc loafer on one and green rain boot on the other: her dad must have tilted the camera. "Dad?" she calls. "Dad, are you all right?"

"What? Oh, hello Murielle. It's you. Can you call back later? I'm right in the middle of something."

"You called me, Dad! I'm about to go out!" She wishes she had more patience. She should be pleased he's finally using the hologramovision, even though probably he just pushed some random button. No matter how often she shows him, he claims he only knows how to work the rotary telephone. He can't help himself; she can't help herself.

But still, she could use a little appreciation. Doesn't he see how lucky he is that even though she could get him a place in La Galleria Senior Mall and Residence Home for the Young at Heart she would never do so? It's a wretched place, not that she would ever say so out loud. The turnover rate is so darn rapid. Once they are accepted and admitted it doesn't take long for them to die. Sometimes less than two weeks. Of course, it is said that way it's painless, probably better than a prolonged existence in the People's Malls.

"We'll be coming over this weekend, Dad!" she says cheerily. "You have enough to eat in the meantime?" There are plenty of people who in this day and age have simply stopped looking after their folks.

11

It's a **Code Lavender** day: this means if Murielle is going to drive the kids to school she will have to take the side roads – the highways are closed. There are still a few local routes not so many know about – but the school is in the opposite direction from the Senior Mall.

If she hadn't thrown Slawa out… but it is too late now. She does miss him in a half-hearted way, plus it is becoming apparent that without him around to blame, she feels more irritated with Julie. Almost two hours late, she drops off the kids in front of Robert Downey Jr. Junior High.

In the car, the screen pops on and she switches to automatic control. "Murielle?"

"Yes –" Who the heck is this? She has a private number after getting too many calls from irate children with relatives in the nursing home.

"Hello, Murielle, hello, A. Jesse March Bishrop here, I'm Founder and CEO of Bermese Pythion where your daughter has been working this summer."

"Oh my gosh yes of course…" She can't see him on the screen – something is wrong with it – but that doesn't mean, necessarily, that he can't see her! No lipstick, hair newly marcelled, frosted gold, and already out of style.

Something is wrong with her auto-pilot cruise control. The car should automatically drive her to her destination. Lately it has developed a habit of heading off the road and onto the shoulder. "Murielle, are you there?" He has a nice voice, a manly voice, although what kind of person calls themselves by their first initial and middle name? One could hardly get more pretentious than that. No, no, do not think this way! "Yes… Is my daughter in trouble?"

"In trouble? No, not at all, she's quite a remarkable young lady."

"Julie?" She's astonished.

"Oh, well, I meant the other one, the older –"

"Tahnee?" She tries to remember, has Tahnee been working there? "Oh, yes. Sorry, you caught me off guard!"

"Anyway, I thought this could be a great opportunity for us to meet… Listen, you think you'll have any time later on?"

"Oh, yes, sure! What time? Is it dressy?"

He laughs. "A quick cup of coffee is what I had in mind; I'm absolutely bumper to bumper while I'm here. I don't know, some time over the weekend? I can pick you up."

"Why, that will be delightful." It has to be a joke, she thinks, as she hangs up. A prank call. The president of Bermese Python calling her? Surely a guy that rich – he's been listed as the richest man in the world, or at least one of them – would not be here in the filthy contaminated East, even on business. And calling her? If only her rearview mirror/hologramphone-o'-vision had been working – she's seen his bright pink face, a boiled little sea-creature, on some program. He is sexy, in a crustacean-like way. She would have recognized him. This way… She shakes her head, angry for being so gullible.

On the other hand, after all, there's always a chance that it's not a joke.

In a sense Murielle's job at the nursing home is that of ombudsman: the parents, the children, the social workers begin arriving at eight, nine in the morning and keep coming, often until late at night. "My mother has been complaining that the food tastes of burnt rubber."

"No, it can't be burnt rubber. It could be methane gas, we cook with gas, as you know we use products straight from the local warehouses."

"Mrs Antrobus, my mother's bathroom, the plumbers were in there trying to fix it, what, six, eight months ago? And it still doesn't work and they left the place full of rubble."

"First of all, the plumbers were not the ones who were removing the walls, so they couldn't have left it full of rubble. It had to be the company who removed the interior walls when they were trying to fix the pipe. Did you see who removed the walls?"

"No…"

"Then why do you think it was the plumbers?"

"But… Whether it was the plumbers or not – the place has been left full of rubble."

"I can't complain to the plumbers and ask them to do it, when I know that it is not their union that comes in to do the removals – and you can't say who was in there taking the walls down. Was there anything else that was bothering you today?"

"I was wondering, if my mom were to… pass, if I could move in. To her room. Even without the bathroom. I haven't been feeling so –"

"Usually there is our waiting list. I would like to help, in your case – if you could get me the right paperwork in the approved format, but you would have to have all of this accomplished before your mother passes on, which, I imagine, is quite soon considering how long she's been here… Our expectation policy is unfortunately based on a rather rapid –" Conveniently her machine rings. "Hello?"

"Who is this?"

Oh God, it's her father. "Just a minute. Mrs Weems, would you excuse me? I'm going to have to get back to you after the board meets to review."

"Who is this?"

"It's me, Dad. Dad, switch on the screen!"

"A screen? Is this a joke?"

"Dad, I'm at work. You called me. How are you doing?"

"I'd rather not answer that until I know who you are. How did you obtain my number?"

"Dad, are you c.k.? As bu?"

"What? I'm not following you. Who is this?"

"Dad, I can't talk now but I'll call you tonight. I really think you'll be happy if you let me come and move you to my house. Don't worry, Dad, I have always promised I will never put you in here." The next person is in her office. She hangs up guiltily.

"Mrs Antrobus? The protoplasm on the walls in my mother's room – it's growing."

"Did you fill out a work order slip?"

"Yes."

"And nothing was done?"

"No."

"That is terrible. What I would like you to do is fill out another work order slip and direct it to –"

"I mean, I am thinking I am just going to go out and buy my own protoplasm-destroyer for her room! It's been months! I did hdg-mail you."

"As you know, we are lucky here to be permitted to have a central protoplasm-destroyer system. It isn't permitted to bring in your own. FYG regulations say it can sublimate the entire building. Check with your local assemblyman to find out more about what you can do to help stop the plasmoidic spread. Thank you for stopping by."

She isn't trying to be mean. She has no other options, no choices, no way out except to attempt to placate, which solves absolutely nothing.

"Mrs Antrobus, once again, my mother's teeth."

"Were they labeled with her name and room number?"

"How can you label teeth?"

"La Galleria Senior Mall and Residence Home for the Young at Heart is not designed for those who have moved beyond assisted living. It may be that your mother's case needs reevaluation and an application for the nursing home for those who have advanced to the non-functioning –"

"But first of all, her teeth were stolen. And second, yes, I agree with you, but I filled out the application a year and a half ago and you said –"

"I see. I wasn't aware that your mother had dentures. As you know, we strongly recommend that patients have implants and veneers installed by our own in-house dentist, for an additional charge of thirty-five cents."

"What?"

"I beg your pardon. I meant, thirty-five thousand dollars. That is well below what an outside dentist would charge. If it has been a year and a half that your mother has been unable to look after herself here, I strongly urge you to find an alternative."

"But… But…"

"I am sorry. I was just about to take my scheduled break. You'll have to come back during the hours."

"But when I got here it was the correct hours! I've been waiting and waiting –"

She is already utterly wiped out. "Karthy?" she calls to the front desk. "I'm going upstairs to the lounge for a nap; do me a favor and don't tell anyone where I am."

An endless procession of children – daughters, sons, grandchildren – who expect her to take care of their parents. Really she tries her best. It is too much work for ten, how do they think she could keep up with everything?

In the lounge the President is on HGMTV explaining – or trying to explain – current wartime regulations. "For those unable to serve in the military it is now permissible to hire a substitute from an emerging nation, for an annual fee of $100,000, some of which will be going to help the family of the conscription substitute."

She flicks channels. The reporter on the twenty-four-hour entertainment news and gossip channel is babbling animatedly about Marie-Therese Rolex, the aging actress who has just been unceremoniously dumped by her much younger husband, the Brazilian playboy Diego LeClery. He is so cute! Of course, that poor actress has long ago lost *the first blush of youth*. Generally speaking, women become bitter around the age of thirty-two!

She switches back. "Strict guidelines will be followed, thanks to the major bill just passed by Congress listing those available and willing to serve, to be found at www. –" A long droning list follows: "Monrovia, Turkina, Nigeraopia, Syria Lanka, Hezbollastan…" General applause from the attentive press corps follows the announcement of each name of each country. "And now on a lighter note, let me welcome the soon to be First Man, my fiancé, Scott Grielgig!" The two men kiss briefly and look into the camera with dewy glycerin eyes.

"Some of you have been wondering about our plans for the wedding and where we are planning to register," says Scott, looking down shyly. "The wedding will be taking place on August nineteenth in Jackson

Hole, the western-most tip of Nature's Caul Valley. Mr President and I have decided that the best gift of all will be if each of you is willing to give to one of our pet projects: the fund to continue research into the terrible disease that has afflicted so many of us here in this country – the Chuntey Bolls Foundation. As you know, Chuntey Bolls has affected more than two point nine billion…"

Murielle turns off the HGMTV. Where is she going to get the extra money to make a donation? Without any help from Slawa, things are going to be even tighter.

She can't sleep at night, it's hopeless. Or if she does, it's only to travel that long lonely estrogen highway which at any moment can get up and wrap itself around her like a python, squeeze, squeeze no juice left then all of a sudden up up yeehaw with Slim Pickens and then down down down with that big morose Icelandic guy outta Journey to the Center of the Earth, lord love a duck you never know what kinda ride you gonna hop that hobo freight train in the dark only to find. When she does wake in the a.m. she's got new hairs on her chinny chin chin and sheets stiff with stale sweat. Can she sleep now, no no so back downstairs to her office. Her job as associate administrator, to ease and soothe the complaints of those people who are paying for their parents, means, apparently, that she is a whipping boy for all the angry people; of course they absolutely refuse to believe the reality, which is that there is nothing she could do to fix anything!

The daughters and wives come into La Galleria Senior Mall and Residence Home for the Young at Heart; she can hide but they always track her down. "My husband's mother, we got the bill this month and we were charged for forty-four bottles of antacid! And, quite frankly, she seems very agitated!"

She has to explain again how, daily, the residents are led into the exercise room, sometimes twice a day, where they can lift weights and run on treadmills. Except that the treadmills of course are permanently switched off, and the weights are only papier-mache. Without the mind, the body can hurt itself rather easily!

Now she has to look up Mrs Rabsom's account. "Yes, that's right."

"I thought she couldn't spend more than her monthly allotment, what's she doing with forty-four bottles?"

How to explain... "If your mother –"

"My husband's mother –"

"If she went to the Supharmacy and didn't go to the cashier, then it's electronically registered via Mrs Rabsom's microchip when Mrs Rabsom leaves the store."

"Are you saying she stole them?"

"Um... she might have put them in her bag by accident."

"That's your problem, then! We aren't paying!"

"Maybe it's time to think about getting Mrs Rabsom's i.d. bracelet changed to Reduced Access."

The doors to the Supharmacy are automatic and only open for those with the blue plastic i.d. bracelets; blue means Still Functional. By the time a person gets to green, they are confined to the fish-tank sized area, they can neither enter nor leave unless accompanied by a security nurse.

Meanwhile the next daughter/cousin/relative/in-law is waiting to see her. "My mother's been complaining about the music, she wants to hear music from when she was young, you know she's older than the others here, she keeps singing Soft Cell's only hit *Tainted Love*, you know. The stuff you play drives her crazy, she says it's for a very uneducated class of people, Aerosmith? Bob Dylan? She wants Duran Duran or, you know, who wrote *Wide-Eyed and Legless?*"

"Andy Fairweather-Lowe. But that's not the point. I can assure you, the music of which your mother speaks is often rotated on our play list; everyone has a chance to hear what he or she likes or wants. Most of our Young at Hearts love Karen Carpenter! And Tony what's-his-name and Dawn! Fitty Cent! James Taylor, Dirty Old Bastard, the Grateful Dead; we have a wonderful DJ for the elderly!" Murielle is spluttering now, this is ridiculous, arguing about music; next the lady will be trying to say, Mozart over Coltrane, or Chopin versus *the music of the immortal genius* Paul Shaffer. None of these things have anything to do with anything, let alone each other! "We try our best to please, but we can't suit everyone's taste –"

Her job is to soothe, to placate, to offer reassurance; nothing would ever, could ever, be done to change anything, what is lost is lost forever, dreadful sorry but the music isn't going to be altered, the dentures weren't going to be recovered: it had long since been made clear to her by those higher up that she is expected simply to string people along, take notes that appear to be of use, if the complaints persist she is to say an inquiry is taking place… Anything to stall for time until they have forgotten, or the relative has… died. Which never takes all that long.

What other senior home has a Supharmacy, which, actually, was her idea? Here the old people ransack the place confidently, revived momentarily at the thought they can save ten dollars on a particular brand of toothpaste *for the next fifteen minutes only!*

On the other hand maybe this was not such a good idea. Because every single product has those automated motion detectors that grab intelligence information off the implant chip of the shopper. "*Please, pick me, Lewis Frumkes!*" shrieks the box of tissue.

"*No, me, me!*"

"*Hey, Beth Savage!*" The antacid is almost in tears. "*Don't leave me here, I'm all alone!*"

"*My brand is preferred by nine out of ten doctors!*"

The cacophony grows louder. "*Feeling a little logey? I'm Fiber Pop! Fiber Pop boosts you up – and out!*"

And the sultry woman's voice, "*For a woman's added pleasure… Hey, stop! Where you going?*"

Those poor poor old people, they are good and kind – or at least they want to be thought of that way – and they are so sorry for the lonely products crying out, they can't bear to abandon a single tube of sobbing toothpaste, they have to be distracted by the public announcements:

"*Attention shoppers! For the next five minutes, our own-store-brand Early Warning Pregnancy Detection kit will be seventy-five percent off!*"

Round the dinner table, talks resume. Is it worth it to spend the extra money on a more popular brand because you're familiar with it, or risk trying a cheap brand to save money? Discussions lead to fights and physical fisticuffs that actually have to be broken up!

In this fashion grassroots politics continue. Capitalism versus Communism. Democracy versus Fascism. Socialism versus Labor. There are Whigs and Wobblies, Shi'ites and socialists, religious right and liberal left – all cooped together in the same young-at-heart center shopping mall! And… nothing is the winner! Everything comes out to one big, fat zero.

Except for the blare from the HGMTV, the house is strangely quiet when she gets home.

"Kids!" she shouts toward the bedrooms. "What are you guys doing, I don't trust you, did you finish your homework?"

There is no reply. She turns down the volume. "Kids?"

"*It is every American's duty to find the financing to hire a substitute. The American people's most valuable asset is him or herself. When, in our covenant, it is stated: 'Unable to serve in the military' we mean we would prefer for those representing the cream of the population not to serve. However, anyone may take out a government loan to enable himself to hire a conscript. Low interest rates are available and financing at an APR73 of…*"

Now she's distracted and forgets what she meant to do. The President is so darn cute! And what a physique; there's a rumor he works out four hours a day, even though he claims he's just naturally muscular. He has to be taking something at his age to have that kind of body. No wonder half the time he is shirtless when he gives his press conferences, the guy is totally ripped…

He's the nephew of a former President and got his start as an HGMTV entertainment reporter; she remembers when he started, twenty years ago.

Now, abruptly, in response to some question from a press reporter he blurts, "The alien immigrant situation? Shit, I don't need this shit, you understand what I'm talking? You know what I'm talking about? I told you all before the press conference, I ain't talking no alien immigration shit! Shit… Now let me move on to some other topics: recounting last night's top hologramovision shows…"

She goes to see if there is any water, even a five-minute shower would help.

12

There is no way Slawa can get back up to the shop carrying his cats unless he has a ladder, but all the stores are, at this hour, closed. Maybe he can find a long rope and tie knots in it? And those poor cats, he can hear them mewing faintly, and a rushing of water. They must be trapped somewhere or they would surely come to him. "Kapiton!" he shouts, "Murka!" but now there is no response.

At the moment he can't think what to do. It is so hot in the shoe repair, and he is miserable. The bitch threw him out! Bocar is the only one who might soothe him. And now this, losing his cats! The sweat is pouring off him, tiny pearls of emotion, each droplet pure suffering in a condensed form. Here he sits, slumped in despair, a bindlestiff in a spindle-backed chair.

What has he ever gotten out of life, apart from Julie and his cats, that brought him any happiness? And once again it feels as if alien rays or particles are throbbing inside his head, or even worse, like someone has taken a baseball bat to his head when he wasn't looking. His eyes are dry and crackly, his sweat is oily, his armpit hair a virtual forest that soon will grow so long it will circle his neck and strangle him.

He might as well throw loaves to the fishes, is how he feels about the uselessness of it all. To cool off, Slawa decides after climbing out of the Smoke-Easy, catless, to go to a nearby bar, where he orders a Moscow Mule.

Here are the ingredients of a Moscow Mule, a drink developed around 1946 and mentioned in one of the works of the great writer Erich Maria Remarque

Vodka
Lime juice
Ginger ale

What you see below is not a picture of a Moscow Mule;
nevertheless it is a drink.

The President and Scott are on HGMTV, standing next to the horse.

"Oh gosh Wes, isn't he gorgeous!" Scott can't help squealing, he is so happy! He embraces the President. Scott, yes, what a man, those muscles, that polished skin, hairless; only his voice is maybe a little offensive, from going to those fancy schools out there where they learn to speak as if their back teeth have been wired together. Scott can't help this, though: is it his fault he grew up in the New Hollywood section of Nature's Caul Valley? Adopted at an early age by Big Momma Taneesqua, star of that never-ending sit-com, *Stand Clear of the Closing Doors*, given etiquette lessons, taught to ride through the green fields and across the Nature's Caul streams, able to ski and fly his own private plane.

He knows how to decorate a home! Is able to give tips on how to frost a red velvet cake in butter cream icing! He can top a cake with candied violets and daisies, and he is beside all that a really nice guy. He is a vegetarian and rescues stray dogs and he is on the board of all sorts of charitable institutions such as, oh never mind. The commentator who has been explaining all of this runs out of time; he has to cut short his praising of Scott and says, "The horse, who is to be renamed Tab Hunter, is a gift to Scott from Mr President. Tab is seventeen hands high

– seventeen hands – now that's a big white hunter! At eight years of age he is still quite young in the equestrian world; purchased secretly by Mr President as a wedding gift for Scott, who is going to give him, shortly, his own gift in return. Let's listen in, shall we?"

Slawa will never get used to this holographic TV. It is bad enough to have the news commentator standing there behind the bar, so real, but now when the President and Scott and the big horse come into the foreground, Slawa recoils with a start. It was one thing when the holograms were teeny tiny little things. But life-sized! When the horse leans forward for a moment he is certain it is leaning toward him, lip curled, about to take a chomp on his sleeves.

But everyone else seems used to this new system; they all laugh when they notice Slawa jump, making it clear that, to them, Slawa is about as sophisticated as those first viewers of the motion pictures, who yelled and ran from the theater when it appeared a train was coming down the track – toward the audience.

"I can't call him Frosty," says Scott, rubbing his face against the horse. "I am going to call him Tab Hunter. Don't you think?" What the President doesn't know – but the viewing audience, most of them do know – is that Scott has discovered the horse some time before and has to pretend, wink, wink! that it is a surprise.

The President shrugs. "Whatever you want, baby. He's all yours. Happy birthday. I hope he's what you wanted."

"Ooh, he is. My big mack daddy." Scott gives the President a brief hug, and in one easy motion places his impeccable left boot into the stirrup and lifts his other leg over Tab's big white bottom. Tab, in a brief power-play neighs and bucks a little, as if he doesn't know what Scott is trying to do! Only Scott is such an equestrian that, somehow, with a firm grip from Scott's strong thighs, Tab settles down immediately, for he realizes now who is in charge.

At a brisk trot Scott waves to the camera, heads out of the White House Fortress and into the grassland beyond. The houses and buildings in the vicinity were long ago knocked down, turned into green verdant swathes to house the bunkers below in an extra blanket of safety.

"Be careful!" the President calls as the two firm bottoms – one belonging to Scott, the other to the horse – disappear from view. "Now that's a pretty sight, isn't it?" says the President into the camera. "And now let me turn for a moment to a more serious matter: in our quest for oil, it has proved necessary to once again set off underwater nucular bombs." Mr President chuckles. "One great thing about my tenure as President was being able to change that word to nucular. Let me pause to say, thank you viewers for your support on this important issue, I received nearly half a million letters praising my action. And now it's time, I believe, to take a break for a commercial. Mr Clean and the Green Giant – I hear **CLEAN PEAS** is a new co-product you're to tell us about?"

Once in a while a murderous rage comes over him. The first time it happened, he had just been released from whatever kind of institution it was, back in Russia. When he got home his mother was no longer there. All the old people in Moscow had disappeared, the babushkas, the toothless granddads with their bottles.

Two men occupied the apartment. Growing up in the Soviet Union, he had not known what homosexuality was. There had been no mention of such activity or such people, because it was illegal. Therefore, it did not exist. And then, on this, his first day out, to be greeted by two men who claimed to have never heard of his mother, to claim they had lived there for fifteen years, and inviting him in for a 3-way. In his grief and confusion, Slawa supposed he had a temper tantrum, or something: throwing the garbage pail, breaking up some furniture, smashing one man, repeatedly, into the refrigerator until the door opened and inside he saw orange juice, and cheeses, and chocolate! Meat and coffee, whole coffee beans in a bag! Tins of caviar, a plump cooked chicken! Then he really lost it, he could not even force himself to think of what had happened. Anyway, it was a long time ago.

Apart from rare occasions, though, Slawa is really a gentle soul. Even though Murielle thinks he drinks a lot, as far as he is concerned he drinks very little. Perhaps something has been slipped into his drink? He is so angry, suddenly. He could kill them. He should kill them. These people, what do they know of suffering? They are the golden ones, inheritors of *objets de vertu* and antique Japanese swords. They dwell in the Lost City of Atlantis, or Treasure Island. The VIP room of Pimlico Racetrack.

For him, Slawa, with anvil and hammer, a lifetime or many lives spent as a serf, a peon, kulak, coolie, slave. The blood of the lowly has run in his veins for a thousand years. What do they know of Beriya and the KGB and his one hundred years of cabbage and rotten fish in the loony bin?

In his youth he memorized great chunks of poetry: Akhmatova, Mandelstam, Pushkin. Samizdat-style he could recite hundreds of pages at a time. Now he remembers none of it. How can that be? It is as if a file up there has been deleted. It will soothe him, he thinks, to find something familiar. He tries now to find something on the computer, types in *Akhmatova*, under a variety of spellings, under a number of search engines, but the only things that come up: BUY AKHMATOVA ON EBAY; EGYPTIAN ANKHS; TOVA FELDSHUH.

It is almost dawn before he drifts to sleep in the hot chemical air of the shoe repair shop; momentarily the cats have stopped their mewling; he dreams of Alga, his first wife. Alga had been young when the first signs of reeTVO.9 began. He would come home and find her standing in the kitchen, staring into space and even after three or four "hellos", she still remained in that kind of trance.

Meanwhile on the stove the butter in the fry pan long since melted, first the honey-gold picking up to a sizzle, browning, browning, growing dark and then, zzzzz! That moment from brown to burnt, nothing remaining but an acrid smell and the dull hissing of the furious pan, such a long trip from cow udder, even to get to cow udder, four stomachs, the cud regurgitated, green and fetid, you could go through each single step, no, it was impossible.

Before they left the house, she couldn't find her pocketbook, her glasses, in the house her glasses disappear, there are sunglasses and there are glasses for reading and there are bifocals, nobody will get any laser treatment any more, not since two million people who had had the lasik went blind overnight! The house keys, she puts them down and the next time she tries to go out they are gone; the frozen TV dinners are underneath the bed, the hologramovision controls are in the refrigerator; the scissors, her left shoe, the steel wool, the list of – where could they possibly have gone?

It is in this sense that inanimate objects are animate. She is convinced objects have lives, thoughts and feelings of their own. And she is convinced, too, they are out to get her. What if she is right? He has noticed tiny quartz crystals appearing here and there all over the house, as if someone had cried and the tears froze; or flaming pieces of toast leaping out of the toaster across the room, flames made solid; knobs spontaneously falling from doors, leaving in their wake a trail of tiny wires, screws, door-knob innards of springs and pink rubber.

For Alga things rapidly got worse – admittedly she was quite young but in a sense this was a relief, whatever is wrong with her isn't his fault. All this time his irritation with her had progressed as well. He could not help himself. "Alga, what the hell's the matter with you! How many times do I have to tell you:

Pick up your dirty laundry from the floor
Bring your dirty dishes to the kitchen
Separate plastic, glass and metal
Turn off the lights when you leave a room
Don't leave the water running
After you take a shower
open the window in the bathroom
Close the refrigerator door
Don't mix coloreds with the whites
Lower the volume or you'll go deaf
Did you hear me?
Are you listening?
Close the cap tightly
Write it down.
Write it
Down. "

It did no good to tell her these things. Whimpering, sobbing, she told him he was mean. Also she had become oversexed, lascivious; she followed him around leering, rubbing up against him, trying to get him, humpity, humpity, twitching bunny.

It did her no good.

They had never had what you might call a passionate sex life; now she was mentally the age of ten, mind going backward, only body headed the other way, rapidly.

One day he opened the front door and a flood of water – which even in those days was gray, though at least it did run when you turned on the tap – flowed out over his feet. Alga had put the stopper in the bath and left the water on, before going out… "Slawa!" she yelled in horror when she arrived home some time later and found him mopping, mopping. "What has happened, what did you do?"

"What did I do? Me? You're the one who is a danger, you turn everything around you into some kind of weapon! What were you thinking of?"

He starts listing her crimes only she starts talking at the same time; the two of them are involved in some kind of weird ancient poetry slam, Keats versus Grandmaster Flash:

"Of? Of? Don't dangle your prepositions at me young man! Of what were you thinking?" "What was I thinking of?"

He never dangled his prepositions again. He gave up, what was the point? There is no choice. He waits months for a place and finally is allowed her admission into La Galleria Senior Mall and Residence Home for the Young at Heart.

In much the same way as the inhabitants are falling apart, so is this place.

It is a nightmare.

Most of the escalators are permanently defunct, the glass elevators often break halfway up or down, leaving ten or fifteen sick and old people – who usually crowd in beyond the maximum number – hanging in mid-air, unable to surmise what has happened. Though sometimes, forces combined, they've been known to gather enough

The Dangling of

Of

Alga, of what you are thinking?
Always before you know my clothes:
Whites in hot water. Whites in hot water!
Not cold. This is not you. But it is you.
You put the eggs on the edge
of shelf! Eggs hit me on head!
And crack. Why you laugh at this?.
But worse, even: you boil six
Eggs. Saucepan you leave on the lit
burner boils away. And the stench
Of burnt eggs, the ceiling black
Why? Alga, Why? How can you forget.
When real eggs are so rare, expensive,
Eggs today like caviar in days of old, but those eggs
Were from a fish.

Eggs. egglike, ovoid and yet
that milk tooth — is that what it is called?
Poking out; a kind of pecking at the universe
trying to hatch or maybe already broken
In hot water albumen turns white —
I do not laugh. There is no yolk.
What is this? Why it's an F — for fish!
There is an O for oval, and there is an F
O, f! O, f! O, f, O!O-F-O-F-O-F-O-F-OF
OF OF OF OF Of, Of, Of, Of, Of, Egg
and Chicken. Chicken and Egg
They are both at the same time
Cluck cluck
cluck

strength to crash out the glass elevator walls and occasionally tumble several stories to the ground floor of the atrium below in what could be mistaken for a group suicide.

In addition to working all day for his uncle, Slawa puts in hours on the weekends and at night as well, driving the "limo", a town car, in order to pay the monthly fees at the home. He has little time to sleep, even less time to visit Alga in the home, though he goes whenever he can.

One day at the Senior Mall he found himself chatting with a guy who also had a wife in there. "They're saying within a few years three-quarters of the population is going to come down with this kind of reeTVO.9 thing, brains slowly turning to spider webs, cotton bolls, ectoplasm, gelatin, candy floss, kapok, what have you, fluffy nebulous stuff; thousands upon thousands are coming down with this disease, this virus, whatever it is, hey, I have inside information they don't want the rest of you to know, pretty soon millions will walk the streets gibbering, still human but without a brain."

Finally he escapes by saying he has to go find his wife; at last he spies her in the Music Room, which had once, in a previous incarnation, housed a Food Court. Today's activity: Sing-A-Long. Generally these days Alga is past being able to participate but this day, as he sat down beside the boarded-up Wok On (where once Chinese food and Japanese sushi sat in their sad world of stainless steel trays), he sees her singing, mouthing, at least, the words to *Like A Virgin*, an old song, perhaps played to her in her childhood, and he finds that tears well in his eyes as he listens to the words: "*Like a virgin, touched for the very first time. Like a virgin, when your heart beats next to mine,*" sung so sweetly and badly out of tune by listless shufflers, the dazed and mentally confused staring off into space, some of whom wear helmets for their own protection, others in wheelchairs, or rolled in on wheeled beds, only able to weakly flail arms and grimace from time to time, either to the music or as indication that sheets are in need of a change.

"Right!" exclaims the sprightly instructor LaVitra. "How many of you remember Gwen Stefani and her number one hit, *Hollaback Girl!*"

No response. But LaVitra is determined, she's got the microphone in her hand and goes from person to person; still no response. "Can you believe this, Keith?" She's talking to the keyboard player; neither of them can believe that this is where they ended up, both of them had such plans and dreams, they were even once on a TV program! Now, in order to pay the rent they have to travel one day here, one day at another place, all the time singing these senior ancient songs, maybe they could even have their own show on TV, like, the *Lawrence Whelk Show* or something? Singing, *I Can't Get No Satisfaction* or…

"Oh, I don't believe this! Nobody here remembers *Hollaback Girl?* Let me try and refresh you all – Oooh, ooh, this is my shit, oooh ooh, this is my shit – come on, everybody join in – oooh, ooh…"

Keith on the electric keyboard tries to energize the crowd, he claps his hands over his head, "Let me hear you put your hands together!" until finally, some dull glimmer of recognition and one or two join in.

"Okay then!" says LaVitra enthusiastically, "How about some requests! Anybody?"

An old lady in the front pipes up, "Do you know *Too Drunk to Fuck* by The Dead Kennedys?" Nervously the music therapist looks over at the keyboard player, "Keith? Ever hear of that one?"

Keith shakes his head, "Oh boy! Nope! My goodness that must be a real Oldie-but-Goody, huh? And to think I thought I knew them all! You got me stumped!"

"How about anybody else?"

"Um… *I Still Haven't Found What I'm Looking For?*"

"Yeah, who doesn't know that one, from that famous Nobel Prize two-time winning pop star who founded Shop to Help the Poor! Okay, this time I want to hear everybody sing, at least on the chorus, a-one and a two – '*I have kissed honey lips, felt the healing in her fingertips it burned like fire, this burning desire. But I still haven't found what I'm looking for*'."

The old people are pierced and tattooed, they have rings through their noses and lips; this is useful because when they wander off they can be chained to their beds or hooks screwed into the corridor walls; the tattoos on the flabby drooping skin have warped, melted, silly-putty shapes of what was once a rose or a faux-Maori symbol, eagles with saggy beaks, skulls with bared teeth that now need dental work from moles and skin tags and warts that look like chips and cavities.

The old ladies have huge breasts, so old they date back to the days when women had them implanted before tiny breasts became the fashion – all the women have them. It's not even their fault. It dates back to some kind of medical/drug company scandal. At one time virtually all women were diagnosed – falsely, as it turned out – with breast cancer. They had all gotten the big boobies. The men are so wrinkly it is clear they date back to the days before men had face-lifts.

And their clothing! It is *so* last year! What could they have been thinking, that styles remain unchanged since their youth when they wore blue jeans and stiletto heels? Or had silky straight hair and plucked eyebrows?

Slawa can't help but fume. He is going to strangle someone! It is boiling up in him, it is all so pathetic. How could they have let a man win a Nobel Prize who doesn't know he has written C- lyrics that include a sentence ending with a preposition!! It should be... I still haven't found the object for which I was looking! English isn't even his first language but he knows better than that! Talk about a cliché! "Honey lips/burning desire". But those old people – well, some of them aren't that old, they are just brainless, missing dendrites, neurons, synapses, glucose – they are all singing along in a funereal dirge, it's not even a song!! It's a dirge! If Bononobo – whatever his name – was here he would personally strangle him!! Long since dead, go on, award the Famous Celebrities all the money and prizes, why?

All that was a long time ago...

And it rains. It rains. Snows, and rains; this is followed by tornado and then one hundred twenty degrees. But mostly, now, the rain. And when it rains the water never goes anywhere, it stays in the troughs of the street that turn into canals. The whole damn place a temporary Venice of spittle, soot, papers, oysters of phlegm, dog poop, the rain water combines with chemical waste and tranny fluid, bilious acid green, luminous, iridescent. Chemical salts, left over from winter, strange rubbery clusters blossom in damp doorways, and the New Yorkers spend all their time scratching their heads, the stuff goes on the sidewalk, dander, flakes, the fingernail parings, bits of old dental floss, earwax scraped out with a fingernail and rubbed off to the pavement. You can put the stuff on an agar plate and blistering forms of life hitherto unknown to man will blossom, not that anybody ever does this but... still, there it is, all getting washed down and mixed together, the drops from an almost empty can of soda pop, dregs from paper coffee cups, bird droppings, swollen crumbs from bagels and pizza rinds.

The original primordial ooze only supercharged and ready to pop even if the entire rest of the planet and all mankind and animal life finds itself nuked! This stuff is so highly ionized – positive and negative – it could burst into life in a day, if given the chance, and a day – or more – is what it took for the soup to drain, even when the sun comes out.

Which in a way is what happens. The grates, the cesspools, the swamp at the corner of each block is... how deep? A foot, two feet, deep with run-off because somehow the city had been designed in such a way that no water ever could run off. Maybe the drains are clogged, or simply higher than the rest of the sidewalk, and meanwhile you have to be extra careful, the battery acid in the water simply corrodes the insulation on the electrics, every other day someone is quite randomly... electrocuted! And on the first sunny day, when the temperature rockets to a hundred and twenty, the water doesn't drain but begins to grow. It has turned powdery yet eggy, like that trick sand under water that stays dry, the lemon eggy color, only a bit lighter, and swells so rapidly it takes over the sidewalks and begins to seep down the steps leading into the subways, swelling and heaving; and if you touch it it burns your skin, just the top layer, but doesn't hurt – but then, at least according to what's on the news, you are prone to infections and this swollen dry yellow... spongiform feeds off the skin, stuff stinks like sulfur and can't be washed off the street by water. Water only makes it sizzle and puff up! It's an ecological disaster! However, a couple days later the temperature always drops, it goes below freezing and the dry mold cracks, splits, crumbles and disappears and within a day or two no one remembers anything.

There is something Slawa is supposed to buy. He has written it down but where is the paper, what is the object? A switch-cable-timer? A quart of milk? And in this filth he heads out once again. Fortunately the freeze seems to have gotten rid of the hard-boiled yolky substance, now once again it is hot and raining; the hot soup pours out of the sky. Hot! Today the rain coming down is so hot they say it is killing the birds – not that many are left – and it is practically raining chicken noodle soup.

You have to wear a self-cooling polyvinyl raincoat and hat in order not to be scalded. Who's ever heard of rain with bits and pieces in it, my God, the worst days he had spent as a kid in Russia when the smoke rose from the factories black and tactile hadn't been as bad as this. Only on the ground the pipe-worms came up, pink and coily. He makes his way gently, picking across the ponds that have gathered in every corner; the puddles are four feet deep in some spots when… all of a sudden, wham! He goes down, flat on his back.

At first he thinks, I must have slipped? Though, how odd, he hadn't felt himself to be slipping, and, my God, his head, which, when he puts a hand to it, he realizes is dripping with something sticky. As if he has landed in melted ice cream? He hit the curb?

But no, someone is standing over him, yelling, pointing, smashing, it's Bocar's uncle, what is he doing here, holding something… What's the old fellow's name, Assam? Kamal? Ibrahim? "Oh, hello…" he says weakly, and holds out his arm, assuming that Aboud would recognize him and help him up but no, all too late he realizes it is Aboud who has brought him down and the guy is holding a bat in his hands, an all-American Louisville slugger, the name of which he can now see as Aboud slams the bat down over his chest. "Ooouuugh!" he yelps, and hears something crunch.

"Listen to me. Where is Bocar? You send him back to me, you understand? I know he is with you. Because of you I am in trouble, I have vouched for this youth and accepted the money. I am not going to jail for no reason, you send him back to me or…" And with one final blow of the bat, this time across the upraised right knee, Aboud disappears into the salty rain, leaving Slawa in the gutter while the traffic lights change from red to green and back again.

He doesn't move. The hot rain stings where he is not covered with the raingear. And when he tries to rise at last, curiously, finds he cannot move. Now the pain replays, fast forward, slow motion, slight variations on a theme. Finally, crawling, a limp invertebrate creature dragging itself through the murk, he becomes aware that people are looking at him oddly. He puts his hand up to his head and finds it is covered with blood. It's hard to breathe, something crackles in his chest, a bowl of rice crisps unsoftened by milk or popcorn, the sharp kernels scraping his throat.

No, he won't go to a hospital, utterly worthless, he had been to hospitals with his kids, emergency room: four, five, six hours of waiting to be taken into a curtained cubicle room by some doctor who acts as if you are bothering him.

Bocar would look after him. Bocar, he has to find Bocar. Aboud has probably already been to the shoe repair shop, he hopes Bocar hadn't bothered to open the place. But how much time has passed, exactly?

Again he tries to get up, again slumps back. The rain is so soft, so warm. The pink pipeworms, freshly hatched, coil over him, devilish things are so quick, up his nostrils! If the rain stops the worms will dry up but there is no sign that the rain will stop. Nevertheless, he realizes he can't lie here. He will have to get back, somehow. Then, thank God, he manages to get to his feet and just then Bocar arrives.

And, as always, when the kid takes him by the arm, this time picking him up in a half-embrace, practically sobbing, he has that peculiar swooning sensation.

"My fry-end, Slawa, Slawa – are you all right?" Tears are curling down Bocar's face, are they really tears or is it rain? "Who has do-ney this thing to you?"

All his attempts to correct the kid's English haven't helped.

"Oh, I am all right. Slawa is strong man. Only just… Your uncle, he is very angry, he is looking for you."

"My uncle did this? He might have killed you, we must take you to the hospital."

"No, no. No hospitals. Now I want to go back to the shop."

The kid half-carries him down the street. "I was looking for you, you have been gone all day! I am thinking, what has happened?"

"I told you not to go out!"

"Only, just, I am thinking something has happened, I came out to look but the wrong way. Finally, I was just about to go back when I espied you. My friend, you are badly wounded, you are bleeding from many or-ifices..."

"Just a head wound." But he is limping and whether or not a rib had been cracked or broken he doesn't know. And then he is no longer there.

It is almost twenty-four hours later before he regains conscious. And when he wakes his first idea is that he is on a beach, the tide has gone out, leaving behind the dying interior of a mollusk – the words *conch* or *precious wentletrap* or *sixteen-chambered nautilus* come to mind – only he now realizes, breaching sleep into wakefulness it is his tongue, hung over, stuck to the roof of his mouth. My God, what is going to become of him, he is stiff and sweaty from sleeping on the floor and far away he can hear the faint yowl of his cats and the rush of the subway train cascading, an underground cataract of metal bones. Coral. Various shells. Variegated shells in shades of taupe and tortoise. Abalone. Spiny urchin. Gooeyduck, gooeyduck, gooey...

Somehow, Bocar has gotten him to the hospital where now, twenty-four hours later, they are still waiting to be seen. It's an entire next day! Bocar has covered him with some sort of hospital sheet, even so he is stiff from having lain so long on the floor. He manages, finally, to get up, drag himself to the filthy toilet, approach a nurse. "Yes. I told your little friend, you don't have insurance. We need your insurance information or cash upfront."

"How much cash?"

"We can keep the money in escrow but we'll need two hundred fifty thousand as a deposit to proceed. I'm sorry, but by law I'm not allowed to touch you unless we know someone will be paying for the treatment. I gave your pal some antiseptic 'cause I felt sorry for him... and you, but... I was about to call the police. You see all these people?"

Through bleary eyes he looks around. There are hundreds of people with stab wounds, bullet wounds, he guesses, moaning, crying, little kids clutching their ears and even one holding an arm in a position as if it is broken. There are old folks with what had to have been Chuntey Bolls or even Derwent Scrubs, faces covered with virulent pussy warts. My God, he is just another in this hideous place. There are mouse droppings. And overflowing baskets of garbage, newspapers, fast food wrappers; he sees his pet SloMoFlies are having a field day. There are people plugged in to their music boxes wearing the video glasses, eating pitha, Yabba Bits; there are children's shows blaring on the walls from the few hologramovisions that still work.

"But I don't understand." He puts his hand up to his head, it is scabbing over but he feels a chunk of something fingernail sized, holy-moley, his own brain?

"When we get one of these hot rains, a lot of people always seem to get hurt and they pour in here. I always feel too bad to throw them out until the rain stops, most of them have nowhere to go. But I have to get the place cleared out."

He drags himself back to Bocar and manages to explain the situation. "Anyway, my friend, I am fine now, come."

Yet on the street he realizes he is weaker than he had thought. Crowds are flowing up from the subways, this means they aren't working; this always happens after a flood. Buses, no, they stopped those long ago when traffic got too jammed. They might be able to take a mini-motor rickshaw, the city imported them from India years ago and they can get around, though slowly, up on the sidewalk, back down in the street – but between the two of them they don't have enough cash and his credit chip is dead... With his arm around Bocar's frail shoulder he manages to slowly hobble back to the shoe shop.

After the attack, Slawa's teeth hurt all the time. A cheap dentist who advertised in the paper only laughs and says it is going to cost at least a hundred and fifty grand, maybe more. Root canal, crowns, caps, bridges... the whole system is rotted, infected. He is a head rotting on top of a rotting body. A rotting head on a rotting body in a rotting country on a rotting world!

And in addition to his teeth hurting, he is furious, with a kind of permanent fury inside him that he can mostly control but then spews out. Almost anything can set him off, a car blocking the intersection after the light has changed, someone cutting ahead of him on a line, it didn't matter. He rarely has a drink, it makes his head hurt even more, his temper is so bad, he is so labile he beats up Bocar and not even for any reason.

He comes in from someplace, finds Bocar with the cash register till open. "What are you doing! You little thief!" He grabs Bocar by the ear, smacks him in the face, knee to the stomach. The kid is sobbing, on the ground, when Slawa emerges from his trance, a trance of rage, because of course now he remembers, there is no money in the till! The cash register is just for looks, because nobody has paid for anything in cash for years! He himself has said it was okay for Bocar to play with the register, the poor guy is just a kid after all! And in the moment of revelation he tries to obfuscate any reason for having struck Bocar. Then seeing the kid on the floor like a whupped dog, he bursts into tears. "Oh, my friend, I am sorry, forgive me."

Now the kid is crying too, "You were the on-LY one I trust, now see, you are like the others! I have been sold as a slave, almost, so that the rich people do not have to fight... and when Uncle took me in I did not know he would be no better – now you. Don't you see how wrong that is?"

Both of them are bawling. He hasn't understood until now that Bocar is almost completely deaf. Why or how has he not figured that out? The kid has said, from time to time, what, or excuse me, I cannot hear, but he never took him seriously. "Yes I know this is wrong," Slawa says. "What they have done to you, enslavement – is wrong, and what they have done to me, Slawa, taking away everything – is also wrong. What do you want me to do, I will do anything you ask of me."

For a long time the kid says nothing, merely shows him.

Now for the first time he learns about the boy and some of what he knows. Bocar is an expert, and he demonstrates to Slawa how ordinary products can be turned into weapons, and how weapons can be used for mass destruction.

There are simple things: how to booby trap a place with trip wires and nails that can be propelled at top speed into a man's head at the opening of a door; bombs using gasoline and soda bottles; bigger bombs made from ordinary chemical fertilizer.

How to replace the safety seal on a bottle from the pharmacy so that it appears never to have been opened. How to do the same with milk, or juice from the supermarket after adding botulism.

You can make your own botulism at home from ordinary food in Mason jars! Ordinary farm fertilizer makes a bomb. You can purchase ricin and sarin from some Japanese people on the Internet, if you join their cult! New friends in Africa can scrape anthrax spores from hides, put it in a sealed envelope so it looks like a letter, it can be mailed right here to Bocar's shop for distribution in free hand-outs of sticks of gum!

It dawns on Slawa little by little. Bocar hopes to produce some sort of disaster that may maim, wound, kill hundreds. Or more. How will he feel, innocent people dead or dying?

But he can no longer claim connection with the rest of mankind, he doesn't care, he can't sleep or he sleeps too heavily, that nightly running of the bulls trampling the Pamplona streets, wakes in a hot sweat with the lingering fragrance of blood, manure, oranges, but why? He has never been to Spain. He must not look back.

"Okay," says Slawa at last, "so I see you are really an expert in what you're doing. But what do you want to do? What do you want me to do?"

"In the name of the people everywhere, who are enslaved to this country, this country who has done such things to me and to you, for their sake and your sake and mine, I want you to help me kill them all."

13

And again no answer at her father's house; Murielle is drowning, the last thing she wants to do is go to see him, but, what the heck, she rounds up the kids, tries to dress herself, but no outfits seem to work. For one thing, she is beyond hairy – maybe she got this from her dad, maybe it is some kind of virus going around. Even though she has had it lasered off, her legs are still hairy, her arms, and my gosh, whiskers, the pubic hair coils mercilessly in ropey knee-length splendor.

Her closets are full of clothes, things that don't fit – okay, well, she has put on weight – or just plain out of style, like the trousers with the colorful codpiece, the dress with puffed sleeves and buttock padding that last year had looked so… chic. Only now seem dowdy, provincial, old-fashioned, or the expensive shirt made from laboratory-grown skin-and-polyester makes her itch. Things that had looked so beautiful in the shop have turned real ugly.

The stuff could, she supposes, be hauled off to the Salvation Army, only it's impossible to get into the parking lot filled with bags and boxes of the cast-offs of hundreds of others. Broken flower pots; donut machines; electric underpants with saggy elastic; stained sheets; hand-crocheted blankets of acrylic burnt-orange yarn, a particular hue bringing back nostalgic memories. A frilled clown to cover a roll of toilet paper behind the toilet seat. Chipped crockery; greasy pie pans; fleece hats; resin garden gnomes. Broken or out-of-date computers; old hologramovision phones; tricycles; jigsaw puzzles missing pieces. Wrappers from gum carefully folded to form colorful chains. A nightmare of human waste, filth, consumption.

She isn't really that much different than her father. She is always happy to throw his things away. It's getting rid of her own stuff that seems impossible. How is it possible to have come from a man who speaks so little and seems to have nothing in the way of feelings? He is an obsessive collector and hoarder – before she forced him to give up driving he would go around the neighborhood to collect old magazines, or to search for discarded yet still viable manufacturers' coupons. On foot he can still fill a shopping cart. His hobby is writing to local chambers of commerce and state tourism boards for information; asking for free catalogs, samples; complaining or complimenting. "Dear Sir," (to the President of a syrup company), "I wanted to tell you of my delight in your product, Uncle Mosley's pure cane syrup. I have been using your syrup for nearly..." Blah. Or: "Recently I had the opportunity to use a coupon valued at forty cents to try your new dishwashing liquid. I found Purity Anti Bacterial Citrus Spring to be inferior in every way to the more reasonable priced Martin's Summer Fresh..."

When she was growing up, these letters had to be read, each evening, to the assembled family – except that she was the only one there.

Often replies would come which enclosed a coupon for a dollar- off some product, or even a free case. God help the company who didn't respond or from whom he had bought some truly defective product, stale or useless.

All of these letters were typed on carbon: he refused to use a printer, a computer, he refused to go to a public copy shop, insisted on keeping his antique manual typewriter, which gradually produced more and more suspicious entries as both he and the typewriter aged, so that at the end his dementia, combined with the bumpy carriage and the difficulty of obtaining a new ribbon, added to that the wearing-away of the letters themselves, (the T no longer had a pronounced top, those letters with dangles – lower-case g, p and q – gradually lost their tails) and the letters, even the positive ones, took on the quality of a terrorist threat: "DeaR sir or mADman: I WOULD LIKE to inform you of the WoRTHiness of your molasses. You may know the old joke 'Mo lasses? How can I have Mo lasses when I ain't had ANY lasses..." And rambled off into a diatribe so ferocious that once a duo of FBI agents came by carrying a letter he had sent – containing a white powder – and hauled him off for questioning. For three days as a kid she was alone in the house, having hidden in the back of a closet, before they believed his story that he had been writing to a flour company, having submitted a sample of Uncle Bubba Purified and Bleached Superfine to inquire what the black specks in the stuff were.

In his way she supposed he had been a good-enough father; he loved her but had in no way helped to prepare her for the modern world. He taught her the Palmer method of handwriting; insisted she take short hand. He made the purchase of an encyclopedia some sixty years old, saying that all the important information could be found in these pages; he was almost sixty when she was born, so it might have been that in his estimation such news was up to date. As for her mother, she never really could get an answer out of him, for all she knew Mom's body was sealed in concrete in the basement.

The house was vast, many rooms, but all of them filled with stuff and dark, facing a gas station on one side and the walls of another building on the other… It wasn't the sort of place she would ever have wanted to bring a girlfriend to and in any event she wasn't allowed.

Pretty early on Murielle learned if she didn't want to starve it was up to her to cook: tuna noodle casserole; chicken divan; mock-apple-pie made out of Blitz crackers (recipe on back of box); Visquit crusted ground-meats crumble; anything that could be made out of a couple of ingredients with one of them preferably being a can and the other a box. TV dinners: Wolverine Mench fried chicken, with a side of corn and another of apple; frozen pizza – there were all kinds of take out in the neighborhood which over the years changed, from Chinese to Korean to Indian – but her father couldn't abide that foreign stuff, though once in a while he would take her to a local diner.

It was her father who had insisted on the validity of Western scientific experiment and research. He thought that unless an event was provable, with sufficient data to back it up, you might as well go around saying the earth was flat! And of course this got her into all sorts of trouble at school, where there were Morning Prayer sessions to the Intelligent Designer. Because the ID was scientific and not religious, they could pray to him in the schools and every morning in homeroom the teacher led the sessions. She liked to call on the class and write the prayers down on the big Wish List. "Okay, O'Jibway, what's the Number One item to pray for today?"

"World peace!" O'Jibway in her blue smocked dress, blonde curls and blue eyes, piped brightly, goodie two-shoes!

"Very good. L'Reign?"

"Um, could we pray I get a new XT174L for Christmas?"

"Yup," said teacher, writing down the request. "JaWohl? Kamal? Mahendra? Zheng-Lee? How about you, Hadassah? Can I see a hand? Hurry up if you want the power of prayer!" As if Murielle was battling her own hand – and lost – hand rose. "Yes, Murielle?"

"But teacher, what kind of Intelligent Designer would have the time to sit around listening to what a bunch of kids want? Wouldn't he have, like, better things to do? I mean, he might have designed us, but that doesn't make him an Involved Father."

The other kids giggling, the teacher irritably shushing them and telling Murielle to be quiet, this was neither the time nor place.

She hadn't wanted to be like her father, but open her pocketbook and there he was in the guise of a moraine of crumbs, hairs, bits of chewing gum and leftovers to feed the kids, the receipt stubs and orange lipsticks missing caps…

In any event her father wouldn't let her go away to school. The local college was nearby. She could live at home. She started with some psychology classes and decided on social work, but before she could get a graduate degree she had met Terry, had Tahnee and found the job as associate administrator for the ombudsman of La Galleria Senior Mall and Residence Home for the Young at Heart, which is how things had ended up.

By the time she met Slawa she was worn out and fed up. Now, it wasn't that she missed Slawa, apart from his fixing things, but on the other hand, half the things he fixed didn't work anyway.

She tries to call her father once again before heading over. There is no response. A company recording says his line is out of order. Now that he is old he doesn't have any friends left with whom she could get in touch. Not that he had ever cultivated many friends, though he had belonged for a long time to various clubs: the Philanderer's Club, the Mono-orchid Society, Emotions Anonymous and so forth.

Still no answer at his house. Maybe once again he has pulled wires out of the walls. She hadn't been there in so long, anyway. She should have figured out an alternative living situation for him long ago – but he had always refused even to consider alternatives, insisted he was perfectly fine and capable on his own – unless she was willing to put him in a nursing home, and there is no way she was going to do that, not knowing what she knows about these places!

"Come on, girls, let's go visit Grandpa."

The girls groan. "Aw Ma… the whole day is wrecked, do we have to…"

Once they had adored their grandfather. They thought it was wonderful when he took out his false teeth and snapped them in the air. They thought it was a real talent to be able to crack a hard-boiled egg on his head. What has happened to turn them so mean? She loves her father, she shouldn't have been so neglectful, it's just that when they are together he seems to know exactly what to do or say to irritate her…

The last visit, she had the girls take him to lunch at the local diner and as soon as he walked in the door he announced, "Where is my Sports Illustrated from 2019?" which is the one item she dared to toss. He has a sixth sense. An ancient t-shirt with an ad slogan, he hadn't worn it in eighteen years: how could he have known that was what she chucked?

She tries not to worry. He just probably hasn't noticed the phone is off the hook. Anyway, she hasn't seen him in at least a month. The two girls whine and mewl, she wants to smack them. "Aw Ma, do we have to… It's so boring there! I was supposed to meet Dakota and Robit and Rumsey at the mall…"

"Aw Ma, I'm gonna be carsick…"

For some reason there is no difficulty in driving this day, up the ancient turnpike. Usually this trip of forty miles can take five or six hours, there really isn't any other way to get there, but today is unbelievable: only two and a half hours later they are there, what luck!

There is no answer when they ring the bell. Now she is fearful. On the way in she opens his mail box. He is probably the last person in existence who gets actual, physical mail, they probably have to keep a postal deliverer just for him… It's stuffed to overflowing, requests from Boys Town, for Save Mikey, the last wild gorilla (Mikey is the only one left in the wild, so what's the point?), one with a note printed on it made to look like handwriting: *PLEASE HELP I am ninety years old and can't cook*. It's a little late for you to learn, she thinks grimly, anyway, why should I pay for your cooking lessons? The next: *Lose up to Thirty pounds in Thirty Days*! Let's see, she figures, if I lose thirty pounds then in three months time I can weigh seventy pounds! Not bad, I wouldn't mind weighing seventy pounds. Still nobody comes to the door; she rings again. "Well guys, I hope Grandpa's okay."

"Ma, I don't want to go in."

"Mom, I'm scared. What if he's like, lying dead."

The house really is in a terrible state… "Dad?" The girls huddle at the front door, wrinkling their noses. "Dad, are you here? Girls, go and open the windows, let's get some fresh air in here." She has brought trash bags, she always has the girls piling stuff in and secretly taking it down to the basement while she distracts him, in this fashion at least she is sometimes able to keep a path slightly clear or to rid the refrigerator of old rancid and mildewed… socks?

"Help! Help me!" he is calling from the dining room; a bookshelf, crammed with papers, junk and magazines, has toppled over, he is trapped underneath gewgaws, a plastic bowling pin, a twirling snow globe with a statue inside of a peacock, an ashtray made from plaster and painted pink.

"Dad, how long have you been here?"

"Grandpa!" They start to pull the papers off him.

"A couple of days. I'm fine."

But he can't get up. "Should I bring some water?" Julie says. He is obviously in shock, Murielle thinks about calling an ambulance but he says he doesn't hurt anywhere. What would be the use, hours in the ambulance just to get to the emergency room, another six- or eight-hour wait once they were there? She might spend the time here, getting him rehydrated, fed. This will be a good excuse to take out the magazines and books without his notice.

"I'll get you a glass of water, Gramps," says Julie.

"Don't bring him the water," Murielle says. "Have Tahnee bring him some water, while you get to working trying to clean up."

"Tahnee's not here."

"Where is she?"

"She went out, she said she was going out to look for her dad."

"Oh feces," says Murielle. She should never have told the girls that Terry grew up in this neighborhood, even though they didn't know each other as kids. "Goddamn it. I told her not to go running off. Doesn't she know this neighborhood is absolutely the worst? She's not going to find her father, she's just going to get mugged or raped or worse, who knows."

"Aw, Ma, Tahnee's pretty tough you know."

"Oh, sure. Tahnee doesn't have a brain in her head when it comes to knowing who's good or bad."

By the time Tahnee gets back, still fatherless but now bleary-eyed, it's time for them to leave, she knows whatever progress has been made will, by the next visit, be undone. "Bye, Dad!" she calls. He is tucked upstairs, in bed, between clean sheets that he will have no doubt soiled by the next morning. "I'll call you tonight! We'll be back next week!"

Things with Dad are deteriorating. Dad isn't even making sense. Dad has hair growing out of his nose and his ears, like some kind of ivy. Every time Murielle sees him she tries to groom him but that hair is the toughest weirdest stuff she has ever seen, more like metal wire than hair, and each week it seems like it has grown four inches, though of course she knows that can't possibly be; still, here she is on a regular basis snipping the stuff with the wire cutters.

Before she can sweep up, or get one of the girls to, the hairs have side-windered, disappear between the cracks in the floor. She must be over-tired to keep having this hallucination. And her dad yells each time she clips; why would he yell, hair doesn't have feeling.

"Almost done, Father."

"Here, take a look at this –" and with such glee he hands over page upon page, printed out… "I received this –" handing her the first pile "– and thereupon decided a reply was in order, tee-hee!"

Murielle frowns. She has come all this way with the kids to try to get the place cleaned up; anyway, she can't read very quickly, in fact, it's an effort for her to read, not something pleasurable at all. "Dad, I'm in the middle of –"

"No, no. It will only take a couple of minutes. I think you'll enjoy it." And with that he begins:

```
dearly beloved
    It is by the grace of the Lord that I send you this
Letter.
    My husband worked with cheveron/Texamco in Kenyaka
for fifteen years before he died in the year 2001. We
were married for ten years without a child. My Husband
died after a brief illness that lasted for Only four
days. Before his death we were both born again.
    Since his death I decided not to re-marry or get a
Child outside my matrimonial home which my religion is
against.
    When my late husband was alive he deposited The sum
of US $190,000,008.37 with a Security company in Europe.
    The funds where deposited as family valuables /
treasures for security reasons. Hence they are not
aware of the real contents of the consignment.
    Presently, I'm in a hospital in Kenyaka where I have
been undergoing treatment for esophageal cancer. I have
since lost my ability to talk and my doctors have told
me that I have only short time to live. It is my last
wish to see this money distributed to charity
```

organizations any where in the World. Because relatives and friends have plundered so much of my wealth since my illness, I cannot live with the agony of entrusting this huge responsibility to any of them for personal reasons.

Please! I beg you in the name of God to help me Stand and collect the Funds from the security company

As soon as I receive your reply I shall give you the contact of a representative who is in Europe as he will be the one to assist you in laying claims for this funds.

Yours Ever.

Sister Melista Pointer

"Oh, Dad. I hope you didn't answer it."

"Excuse me. Please allow me to continue, madam."

dear Sister Melista

thanks for your generous offer; but I really think you should give the money to your relatives, particularly if they are related to your husband. I really don't think they can be much worse than I! for one thing, I am not a Christian. I am a Jewish person, and about Christianity, I cannot make that leap of faith that would allow me to believe in the Virgin Birth. To look at facts, a young woman — let's call her Mary — is alone while her husband goes off on a job. And when he comes back she tells him she is pregnant, but there haven't been ANY guys around. Do you really think that's what happened? Probably to save face the husband — "Joseph" — said, "Oh, wow, that's unbelievable, God must have done it."

Misty, I don't want to upset you on your death bed. But do you really think God would do that with a young virgin? That is really sick. And there's something else: don't you believe, as a Believer in Judas Iscarious as

135

Your Savoir, you should make peace with your relatives, the ones who are robbing you blind? You must TRY at least to forgive them. Why give the money to a complete stranger, one about whom you know Virtually Nothing! I want to tell you, Melista, I would have no problem with Abortion or having a Child out of Wedlock (after all, Mary did, didn't she? I mean, it is kind of Adultery, right, to get pregnant with someone who's not your husband!! Or do you think she was raped? Would God rape? My guesstimate would be, yes, because He has also smote people, caused the plagues, a rain of frogs and so forth!).

I do have a problem however with some Jewish guy going around saying he is the 'son of god'. There are all too many of that type of fellow here in Jersey! It is true that sometimes that is the fault of their Mothers, but a lot of times, it is just these guys who are so stuck on themselves and they want to go out with a woman who is like, thirty years younger than they are — just like G-d with Mary! However, if you feel that even though you are about to die you can't possibly see your way to forgiveness, how about donating all the money to the charity of your choice? I am sure there is a Ballet or Opera Company in your neck of the woods, or you might like to think about giving money to an Animal Organization. There are a lot of animals who should be Neutered and Spayed to avoid further overpopulation of animals.

Best

Almuncle Antrobus

P.S. I see that your hdg-mail is entitled, 'trusted assistance needed'. I really wouldn't trust strangers so readily, Melista. If I get the money i would probably spend it on a little geisha. They are so so so cute and I hear can do amazing things with their mouths!!

Her father looks at her attentively and when she doesn't laugh begins his own cackling. He has really lost it. What is the use of any of this, surely there has to be a God at work who had long since gotten bored and moved on to another part of the universe helping to improve the lives of some alien species. The captain has abandoned ship!

"But Dad... You're not Jewish."

"Oh... My mother was; I could say I am half-Jewish. Just so you know, I'm leaving my money to the state of Israel to plant sequoia trees."

"Sequoia trees," she says, aghast.

"Another possibility is Franklinia. This unusual tree discovered by Benjamin Franklin was found in the wild only once. All trees after that are descendents of the original. With its broad glossy dark leaves and fragrance redolent of allspice –"

"Cut it out, will you, Dad!"

"Bear with me, then. Envision, if you will, next to the Mount of Olives, overlooking *kol Yerusalem* a grove of Bodhi trees, beneath which the young Buddha sat –"

"Dad, they wiped out the Middle East years ago! There's nothing there that will ever be inhabitable again."

"What?"

Dad doesn't even know that nowadays this kind of thing will get him in trouble! Mostly the Jews are gone. Oh, maybe some people with a few drops of Jew blood left, but if he goes around talking like that, or if his letter ever leaks out... Oy, vey.

Two blocks away a sinkhole has mysteriously opened up and according to the local news this sinkhole is growing larger on a daily basis; it has already swallowed two houses with the third almost about to topple in.

It isn't just that Dad has never thrown out anything; he continues to scour the streets for things. A black and white television with two knobs, UHS and VHF. An AM radio. The rotary phone.

Judas, the place could have been turned into a museum, there are actual books and receipts and magazines, all of which are long obsolete.

There are sacks of pennies, which haven't been a valid currency for fifty years. Vintage cans of food pre-dating when meat was grown from cells in great sheets in hydroponic factories, instead he has "Vienna sausages" and "devilled ham"; "pink salmon"; "artificial crab". Tins that have to be opened with can openers and – had Murielle done so – probably would have exploded their antique contents into the room.

The kids find him on the street, rummaging through the neatly tied garbage bags each of which is going to cost a hundred bucks to have taken away, and which, if not tied in the correct method, will be tossed back onto the front lawn.

"Ma, you have to stop him, or I'm not going to help any more!"

"Yeah Mom! We've been spending every weekend trying to clean up and then he messes it all up and takes everything back in!"

"Plus, Ma, Grandpa smells! I mean, I know he's old and everything and it isn't his fault, but can't you spay him?"

Oh dear, Murielle supposes she will have to take him home to live with them, she has long ago sworn he will never have to go to the Senior Mall! He keeps saying he will never live with her; if he has to live somewhere he wants it to be a Young At Heart Shopping Mall. But there's no way she can do this to him. No, she can't envision this.

"Dad, you've got to quit taking stuff back in!"

"Who keeps throwing it out? I need all these things. Why don't you ask me first? Have you seen my *Golfer's Annual* from 1997? I've been searching everywhere."

"Dad, every time you rip open one of those garbage bags it costs me twelve dollars, those bags are not cheap! I could be spending the weekends making overtime, instead I'm here throwing out TWELVE ROTARY PHONES when you know anyway, they don't work any more and I bought you new hologramovision sets. And meanwhile I'm struggling to make ends meet."

"To make ends meet what?"

"What?"

"To make both ends meet what?" he asks.

Momentarily she is distracted. "Well, I dunno…"

"Do you mean you want them to meet each other? Or the middle?" He seems very angry.

"Dad – your blood pressure!"

"Let me see those checks. Oh, these are my Social Security, the reason I didn't deposit them is they always bounced and then the bank charged me, so I stopped."

"Social Security… I know you told me, Dad, but what is it?" Maybe by distracting him he might calm down. How he loves talking about the past, which for him is apparently much more vivid than the present.

"Oh, I must have told you, no? That's from a long time ago when they thought people weren't grown up enough and so they wouldn't be able to manage their own money."

"Ha! That's so funny!"

"What's so funny about it? Nobody has any money now, either."

"Dad, like the President says, that's their own fault, they should invest wisely and save."

Now he is nearly apoplectic. It is all too confusing. Who knows what the heck might set him off? Fortunately just then the girls come in and slump wearily on the couch in the living room. Tahnee is throwing a plastic thing in the air.

"What have you got there, Tahnee?" says Dad in a calmer tone.

Tahnee doesn't respond, just sits with her hair over her face.

"Say, is that a lanyard?" He chuckles. "Used to be pretty good at making those things, back when I was a kid. Let me see…" Whatever Tahnee is holding is unspooling, a shiny brown plastic tape; a fight breaks out as Grandfather tries to take it and initially, at least, Tahnee will not release her grasp. "Why, that's a real old cassette, what they used to call an 8-track."

"So Grandpa, what's this?" says Julie, holding up an album cover and removing the record.

"That?" Grandpa grabs it from her hands. "That's a record; you don't know what a record is? Back in the old days, you put one of these on a turntable, put the needle on, that's how you got music."

Julie laboriously reads the title. "Madonna. Who was that, Grandpa?"

"I'm not sure. I don't think that's worth anything much. But I got an old ZVD3 somewhere, that one's worth plenty. That'll be your inheritance someday, Julie."

"What is it?"

"It's a documentary of the Great Westside Stadium disaster of 2020. The terrorists only got to release a few hundred copies before it was banned."

"What was the Westside Stadium, Grandpa?"

"Oh, it was a football and baseball stadium on the West Side of Manhattan. Nobody wanted it but every single mayor kept pushing and pushing and finally it went through. After it was built the insurgents occupied the stadium and began slaughtering the people who were there for the game, one by one, in the most horrible ways you can imagine. They murdered one per night just before the evening news and then sent the videos over to the local TV channels."

"The video of the person being killed?"

"Yup, and the footage had advertisements from the terrorists' backers. Finally after three months or so the Homeland Security Seals bombed the whole place and wiped everyone out. It was kind of a shame, though, because the terrorists had only killed thirty or so people by that point and there were still thousands and thousands left. Good thing it was a Mets game and not the Yankees, or the place would have been more crowded."

"Cool." It is the first time in ages that Murielle has seen Tahnee exhibit interest in anything. "Can we watch the ZVD3 later, Grandpa? Does it show stuff?"

"You better believe it."

"But why did it happen?" Julie's eyes fill with tears.

"Oh, well, some people said it was a setup because as it turned out the Westside Stadium never brought in the expected revenue."

The kids are getting restless, Murielle can see they want to go home – probably so they can sniff some more inhalant. She knows what is going on but what can she do? Besides, more than one report has come out that in chronic sniffers there is no sign of reeTVO.9, the gluf maybe protects the brain or something, hardening its surface like old Teflon.

"You know, back when I was growing up," her father begins; now that he is calmer there isn't going to be any shutting him up and the girls are glaring at her. "We used to have fifty states, yup, believe it or not. The coast used to be along the states of California, Washington and Oregon, believe it or not. And then came the earthquake, followed by the tsunami, which I believe was the President's nuclear –"

It is the same speech he has recited a thousand times before. "Dad, we have to get going. We've left the dog alone." She bends to kiss his cheek. The hairs are already twisting out of his ears and nose, geez, hadn't she just cut them? "We'll be back next week, Dad, see if you can get rid of some stuff on your own, and please! Don't bring in any more junk! Girls, give your grandfather a kiss and a hug before we go."

Behind his back the girls wrinkle their noses at her and scowl, but at least they obey. She's told them that there's no room at present time for him at the Senior Mall but the truth is she would never send her father there. Corners have had to be cut, she has had to fire staff members. From now on in order to be admitted, residents have to be able to clean up after themselves; feed themselves; let their activities be shown live on the *24 hours a day of sex, drugs and Rock-'n-Roll Network, all real, all the time!*; and play an okay game of bridge.

She hasn't told the girls yet, but next week she knows she will have to finish getting rid of the stuff and bring him home, to live with them.

14

Murielle is going on a date with A Jesse. She has told the others it is a date, even if it is only a cup of coffee. She has spent several hours getting ready. Several hours? At least. Here it is, already fall and none of the new fashions to wear! Every item she pulls out of her closet is wrong according to the standards of Julie, Tahnee, Cliffort and Dyllis. But since each of them has a different idea as to what is appropriate, or looks good on her, it appears there will be no consensus.

There isn't one item that goes with any other. And during the time the things have been in the closet, they have acquired spots, stains, tears, ripped hems. Had the girls been borrowing her stuff? She simply doesn't understand why everything is so full of holes until a moth-like thing flutters by. Oh, no, it is a SloMoFly! Those stupid flies that follow Slawa around, that according to Julie are supposed to save the world by devouring polyester, rayon, everything synthetic that would never disintegrate.

She can't bear it. She turns in front of the mirror: Look at this ruination of a body! What the heck has happened to it? Someone has taken her head and placed it atop this... this... she doesn't even know what to call it. A body, yes, but so misshapen, lumpy, flabby. Breasts that once stood taut and firm now end at the navel. Broken capillaries cover the corpus like a child's dot-to-dot game. It has to be some kind of joke. Mentally, she doesn't feel any older. She's got the same expression as some of her seniors at the home, with that desperate look as if they had been trapped against their will inside a human body.

Oh Intelligent Designer, Murielle thinks in silent prayer, *please let A. Jesse be the type of man who loves fat, hairy middle-aged women! Let him be the sort of man who is only turned on by the flabby type!*

It seems impossible; a lifetime spent waiting. There is no use in seeming too dressed-up; on the other hand she wants to make sure this guy knows she cares about her appearance!

At last the group selects a polka-dot halter-top dress in shades of pink; it has a matching bonnet, so very *a la mode*, pettipants beneath, also *au courant*. The holes are quickly glued together so it will look presentable, temporarily at least; but to Murielle it simply isn't flattering. Her ample breasts sway in the sacks of the dress's top; she has on pink pumps and because her legs are so white, he has rubbed them with that very fashionable self-greening lotion which has turned them green but, alas, also streaky and odorous.

The five of them sit in front of the house on lawn chairs, waiting for A. Jesse's arrival, munching on a bowl of some snack that Cliffort has prepared. "Benito Intelligent Designer," Dyllis says between crunchy mouthfuls, "Aiiee, I can't believe he is coming here to have coffee with you, Murielle. Ju know, I remember when we was growing up, and eet was like, we never going to get of here! Thas why I always thinking – say, Cliffort, what is this snack anyway? Eet's so good!"

"It was something I thought up, using cockroaches," Cliffort says, grabbing a handful.

"Oh my gosh," says Julie. "Cliffort, you know about the cockroach Greg, don't you? With the red spot? You didn't cook him, did you?"

"Don't worry, I clean out their systems first, a couple of days till they voided themselves. You see we are so used to eating only processed cellulose texture products, when you finally get to have something that was alive –" His tongue is so long he can almost snatch one from his hand from far away. "Heat the oil very hot, garlic, fresh squeezed lemon and chili pepper – doesn't completely cover the slight hint of pesticide and doom, but I kind of like that."

Julie is about to run into the house in search of Greg, when a **Gigantor Monster Smash Truck** pulls up over the dirt lawn.

"Bowel movement, look at that truck," says Tahnee. "I hope the neighbors see!" The truck is so huge that the wheels are the height of the house, you can't even see who is inside.

"Hello, A.," Murielle says, getting up and going over to the car as A. Jesse throws out a rope ladder from the driver's seat and waves. "Did you have any trouble finding us? How was the traffic?"

"You know what I'm doing these days?" he says. "I just drive right over the other cars. I mean, not the ones with people in them, of course, but the ones that have just been left there, stuck so long the people walked home. Yup, this is the way to go these days!" He appears older than the way the girls have described him.

She can't remember meeting a man – he's at least her age – with such an animal magnetism. On the other hand, he is wearing a very strong after-shave, so perhaps that's it. His eyes are kind and admiring: she knows at once he has suffered a great deal, he hasn't had an easy life. Seeing him makes her nervous. When she gets nervous, though, she involuntarily recites from *101 Greatest Scenes For Actors*. "Ida Scott?" she tilts her head winsomely. "This is Amanda Wingfield!"

Tahnee is glaring at her. Murielle can't stop: it's so stupid, but what can she do? She isn't alone in this only recently recognized medical condition, which is due to a tiny glitch in the brain, kind of like an electric hiccup. "Look at my hands! These hands are worse than a foghorn for reminding me." Now she's getting the skeeves, hands shaking, head filling with ice and tar. Mumblechuks, she thinks, mumblechuks.

"How do you do, I'm A. Jesse March Bishrop. Tahnee and, um… her sister didn't tell me they had such a young and gorgeous mother…" His feet are killing him, these darn platforms! But they looked so pretty in the store. He should have stuck with the court heels. He takes Murielle's hand and presses it to his lips. The kids are smirking. Somehow the whole event, a simple cup of java, has already escalated into more than she is prepared for.

"Would you like to come in?" Murielle says. "Have something to drink? We're not air-conditioned, I'm afraid, but it's a little cooler inside."

"No, no, thanks, if you don't mind, I think there's a place near here we can have a drink, I think I mentioned, earlier, I'm on quite a tight schedule –"

"Oh! Never give a sucker an even break!" It's almost a tic.

A. Jesse March Bishrop raises his eyebrows, puzzled. "Excuse me –"

"Oh, I'm sorry you had to come all this way then, I didn't realize."
She is blabbing the way she always does when she thinks a man is highly

eligible. For once, though, Dyllis is silent, no doubt at the presence of her boss.

"So how come you're allowed to drive a Gigantor Monster Truck?" Tahnee says, almost belligerently.

"Guess I just know the right people!" he says with a wink. "And, you know, I hold the patent on the anti-gravity Sonambula, it's just that, well, keep this a secret, okay?" Everyone nods eagerly. "We just can't get them to stay up very high!" There is silence, this has to be mulled over. A. Jesse doesn't trouble to explain how the hole through the earth screwed up a lot of things, what's the use? This weird crew would never understand. Still, he supposed, he could have gone on to explain, patiently, simply, how like an apple without a core (even though the extraction of the earth's core wasn't proportionate) Isaac Newton was dealing with a different object. "And is this little, um, little sister?" A. Jesse March Bishrop says, going over to Julie. Julie sits with hunched shoulders.

"Julie, get up! Say hi!" Murielle commands.

"That's okay, she doesn't have to! Next time, honey, you'll come with your sister – and your gorgeous mother, too."

"What does 'honey' mean, anyway? I always wondered."

"Good question." He is always happy to explain. "It was something people used to eat, back in the old days – made from insects. Bees or some such."

"Yuck!" The girls shriek in unison. A. Jesse is delighted.

"Oh, before I forget." He returns to his car, reaches into the back seat, pulls out a bunch of lilies. "These are for you."

"Just beautiful." Murielle holds them wistfully in her arms, inhaling deeply.

"They don't have a smell, Ma!" Tahnee says contemptuously. "They're flowers, not perfume!"

"Yes, they do," Murielle said. "Of course… there's rosemary, for remembrance – but these have a beautiful scent. Kind of like something very old-fashioned, nostalgic. Something people used to have at the turn of the century. I don't know if they still make *Paris* by Paris Hilton?"

When Murielle and A. Jesse have departed, Tahnee heads off to meet Locu at the shack and Julie goes up to see how Sue Ellen is getting along. "Sue Ellen? Is that you?" In the corner of her bedroom Julie can hear some… something soft and slimy, mucking around. More at night, it's true, but even during the day, lately. It's Sue Ellen. And those little suctioning sounds – at first Julie had been afraid; now she kind of understands.

Sue Ellen is a ghost – or maybe just a wet spot – who lives in a corner of Julie's room.

Sue Ellen makes one corner of Julie's room very unpleasant, but then, so many corners of the house are unpleasant and there seems to be nothing anybody can do; sometimes Julie suggests to Sue Ellen that she go to The Other Side.

Wet spot

Sue Ellen has tried to, but when she got there she was sort of lost: first there had been a lot of people waiting on line, to use the bathroom? – but she didn't have to go – then there's a test – in a… room, endless row of – what the heck were they, desks? And something like a pen and paper – and a kind of a bad smell and finally nothing seemed to be happening… And then there were questions that didn't make any sense… alive – either that or a damp area, Julie still isn't certain – when Sue Ellen does seem to talk, she explains, kind of, that over the course of history so many people had died… people, and then in other categories, animals and trees and grass, they had sort of… run out of room. It is too crowded and kind of… spongy.

Sue Ellen has told Julie that at the time when she did try to Cross Over, she thought, *I'm not going to stay around this dump here!* And even though they were all screaming, wait, come back! Don't be scared – there was no way Sue Ellen was going to take a test she was clearly going to flunk (which Julie could sympathize with) and so she kept going and that was how Sue Ellen ended up here in the corner of Julie's bedroom, making it damp.

Every few days her father – before her mother kicked him out – would come into her room, inspect the corner. "I do not understand! What you do here, Julie! You spill something? Why always, in this corner, wet? No leak from outside wall, no pipe here… no plant in pot. You do this? But why? Here is the mildew, this blackness – no good, I say!"

Once in a while he gets out the sander, sands down the **Renewable2%** floor – it is getting kind of worn out there – spritzes the wall with bleach… A day or two later, it is back to being slimy. She feels kind of bad, maybe she could have explained to her mother and sister, "It's a ghost –" but not to her father.

Even though her mother and sister believe in the existence of ghosts, and coffee enemas and the kabbalah and channeling past lives and paranormal phenomena and holistic medicine; astrology; psychic abilities; mushroom-quinoa intestinal implants; telekinesis and that the government is covering up the existence of aliens, somehow Julie doesn't want to tell them about the wet spot. She doesn't have the strength to go into all the details; they would have kept questioning her, plying her with questions – and probably gotten the HGMTV crews to visit.

One thing about Sue Ellen – Julie knows she isn't happy. Sue Ellen keeps saying there doesn't seem to be anything to eat around here – not that she is exactly hungry, but at night she often accompanies the person she called "that wady" meaning Murielle, to the fridge and makes sure the "wady" keeps stuffing her mouth full.

Maybe its Murielle, maybe Sue Ellen, but one or the other has terrible cravings! Salt and fats, salt and fats! Salami and swiss cold slabs of eggplant parmigiana; potato chips, jelly donuts, cheese enchiladas, hot buttered toast, peanut butter and bacon and mayonnise and whipped cream. But it is never enough. If only there were fried pork dumplings, even cold! But there never are.

And so when Murielle says, "I can't understand, I wake up in the morning, I am so thirsty, and who keeps eating everything in the fridge?" Julie knows there is no use in saying, *you ate it, because there's another… person… in the house, or more like a sort of… wet spot… that is trying to eat vicariously through you…*

It wouldn't have made any sense, would it?

When she has finished trying to soothe poor Sue Ellen, Julie goes to the basement and one by one lugs the cages upstairs and out, so the animals can have some light and a little hop around the yard. No one else cares, is how it seems to Julie, and it is up to her to rescue dying plants and sick animals and volunteer in the old age home where her mother works; if she is taken out to eat and there are two restaurants side by side, one well recommended and full of customers, the other empty and smelling of grease, Julie asks to eat at the latter. Because she feels sorry for the poor people who run such an unsuccessful place.

She is a good student by virtue of the fact that she studies hard but even so she never gets the right answers. Nor do the teachers really like her – too plain, too plump – her sister, it seems, has gotten all the looks. The height. The blonde hair. Julie doesn't resent Tahnee for this, the opposite, she admires her and thus when Tahnee says, "Let's go steet," or needs a companion in drinking or a lookout if she is going to have sex in the shack with Locu, Julie is always grateful to be included.

But Julie is happy enough, not like Tahnee; she has everything she needs: tonight her father will take her to the mall; since Murielle is out, he is going to come over and visit, cook dinner, do some repairs… He still has the keys; fortunately Murielle hasn't had the locks changed, and when he comes in, looking around nervously, Julie runs to greet him, grabs him in a big hug and throws her legs around his waist. "Oh, Daddy! I missed you…" Then wrinkling her nose and taking an involuntarily step back she sees her dad is looking at Cliffort who has draped himself in a number of damp cloths and is slumped on the sofa in front of the TV with his feet up on the table…

"Oh, Dad," says Julie, "This is Cliffort, he's been staying here. Cliffort, this is my dad –"

Cliffort rises, the damp cloths dripping. "My apologies for my soggy state, Comrade," Cliffort says. "I find I thrive under moist conditions."

"No need to get up," says Slawa quickly, but Cliffort has already crossed the room and is grasping his hand; Cliffort's skin is pale and soft… How many of these poreless, uncallused fiends now occupy the planet, Slawa wonders, what has happened to all the testosterone?

"Right, Julie, I have to go out, I'll leave you and your dad to it," Cliffort says, grabbing his things on the way out. "Very nice to have met you, Comrade, Julie talks so much about you."

"Daddy, Daddy!" Julie hops and dances as she wheedles. "Daddy, can we go to the mall so I can go to Shrimp Chips?"

"Julie, what did I tell you? No!"

She has been bugging him for months. "But Dad, it's not fair! All the girls in my class are doing it."

"I'm not giving you the money, Julie." Slawa had planned to sand the floor in Julie's room where it was always damp, and maybe cook some borscht: Julie loves his cooking. Certainly he hadn't planned to go to the mall. He needs to do chores around the place, he doesn't want his daughter growing up in squalor. Should paint the driveway, although it looks, at any moment, as if it were about to snow... which it does, sometimes, in August.

"I have my own money. The place at the mall, Shrimp Chips, you don't even need to make an appointment."

"I am not taking you! Julika, it's awful! It's going to look terrible. Why you want to do this thing?"

"I just do! It's the style, Daddy."

"Right, and then in a few years they're going to start sagging and... what did they say, they're going to be pendulous, and –"

"You can't talk! Look what you did when you were my age – you had your nose pierced, and your eyebrow, and your tongue slit, and your belly button. And you thought it was terrible to have a microchip implant, but look, now everybody has one and it's no big deal."

"This was stupid of me, Julya, because then when I arrive in this country the piercings were already out of style, and it just made me look dated. Like an old guy wearing white shoes."

"So what, it's my choice!"

"So it is your choice, but why you can't learn from me? Look what I had to go through, the stupid hole in my nose that people always point at and say, 'Excuse me, sir, you have something on your nose'."

"I know, I know, you've told me that a million times. But Mom is glad all the old people at the nursing home have nose rings – that way the aides can chain them to the wall. Dad, this is different. Guys now are only interested in girls who've had it done. It's totally safe, they inject them with FBI-DA-Homeland approved lichoneÑÒ –"

"That's the style this year that you think guys want. Then when the style changes, you're going to have to have them shortened." Slawa adores his daughter. He never wanted her to suffer, nothing bad must happen to her, yet there is nothing he can do, life is going to happen to her anyway. "Listen, you know the saying: the lord is with you, getting and spending. But now is not the spending time, not on a foolish fad!"

"I don't care!" She is petulant. "There are lots of places that do it; you just go there and they inject them with the stuff and that's it – I mean, you can go back for more, if you want them bigger – all I'm asking, Daddy, is for you to take me there. There's no way I can wear a bathing suit otherwise –"

Slawa gives up. He has never thought he could love someone so much. How he worships her, she provokes an emotion he has never imagined possible; he had been such a tough unthinking kid, desperate for basic survival and here she is – when he still lived at home, when the washing machine still worked, he would go through Julie's pockets before doing the laundry and find them stuffed with seeds, nuts, bits of bread. She always carried something to feed the rats in the park. And now with her poor puffy hands, that somehow got all burnt; let her do what all the others her age want. "Okay," he sighs, giving up, "not this time, but next. Right now, I got no money."

"Ooo, yay, yay Daddy!" She jumps up and down exaggeratedly.

She isn't pretty but to him she is beautiful, a fat, plain serious little child with dark, close-set eyes – he never saw what she actually looked like. He would croon to her in Russian while she slept, his little dumpling, his stuffed cabbage, and songs he did not even know he knew came back to him, Russian songs from his childhood.

He thinks about her during the day, the way she twinkles through a room, no more solid than the shifting light or dust motes, an electron floating capriciously and speeding up to the ceiling and then the floor. When she was little he found her crying in bed one night after she read how pearls are created. How old then, six? Eight?

"And they take the oyster and put a grain of sand in it, so it has to live with constant irritation, that's what people go around wearing, a poor oyster's drop of torture."

"Okay, but now, you know, don't worry, there are no more oysters."

That only made things worse; she sobbed and sobbed. He had to sing to her for hours to get her to calm down, fragments of songs that popped into his head: "*And there we had a collective farm, all run by husky Jewish arms, who says that Jews cannot be farmers, lies?*" and "*My father was the keeper of the Eddystone Light and he slept with a mermaid one fine night. From this union there came three – a porpoise and a porgy and the other was me!*" Finally she slept, her face flushed and puffy from salty tears, he had never loved her so much.

And now his baby wants to have something done to her... bits. Of course it is the fashion. Or is it? He worries about Tahnee's influence. He had known her since she was tiny but he had never exactly liked her. Tahnee was always beautiful to look at but after a short time he no longer thought so... There was something in her eyes, an inward glance, as if she didn't see the world or other people, she has no need for them, a little spoiled face begging to be smacked. He never did smack her, but she never warmed to him, either, no matter what excursions he took her on. And he had tried!

Once he had taken them on an outing to the beach, which for him was something very special; growing up in Moscow he had always wanted to visit the ocean... They set off early in the morning but... the public parking lot was full, there was a three-week waiting list. Otherwise it cost almost a thousand dollars to park unless you had a summer home here. Finally he let them out and drove around for seven hours before at the end of the day, when the sun was setting, he managed to find a public spot.

His family: Murielle, the girls, perched on a plaid blanket on the middle of the... beach.

Only it wasn't so much sand as rubbish, mile upon mile of plastic bottles, condoms, rubber balls, crushed cups, garbage cans full to overflowing. The sea was miles away, apparently it had shrunk. Certainly it was not the way he had envisioned it from childhood storybooks and old movies.

And when he finally did get to the water's edge, he could barely push his way through the water which was more garbage than liquid, viscous,

A Sea Dirge

By Lewis Carroll

There are certain things – as, a spider, a ghost,
The Income tax, an umbrella for three –
That I hate, but the thing that I hate the most
Is a thing they call the Sea.

Pour some salt water over the floor –
Ugly I'm sure you'll allow it to be:
Suppose it extended a mile or more,
That's very like the Sea.

Beat a dog till he howls outright –
Cruel, but all very well for a spree:
Suppose that he did so day and night,
That would be like the Sea.

I had a vision of nursery-maids;
Tens of thousands passed by me –
All leading children with wooden spades,
And this was by the Sea.

Who invented those spades of wood?
Who was it cut them out of the tree?
None, I think, but an idiot could –
Or one that loved the Sea.

It is pleasant and dreamy, no doubt, to float
With 'thoughts as boundless, and souls as free':
But suppose you are very unwell in the boat,
How do you like the Sea?

There is an insect that people avoid
(Whence is derived the verb, "to flee")
Where have you been by it most annoyed?
In lodgings by the Sea.

If you like your coffee with sand for dregs,
A decided hint of salt in your tea,
And a fish taste in the very eggs
By all means choose the Sea.

And if, with these dainties to drink and eat,
You prefer not a vestige of grass or tree,
And a chronic state of wet in your feet,
Then – I recommend the Sea.

For *I* have friends who dwell by the coast –
Pleasant friends they are to me!
It is when I am with them I wonder most
That anyone likes the Sea.

They take me a walk: though tired and stiff,
To climb the heights I madly agree;
And, after a tumble or so from the cliff,
They kindly suggest the Sea.

I try the rocks, and I think it cool
That they laugh with such an excess of glee,
As I heavily slip into every pool
That skirts the cold cold Sea.

slimy, as much sugar as salt. It was a sea of hair.

The entire ocean had filled with human hair flushed down the lavatories as people cleaned their brushes.

A man was giving a nature lesson to a group of others who watched him as he emerged covered with hair and used condoms. "It is so much better now that we are able to raise our food products in factories, no creatures are killing any other creatures… And can you imagine having to swim with all those things in the water around you? Fish, sea urchins, electric eels –"

The group gathered at the shoreline shook their heads in disgust and disbelief.

They drove home in sticky silence and no one ever made a request to go back. But he never forgot the seaside, how he had taken the girls, one at a time, into the soft gray waves filled with garbage and oily soap, and when he picked up Tahnee to carry her out he saw her lip had curled and she said with disgust, "You are so hairy!" If it was possible for a child to be born bad; anyway, he hadn't liked her even when she was so little.

It was absurd, she was only a child but he couldn't help but feel there was something evil about her. Still, he would never forget the taste of the air and the flat slap of the waves lapping on the sour brown sand.

God knows he had tried, but what had it led to? His wife hated him, she was trying all the time to throw him out. And Tahnee, older now, had appreciated nothing he had done, either. He suspected her of being a bad influence on Julie. It was thanks to Tahnee, no doubt, that Julie – who was smart – wasn't interested in beauty school to become a hairdresser or a product marketing stylist, something like that. What will become of her?

The years went by so quickly. No more little girls; sometimes he came back and the house had a funny smell and Tahnee and Julie sitting there with a shiny polyurethane expression in their eyes: "What have you two been doing?" he said. "What is that smell?"

"We were painting, Daddy, painting and playing with Sue Ellen… dat's de paint smell."

Now that he is no longer living at home it occurs to him the children had not been painting, they had been taking drugs of some sort. How stupid could he have been? Abruptly he can feel his own liver, a large spongiform entity, occupying more than its fair share of space on the lower right side. He has accomplished nothing he had planned and now the bubbling… whatever it is, a bubble of rage, coming up from his stomach, blocking his throat. He has to get away from this place, especially before Murielle gets back, even though he hasn't helped Julie with homework nor any of the other things for which he had come, he has to get out of there.

Especially before Murielle gets back. Though his past remains fuzzy he can see his future, his hands as alien and thick as that of a gorilla's, joining the plump flies in a stubby circle around Murielle's neck.

15

No time is wasted. Important and rich men cannot afford it. Besides, her dress is only half on! Or half off – it's more than that, the whole thing is unraveling, more holes than fabric. Dumbest seduction ploy he has ever heard of but she is giggling coyly, "Oh, this is so embarrassing," clutching the threads of shreds, "I'm coming unglued!"

Jesse pushes Murielle backward, onto his king-sized bed, pulls up what is left of her skirt and down with the peplum then goes to work; it is some time before he lifts his head. "Sweet Intelligent Designer! Murielle, you are my dream come true, I don't know how to say this without sounding insulting, but believe me I mean this only in the nicest possible way, it's like… when I eat you out, it's like a Swiss cheese and salami sandwich, you're my pudding, my hairy meat pudding sandwich, oh don't be offended I mean this in the best possible sense, Murielle, I haven't had any problems with getting overexcited like this since I was a kid, I started to dribble as soon as I saw you." As he says this, he pulls her breast free from the brassiere on the right side and bites it, hard enough that she thinks he might leave tooth marks.

Gently, dreamily, she bats him on the head like an irritated lioness with a cub. His head flies back sharply. "Aw honey, honey, honey, be nice." He returns to his activity, slurping beneath her dress and thinking, *it better be worth it, having to do this!* The woman has pubic hair nearly down to her knees, black and coiled, kind of sexy in an odd way, if a person wanted to get down in the primordial ooze and fuck the universe into existence.

There are mirrors on the ceiling, which alarm her slightly, particularly as she finds it uncomfortable to have the one breast swinging free while the other is still caught in the fabric cage of heavy-duty nylon.

It is a shame but A. explains that due to his Sausberger's and heavy dosage of Verisimilac, he is impotent. Nevertheless, he hopes he has gratified her to some extent and he would like to spend more time with her. "Perhaps, Mommy," he says, "You might want to come out to Nature's Caul and do some skiing, or the beach."

The West Coast really has a beach, a very nice one, because at great cost to the taxpayer, sand has been placed on the broken edge of what was once inland California. And many miles out to sea, a great net of indestructible steel has been built to act as a garbage filter and hairnet.

"Nature's Caul?" Murielle sits upright; it is impossible. No one in the world she occupies has ever been to such a place, not inside anyway. It is for the rich, only the very rich, and in Nature's Caul there is grass and sunshine and fresh air and little tiny multi-layered pastries in a myriad of colors, delicate as butterfly wings and petals. He even says he will send his private plane back for her; and she can bring the girls! "When do you think you'll be able to get some free time?" he asks.

"When? Why... I dunno, I can come with you tonight. I'll just call the office and..."

"And the girls?"

"Oh... sure, they can miss school."

"No, no," says A. Jesse firmly. "You know how much I believe in education; I could never allow that. I think it's fairly obvious your younger child is happy at her school and her work. She's also very sick. She needs your attention and I don't want to disrupt anything, at least not right now. But I tell you what: I can take the older one, I'm a board member of the Nature's Caul School, I'll arrange for her to have a scholarship. And when the little one is better and finishes the semester you and she, or just you, can come out to join me later. What do you think?"

She will join him later, she thinks, and lies back pulling the fluffy white comforter over her, a comforter that smells so sunny and fresh. Oh the happy contentedness of a sea cow, princess of the water, landed on some rocky beach and basking in near zero warmth, the thin trickle of Arctic sunlight, a warm yellow-gray paint tasting of mackerel and kelp, being oh-so-gently prodded into warm gelato.

"You know, Murielle, you might really want to talk to my lawyer about a lawsuit. Just the other day we got an amazing settlement for a little girl who had a case similar to your younger daughter."

"What?" She is startled. With an alarmed groan she slides back and opens her eyes to find two pink freckled hands like starfish, one on each bosom, in a kind of kneading motion. Peeping up from between her legs, the swiveling eyes of... a crab? Some sort of light blinks from across the room. "Are you sure the hologramo-camcorder cam isn't turned on?"

"You sure are paranoid, Murielle. Just relax. I am enjoying my work. I don't like to rush things." The earnest crab eyes, as if on retractable stalks – only these were fringed with pink lashes – disappeared into... the sand. She lies back but more terrible images... legless things washed up on the beach... appeared in her head once again.

"No, no, Jesse, stop... What were you saying? What kind?"

"What kind of settlement?"

"What kind of defect?"

"The baby was born with a partial brain. The baby got to be about ten years old when they found out. The remaining brain was rotting away... That's called anencephaly. In this case there was a basic cortex. The child was able to sleep, defecate and eat; actually it was pretty much like an ordinary person! I think that may be something similar to Julie's problems." He is relieved to remember Tahnee's sister's name.

"But what are you talking about? There's nothing the matter with Julie."

"Oh." He pauses. "I'm sorry. I saw her a couple of times, I just assumed."

"It's true she hasn't been herself, not since the plane crash."

"I'll arrange for Julie to get into my hospital here, if she gets better you'll bring her with you; if not, you'll come by yourself. Meanwhile, Tahnee can get something resembling an education out West; you know, that is one bright girl, I hate to think of her being squished by the school system here. I have a daughter or two just about her age, they'll be happy to help out, kind of a long-term Fresh-Air kid project."

"Tahnee is quite smart but... she's no scholar, you know, she's not much for the studying!"

"Nor my girl. Maybe they'll be a good influence on each other."

Of course, if Tahnee is gone for a while, she will have a room for Dad, and after all isn't she finally entitled to some happiness of her own? Imagine that, Tahnee already out there in Nature's Caul and she will join her! It's a boarding school, she can see Tahnee on the weekends, and, my gosh, it is so good to get the human touch. A. Jesse strokes the back of her neck. It's strange, but certainly there had never been much physical affection between herself and Tahnee, even when the girl was only an infant, she would not allow herself to be cuddled, she held herself stiffly. But then Julie, who had been cuddly, somehow just didn't do it for her, she always felt there was something slightly sodden about Julie, or heavy, or just plain uncomfortable. In any event if you had a child and it was affectionate, it was only for a few years, by age eight no kid wanted to be kissed by a wet-lipped adult. Now the only affection she gets is when Breakfast wants to sit on her lap, but even that is highly unsatisfactory. The dog hits her with its paw, "Feed me. Feed me." Or "It's too crowded! I'm not comfortable."

Now she has Jesse! It's kind of like having a teen obsession. All the little presents he might like – a new sweater, or fancy golf balls, yes, she will buy him little presents; it is a drugged state of bliss. Scrotonins?

There's only a day or so before the sinkhole will reach Grandpa's house. It's probably a good thing, Tahnee departing: the police call and tell Murielle it's time to come to get him, his house is condemned.

When she arrives, Dad is being held back by a cop, apparently he tried to jump into the pit that is now perilously close to the house. "Your father keeps saying he'll only go if he can go to the nursing home," the officer says apologetically. "I had to cuff him."

"Oh dear," Murielle says. "I'm sorry. He's just a bit confused. Dad! Dad! It's me, Murielle! Don't worry, I'm not going to put you in a nursing home! You'll come and live with me!"

Dad is writhing, his arms behind his back. "I'll be goddamned if I have to live in that house. I spent my whole life saving money to get inta that Young At Heart Retirement Center and I'll be goddamned if SHE keeps me at home so she can drain my funds." He spits into the depths.

What's down there at the bottom of the sinkhole, anyway? A crowd has gathered, watching the widening maw. It seems to be a slurry of broken ceramic, cups and plates, roiling and on the move, and each bit containing part of a man's face, broken or whole. At first Murielle thinks it's a repository for Gentleman's Relish, piccalilli, and anchovy paste, then, staring more closely, is it the Quaker Oats Man? No. The porcelain is printed with pictures of Chairman Mao, at various stages of his life!

The police push Dad into her car, his hands in plastic cuffs Murielle can snap off when she gets home. Cliffort has agreed to stay in the house, room and board free, in return for looking after Dad. That's a relief, he can't be left alone even for a minute. Doors and windows have to be covered with stronger metal gates and bolted on both sides.

Cliffort has promised he will wash Grandpa and bathe his feet and massage them, and clip his nails and promiscuous hairs. Grandpa moves into Tahnee's bedroom. He calms down right away, thanks to some pills that Cliffort has.

She's so relieved he's not angry, she doesn't mind when Dad reads another bunch of letters to her. "Listen to this!"

Dear Good One,

I am Lady Juan Aishat Ummah, the Proprietress of J.A.UMMAH DAY CARE ORGANISATION based here Hoek Van in Netherlands.

I was contacted few days ago by the lawyer to my In-law, who told me in confidence that my In-law Lodged some funds as consignment with a Security Vault there in England.

Moreso, he says that, for the past years, he has been keeping the (SAFE) Where my In-law keeps his Valuables, and now since he has not heard from anyone till this date, he then decided to force the Safe open and while going through the files, he got my contact.

Besides, we have all forgotten about my Late In-law and families, hence they all died in the Plane Crash years back, but the Lawyer Convienced me, thereby assuring me that if I can be able to get a "TRUSTED & HONEST ONE", who can be capable to Recieve and Handle the whole funds, that he will forward Prooves like (THE CERTIFICATE OF DEPOSIT AND THE VIDEO CLIPS OF THE SAID FUNDS, when they were Packaging it into the Trunk Boxes.

As soon as I recieve your acceptance letter, I shall Also forward to you:-

(B) The website of the plane crash, where my late In-law and family involved.

(C) The total amount that was disclosed to me by the Lawyer.

(D) The Percentage that will be for you.

(E) My photograph

I will be very glad to recieve your most urgent reply.

Thanks

Lady Juan A.Ummah (Proprietress)

J.A.UMMAH DAY CARE ORGANISATION

REPLY TO: ladyaishat33@yahoo.ie

Dear Lady Ummah,

I was very upset to hear about the plane crash in which all your family members were lost. That is so so terrible! I can't believe you had forgotten all about them until your lawyer broke open a safe!! With the Money! Do you know how much money is involved? I think it is wonderful that you are running a day care center in the Netherlands. I feel quite strongly that there must be a way for the lawyer to send the money to you, directly. You are perhaps the most deserving, although were your son-in-law's parents also involved in the tragic accident? ANd your daughter, who I presume was married to your son in law, did she also go down? Did they have any kids? If they all died it is really terrible you forgot about all of them until now when the safe was opened. If it was just your son-in-law, well, I can understand that more readily – but in that case, mightn't you be better off trying to get the money to your daughter? Even if you forgot all about that miserable son-in-law (and I am going to have to make the assumption he was pretty miserable character, else surely there would be more mourning on your part, and besides, as we both know, Men are Usually Pretty Useless!) i think you should have gotten money from the insurance company that is running the airline. I have a lawyer in mind for you to handle it if you did not. Seems to me like a couple hundred grand at least, for the son-in-law, should be coming your way; and more if there were others! If you could let me know a little more about the whole event. My lawyer will not charge but receives payment only when he wins.

Best

Mr A. Antrobus

Dearest Mr Antrobus,

Thanks for your urgent reply to me and your concern about my in-law and family members. I mean it was a tragedy that I never expected.

Sir, one thing I want you to know is that you can never can tell what will happen, so I did not just forget and wait till the company gets in touch with me or destroys the safe.

If I may ask you, how do I would have known that my late in-law has such deposit if he did not tell me?

Now, the question is not only that they contacted me for the claims, but can I be able to make the claim, when I cannot afford to travel to UK.

Yes, I am running a dare care, which needs funding, but now if I cannot go to Auk or send someone that I will trust to represent me, I am sure that the company will not attend to me.

Besides, his lawyer has assured me that if I cannot come, that I can send anyone that will represent me and on trust, so if your lawyer can do it, I mean travel to Uk to represent me, I will appreciate it also, so kindly reply and let me know so that I can get back to his lawyer.

Thanks
Lady Aishat

SIR,
I AM STILL WAITING TO HEAR FROM YOU.PLEASE REPLY TO THIS MAIL.
THANKS
LADY AISHAT

"Anyway, this was the correspondence until I got here. I wasn't able to get back to her right away." He keeps reading, Murielle thinks she is going to strangle him or herself!

Dear lady aishat,

You are right and I am sorry not to have responded to your last hdg-mail. Since our last communication I have fallen on hard times. I have been feeling depressed – why, I am not certain, it is nothing so terrible as what you must have endured, losing your family in such a tragedy as a plane crash! Nevertheless my home was destroyed in a sinkhole and my daughter has dragged me to her miserable house instead of allowing me to enter a really fun Nursing Home. My doctors advise me to get away, take a trip, to distract myself. I have spent time in Amsterdam and I also have a dear friend in Antwerp (in Belgium). Do you think if I were to take a trip to the Netherlands I might be able to visit you in van Hoek, and see the wonderful things you are doing with the children of the poor in your day care center? At this time of year I should be able to get a fairly cheap ticket, and I would be delighted if you would join me for lunch or dinner. This may seem a little forward of me, but maybe you have an extra room in which I could stay for a night or two? Or, if not, is there a local inn or hotel, charming but not too expensive, that you could recommend?

I hope to see you very soon –

Yours truly

Almuncle

At least he's keeping himself entertained, though really it seems kind of dangerous.

Cliffort sleeps on the couch, even though he would prefer to stay in his van at night; he finds he prefers the vehicle's humidity. But after only a few days, "I need a break," Cliffort tells Murielle.

"You want the day off? That's okay, I'm not going in today."

"Mind if I take young Julie here out to a park?"

"Which park?" says Murielle. "The Bermese Python one where the plane crashed is still closed."

"Dunno," says Cliffort. "**Maybe the Wilfredo Rosado Memorial Fun Park** and **Paterson Silk Factory Outlets?** Julie's looking a bit peaky, isn't she?"

162

"All right," says Murielle, "But don't be long, Julie, you really should be studying for your eighth grade test."

"Oh, I'm sure she'll be fine," says Cliffort, giving Julie a wink.

"Yeah?" says Murielle, "Here's a practice test booklet, you take a look."

Cliffort picks it up and reads a sample question. "'The Ottoman Empire' refers to:

a.) a tuffet; a style or type of furniture

b.) the period of history during which Atahualpa ruled the Inca peoples

c.) a kosher brand of chicken breast

d.) a young Turk.'

"Right," says Cliffort, "That's simple enough. I can easily help her prepare. It just involves simply thinking it through."

"Ooo, can I go, Ma? Please? Let me change into sneakers," Julie says, "My feet are sore."

Aw, come on," Cliffort says. "My van's only a block away."

"Fine, I'll wear my flip flops."

Cliffort grabs them before she can get them on. "Whose shoes are these?" Still holding Julie's flip-flops, he picks up a pair of Tahnee's sequined green platform sandals that she had left by the door. "Here, put these on, if you can't walk, I'll carry you."

"But those are Tahnee's shoes, she'll kill me." Julie is frightened, frightened of everything but at the moment she is afraid of being alone with Cliffort. Must her life continue this way forever, simply because she was born in the month of Phobias under the rising sign of the Closet of Left Shoes?

"Right, but your sister's not here is she?"

It's true, Tahnee is gone, without even saying goodbye, only leaving that ring with the finger still in it on Julie's bed. If she had wanted the shoes, she would have taken them along, wouldn't she? If only Julie could be more like her sister, who was born, according to the New Revised Zodiac, in the month of Indifference and with a rising sign of Burnt Edges.

"And by the time Tahnee comes back, I'm sure the shoes will be out of style and she won't care. Go on, put them on. Do it for your Cliffort."

But… they're men's shoes, Julie thinks uncomfortably. Still, Julie's had a crush on Cliffort for ages, or so it seems, there is something about him that is so… sexy, dirty and dangerous at the same time. She is scared though; she doesn't want to come across as a little girl. If only her sister were here to give advice! She and her sister wear the same size shoes, though she would never have bought men's; it's too kinky, but she puts them on. Upstairs, Grandfather is moaning in what is now his room; he's barricaded the door and keeps yelling that he's trapped.

The street is tarry, she sticks with each step, and her feet are still sore from walking on the prickers, the sharp tips are still embedded in her soles. The last time she walked on the prickers it had taken her mother hours to prize them out. She doesn't want to whine, though. Cliffort might lose interest in her; at least she hopes he is interested.

He walks about a block ahead, a jumpy erratic gait, and doesn't seem to notice that she can't keep up, surely if he had been interested he would have walked alongside her? She is only thirteen, but her breasts began to develop when she was eight; still she hasn't gotten her period, so maybe she doesn't really count as a woman. She keeps stumbling and it seems to her that night has come on very quickly. Everything is so gray and dark, she can hardly see. Except, she realizes, Cliffort is now green. He is a kind of glowing orb of green, emerald-green with yellow edging; beyond this a funny kind of orange. And in the middle of the green, in the middle of his legs there are fuzzy pink spots. Does Cliffort know what has happened to him? Or is it something that is happening to her? She hurries to catch up. "Cliffort? Can't you please walk slower?"

He turns. For a moment it seems as if he had forgotten who she is. "What?" he says. "Walk slower, yeah. Sorry about that, nackets!"

She winces. If her sister thought something wasn't cool, so did she. On the other hand, Tahnee had seemed to be impressed by Cliffort. She had made none of her usual jeering, sniping comments about him or his clothes or his taste in music. If Cliffort really does like her, it would be the first time someone had ever preferred her to Tahnee, but perhaps it is simply that Tahnee isn't here.

Down the block there are still crews of men looking in the marsh for bodies. Or body parts. They wear tall boots and are wandering around up to their waists in the muck with scoops and dredging hooks and nets.

She looks at Cliffort. She deserves to die. All this is her fault and if she confesses she will go to jail forever; but isn't it Cliffort's fault, too? "Cliffort, should I say something?"

"Like what?"

"That I shot the plane?"

"Nonsense." For a moment he crumbles into cubist blocks, the bits don't fit, either with panic or... Julie doesn't know. "Listen, nacks, you don't... uh... you don't think the Kamikaze launcher had actual bombs in it, do you? That's ridiculous, I'd never let a little kid shoot real missiles; everybody knows the Kamikaze is pretty feeble and out of date, nobody pays any attention to it in the world of weaponry, that's how I was able to obtain one."

Though she only half-believes him she is relieved. His van is just across the street. He unlocks it and she climbs in. From the passenger seat she turns to look around. A not unpleasant fecundity: of gym shoes, skunky feet, yeasty beer. A bogginess. Still, it is beautiful. There's a chandelier hanging from the ceiling made of glittering crystal butterflies, a mattress covered with pink satin, a mini fridge, an HGMTV set and stereo system. The windows are smoky gray-green.

"Wow," she says.

"Nice, huh? Come on, I'll take you for an ice cream."

He turns on the holograph; the President is talking about the latest terrorist attack, the downed plane – he will not say what airline, until the families of the passengers are told. All on board are presumed dead. Retaliation would be sought against the remaining Israelian Mishpucha, if there are any left.

"I urge the American people, in the name of the Congressional Institute of Creative Security, to turn to the home shopping station, either on radio, hologram or Internet, to purchase items to support our great nation and its endeavors. With each purchase is an opportunity to cast your vote, for an additional eighty-dollar charge, for who you'd like to see bombed. Coming up next, *The President's Choice Tea Party*"

The show returns to the two announcers. "Rich, do you think the President had prior knowledge of the attack?" asks Swootie Charles.

"No, I don't, Swootie, but we're going to take a break now for the updated traffic and weather report, and we'll be right back with more on this story after this important message: folks, do you suffer from Dwitney Scrubbs? Do you know this can easily become Derwent Chumbles?"

"Um, Cliffort?" says Julie. She wants to tell him that she can no longer see him, only this massive green blob, with darker green dots where his nostrils would have been. And a blobby translucent jellyfish-like image over his crotch. What the heck could it mean?

"Let me just hear the traffic and weather," says Cliffort. "Do you mind?"

"Hi, I'm Brettny-Amber Boyle bringing you the 24/7 Traffic Report. The twenty-lane highway from the Holland Tunnel continues to remain closed after seven years. Traffic on the G.W. Bridge, you're looking at a ten to twelve hour wait on the lower level, seven to nine on top. An accident on the BQLIE has slowed things down there to a possible two to three day wait. Heading out to Connecticut, traffic appears to be at a standstill, due to road construction..."

"Aw, never mind," says Cliffort. He flicks off the radio.

They park at Dream-Queen Castle, with a pick-up window in the middle of two mound-shaped heaps that are supposed to resemble soft serves, topped with gigantic pink plastic cherries, visible from miles away. Cliffort walks up to the glass. "Two large vanilla cones," he says, "Oh, and um, golly, let me have some Yabba bits, extra crispy."

"Schlee-sssuslh?" says the girl behind the counter, which means either, "Do you want the sauce on the side?" or, "What kind of sauce do you want with it?"

"Ne shuggh kig," says Cliffort.

"That will be thirty-eight dollars," says the voice. He reaches into his pocket. "Damn," he says. "Do me a favor, look in my pocket book, it's on the back seat, and see if I have enough money to pay for these?"

"That's okay," says Julie, "I have forty bucks."

She passes over the money. "Is that all you've got?" he says, grubbing around in his pockets some more. "Looks like we're totally wiped out for cash!" he says. "Hope we make it back before we run out of gas!"

The hand that emerges from the window with their cones has a strange blue band around each knuckle. Julie doesn't know if anyone else can see it, but she realizes this person is going to get, or has... "Cliffort... What does it mean that I can't see?" Julie tries again.

"And, um, on the ice cream, gimme the sprinkles, okay? The ones that look like little bugs? Julie, ya want sprinkles?"

"No, thanks."

"What's a matter, you don't like sprinkles?"

"They don't have any taste!" she says.

"Oh ho ho ho," Cliffort says. "They have a taste to me, kind of, you know, peppery. That's very funny, that you say they don't have a taste!"

She can't figure out why he thinks this is amusing. But then, so often people laugh at things she says that aren't funny. He asks Julie to hold his ice cream while he tips the nuggets out into his hand and somehow, Julie doesn't quite see how, pops them into his mouth even though his hand is green ectoplasm. One green hand on the wheel, the other feeding his face, Cliffort makes a turn a few miles away into **Wilfredo Rosado Memorial Fun Park**. Some years earlier the State Homeland Conservationism Partnership required all the NJ schoolchildren to collect money to fund the construction of a mountain built with New Jersey garbage. The mountain, close to half the height of Everest, and a quarter the length of the Himalayas, is covered with a simple layer of rubber from recycled tires. There will, some day, be bicycle trails, hiking and climbing areas, spelunking caves, rubber luge runs and so forth.

The dumping ground is already a quarter of its predicted future height. A vast mountain visible for a hundred miles, swarming with the only birds tough enough to survive, bio-adapted seagulls, some of which have four or five legs; beaks resembling needle-nosed pliers. Others are a mixture, some of which were someone's stupid genetic muddling of seagull-chicken-hawks. These are basically the only birds left since the bird 'flu of 2018 wiped out one billion people. These birds will attack like hawks, and eat anything. They have dandruff, which is white; along with their white droppings, the whole black rubber surface is speckled.

Cliffort is slurping on his vanilla cellulose ice cream, oblivious, apparently, to the fact that the inside of the van smells and feels like a damp tropical swamp. She unrolls the window but the odor is so hideous she quickly rolls it up again. "Come on, let's go out for a little walk," he says. "Ya better not wear your sister's shoes, they'll get filthy."

"I can't walk out there barefoot, what if I step in something?"

Julie's nervous, the Wilfredo Rosado Park has a bad reputation. People leave bodies here. The gases continuously produced, the oils and unguents that form the slurry, the plastic bags and shredded papers, sections made of rotting clothes... cans, plastic pop bottles, pikes, peaks, faux karst, cairns, ridges, alluvial deposits. A dry river of glittering glass shards, white and green and brown. A volcanic outcropping emits a greenish snot-like material that boils up and oozes down one side.

"Don't worry about it, I'll make sure where you walk."

The peculiar smell, the burnt sourness, brings back all the horrors of the plane crash. Her nose begins to prickle, her eyes sting. Beneath her feet, the tops of soup cans, rusted bedspreads, rotten compost, piles of green meats. From the top of a pile of stuff in thick black trash bags he looks around and calls to her, "Damn, there's some good stuff down there. Look at that sofa, looks like it might be vintage Sears."

"Cliffort," she says, "Everything's looking so odd to me, I think I can tell what's wrong with you, you sort of have, I dunno, extra nostrils on the side of your nose. Or, is that like because you once had piercings there?"

"What? Piercings? How ancient do you think I am?"

It takes all of her strength but she blurts it out, he is so cool, "I really have a crush on you, Cliffort, please don't let anything happen to you, I think I might be in love with you."

He scowls. "Right. Let's get something straight. I likes my women tough and independent, not whinging and needy and lovey-dovey. I have a crush on you, too, but I think it will be better if we call things quits now, okay? 'Cause you're just too soft for me."

He has a crush on her too! Only… she has screwed things up, big time, by being needy. Panicked, she changes tack and asks, "Can I ask you something? Do you think I should have my labia done?"

"What, the labia minora stretching?"

"Mmmm. Like, a lot of my friends have done it at Shrimp Chips?"

"Wouldn't know about that. I'm a toe man, myself. More on the receiving end, if you know what I mean."

"Ouch!" Something sharp jabs her foot.

"Now what's wrong?" he says irritably.

"Nothing. I mean, I cut my foot, like, no big deal."

"You cut your foot? Oh, Julie, ya didn't get hurt did you? Is there blood? Oh dear oh dear, let me have a look."

She doesn't know what any of this is about, why is he acting so nice to her? He carries her back to the car. "Curp!" he says, "Just look at them tootsies, absolutely filthy, aren't they!"

Julie loves being carried.

"You'd better let me have a look, make sure they're not hurt, clean 'em off a bit."

To her surprise, horror even, he positions her left foot in the middle of his lap, then picks up the other with his webbed fingers and begins to lick. His tongue is sticky between her toes; from time to time she sees it, fried-bologna pink, a slender tubular shape. Having her toes suckled doesn't feel particularly pleasant and she is nervous that, since they are so dirty, he might get a disease.

After a while she tries to get free. All she had been hoping for, really, was that they would kiss. Surely this is not what lovemaking is supposed to be?

"Oh fuck, Julie," he says, eyes glassy, "Julie, don't pull away now, you've gotten me all aroused, don't do this to me. I want you to stick one in my hearse."

"What?" she says. "Your hearse?"

"My arse, Julie, my arse. You've got the fattest toes I've ever seen and from the moment I met you I knew how funky they were going to be. Plump little bugs! Julie, I'll do anything for you, you gotta help me out."

She is nauseous. "I want to go home," she says in a peeved tone.

"Just help me out then, Julie, I swear, I'll do whatever you want," he whines, unzipping his fly. "Look, nothing down there," he says, cheerfully fierce, as he tugs down his pants.

"Oh, Cliffort." A queasy sorrow sweeps over her. She doesn't know what to say, really, the dry crumbling of dead beetle wings, a crackling of tired stars.

"See? I gotta tongue, though, and I still got a prostate! That's why a good toe fuck is fun, right up my little pink cloaca, see it winking at you? Otherwise, there's nothing down there. Let poor old Cliff have a little pleasurable frottage, if you're so unkind you won't do the other. I'll just rub along your backside, save you the worry of premature deflowering."

She's too embarrassed to ask him what deflowering means. Something to do with waxing, she thinks, trying to distract herself. It's kind of horrifying: he is completely smooth between his legs. Before she can stop him he's got her doggy style and pulling her shirt up and her pants down he grabs her arms with his, holds her down and begins to rub up and down on her. His skin against hers feels so soft, hairless and moist. He rubs and grinds and something hot and fetid spills out across her backside, the area between where he has yanked her shirt higher and her pants lower. He takes her hand and he twists it behind her back, rubs it into some hot sticky stuff.

"Crapaud!" he says. "Excuse my French, but behold! My spawn. There's quite a bit of it, too, going to waste, alas." Turning business-like: "There's a paper towel in the back, or maybe some tissue in the glove compartment. Give me a little tidy, my special lady, and you probably need to clean up, too." She wipes his smooth pale skin, so sticky the tissue clings to it. "Tomorrow if I can get some quosh I'll take you for a pedicure. Maybe you can lend me?" He sits up. Then an odd expression comes over his face and he begins to cough, again and again, a desperate sound. "Damn," he says. "That stupid mucormycosis amphibiarum. It's back. I thought I was through with it. They say the climate's too dry for me, I should live where it's moist. That's why I settled by the swamp but it doesn't seem to be doing the trick, does it?" He coughs again and with a pained expression begins to search around for a drink.

But on the drive back to her house, Cliffort starts to seem pleased with himself. "Didn't think I could get aroused any more without taking Erector," he says. "You must be quite good for me, haven't heard of any landsmen not needing Erector or something else, not in years. Don't think I could fuck a pussy, though, not the way I'm built. You won't mention it to anyone, will you Julie, about my being microcephallic? I can still gratify a woman, I've got quite a tongue, after all, compensates a bit. But I tell you what: if you can get yourself some birth control, I'll get myself a strap-on prosthesis, we'll have a go at it, shall we?"

A pleased young man

Julie's not sure what this means but she doesn't like the sound of it. A few hours later they pull up in the drive. Murielle hasn't been worried, exactly, but if Dad is going to stay in her home she realizes she now needs Cliffort more than she previously thought. She can't get into Dad's bedroom and Dad won't come out; he is either smoking crait in there or has set fire to something. "Oh, where were you?" she says. "What took you so long?" Then she sees Cliffort's expression, that of a cat who has stolen a particularly savory bit of sausage from the kitchen counter. Julie is looking queasy.

"Cliffort, see what you can do about Almuncle. I'm afraid the whole house is going to go up in flames. He's smoking crait, I don't know where he got it, but it sure makes him nasty."

"Dear oh dear oh dear," says Cliffort. "Can't imagine where he got it, that stuff's dangerous. I'm just going to brush my teeth and then I'll go and have a word with him."

On the top step Julie leans over and throws up into the dirt at the bottom of the steps on top of the plastic rhododendron.

16

Out the window of the plane a wall can be seen, made of old cars, hundreds of stories high. Then, beyond this, a terrible boiled area, fissured oozing primordial stuff, black and tarry, steam rising here and there. "What's that?" Tahnee says.

"What?" says A. Jesse. He is surprised Tahnee has not been squealing with excitement: her first airplane ride, the private plane (which even A. Jesse has to admit is pretty splendid, lined as it is in rare and exotic reclaimed tropical woods allegedly found in old barns and railways and hand-knotted Oriental carpets, where each square inch takes an eleven-year-old girl up to a month to knot, eventually permanently crippling her hands, etc.). But this has had little or no effect on her; only now does she express even vague interest.

"All that stuff... the black glop... what is it, how long does it go on?"

The plane has risen now through the clouds. "Don't they teach you kids anything in school these days? That's from when the USA lost the war."

"The USA never lost any war!" Tahnee says. "They taught us that much, at least."

"You're kidding? Well, that's not true, we did lose a war, after we turned over what they were calling Israel to the Palestinian peoples and then the Palestinians joined up with Syria and..." He can see she's tuning out already. "I did tell the President at that time, all we needed to do was give every Palestinian a house and hologramovision and computer with unlimited free wireless access and a halal McDonald's, that would have been an end to the fighting."

"That's not something they ever told us in school. You're just making it up. The land between New Jersey and Nature's Caul is Our National Forest for the Preservation of the Snail Darter."

It is remarkable, watching an empty mind struggling to think. A clock casing without any mechanism inside, so you had to push the hands to make them go around. Either that, or wait until it was correct – twice a day. A. Jesse gives a snort.

"Anyway," says Tahnee, "you're boring. All I wanted to know is what is that glop down there?"

"If you'd listen to me…" She is so beautiful, he can't bear it. Milky pearls, oh Lady Guineviere, is she the same as the Lady of the Lake, blue and cold, eyes the color of crushed moonstone? All that and her little rump, sassy as a filly. He sighs with appreciation. "As I was saying, we lost that war and we had to agree to take their garbage and radioactive waste for twenty years and unfortunately it kind of filled up the middle of the USA because we didn't have anywhere else to put it. What a mess, I told them not to but they insisted and covered it over with used tires that were melted down; they said, 'Oh, this will be great, the whole Midwest will be drivable surface.' Well, look what happened! The rubber stayed liquid, which I told them it would when the nuclear waste heated up the garbage. But did they listen?"

"Oh, yeah," says Tahnee, "That's exactly what they're doing in New Jersey, not too far away, a garbage mountain covered with rubber. It's really cool, it's going to have mountain climbing and…"

"Covered with rubber tires?"

"Yeah, they liquefy the tires, and pour it over the whole place and –"

"Great." A. Jesse sighs. "Same old, same old, eh?"

Tahnee sneers, a barely imperceptible curl of the lip upon which he surfs, higher and higher before being abruptly tossed, face down into the cold sand. "Don't you listen to anybody?" she says.

Even as she glares, he is smitten, he will ride her every emotion. He can't bear her ignorance, the dichotomy between her looks and brains is too vast. He shifts, trying to balance. He will teach her what she needs to know! "Then, right after that, we lost the West Coast states. They were aware of what might happen if we kept setting off those underwater explosions, but they expected the other countries would break apart, not ours."

"I'm going to sleep." She looks at him with disdain, a dainty twitch of the nostrils, and shuts her eyes. He can't believe he is finally alone with her, and will be, for as long as he wants. But he needs time to think. Perhaps she is clever, far cleverer than he had imagined. The gaping ignorance is an act, the bird pretending to be the hungriest in the nest to get the worm. She cannot be forced into anything, he sees that now, even if she is, for all intents and purposes, his property.

The evening fades from ochre to umber, or perhaps from pale-violet to foamy-blue with vestigial wisps of cumulonimbus clouds and in the distance the sun, a risible bloody eye, glares balefully on its descent to the horizon. "Wow, now what do you think that is?" says A. Jesse, hoping to get Tahnee's attention somehow. In the distance a plume of brilliant red and yellow fire spews straight up into the sky and spits out chunks brighter than the mournful sun. "Do you see that?"

"Yeah, so?" Tahnee is uninterested. "What is it, like, an amusement park?"

"That's the volcano!" says A. Jesse, using a tone of voice he might use in addressing a three-year-old and one he instantly regrets when he sees her even more disgusted expression.

"If you knew what it was, why did you ask me?"

But he is unable to stop himself. "Watch, oh, look look! Thar she blows, good old faithful, Mt. Dallas-Ft. Worth Volcano! Isn't it exciting?"

"You got any steet?"

"No." Should he tell her she's not allowed to use any while she's around him? But then, no doubt, she'll just go out to do it someplace else. "Anyway, in a few minutes we are going to make a stop to allow someone very special onto the plane, would you like to know who?"

"No. So, then, got any crait?"

He shakes his head. "Not with the Special Someone about to board! But, before I tell you who, there's just one other thing I think you'll be interested to learn. Now, in the Nature's Caul Morphew Valley, many years before California was destroyed by the earthquake and volcano and tidal waves, the new Idaho coast formed; the wealthiest, most

**Mt. Dallas, Ft. Worth
volcano erupts**

forward thinkers bought property and secured protection for themselves by building a canal to the East! And here all was lush and verdant. Admittedly the coastline was rocky except where they had put artificial sand beaches and the water not what it once was in terms of cleanliness. Still, the best people, our kind, had the coastline and they were only minutes away from the Grand Tetons, just a short distance for excellent ski conditions. It was a natural reserve for wildlife even though it was not open to the other side on the east. The West Coast tragedy left a huge spit of land, Nature's Caul peninsula, inland from Boise, and up through the mountains where a narrow spit ends before the rest of the New West Coast. So, the garbage and radioactive material in the long run proved for the best for the American people, since it ends exactly where the Happy Nature's Caul region begins and therefore it remains a private and secluded enclave for those who can appreciate it!"

"Whatever." She is watching the President on HGMTV, who is asking the audience to select A, B, or C on their remote to choose their favorite spot where the wedding will take place. For security purposes all three locations are within the Nature's Caul, but terrain is so varied inside the perimeter that the choices are breath-taking, be it the pink sands and palm trees of the turquoise ocean; the magnificent snow-capped mountain range; the open skies and vast prairie of the plains.

"I pick the turquoise ocean," says Tahnee to the HGMTV.

"Good choice!" says the little 3-D hologram guy who pops out of the corner of the screen when Tahnee presses A. "Why did you pick that, Tahnee?"

The President is still babbling in the background.

"I guess… I don't know. I guess, even though I burn really easily, I like to swim?"

The plane has now descended in the darkness onto an illuminated runway strip. The doors open and a foul smell blows in, that of things burning that were never meant to be burned, plastic and polychlorides, batteries and aerosol canisters; but it is only for a minute, long enough to let the US President in and the doors are shut once again.

"Hi there!" says Mr President. "Good to see you, A., and thanks for the lift!" Of course he is accompanied by the SS men, but thanks to the President's fiancé these guys are much better dressed nowadays.

"Jesse, we really don't have all that much time before we land, so shall we get started?" The President looks at A. Jesse meaningfully.

"You know, Tahnee, maybe you better go and sit in the back, Mr President and I have much business to discuss!"

Tahnee likes having a flight attendant all to herself and the couch in the back folds out into a bed with the softest white sheets. The sheets are *pure cotton with an eight hundred-thread count*, according to Marie-Therese who is wearing the cutest little attendant's uniform by Tark Bocaj. Tahnee has never before lain on 100 per cent cotton. Cotton is a luxury fabric, they don't grow it in the laboratories. She is learning rapidly. Marie-Therese brings her crab cakes, which are made not from processed imitation crab but the real thing; likewise the cheese, these cheeses are *artisanal cheeses aged up to seven years in temperature-controlled caves.* And the orange juice is made of freshly squeezed oranges. Although she's not of drinking age, Marie-Therese has been told to give Tahnee whatever she wants; thus Tahnee is able to select from an incredible variety of vodka. Among the brands are: Grey Goose, Sky, Smirnoff, Russian Standard, Imperial, Cristal, Absolut, Stolyichnaya, Finlandia, Royal Scarab and approximately eighty-seven more. There are also flavored vodkas: pepper, orange, citron, pomegranate, mushroom, peach, lime, vanilla and quite a number of other flavors!

By the time the plane lands Tahnee is woozy, her eyes bright, her cheeks are the slightest bit flushed, almost the color of dawn. He likes it this way. He doesn't exactly ply her with more, which really would be tacky and beside, he is not in any hurry.

"You see," A. Jesse tells her, lighting up a blunt, which, after all, compared to steet – and crait – is perfectly natural, "the meeting: well, so the President says to me, 'Listen, A., let's set off another underwater bomb'." He hands her the joint. "To prevent war, but in actual fact he's got his science department telling him it'll raise an island and we can relocate Vegas there. Of course any new land coming up is going to be contaminated – at which, of course, Wesley almost has a cardio infarct, he doesn't want to hear it – but East Coast citizens will be allowed to go there, spend their money and feel like they're somewhere. Actually, this isn't such a bad idea, we'll have casinos, ship in some sand, slap up some palm trees or pine trees – whatever. These people, they haven't seen a pine tree before, so, anything will be like a vacation for them!" Tahnee is fixing herself another drink before she takes the blunt from him. Nothing seems to have any effect on this kid. "We'll have, I dunno, replicas of things. This is agreed. Problem: my guys say it will cause a tsunami and destroy a lot of the country that we're claiming to be at war with. No problem, says Wesley, we're gonna say that they have biochemical munitions that we have to get rid of. Point to him. The devastation will slow them down; we'll go over with soldiers to blow up the rest of them and turn them democrat. Afterward, the aid from American peoples will make them realize that they are much loved by us."

Oops. The plane is landing and as they exit on to the tarmac and A. Jesse's waiting car, Tahnee is looped out of her gourd, she is not used to smoking such quality marijuana. And it is cold here, in fact, it is winter here, with beautiful clean flakes of snow floating and floating, so clean and white and Christmassy that in her tiny satin hot pants she can't help but shiver. "Oh, gee, are you cold?" says A. Jesse considerately. He leans forward to turn up the heat and puts his arm around her. To his surprise, Tahnee cuddles into him with a purr. "There's a nice shop here for fur coats," he says, "We'll go and pick out one for you tomorrow."

"Gross!" says Tahnee, giving him a shove. "I would never wear fur, do you know what they do to those poor little animals?"

"Oh no, sweetie, out here that's not something you have to worry about. The fur comes from dead animals."

"Yes? And your point is?"

"I mean animals that die of natural causes; and they all programmed to keel over when they reach the age of two-and-a-half or three. At their peak. Mink, fox, chinchilla. Until then they lead happy happy lives! I'll show you tomorrow. You see, out here in Nature's Caul, the animals are all so tame and gentle, they come and go as they please. And when it's time for them to go, they go back to where they're used to being fed and drop dead in full coat."

"Oh."

For the first time he has the sense he has genuinely engaged her, impressed her. "Anyway, as I was saying." He is used to women acting attentive, but she offers no encouraging murmurs of interest, "In addition, the decimated country will be required to use the money to hire American construction and contracting firms and buy US food supplies such as peanut butter and macaroni and cheese. So what's in it for me? My hedge fund is going to quadruple, at the least, overnight. But do I need the money? Not really. What's my private… oh gosh, what is the word I'm looking for? You know how each person has a…"

"Dream?" says Tahnee, snuggling more closely into his side. Marijuana always makes her affectionate.

"I guess." Oh God, he will absolutely swoon now. Swoon? What the hell is wrong with him, and at his age. He presses his nose and lips to the soft area below her neck, and as he does so he has a sensation something akin to his two frontal lobes being gently parted. Or a massage by a thousand fluttering feathers? He suddenly hates her. "Let me move you over a little bit, honey, I got your elbow digging into me."

Miserable now, he looks out the window. As the car climbs the mountain round the trees change from deciduous to fir, covered with snow.

The girl snores gently, dribbling a little drool on his custom-made white shirt. He has had a big stiffy for the past four or five hours, off and on; it's been goddamn painful, but now finally it goes away. Maybe he's lost interest in her altogether, who knows? He's never had much of an attention span for people. And now he realizes something else: thin rips, or maybe ridges, have appeared in the universe's fabric. If not the universe, the skin around the earth. He unrolls the window and looks out at the night sky. The stars twitch above. You can still see them here, maybe the only place left and the air is so clean and fresh, thanks to specially piped-in ozone and ions and special plug-in scents every few feet along the road.

He is a scientific genius. Or a financial genius, but then, who can tell the difference between them? Or anything, for that matter. It's the process. His mind has now made the leap, this understanding about the fabric of the globe, similar to old underpants. It's a pair of boxer shorts washed too many times, or with too much bleach. It has something to do with the surplus of electronic devices. Or that too many people and things have died, there's no room left for them or their electrons, neurons, what have you.

The marijuana really was too strong. At least they have arrived at last at his house. "Here, honey," he says, nudging her gently. "We're home."

His lodge is ski-in, ski-out, and a big roaring fire in the stone fireplace has been made per his orders in the vast reception hall; one of the staff comes to take the luggage while another carries steamy drinks on a tray that might be glog or grog or gluwein or hot mulled cider. "Why aren't these toddies hot?" complains A., taking a sip.

"Sorry, sir, we're having trouble with the stove, it doesn't seem to be working at present, nor the microwave, the remote system has its wires crossed and when we press the button the sliding doors open."

"Don't bother me now, with all that – can't you see I've got company?" he says, indicating Tahnee as a big dog comes in, who might be a Scottish Deerhound or an Irish Wolfhound or golden retriever or a Labrador retriever or a Newfoundland or a hyena.

Hyena

The hyena's reputation as a skulking, craven coward is not justified

Scottish Deerhound

Whatever it is, it crosses the slate or bluestone or ipe wood floor, wagging its tail, claws clicking, clickety, clap, tap, tap, tap. "Hi there, Boss, he says, though it is unclear whether the dog actually knows him. "Don't worry, he's friendly." He has arranged all these things specially, it is just that he can't remember whether he has selected items a, b, c, or d, for this particular residence.

All Caul is divided into three parts. The richest of the rich have custom-built homes from which a person can **choose from items listed below**

- heated outdoor infinity pool with view of mountains and valley below or indoor pool with waterfall
- glass greenhouse redolent with rare exotic orchids or fragrant citrus or unusual sedums and succulents resembling stones
- heated barn with pure Arabian horses or gaited Pasofinos or Lipizzaners (your choice of color except for the Lipizzaner which change from dark to white as they age or possibly the other way round)
- living room decor: paintings by Rothko, Agnes Martin, Alfred Jensen, and furniture by Herman Miller, Knoll, Eames and George Nakashimaya or collection of Legeres, Braques, Brancusis, Picabia accompanied by zebra wood furnishings by Ruehlemann or works by Matthew Barney, Ed Ruschka, Damien Hirst, Andy Warhol diamond dust silkscreens of shoes and furnishings of (tk) or Elfrieda Biondi sculptures, Dewey Whitefish installations, paintings by Sorbet Finkelstein, Toppy Bleck, Erna Meisterstuck and furniture by Mississippi Ralphman, Stephen Jonas and Lucash Amelio.

Someone has his private number. A woman's face with three dark chin hairs four feet high, nostrils the size of buckets, emerges on the screen. His ceilings are eighteen feet high, at first he thinks he is going to scream: that face is so darn huge! Who the heck could it be? He has forgotten to do something – press a button? utter a word or phrase? – to reduce the image to a corner. Oh, gosh, it is that darn Murielle already bugging him.

"Darling, it's me." The breathless fakeness of the voice on the other end, who does she think she is fooling? "I've been so worried, I've been trying to reach you, of course I'm wondering how Tahnee's doing and all, but I know you just got there, I'm sure she hasn't even settled in. The thing is, I really miss you, I can't wait to see you. When do you think you can send the plane for me?"

It occurs to him he doesn't have to put up with this. "Honey, I am right in the middle of a meeting, that's why I haven't turned on my screen for you to see me – let's talk later."

Tahnee comes down the stairs pink and freshly showered, dressed in a luxurious qiviut robe he provides for all his guests. It is true that the underfur of the musk ox is the softest fiber in the world, though there is also vicuña and shahtush, then there is cashmere, which is not quite so soft though nearly; there are various other types of furs that can be woven into knitted coats, soft and light, marabou feathers are mighty soft too, and warm!

There is a limit however to the kinds and varieties of soft, exclusive material that exist, not that Tahnee knows bespoke from off-the-rack; she is very ignorant, all she knows is she can't believe how good she feels, the never-ending stream of real water, and hot and clean at that. She feels so good she even sits down next to him. Oh she smells good with that clean hair and freshly powdered skin; gently he strokes her arm, traces a delicate pattern along a blue beating vein. "Mmm," he nuzzles, "Shall I take you up to bed?"

"Oh, heheh," says Tahnee, abruptly sliding away. "Did you know there was something wrong with the hot water, or, I mean the cold water? I practically got burnt! Good thing I didn't try to give one of our pets a bath, I would have cooked it. And so strange to have water without lumps."

"Mmmhmmm." He nuzzles softly, oh the tender stem of neck and how good she smells, uncontaminated by anything other than the lightest sprinkling of hormones, so delicate she might have been a pre-pubescent boy, no funky testosterone here, nor that sour slap slap slap of estrogen breaking upon the seaweed-strewn shore...

"You know, my sister… she was always taking home all the animals from the lab? Like, animals that were either going to be killed or got thrown out before they were dead? Like, we have these rabbits, with feathers, so so cute! And one time, like, we found this dog – we still have him. Its name is Breakfast. Anyway, my dad taught him how to talk! Not very well, of course, and it's not like he has anything particularly interesting to say –"

"Jackass Designer!" he curses and sits back. "You're telling me that you and your sister have the animals from my lab? Nobody is supposed to have those! They're supposed to be top secret. What else do you have in your house?"

"I dunno. I'll have to try and remember. Um, some big flies followed my dad? He's not my real dad, but…"

"Flies? What kind of flies, there must be stuff going on in there I don't even know about. Try to remember what else."

"Jesse, do you think I could have my own geisha?"

"We'll talk about it tomorrow, okay?" he says, "You have to realize, this is all a shock to me."

"Ohh, please?" She's now stroking his hand, bringing it up to her lips. What a little tease, he feels himself getting flushed and begins to slide closer once more just as the door opens.

It's his first… he doesn't want to say… son. B. Jesse isn't really his son. On the other hand he is the only father or parent B. has ever had. It's just too fussy to call B. his clone, it's like introducing someone as your 'second' cousin, rather than just saying cousin. Besides, it's embarrassing to think B. is him, twenty years younger.

"Hi, Dad!" says B. happily. "I was just over at Tanky's Roadhouse and I thought – whoa, who do we have here, who's this little minx? Jeez, Dad, what is she, sixteen?"

"Actually I'm almost fifteen," Tahnee says, sitting up primly and folding the robe tight over her legs. She can't take her eyes off B.

"What?" Now A. Jesse is bolt upright. "I thought you were eighteen?"

"I don't know where you got that idea."

"Okay, almost eighteen, you said this was going to be your last year of high school."

"Listen, I didn't mean to interrupt nuthin', I just wanted to ask, Dad, if I could borrow the plane, me and a couple of friends were thinking..."

"You didn't interrupt," says Tahnee coolly. "I was just heading up to bed, see you tomorrow!" She gives A. a wink. "Nice to meet you!" she calls to B., though A. doesn't remember making any introductions.

"See you around," says B. "She's too young for you, Dad," he adds once she has left the room. "She sure is hot, though, I guess we have the same taste in gals, huh?"

B. could lose thirty pounds, thinks A., he's like an overgrown frat boy. And those stupid shoes! He would never wear high-heeled sandals at this time of year – especially red sequined ones! "Do you really need to wear so much eyeliner?" snaps A. How is it possible that he gave birth, well, not gave birth, exactly, but how is it possible he had such an idiot when they are one and the same? He is a genius, therefore how could B. not be? They are the same person, after all, even though B. is thirty and A. is fifty; well, he was only twenty when he had B. and that was too young to be a dad, let alone a single dad. His own parents had been so strict and rigid, he always thought when he was a parent things would be different, he would never treat his kid the way they had treated him.

But B. hadn't been like him at all. From the start the kid was disobedient, refused to study. The boy wanted to be 'an artist'. Artist is a hereditary position, just like movie director or movie actor or pop star, they weren't going to let someone from outside come in. Particularly someone like his pudgy son/clone who had no talent whatsoever, at least as far as he could see! B. hadn't even bothered to finish art school, he expected a free ride through life from A. just because he was in the one percent and A. indulged him, now to his regret. Unlike the way A. was raised, he gave B. unlimited funds. A. had grown up middle class, to one of the poorer families in Morphew Valley (his father was estate manager and they had a cottage on the grounds of Wolkingfordshireham

Chateaux-and-Castle). He knew what it was like to be looked down on. Was it so wrong to let B. spend the money when they had so much?

"Uh, A.?" B. has a plummy voice, a stagey voice; he should be wearing a raccoon coat and carrying a hip flask, yowsah, yowsah, yowsah, "I was asking you about the plane?"

"No, you can't borrow my plane," A. tells him in an angry tone. "I told you if I didn't see some real effort to improve on your part, you were going to have to work for me. Look at you, you're thirty years old, hanging out at Tanky's Hide-Away –"

"It's Roadhouse, Pater. Tanky's Roadhouse."

"Whatever. What have you done with your life? What have you managed to accomplish? Not much, from what I can see. You know, by the time I was thirty…"

"I know, you've told me one million times. And I said, if you want me to come to work for you, I will, but you never wanted me to! You never give me a chance, you just ruin my self-esteem by saying all that stuff like I would put Bermese Python under in a week."

The two men are shouting, a rutting elk battling its reflection, antlers smashing into glass – they sure have that in common. Finally the phone rings, giving B. the chance to sneak out. Whinging blubber-boy, thinks A. Jesse, the only reason the kid left is because he knew A. would deduct his allowance if he kept it up before taking the call.

All he has to do is wave at the screen to answer it, that one tiny chip embedded in the web between his thumb and index finger, it is amazing! It can operate up to nineteen hundred electronic devices by microchip implantation. "Yes? What is it?" he barks before he finds out who it is. At least this time he's shrunk the image down to a more reasonable size, no more pores as big as tennis balls, no more faces to which the camera has added pounds and years and changed to a weird color, no matter how amazing the number of pixels.

"Oh, A. I'm sorry, I hope I'm not bothering you calling again."

Nuts, it's Murielle. "What's going on?" he says.

"I just don't know what to do! These flies, or moths, you know, they've eaten everything, I have a feeling they've mutated and it's not just synthetic fabric they're eating now, I mean, it's like, anything plastic, the vinyl siding, the rubber on my shoes."

He has an idea. "You know what? I'll come out to take a look."

"Oh, Jesse, really? I feel so terrible, to interrupt your work. I mean, I could just close up and come to you… There's practically nothing left here anyway."

"No, no, I have to go back to headquarters at some point, something's come up. Besides, you want to know the truth? I miss you. It'll be a little while, sweetie, but just hang in there."

After he hangs up he puts in a call to the Head of Security over at the laboratory in Jersey, asking him to look into the possibility that some of the genetically modified animals might be missing. Since they are patent-pending the whole thing is very alarming. Another company could have stolen the secrets. He'll be heading back pretty soon, he says, and he hopes the matter will be taken care of by then. Any animals – stolen, or escaped – that cannot be recaptured should immediately be euthanized; a lot of them aren't particularly safe anyway. Example: Murielle Antrobus, her kids used to work as interns, now her nearby home is infested. Her place really should be exterminated before the infestation escapes.

How long, he wonders, will it take his clone to lose thirty pounds? He'll lock him up in the gym and have slimming meals sent in a couple of times a day; if the kid stays off the booze, the weight should come off pretty quick.

At least, it always had for A.

By Phyllis Janowitz

Elect me president, why not, why not,
I promise you'll be driven in servile
limousines to watch croquet balls tumble
on unimpeachable greens. Your daughters
will cavort with cellos through mellow

Afternoons, while you, reclining,
compose concertos on fresh hay.
This will keep your thoughts away
from mortar and from butter; when you
sketch with sticks on dusky walls,

depicting antelope and buffalo
lurching gracefully over nothing, no
piles of stock and venomous ilk
will coil in your way. I promise
each citizen an equal sum to write

lyrics, sonnets and loony tunes,
to put a bee in every bonnet humming
in iambics; strophes and tropes adding
root and bloom will exude exotic
aromas in a jungle of golden freesias,

a garden of tropical fruits. My dear
brethren and sisters (I will say, raising
long arms as if to fly), do we not belong
to the same flock, all of us pariahs,
white and black? Once, fast asleep,

did I not awaken in a bed which rocked
like a ship going down, a rumble like
loose lions in the dark? The term
"earthquake," missing from my brain, by
its lack increased the residue of shock.

Oh elect me, if not president, then
present dick, then take stock and dead lock,
your local tic tic toe, tickets toc. If
I am elected we will play together
a game called the learning of names:

Porbeagle – a small shark of northern
seas noted for it for its voracity. Pooh-
pooh – to make light of. Trumpet wood –
a musical tree of the mulberry family
with hollow stems and shield-shaped leaves.

Oh let us, benevolently, look after
the charges of that astonishing mother
nailed to the beak of the barque;
she has given us slippery words to tend,
squirming infants swaddled in vulture skin

who know nothing about political aims.
We can unwrap and release them
to seed in sweet water. We can train
the small minnows to swim. Ah,
we can do whatever we like with them.

17

A full orchestra is playing the Presidential Suite as the President and Scott walk down the aisle at the Temple of the Intelligent Designer (Christian-Orientation). Scott wears white tie; the President in black. The newscaster explains how Mr President and Scott chose the minister, Reverend Murray Washington, who is head of the Ministry of Family Homeland Values and a former CIA operative who left the CIA after taking a science course which led to his conversion to the Church of Intelligent Design.

"This is really a star-studded event," says the announcer as the camera pans the audience. "T. Dakota Gunnerson Jr., Kelvin Winter Redstone. I see behind them Barbra O'Neil-Gandolfini, DJ Woofty Woof Bambatta, Little Theresa of The Flowers, Amber-Daisy von Thiessen-Leoni."

Grandpa turns off the hologramovision in disgust. "Elect *me* President" he mutters, "Why not?" The whole darn country is watching this stupid show, what a lot of rubbish. The collective unconscious has been drugged, a faint whiff of chloroform lingers on the surround – else why would it have been unconscious? "Back in the good old days," he announces to no one in particular, since no one is there and he has been left alone again. "Back in the old days." Then stops. What exactly had been so good about the good old days, anyway?

Except he knows things were better. Or at least not as bad as now. He has always said, they never should have drilled that hole through the earth's core; ever since then things had gone askew. But why is it no one else seems to have noticed? And whenever he brings it up, they all nudge each other and wink and he knows they are thinking, *there he goes again on one of his paranoid conspiracy rants.* He is not paranoid, something really is wrong!

He had tried to raise his daughter with old-fashioned values, but what the heck were they? And anyway, he obviously hadn't succeeded or else she wouldn't have trapped him here in this wretched little house, all alone except for that constipated dog who, he could swear, kept muttering things to him. He knew better than to tell anybody, or who knew what kind of meds they would start him on. Here, his own flesh and blood worked at that fancy Retirement Home, he had seen the place, there was shopping and fine dining, indoor track and field, all kinds of night life, what the heck did she keep him here for, some kind of punishment because he had once borrowed a lot of money from her? He hadn't yet been able to pay back. Why had he needed to borrow money from her anyway? Then it comes back to him, back in the glory days when he had his own Monument Design company, drawing plans for the most intricate gravestones which were made right on the premises. That was before the whole business went high-tech and he scrambled, unsuccessfully, to stay in business while all over the place, thanks to that indestructible plastic that could be etched with the person's holograph image and various buttons you could press. "*Hi, my name is Wyatt Corey Durango, and I was born in 2034 and died in –*" etc. The general text could be prepared, basically, at any time prior to the event. "*Press One to hear my life story. Press Two to hear the genealogy of the Durango Family. To view a slide show of the life of William Corey*

*Durango, press Nine. If you'd like to leave a message, press Five, followed by
the pound symbol. For Spanish, or to repeat this menu..."*

Now she's angry because she wasn't even going to be able to sell his
house, which she had made him sign over as collateral, because since the
whole damn place is about to be swallowed up into the sinkhole. That
isn't his fault!

He begins to rummage through the one suitcase they had let him
bring with him; she had thought it was his clothes and toiletries and a
few old family photographs – hah!

Dearest Almuncle

Thanks for your reply, though it was a little bit late, but all the
same am happy to hear from you.

Sir, I really appreciate all you have said in your mail and which is
fine, but sir, if I may suggest, can you let me have your contact details
to enable me forward it to my late in-laws lawyer and he will be in the
better position to let you know all that the transaction may require,
because I know that it will cost both of you some money as he rightly
stated to me, since they will go to the High Court to make changes of
ownership into your name as now the beneficiary to my late in-law.
Please it is just the favor that I am asking from you.

Kindly reply now.

Thanks

Lady Aishat

Almuncle rummages for a pencil, one of those good old-fashioned
writing utensils, and a scrap of paper, on which he replies hastily, before
anyone returns and sees what he is doing –

dearest lady,

*so do you have room to put me up in your home? do you want me to bring
anything from new york city, like, i don't know, some bagels or something? new
york is kind of known for its bagels, you know, or maybe you would like some
t-shirts that say I ♥ New Jewsey? if it is a problem for me to stay with you,*

i could bring my own sleeping bag and sleep on the floor — that way i won't get your sheets dirty! at this point i am hoping to arrive sometime early next week. what i'll do is, when i get to amsterdam, i'll take a train to hoek and from there get a taxi right to your day care center, or do you think it is within walking distance? also, what is the weather like right now? should i bring one 'evening wear' outfit in case there are clubs or parties we might be going to, or will it all be kind of casual? either way, i look forward to seeing you next week and hope we can work out all the financial stuff once I get there —

best —

Almuncle

And so on and so forth. After all, what the heck did he have to lose? He was fairly certain that this offer, unlike so many others, was sincere, if only because of the picture Lady Aishat had sent him, which was goddamn sexy, though in a demure rather than provocative way. A nice old-fashioned gal.

Of course then there was the matter of finding a stamp. Mail was always safer, if you could ever get someone to collect a letter. Fortunately in the bottom of the suitcase he had saved some, over the years; nineteen cents, twenty-two cents, thirty-four-cent stamps, on and on, a couple from each era. Only now realizing that in order for there to be enough postage to the Netherlands, my gosh, that would be… what, a hundred eighty dollars or so? And no room on the envelope: he would have to find something larger to put the letter into, but then, of course, the postage would go up, and so many of his stamps were two cents, or three. He shuffles down the stairs. There's what's-his-name and what's-her-face, smooching away on the sofa.

"Hi, Grandpa Almuncle!" It is Julie, nervously she breaks loose from Cliffort and jumps off the couch. "What are you looking for, can I help?"

Almuncle is distracted and forgets what he was doing. For a moment he remembers how, when he was young, grown-ups appeared so very old; someone his age must, to Julie, appear like a completely different species, a kind of ancient reptile on the verge of extinction.

"Believe me, it may seem unbelievable," he growls. "One of these days you people are going to end up just like me, hah! That is, if you're lucky! Yup, your breath turns bad, your skin all dried out and wrinkly."

How odd it all seems now, how quickly the whole thing went by, none of it ever seeming really life-like. A kind of facsimile or replica. And perhaps the next time around, things would be different. But if there was a next time, what, indeed, would be the point if he couldn't remember anything from this life? He would simply have to start all over again. "Who's this inflated amphibian, what are you doing here, sir?"

"Grandpa? It's Cliffort, remember? Hello!" She is waving at him, he must have zoned out, what was he doing, anyway?

"Mr Antrobus," says Cliffort, "Maybe you're hungry. I'll go fix us a little snack, oookay?"

Now Julie is alone with her grandfather. She tries to hoist her pants. "You promise you won't repeat this to anyone?"

"What's that? No, no, of course not."

"So... well, Cliffort was showing me how to shoot, only he didn't know that I had, like, straight As in munitions and stuff? And so, I think it was because he put his hands on mine, and, and, anyway, it was right after I pulled the trigger that the plane crashed – I didn't mean to do it!"

"Oh my gosh, so you were the one who pulled the trigger that brought that plane down? That is terrible. So many people killed! That is something you are never going to be able to forgive yourself for, so many lives destroyed and not just the people that you killed, but all their families!" He loves people, Almuncle thinks, it's just his own family he can't stand. Geez, one little nanosecond of fun, one little squirt of jism and he's supposed to feel related to these offspring and their descendents forever? Even a damn dog wouldn't bother.

Julie begins sobbing. She had been so certain Grandpa would reassure her and say it wasn't her fault, or at least make her feel better. She never would have confided in him if she thought it was going to be like this. "But I... I never..."

"You never what? You never considered there would be repercussions to your actions? Julie, I don't think this information is something I can keep to myself. Not when it involves the deaths of so many. I am going to have to have a think. What shall I do?" Meanwhile Julie's got that gosh-darn red spotted cockaroach climbing over her shoulder waving up its feelers in alarm. "Oh for heaven's sake, why don't you keep that thing in a box, you know it's going to get squished. Here," he rummages through his treasures, "keep it in this."

Snuffles. "What is it?"

"It's what they call a matchbox. In the old days you rubbed a wooden stick against the side to make fire."

"One stick? I thought they rubbed two together."

"Whatever. It was a long time ago, anyway, before people had plumbing."

At least her snuffles have diminished. She holds a blistered, blackened finger up to her shoulder. What the heck is wrong with her? The roach steps onto it and she carries it down to the matchbox.

"Oh, don't tell anyone, Grandpa, please! You promised! And… and besides, tomorrow's the day of the big test, can't you at least wait until after it to decide, the big test will decide my entire life, just about!"

He agrees he will wait until after it is finished to decide what he should do.

The big test is the one that all the eighth graders have to take; from the results only a few would be selected, though selected for what, Julie – nor anybody else – doesn't seem to know.

Anyway nobody from her school ever was selected, has ever been selected. Being selected is for the rich people who live out West, so why do they even make them take the test? And some of her friends are feeling as sick as she, though others are like, yeah, whatever. Knowing it is all hopeless anyway.

Of course with her mother, it's, like, you'd better do well or I'll kill you; but then her mother would always add, "I don't know why I bother, you're going to flunk, I'm sure."

A lioness swats her baby for no reason that the cub can determine; so it was with Julie and her mother. But even if she had done fantastically her mother wouldn't have been able to come up with the money for whatever it was that being selected would cost. She can't sleep, between worry about the test and what her grandfather is going to do; Julie can hear him and Cliffort talking in the kitchen. Finally she remembers Tahnee has a few pills in her top drawer and she takes a couple of these, which do have a calming effect, so calming, in fact, that she oversleeps.

By the time Julie arrives at Robert Downey Jr. Junior High she has already missed first period, homeroom. At school the Christian Fundamentalist Survivalist kids are at war with the Iscarians, who believe that Judas Iscariot is the good guy and Christ was a promiscuous Jew, a belief that has become more and more popular. Strip searches are conducted daily on the kids to make sure no munitions are brought into the school. It can take an hour, waiting on line, girls separated from boys, sniffer dogs, and so on.

On the other hand, in case the Homeland is invaded, every child is given an assault weapon, which you are supposed to keep in your locker. Of course no one does, most of the lockers are too small to hold them, anyway, you can keep it at home. You are supposed to attend weekly practice, but it is so boring. There are ways to fake credit in the course or at least make up for it by going on a two-day sleep-away camp two or three times a year, where, like, you sleep in these bunkers and all the kids get high and stay up all night and almost always some kid gets his or her head blown off or drowns.

Robert Downey Jr. Junior High was built in the early part of the twenty-first century at a time when there was an unusual numbers of shoot-outs and bombs, and thus had been designed prison/Stalinesque in style, originally supposed to be fifty stories high with offices and stores on the top floors; this had never happened though, nobody wanted to rent office space way out here and the school didn't have enough money to keep the whole place heated, lit, etc. so now only the first three floors are in use.

Julie always thinks the sprinkler system in the ceiling was constructed so the place could be flooded if things got really bad or the kids rioted. Then the halls, the cafeteria, the classrooms where no windows can be opened – would fill with water, a giant fish-tank or sewer system, with the kids clawing their way up to the ceiling for the last gasp of air. Trapped even without a flood, so trapped, the smell from the cafeteria wafting down the hall; ancient food steaming for days atop the steam trays; untouched string beans, watery, overcooked; instant mashed potatoes, Salisbury steak, tuna salad, and all of it reeking of peanut butter. Some years back something had gotten screwed up in the laboratory where they grew the school food. Some of the kids majoring in the Chef's Institute work there, and they say that peanut butter enzyme – or flavoring? – had gotten permanently embedded with all the starter-yeasts so there isn't one thing that doesn't taste like peanut-butter. The kids joke about it, peanut butter and hamburger day! Peanut-butter sushi day! There had been a clean up over the summer but… it still hadn't worked, even with new starter-food spores and growth-medium from the suppliers.

The problem is, if you want just a plain old peanut-butter sandwich, which is grown in loaves with layers of peanut-butter between layers of bread layers, it tastes like raw fish. The tomatoes, which grow in a sort of gelatin block and can be sliced, taste like fish and peanut-butter.

Outdoors it is no better: the playground was designed eons ago by a landscape architect hired by the Bermese Pythion company as part of their Art for the People public works which meant that they didn't have to pay local taxes.

There are eighty kids in homeroom and it is impossible for the teacher to keep order, especially today, when all the kids are wrecks, knowing in a minute they will file to the auditorium for the test. Julie arrives and takes a seat in the back of the class. This is where the kids sit who claim to worship Deepak Chopra and Tupac Shakur.

And then it is time, the auditorium, the sheets passed out, the whole thing made to seem… scary. "You may now open your test booklets which you will find in your computers on www.EighthGrade Education.com!" The principal's voice cracks through the air. "And…

you may begin!" Loud music comes on over the speakers, some of the latest hit tunes the kids have asked for.

Three whole hours; a quick lunch break and then more.

MATH:

If the time before Christ is B.C. and after Christ is a.d., what is the time during which he was alive called. A) D.j. b) d.c. C) J.C. D) the twelve thousand forty-five days

Gladys bought two shares in Bermese Pythion stock. Over a one-year period the 52-week high was 84.8 while the low was 63.29. If the quarterly dividends were .68 of a share and the last change was +8.01, what is your prediction for the next annual report in the event that the Warren Buffet clone is twenty years of age and available? Show all work.

ENGLISH:

A cat-o'-nine tails is to the English as

a) Hologramovision is to an American b) Lala Rookh is to Muslims c) Perl Mista is to a dinner party d) Teapot Dome is to taffeta

An olive is to a chair as a) an umbrella is to an algebra equation b) as buttered toast is to an alarm clock c) a cataract is to a catamite

A borsalino is to an isotherm as a) gaiters are to a monstrance b) ontology is to a philanderer c) an anchorite is to a hectare d) a pood is to a jeroboam

Suttee is to a suicide as a) a suture is to a surgeon b) sewage is to a sturgeon c) a surge protector is to a superior d) solution is to a servant.

Oh, bowel movement, she thinks, she'll try to guess – that gives at least a one in four chance – maybe it is sewage is to a sturgeon... then realizes, she doesn't actually know what a sturgeon is, something to do with a boat? An old kind of sailing ship? In which case, they would have plenty of sewage on board – unless the toilets in those days went right in a hole down to the water – but then, in that case, wouldn't the...

bilge, yes that's the right word, wouldn't the bilge come up, back into the sturgeon?

The ship's sturgeon... her head really hurts, and to make matters worse, her laptop – on which the test is – emits an odd sound and the question is... it isn't lost, exactly, it has mysteriously converted into a little table, a diagram of some sort, and she can't revert it back to its original shape. Now so much time has gone by she knows she is going to flunk. Flips through the test, a picture!

SPORTS MARKETING:

In this famous work by Jean-Louis David, entitled 'The Tennis Court Oath' discuss the use of foul language at Forest Hills and Wimbledon in the centuries since this was first painted and how it compared to what was being said in French. Describe the similarities and differences in clothing style and logos, advertising and sponsors.

There are almost two thousand kids in her school who are in the eighth grade; only half can fit into the auditorium so the others will take the test, a different one, tomorrow. Most of the kids are illegal immigrants, and it is obvious the only jobs that will be open to them are at the fast food franchises, and nowadays you have to go to a two-year college for that, or else get all the service positions out in Nature's Caul Valley, working for the rich people. Sitting next to her is one of the Chinese girls, for some reason they are mostly named Maya. If only she had been adopted from China, it really isn't fair, how come her mother had found, like, the only two fertile guys left on the planet who naturally had no brains... And all those Chinese girls, when they grew up, they got to go to China where there were like, a billion guys for every girl.

At this rate she is going to fail completely. "Psst!" she says. "Maya… you gotta help me. I can't do an essay! What am I supposed to write?" Maya ignores her… maybe she should just go on.

LOGIC:

What comes next in the following list?

High boy; cowboy; toy boy; rent boy; drummer boy; delivery boy; cabana boy; whipping boy; head boy; dough boy; Boy Wonder; cabana boy; dog boy; down, boy! fat boy; charpoy; golden boy; The Beach Boys; Boy George; cabana boy; po' boy; tom boy; bugle boy; hoi polloi; house boy

Logic? Is that something they even learned? This isn't working, if you can't answer a question keep going but… there is another goddamned essay section of the test!

In Song of Solomon, Solomon says, "Of the writing of books there is too many."

What were the names of the books? Use your best judgment. Defend your position.

Holy intestinal extrusion! Where has she been all semester? She can't remember ever being assigned the Song of Solomon. Was it something in her Musical Theater and Film class? The whole thing is a nightmare, she could look it up but obviously, all ZiplineNet 23 service has been cut off… Everyone else is writing eagerly. Keep moving, keep going forward, then if there is time she can go back to check the work…

What was the largest grossing movie of 2029? Write a plot synopsis, explaining why you think that movie was so effective. Explain the difference between net and gross profit. Extra Credit: provide biographical detail of this film's producer.

For Miss Fletsum's Class Only!
Just for Fun
(I wrote this for you myself. Remember, some of these can be tricky!)
Match the descriptions to the picture (80 points)

a. ventilation passage
a. shell
a. tripping lever
a. discharge pipes
b. leather collar by which motion is transmitted from the upper to the lower cone
b. field magnets
b. floating flap
b. base
b. primer case
c. anus
c. valve
c. entrance
c. sliding rod carrying the collar and regulating the speed
d. inner tube
d. bulkhead
d. right bronchus
d. liver
e. shafts
e. joint ring
e. heart
e .neck
f. adductor
f. buoyancy-chamber
f. triglyph
f. portico surrounding the courtyard
g. piston-rod
g. valve gear compartments
g. stomach sac
g. sectional side view
g. bevel head bolt

Dynamo

Oubliette.

A Side-suction
Force-pump.

Oyster with Right
Mantle-flap Removed.

Cone-wheels used in Regulating Speed.

Bliss-Leavitt Torpedo with War-head.

Nomenclature of the Sheep.

Scotch Bagpipe.

Just for fun? Just for fun? My gosh it is so difficult to do anything with her hands all bandaged up…

Oh b.m., b.m., British museum! Why had she been such a rectum and not studied more; *let there be a fire drill, let there be a bomb threat, something has to happen, she is going to end up with a big fat zero and nowadays you gotta do better than that even to be a bathroom attendant.*

To her horror, her computer is eating everything in front of her. It is just swallowing up the whole text, little bugs are crawling out from under the keys, not fake bugs but the damn cockroaches!

Not that she is the only one to have cockroaches in her laptop, mind you, it's just that she isn't as tidy as the other girls, something sticky is on the keys and maybe if she had spritzed with that disinfectant the teacher kept telling them all to use…

She gives the laptop a shake; man that thing stinks, piles, clouds of cockroach droppings, like pepper flecks, come tumbling out of the holes in the back and the stench is tremendous, that cockroach smell of death, along with a nasty collection of dried legs, feelers, fragments of carapace. She's about to start smashing the emerging newborns (very new, since they are still in their just-hatched, newly white stage) when a big guy comes out and just in time she realizes she's about to smash Greg! He's got that red spot and he's waving his feelers at her; quickly she scoops him up and zips him into her bag.

Chateaux, the girl next to her, wrinkles her nose: oh, come on, there is no way Chateaux lives in a place that is any cleaner, those damn bugs are everywhere, she only wishes Chateaux hadn't seen her rescuing Greg, it's going to get around school, she bets.

Maybe her prayers have been heard: the giant hologramovision screen on the wall in back of the stage, which is constantly turned on, goes blank.

The kids applaud, they are so sick of the Educational Station: pictures of canyons filled to the brim with beer cans, dying elephants, effects of drought where lakes are drying up, animals being euthanized in shelters, hurricanes wiping out villages, the polar ice-caps melting, irradiated kids dying where nuclear power plants have exploded, etc. etc., and while these scenes play, at the bottom of the screen is the number you can call to donate money – anyway, all this goes blank.

When it comes on again this time it is the President. The kids taking the test begin to cheer; if he is interrupting the educational channel they had better listen! Even if it means not completing the test!

"Today's security has been upgraded to Code Lime/23," he says. "I urge you all to return to your homes and remain calm. We believe the threat of terrorist action to be very real. We believe this to be a very deliberate attempt to sabotage the coverage of my wedding. Nevertheless we have no plans to cancel this evening's hologramovision broadcasts of the wedding supper followed by dancing to the Duchin-Haywood Orchestra, and this morning's ceremony, as you may know, has gone smoothly. However, at the present time for your own safety, details cannot be released. As citizens of our great nation, I suggest that you make sure your Homeland Emergency Supply Kit is fully stocked and has not reached its expiration date. While you stay close to home this afternoon and evening, a helpful hint might be to turn to the Shopping Network. To keep our economy strong, for a limited time only the updated Emergency Supply Kit 2200Q will be available at a special price. Shipping and handling not included." The sound grows fuzzy, maybe something is really wrong?

While he is blabbing the kids begin to print out whatever part of the test they have finished and fold up their computers. At least this way maybe Julie can re-do the whole thing, she'll have the excuse that, as a Homeland Girl Guard, she has security duties to perform and she can say that somehow in her haste the print-out got lost, they have to schedule a make-up test, right? Nothing ever happens when the President says there is going to be a terrorist attack anyway.

The war has been going on now for... what, thirty years? Sixty? It isn't always the same war but close enough; different countries take over from time to time on one side or another, mostly to get their turn at off-loading some weaponry they had been forced to buy or manufactured themselves that is rapidly becoming outdated.

The buses are lined up outside the school and she is about to get on when her mother pulls up. "What are you doing, Mom? You're not supposed to be out, you should have gone home, didn't you hear it's a Code Lemon?" She looks around at the kids lining up to get on the bus.

"You, young lady, are in big trouble…" Murielle is white-lipped.

Julie doesn't dare speak. The car is full of rage, they are sealed in together in an airless room filled with wet concrete. They drive in silence. The house is not far from the lab and her mother's work, La Galleria Senior Mall and Residence Home for the Young at Heart. Her mother knows the back routes.

Maybe her mother can be jollied out of whatever mood she is in. "Sure is hot out here, huh?" Julie says. Her mother doesn't respond.

Usually the weather is far more changeable. This heat has gone on for months, no rain at all or when it does it has higher-than-usual acidity. The raindrops sting your arms, blister the siding of houses. There is nothing left alive outside the car, even where things are not paved over, the plants and trees have died long ago, except for the property around the Bermese Pythion laboratories, where specialized trees and grasses have been planted, also genetically engineered.

Her mother is definitely in a sulk. Now all Julie has to look forward to is a long evening of cleaning out her own animals' cages in the basement, and then, before getting to play with them, she will have to fix dinner. It seems odd that her mother is not berating her or telling her what a difficult day she had. Murielle is in a deep black funk, speechless, a sack of skin filled with rage, slamming doors, maybe not speaking to Julie for days, weeks upon end… leaving Julie unable to figure it out. "Ma," she says at last, nervously, "Ma, is everything all right? Is it that Grandpa told you?"

Her mother acts as if a cork is pried from her mouth. A gassy explosion. Julie flinches. "Grandpa? Why? What did you do to him?" Murielle drips with cold sarcasm. "Listen to me: I had a call today, from A. Jesse. He says things have gone missing from the labs at Bermese Pythion, things, I mean animals and did I know anything about it; you are suspected… Lucky for you I didn't tell A. Jesse that I figured you probably had done it. I told him, 'If she did take anything I don't know anything about it, yes she has some pets at home but she's had them a long time.' Believe me Julie, if you did something and you get caught I'm not gonna be there to bail you out! Why can't you be like your sister?"

Julie bursts into tears, she begs to be forgiven. "Ma?" Julie is frightened. "What's going to happen?"

"I don't know what to say, Julie, if they decide to come over and search and you have their lab experiments, that's the main thing they're afraid of, that the projects will get in the hands of the wrong people or infest an area. Dyllis will probably lose her job, and I guess if you have their things, they'll send you to juvenile detention or prison, whatever a judge decides."

"Ma, I don't feel so good. You better pull over." She is out the door, vomiting copious amounts of what appears to be lime Jell-O. Small raspberry-colored things writhe in the transmission-fluid-green pool.

"Julie, you look awful. All kind of… Oh my gosh, ugh, you got pimples! Lots of them. Holy Excrement, it's that Cox-Weems Pox, what should I do?" Murielle peers intently. Boils are rising as she inspects.

"I'm fine, Mama. Maybe something I ate."

"They said on HGMTV that it was a terrorist biochemical attack. We're going to the hospital."

"Ma! I just puked, that's all."

It's no use.

The hospital it is.

It is so nice of Cliffort to visit her for a while and give her mother a rest. Murielle goes to the cafeteria for a quick cup of coffee and some green jelly. Cliffort is so dreamy, she can't help but smile when she sees the nurses and doctors do a double take, he really does look like a movie star. He gently pats her on the tummy and then bends to her ear. "My gosh, Julie… you've got quite a little tum-tum there, there's no way you think you might be… you know."

"What?"

"Um, how to put it? In the family way, enceinte, preggers, knocked up, a bun in the oven, big with child."

"But how could I be?" She can barely speak, her voice is a whisper and for some reason she is not allowed anything to drink. But she manages to whisper, "I mean, I'm too young, I never even got my period, how could I be?"

"Stranger things have happened," says Cliffort with a wink. "As the actress said to the bishop." He takes a step back as the nurse enters the room with two giant objects resembling pills, or coated candy, each a bit bigger than a fist. She shoves the first into Julie's mouth and tells her to bite down. Then the nurse turns her over and inserts the other in her bottom.

Julie wants to scream but instead she bites down. The thing in her mouth is full of a kind of liquid chalk with the flavor of blue cheese. She wants to say maybe the nurse got the two things mixed up, put the suppository in her mouth by mistake? But she can't speak, she is half-choked and in pain.

"Nurse Dawn?" Cliffort glances quickly at her nameplate. "Perhaps you can answer the question: a friend and I have a little bet going. He says a woman can't get pregnant before her first period."

"Untrue," snarls Nurse Dawn, as she yanks out a chunk of Julie's hair. "The lab has asked for this for analysis before the intubation. Then we'll have to do another, after."

"And, part two, could the mere presence of spawn in the vicinity of the vulva find its own way up the vaginal canal?"

"Spawn?"

"Sperm, semen, jism, spunk, cum, ejaculate, tadpoles, manly nectar –"

The nurse is distracted. "What? Oh yes, I s'pose it could happen." Julie can't help but think that her mother and Cliffort are taking a secret delight in what is being done to her. They watch her expression as plugs of skin are removed with some sort of device resembling a hole punch; then, most horrible of all, Nurse Dawn inserts a speculum so that scrapings can be taken, to prepare her for the intubation. A group of medical students enter the room in order to watch.

By stretcher she is taken down the hall and placed in a narrow tube that slowly slides into another tube for resonancing of some sort, which wouldn't be so awful except her body has to be practically frozen to reduce her temperature, she has to lie naked on a bed of ice for nearly an hour. They put a nasty suctioning device into her ear and painfully vacuum stuff out which hurts an unbelievable amount.

Still they keep saying they are trying to lower her temperature; she is sure she has heard a doctor say she is to be given some pain medication but no one does this and instead, still naked on the bed of ice, she is deposited on a stretcher in a hallway where everyone who walks by stops to stare.

Hours go by. More and more people – doctors? Interns? Official-looking men in drab suits! And someone claiming to be the Head of Security for Bermese Python – he wants to talk to her, even though she is stark naked and shaking! But curiously he disappears when she pukes, this time a lemon-yellow material, spongiform in appearance, dappled with holes from which protrudes something resembling waving, wiggling antennae…

At last it is decided she probably doesn't have the Cox-Weems Pox; nevertheless, she should be admitted overnight. It may be some side-effects from being near the airplane crash, the fall-out of frozen sewage. She keeps protesting, she doesn't feel sick! But after a while with the patronizing smiles and the peculiar-smelling air: a rubbery odor of powdered latex examining gloves, of Band-Aids, of rubbing alcohol, of recycled air, she slowly begins to think that, after all, maybe there is something wrong. In the next bed a woman is moaning behind curtains and buzzing for the nurses over and over. "Madam," says Cliffort, "don't you get it? Nobody is going to come!"

Around nine that night her mother announces she is going home. Cliffort lingers. "Don't worry, Julie, if you are pregnant I'll be happy to practice couvade," he whispers, pulling the curtain closed as he crawls into the bed alongside her.

"Cliffort, what are you doing?" His tongue is in her ear, his soft webbed fingers are caressing her, making fluttery circles on her hot skin.

"Cliffort loves his Julie, Cliffort wants it real bad. Cliffort can't wait any longer."

"But Cliffort." Julie is nervous, someone can come and pull the curtain aside at any moment. "Not here, not now! There are other people around!"

"Ssshhh, ssssh, it's okay." His pants are down, he's peeling back her hospital gown.

"Please, Cliffort, you gotta go now!"

"Don't you know what this does to a man, Julie? I'm starting to get green balls! Come on, just play with me down there a little bit."

"No, no, I don't care! Cliffort, get out!"

He stares at her coldly and gets up. "Very well, if that's how you feel," he says. He pulls on his pants and stalks out.

A nurse comes into her room; this one is tremendous, dressed in white, an overgrown loaf of pumpernickel, sour and yeasty. "Turn over," she says.

Now Julie wants to call Cliffort to come back, but it's too late, the nurse angrily pulls up her hospital gown and jabs her a number of times with something that burns as it goes into her buttock cheek. "What is that for?"

"Never you mind," says the nurse. The nurse is furious but what did she, Julie, do to make her so angry? Julie has tried her best not to bother anyone, not to ask for anything to drink, not to buzz to use the bedpan until it is imperative; Julie smiles when the nurses come into the room, she tries to be helpful and informs them that the woman in the next bed is dead but... they obviously don't like her!

The injection makes her itch; she scratches herself uncontrollably until, around three in the morning, just as she is drifting off to sleep, two different nurses come in, give her another injection and then, this time, tie down her hands. "No more scratching!" one says glibly. "It will leave scars!"

"You were lucky that the airline company agreed to pay for your hospital costs," Murielle says when, back home, Julie complains. "Besides, that's how it's supposed to be in a hospital, and you were in one of the best."

"But Mom, I can barely see – and I feel little teeny explosions inside."

"Keep the bandages on, your eyes might get better. I don't like to have to leave you alone, but I have to go back to work. When I go off to be with A. Jesse things will be different, and I think he can help us get you girls a settlement from the airline."

"No!" Julie doesn't want to explain she doesn't want a settlement, it should be she who makes restitution to them! She is sobbing but no tears come out.

"Look, don't cry. None of us can afford to cry right now. Why don't you watch hologramovision? I left you a can of soup on the counter, all you have to do is put it in a bowl and turn on the microwave, just be careful when you take it out. You don't really need to see to do that! And there's tuna-fish, from the deli. You'll be all right. Just call me if you get scared."

Julie feels her way to the kitchen, opens the door to the fridge. Then pries off the top of a plastic container, sticks in her finger, pulls something out, maybe an olive? But when she tastes it, a color, sky-blue, or... no, it's closer to rich deep purple, filling her mouth and in the air hangs a yellow 11. What the heck is that all about? 11. An idea of... egg-flavored icebergs, maybe sort of like meringues... ovoid shapes... a whole lot of information is getting scrambled up... maybe her ear-microdot is coming loose or the battery getting low 11 11 11 11 11 11 11 11 11 11 11 Somehow her wiring might have gotten switched to... a cooking show? All she knows is, it is awful and when a bell rings in the distance – the doorbell? – it smells meaty. Rotten meat at a low temperature. Or... chalky stale bird droppings?

Maybe it is just the stupid disease.

She is panicky restless. Shaky. Everything is all wrong. Something comes back to her, one of the doctors saying to another, if the pustules don't erupt there is a strong chance of lesions in her head. What if everybody started feeling this way? Slimy walls, custard mattress. Nasty floating motes, the size of gigantic amoebas and whole paragraphs out of books, just hanging up there.

Hours pass, she is alone, it is dark.

"Julie?" A banging on the door. "Julie, it is me, Rima Patel, I heard the news that you are ill –" Mrs Patel is so so nice, she has brought her dhal and homemade puri and raita and rice, rice pudding and carrot halwa, things with cardamom and rose water. "Julie, I am here also, Mahendra Patel, from next door. We did not mean to disturb you, but Locu has been asking us to see how you are doing, he is worried about your sister, but he knows your mother does not care for him. Julie, where is Sister, he is driving us crazy."

"Mahendra, the child is looking terrible, how can they leave her alone like this?"

Cool wet rags over her face... She sleeps, mostly... Someone comes into her room in the darkness and stands by the door... She is sometimes, dimly, aware there is noise, there are people blocking the doorway. It now seems that Mahendra and Rima and her own grandfather are taking care of her, but where is her mother, where is Cliffort, why does he hate her now, where's her dad? Sometimes in her long trances she, the original Julie, emerges briefly, wondering whose voice is banging on, sinks back down again. Sometimes, Sue Ellen is there beside her, but who wants to have a wet spot that thinks it is trapped in a dirty ashtray, as a friend?

It is exhausting and each day her head hurts more than the last. The headaches now almost never go away. And yet her condition is not completely without pleasure. The root scent of a forest truffle, combined with the color blue, and the c-chord played on a slide guitar connected each time she hears the words "multiple ulcers" and "watering-can" along with the soft mouse? Or is it a hamster?

Okay, so things are not exactly right.

When everything is quiet in her head she turns on the HGMTV. There has to be some show on that can distract her and at least she can still see the picture, kind of, it is in 3-D from floor to ceiling...

The President is saying, "War with the Liberiayanesetrian people has escalated and it has become necessary..." Suddenly he puts his hand up to his ear... "What? Oh, I beg your pardon... The war with the Burkina-Bissau-Guinean-Faso (kind of complicated, but for your folks listening out there, 'Faso' gives you a clue as to what kind of system they believe in) people has escalated as once again they have refused to accept democracy and the decent way of life…"

She turns to another channel but he is still there, and on all the successive channels, it's the State of the Union, except for the shopping show: he has pretaped his news conference, but is Live- on-the-Shopping-Network. "Hello Julie, and welcome to the diamond show," the President says. "Folks, we have a new viewer who has just joined us… Does anybody want to tell her your feelings about diamonds? Yes, we have a caller!"

"Hi, this is Ashley, and I'm calling from North Carolina. You know, I bought the diamond ring, Julie, and it is just beautiful! I really hope you get one!"

Someone's come in through the front door; maybe it is Cliffort, saying he forgives her. He is rarely around, he spends his days doing something, but she doesn't know what, she thinks it has something to do with insects. When he is there he hardly speaks to her, he makes sure they're never alone together, she feels awful! Julie picks up the remote control to turn off the HGMTV. "Hang on there just a minute, Julie!" says the President just before Julie switches him off.

"Daddy!" she says with delight.

Slawa strokes her upper arm, one of the few places they haven't bandaged. "My little Julyka, my little my wixen, my wermin." When she was little Julie would howl with laughter whenever Slawa pronounced his 'v' as 'w', he is doing it now to try to cheer her up but it has the opposite effect. He's so upset at seeing her he doesn't know what to say. "So how is Mother? And your sister?"

"Mom's fine. Tahnee, you know, she's at boarding school. She got a scholarship. Daddy, Daddy, see my ring?" Tahnee has lent her the ruby ring while she is away and Julie has wrapped it carefully in a bit of tissue, so that her dad can't see there is a finger in it. Even though the finger has shrunk, she still can't pry it out. Fortunately he merely glances at it before she tucks it away. "Oh, Daddy… oh, Daddy."

"What is it, my little cabbage?"

"Oh Daddy, there are so many things, like, I shot down the plane –"
Without thinking she blurts it out, oh Daddy.

"No, no, Julie, that is nonsense. Your grandfather has spoken to me about this silliness. He is miserable old man, Julie. You shooting, maybe, but not your fault plane is crashing. Cannot happen this way."

"Oh, Daddy, are you sure?"

"Yes, of course you tell police this is what happen, they laugh at you. No one will believe this, or peoples not receiving insurance money from plane company. What else, my shapka?"

"Oh, Dad, all those animals I took home from the lab, Mom says I stole them and they're really mad at me and I'm going to be locked up –"

"What, all your little pets you find outside laboratory, or dying inside? And only now they are finding out some things are missing? No one will say nothing, Julie, you will see, this kind of place no want the publicity on what they are doing to animals, and you find them mostly outside in garbage –"

"That's true, Daddy, and I never took anything that wouldn't have been thrown out anyway because it was almost dead –"

"And so they don't notice an animal missing; how you think they will look if they announce now, for six years he has been missing."

"And we really did find Breakfast outside, Dad!"

He clutches his head in his hands.

"Dad? Are you alright?"

Since Bocar's uncle hit him with a bat, he has these terrible pains, not all the time but when they come they are excruciating. "No, it's nothing. I am thinking. This is true, yes, we finded the dog outside, he is stray. Don't worry, I am your father, I will take care of everything. I am here to look after you."

"Oh, Daddy. I love you so much." She sighs happily.

"Julie my love, I gotta go, I'm not supposed to be here. So, you feel better now? Is there anything else?"

"Oh, Dad, there is one more thing – promise you won't be mad?"

"No, of course I will not be mad, you tell me."

"I think… It was like this, I am kind of in love with Cliffort? You know, the guy looking after Grandpa? And so, one day he took me out, and I didn't know what was happening, exactly, 'cause as it turned out he didn't have a thing –"

"A thing? What kind of a thing?"

"You know…"

"No, I am not knowing. What is this 'thing'?"

"His, um… private parts… You know, the part that men have."

"His cock? He missing his cock?"

"Yeah, I guess…"

"Thank the Designer, Juliana, you know in this country if something happen, there is no abortion, no health insurance, Yuliya I don't know how to explain, but for the people like us – we are never going to get out of trap, and that is where they want us to be."

She doesn't really know what he is talking about, only that he is upset. "But Dad, I don't think he has a thingy, but… Dad, I didn't really know what was happening, you know, but then, when stuff came out of him, which he said was, like, spawn or something, I think some of it got up into me and, so oh, gosh, now he's mad at me and he's not speaking to me. I want him back! I might be pregnant."

She sees her father has turned pasty white, eyes narrowed in a pure blue-steel rage.

18

Oh, he is happy.

"None of this hydroponically grown slabs of tasteless tissue for us!" A. Jesse pontificates as Tahnee sits across from him at the long dining table made of polished petrified wood, where they are eating hand-massaged beef the texture but not the flavor of ripe bananas. "You don't need to worry about being a vegetarian. Here in Nature's Caul there are people who have full-time jobs pampering and massaging Kobezebu cattle, and when it is time for these cows to be slaughtered, they are slaughtered so gentle, so loving, in such peaceful surroundings: soft music plays while the cows are quietly chomping away on tasty morsels, and the massagers are stroking, the autistic people are soothing them, so that these steer don't even know what is about to happen. They get to live long and fulfilled lives."

Unfortunately Tahnee is merely toying with the food! There is real asparagus, real enough in that it is grown in a field, not in a tissue culture center, though it is true this kind of asparagus grows on trees. There is real Hollandaise sauce made with fresh creamery butter and eggs from the happy chickens that wander freely within the parameters of Nature's Caul, scratching and pecking.

Doesn't she realize how lucky she is? He would like to reach across the table and smack her, her manners are so appalling and later, he knows, she will take a frozen pizza from the deep freeze to be microwaved.

"In order for there to be rich people there have to be luxury items that no one else can afford. If there weren't, nobody would ever bother being rich, they would just lie around like everyone else. And it is no good if the poor people have the same luxury items as the rich people. It is okay if they have poor imitations, or cheap knockoffs or even items that only the privileged would know are fake because the detail is not the same."

"Like, whatever," she says, bored. "Trepan me with an ice pick, you exfoliated parvenu. Blah blah blah is all you ever do."

Stupidly, tears fill his eyes. What is happening to him, anyway? He is like a bunch of soggy crumbs these days, try as he will, he just can't squeeze the crumbs back into a loaf. It's like... it's like... why, it's like being a female, one who's about to get her period, all soggy and sappy and weak... Even his little bosoms are feeling tender, is it possible he is getting some kinda female hormone, estrogen or something, from somewhere? Pregnant butterfly urine?

"I'm sorry." Tahnee gets up and goes around the table to sit on his lap, where she now tenderly brushes the few strands of reddish hair over to one side of his pate, which reminds him, would he be more attractive with Hair-A-Tick, he can get the hair back on his head, it's just that there have been so many side effects with that damn method.

"You see, in a fair democracy, one based on all men created equal, the only luxury apart from material goods allegedly made of slightly better quality, access to activities limited to the general population because of exclusivity as well as cost, is slaves. Not slaves in the sense of ownership but in the sense of servants. In a true democracy servants feel and believe themselves to be equals. However, to feel more important one must have people below oneself who are both humble and desperate. Let us look at a country which is a dictatorship and another that was Communist."

Tahnee yawns. Obviously she's not listening.

He can't stop now, though, he has to try. "It has never been about government. It has never been about political ideologies. It has – always and only – been about business. Money is made by the corrupt whether the system is communist or capitalist. There will always be someone skimming the cream, legally or not. Factories, farms, oil, land development. Those who are rich have power and all the fun toys. There is no point in raising money to save the Bono monkey. Bono monkey he long time bought and dead."

"Oh whatever. Spare me the rhetoric." She is so rude he would so much like to turn her over and smack her plump little behind, spank it until it is hot and pink and she begs him to stop; only, he is certain, she wouldn't let him, she would kick and scream and hit back. "Oh, Jesse, that reminds me of something I wanted to ask you. You know about the geishas you can have, like the boys who will wait on you, or the girls, what you called something like a varlet or a ladies' maid?"

"The word is valet."

"I want one. You promised, remember?"

"No I don't remember but of course, that can be arranged. I'll ask Striosa." Striosa is the head housekeeper. She has a million nephews and nieces living in the slums of some anonymous country – is it Nicotinga? Guyanaba? – one of those places where every other year or so a mudslide wipes out the cardboard and tin shelters, and obliterates a half million blah blah blah, a cause for celebration among the wealthy. Thank God the population is reduced, and then the rich ladies can host the benefit committee and obtain donated flower arrangements for the tables, dinner followed by dancing and a silent auction.

"But why can't I choose who I want?"

"Who were you thinking of? Did you see someone here you like? Striosa's niece, Onchantay, is sweet, she's your age, it would take a few years to train her, probably, but…"

"No! I want a friend from home."

"That's sweet, but these people, they have their own systems for who gets hired. It's very complicated. It's based on who they owe favors to, they get a percentage of the geisha's pay. The kids have to take classes, that costs money – it depends on their relatives back home."

"I don't care! You promised I could have Locu!" Locu. Who? What? Jesse has no memory of anyone named Locu, what is she talking about? "I didn't mean to hurt your feelings, I forget you are, like, so so sensitive! It's just that, honey, I am lonesome, when do you think Locu could come out to start as my geisha, I know you could organize it!" and she adds slyly, "Otherwise me being this lonesome, maybe I should go to school. It sure sounds great!"

He thought they had discussed it, she can tell her mother she is going to school but she doesn't have to go, school would be so… boring for her, though of course the real fear, for him, is that she'll meet some high school boy, would blabber to her friends that he is a pedophile, or worse; the little vixen is capable of anything, he now knows.

He is suspicious. "Is this a guy or a girl?" As if that would somehow make a difference with these kids today?

"A guy."

"Is he your boyfriend?" He almost spits out the word.

"Um, no." Knowing A. Jesse even a bit, Tahnee has prepared this in advance. "But I'm lonely. I want to talk to Mommy. There's nobody else here my age, you said I was going to go to school. Locu is just my friend. He likes other guys."

Jesse is placated, somewhat. "I tell you what. In that case, maybe I'll see about getting him sent out here and I'll have him work over at Benezer Salamonder's and that way Ben can train – what's his name, your little friend? – until he gets tired of him, and then he can send him over here." That is, if the kid lives through it, Jesse thinks, then adds, "But I should warn you, I hope your friend won't mind a little rough stuff, though I'll ask Ben if he can tone it down a notch or so –"

Tahnee looks pouty. "He's my best friend in the whole wide world. Why can't he come here first?"

"Believe me, all the young boys love it over at Ben's, and you're not exactly knowledgeable about etiquette to be able to train staff yourself."

"Oh please, let me try! I promise I'll be nicer to you!"

"We'll see how you act over the next few days."

She reaches out to stroke his cock through his trousers. "Oh, Jesse," she murmurs contentedly, "I love it here so much and I hope when Locu comes I'll be more comfortable and I can make you happy."

The rich kids have no education either. The rich don't have nicer manners, they swear just as much and are as tattooed, pierced or whatever the latest trend is. None of them read books, they all see the same movies, they all eat McDonald's.

Not only would teaching Tahnee to read make her a freak, she would refuse – couldn't – do it. Generations of ancestors playing video games have frozen any ability to read. Apart from minor things – like hand-waxed dental floss, for example – and sports that are unavailable to the poor (tennis; horseback riding; golf on real courses; mountain climbing; skiing on real slopes; swimming in genuine water – hey, the poor can do all things with virtual reality programs, so, after all, it's not that big a deal!) the rich kids don't live lives any different than the poor.

Tahnee loves her room. The sheets are folded neatly just beneath her chin, topped with a genuine camel-hair blanket and a feather duvet so light and fluffy and soft and warm. And, for the first time in her life a bed where roaches don't crawl over her in the middle of the night! It is so cozy here but now Tahnee is actually sick of Murielle's calls, is there no way to get rid of her? She was only pretending to miss Mommy; now that Locu is with her she has what she wants.

Murielle can't understand what is taking A. Jesse so long, she is frantic and calls Tahnee, like, every five minutes, since Jesse mostly doesn't take her calls. He is really going to have to come up with something.

A. Jesse is sorry he let Tahnee have Locu. The two of them spend all day together, giggling, cutting pictures out of magazines and dressing up in silly outfits made from shower curtains or umbrellas; to be honest, he can't stand the kid. The way Locu stares at him with those lucent amber eyes, Jesse never knows what he is thinking and the house is perfumed with the strange spices, cumin and cinnamon, cardamom and mustard seed, flavoring the steamy pulses that simmer on the stove. Jesse can't stand Indian food! Only Tahnee eats and eats.

One evening after one of these dinners, dhal masoor, matar paneer and mushroom bhaji, A. abruptly turns to Tahnee. "Where's the sapphire necklace I gave you? Why don't you ever wear it?"

"I don't know," she says.

"Where is it?"

"I guess I lost it."

Locu glances down, his gold-flecked eyes have lashes petal-thick, chrysanthemum, spiky aster, he could be a movie star, surely there is something going on between them? "You what? How could you lose it, do you know what that cost? Where were you when you lost it?"

"How come you're looking at Locu?"

"I'm looking at him because he's supposed to be your geisha, he's not supposed to be hanging out with you while you eat in the kitchen, he's supposed to eat in the kitchen while you eat in the dining room. And generally speaking, only older women or gay men have geishas that are male, for reasons I'm not about to go into here. Anyway, that's not the point. Where is the necklace, when was the last time you saw it?"

"I don't know where, maybe on the ski slope or something."

"On the ski slope. You were wearing that necklace to go skiing? What were you thinking?"

"Well, probably it wasn't on the ski slopes, its just here someplace. It will probably turn up."

A. Jesse searches for hours with the housekeeper. At last she finds it in the pocket of one of Tahnee's jackets. He storms in the art room, "See, I found your sapphire necklace, I spent hours looking for it! Next time –"

She and Locu look up guiltily. "How cool is this? Locu is sewing my new dress, I think he should have been a dress designer even though, actually, it was kind of my idea." She is talking fast and it is so irritating. He has spent hours looking for that necklace and rattles it in her face. "See how materialistic he is," she says to Locu who takes the necklace from Jesse's hand and begins to wrap it through her hair in an elaborate style, the ungrateful little bitch.

Next he finds them standing in front of the one-way mirror in front of the gym, watching B. Jesse. A. Jesse has the housekeeper feeding the poor schlemiel calorie-free food, you can eat as much as you want, it's nothing but air and textures, but... put on enough ketchup or mustard, it has a vague resemblance and taste. "He looks like a piglet," Tahnee is saying.

"He is almost ready for the barbecue," Locu giggles.

"You could put an apple in his mouth," Tahnee says, "The skin should really be crispy, though, there's so much fat you'd probably want to stick him with a lot of pins while he's cooking."

They haven't even noticed A. behind them. "Do we look the same?" he asks Tahnee.

Locu giggles. "Who asked for your opinion?" Jesse snarls.

"Oh, no, I was just... it was just a nervous reaction, sir, I cannot tell you how grateful I am to be here in training as a geisha, that is what I always wanted. Especially to be with Tahnee and..."

He turns and catches Tahnee sniggering; what a pushover they must think he is. Inside the gym B. Jesse is pacing, orangutan-style, red ape, the clone still has a pot belly, tufts of fur, and B. shoves his face into the glass; from B.'s side it is a mirror. "Is that you, Dad?" says B. "Who's out there? I'm sick of being locked up in here, are you nuts? Let me out already!" His mashed face is squashed against the pane. He's not ready to take A. Jesse's place yet, it's true.

He knows Tahnee and Locu say mean things about him behind his back. He hates her. And yet... All the women before were simply... He never felt much of anything but he figured that was all that there was. This is different. To have that sensation once again, of wanting something; it has been so long since he *wanted*, it is unfamiliar, it is giving him a panic attack. Abruptly a moment floats, unmotivated, a flimsy scrim into a parallel existence where everything that has ever taken place is stored: a moment when he was a kid. Of his family, gathered around a table.

Could that have happened, all his family gathered at once around a table? But who the heck are these people, what are their names? There is Mom, could her name have been Gunny? Jinty? And – my gosh, yes, there is a dad, Dad's name is Bolly or Kaylie. And... here is Sissy! Or... it could have been a brother. In any event, that is his family, after the meal or... the family conference... Dad going off to the HGMTV room to smoke a joint, Mom must have just had... her face is all bandaged and oozing, has she just had a face-lift? Or maybe she's been in another car wreck? Whatever. Oh, and there is the dog. The dog is named Chip, or Max, or Steam, something like that. How he loved that dog! It must have been wonderful, his childhood. Because he was so contented, yes, remembering this happy moment, happy.

Unless he has only imagined it.

Now, if he can get rid of Murielle once and for all, he could be happy like that again.

A. Jesse has a gift for Tahnee, something so rare there are at present only two in the world, an invention straight from the lab, the palm-sized lion… He'll bring the little male to her, my God, it is the cutest thing in the world! Fits into the palm of your hand, there isn't going to be one kid on the entire planet who doesn't want his or her own pride of lions, you can feed one on a couple of raw chicken legs and a pound of chopped meat would last it two weeks!

He's got the little guy tucked under his arm, he's a feisty little thing; even though the lion has been hand-raised from birth, the stupid critter is roaring and scratching, feisty as can be. A. Jesse is laughing and trying to hold it under control when he pushes open the door to Tahnee's bedroom. "Oh, sweetheart! Wake up! I have a surprise for you!"

Only, what the fuck, she's all the way under the covers, which he peels back and there's the kid, Locu: queer? Yeah, right, the two of them are going at it! So much for her virginity and Locu's lack of interest in the females!! What a sucker he's been!

Locu looks up sleepily, "Oh, heh-heh, sorry," he says.

"Go away," says Tahnee, "Don't you know to knock? What are you doing here?"

For a moment he is almost about to apologize, then he grabs Locu by the neck and yanks him off the girl; the kid is giggling nervously, still holding the sheet, then – still with the lion in his hand – he backs out, into the doorway. He calls for security; Tahnee is scrambling into her clothes and Locu's pulling on his blue jeans, three big guys come running and A. Jesse tells one to take the lion and another to grab Locu; he will figure out what to do with Tahnee later. In the meantime he waves his implanted microchip at the various equipment to turn them off.

She is going to have to stay in there without a computer, hologramovision, nothing she can use to communicate. He points at the windows and the metal security gates come down, then he points at the kid. "Throw him out," he says to one of his staff.

"What?"

"You heard me. Tie him up and dump him outside the gates."

"Your gates or the whole outer wall?"

"The whole place. What good does it do me if you dump him outside my property? I want him out. And make sure you get his entrance papers revoked. I don't want him sneaking back in."

"But is that really what you want to do, yo, Jesse, sir?"

"Do as I say."

Outside Nature's Caul and Morphew Valley Holiday Spa and Resort, beyond the thousands of miles of electrified wiring which is patrolled twenty-four hours a day by guards, there is a strip of land before the garbage-zone that was part of the war reparations. Here, he has heard, in the no-man's land, live people who have come up in through Mexico, or hoping perhaps to get a job on the inside; some of them even have relatives who support them, tossing leftovers – illegally – over the fence, or they survive on recycling rubbish trucked out, picking through it to find anything edible.

It's supposed to be pretty rough out there, but what's it to him, the kid can either survive out there or somehow figure out how to make it back east.

A. can't seem to calm down, even once Locu is gone and he knows Tahnee is safely locked in her room. He tells everyone he will be in his office, he is not to be disturbed. Of course he can't get any work done, all morning he paces, trembling.

He unlocks her door, the room is musty: sweat and goat. She's huddled under the blankets. He crosses the room and says, "What did you have to go and do that for, I was asking for so little in return for giving you everything. You know that, don't you?"

Tahnee shrugs. "I don't know. I'm bored. You're boring."

"I've never stopped thinking about you, since the moment I saw you; you're the most beautiful thing I've ever seen, you're like a fawn or some kind of gazelle, you know what I'm saying?"

He leans forward and starts to kiss her. His tongue feels thick and bumbling and for no reason he pictures a bee drowning in the pool, buzzing and soggy.

"Ugh, just get away from me." Her tongue unfurls, snailish, from her shell of a mouth. He sits back, stares at her, rips off her halter-top, the strings welting her neck before they break. "You are so disgusting!" she adds.

"Look at these sweet little titties," he says. "And all this time you were stringing me along."

"Just get away from me, you cretin, I'm going to call the police and tell them you're raping an underage minor."

"Raping you? I was willing to wait years for you. You stupid, stupid idiot, you had it made, now you totally blew it. At least one thing is still true," he tells her as he waves the chip at her door, making sure it is locked, "If you're rich enough or famous, you can do pretty much anything you want. What did you think, you could play me and I'd never catch on?"

For the first time since he has known her, she looks scared. Maybe something is finally sinking in.

"You don't understand, we just mess around. He's just an old friend," she mutters. Then, dispiritedly, "I'm still a virgin."

He forces his tongue into her mouth, he knows now how much she hates him, she is lying like a corpse with his thumb and forefinger pinching her nipples. No one has touched them before! When Locu tried she always screamed and kicked him, or slapped him – he was allowed to look, that was all – now, with fat tongue in her mouth she can't verbally protest, though she tries to pull away.

The breasts are so sensitive to the touch she doesn't know whether it is pain or pleasure she is feeling but the sensation makes her momentarily homesick and filled with longing – for something she can't place. A. Jesse's mouth is on the right nipple, it is even more tender than the left, she wonders if it will help it grow but something about it, the bud, in his mouth, makes her queasy.

Somehow he has also pushed the *chinchilla spread* onto the floor while he pulls off her pants; she tries to keep her legs together but even though her nipple is in his mouth, he has her legs apart. After all, what does she care, but her legs seemed to want to squeeze shut by themselves and then he has his tongue down there, slurping, not half as nicely as Locu, this guy's tongue is… too thick, a bludgeon, not delicate. A ham sandwich.

A. Jesse forces her hand between his legs, which has a huge erect prod sticking straight out. At some point he undoes his fly, freeing a big bluish trunk as thick as her forearm and almost as long – and he wriggles out of his clothes, pushes her flat, begins to shove himself in; he is going to make this as ugly for her possible. "The head is going in, you like that? Ooh, baby, you are sooo tight," he says, and as he forces he murmurs, "You stupid, ignorant cunt. Who do you think you are to disrespect me?"

"Jesus, let me go why won't you just let me go, you don't want me why can't I leave –"

Shut up shut up he holds a pillow over her mouth and holds her down at least to shut her up shut her up does not take too long she thrashes a bit and when the thrashing has stopped he stays there, holding the pillow over her mouth and nose for a few more minutes, only then does he stop pressing.

She lets out a scream muffled by fluff. "Hurts, hurts," she says.

"Sshh, sshh, its all right, just relax, relax," he says as he gets the rest of himself inside.

"I can't breathe." She keeps trying to wriggle out from under him.

"What's the matter, huh? You don't like it?" And when her arms start to flail he turns her over, still holding her onto him, so that now he is on his back and she is on top of him, and he begins to move inside her again, only very slowly now, in and out, jigging her slowly.

She might have been a big dolly except she spits at him so he hits her in the side of her head. "How does that feel honey, hmmm?"

What an asshole, what the fuck is he thinking, the pain is so terrible, this sense of being burnt inside? Up and down, up and down, with each thrust or motion the dry burning tinder, only she can't get away, no matter how much she flails, his hands force her down.

"Uuuuh," he says suddenly and she is filled with something liquid, but it doesn't sooth the burn. "Oh, honey." And he is motionless. "Oh, honey. That was amazing." And finally he softens and she crawls away, shaking with pain. "You okay? You liked it, huh?"

"No I didn't like it! Are you nuts, you slimy muckrake?" She reaches down to the floor, tries to find something under the bed. "Can I get up now? You shrimp dick. That was about as nothing as you can get."

"Stupid, ignorant cow, who do you think will ever want you? I picked you out, all I have to do is tell them to put you out and you'll be crawling back to your ordinary nothing existence, who do you think you are to disrespect me?"

"Let me go why won't you just let me go, you don't want me why can't I leave, I never wanted to come here."

"Fourteen years old, you tell me one minute you're eighteen, then it's fourteen, then you have a friend who is 'gay'. You've already been with a man, right? You think I believe you aren't fucking your boyfriend?" He has never been so aroused in his life. How odd that it took so long for him to really want it.

"No, no, Jesse I told you!" she says as he sticks his index finger into her. "Don't do anything to me again, I'm too sore, it hurts."

"Sssh, sssh, relax," he says, putting another finger in her tight bottom. "I'll take care of you."

"Please! No, not right now, it's, like, it's burnt in there. Get off me you wrinkled-up prune, you're an old man, what makes you think I would ever want you to touch me!"

Tahnee's got something in her hand, what the fuck is it? She starts clobbering him over the head with it. "That hurts!" he yelps, though it's as much the shock as the real pain, being clonked on the head by a big heavy flashlight. Before he even knows it he grabs the weapon away from her and puts his hands around her neck. "You like this? Huh?" He presses and presses for the pure pleasure of watching the panic in her eyes, at least finally those dishwater ignorant marbles have a new look on them. Finally she's having an emotion! Now, isn't that nice, she knows what it's like to feel something other than disdain! Only he doesn't seem to be able to stop.

She gurgles, and a strange sound comes out of her throat as he releases his grasp. It's surely not that easy to kill someone and phew, sure enough, after a minute or so she lets out a little gasp. She's been faking, all right, he knows he went too far but she started it. She was asking for it.

He arranges her beside him and covers her tenderly with the soft chinchilla. Strokes her hair and her tender nipples and together they lie there in the darkened room. Then after a time he says, slightly uneasily, "Are you okay?" But there is no answer. "All right, quit kidding around," he says. "I'm sorry."

He turns on the light. In front of him, her face, it is so beautiful and perfect, an angel, really, he has never seen anything so perfect in his entire life. "Quit fooling," he says, more sharply. He has the skeeves, he can't stop shaking. "I said I was sorry. If you want I'll tell them to go get your stupid geisha back." Something white and tremulous is in the middle of the room, the sound of a sigh or a bell quivers in the air and disappears.

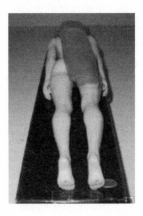

19

Murielle watches out the window. <u>He</u> has called from the airport, saying he will stop in at corporate headquarters and then call her when he's ready to swing by. Now she wishes she had more time to prepare, nursing Julie and trying to cope with her dad, it's been too much; she hasn't had a chance to have her nails done, nor attach new false eyelashes: these things take hours, not including getting rid of crackling black body hair, almost impossible really with her rampant hirsutism. Fortunately the last time she saw him, A. Jesse seemed to love it.

How absurd at her age to be in love. Love at any age really, but at least when you are young you don't know any better. Just to think how in a brief instant her whole life changed, at a time when she truly felt as if nothing would ever happen to her again!

Two men are in front of her house cutting off the tree branches.

"Hey!" she shouts. That tree is the only one for miles! It's true, it is kind of dead. She and the kids pasted some artificial leaves and flowers on it, when the girls were little. But who gave permission? "Stop! What are you doing?" By the time they can hear her over the noise of the chainsaw, it's too late: both branches have been lopped, only the leafless trunk remains. "Who told you you could do that?" But they are gone.

The sun burns down, there is no breeze, the ground is baked; here and there through the cracks protrude cans, hubcaps, the edges of heavy-duty trash bags. Transmission fluid and used oil welter out from the substrata. Pre-Columbian pottery, Tang statuary. The planet's garbage is on the move.

A man wearing one of those compact helicopter backpacks circles overhead and lands on the drive. The man, prawn-pink and glossy with importance, ducks his head as the blades of the heli-pack putter to a halt; he undoes the straps that harness the equipment to him. Wait a minute! Is it…

"Oh my gosh! Jesse! What are you doing here?" She runs into his arms; not exactly, but she has to be careful not to knock him down. He seems somehow different. My goodness, he has really gained weight! Yet, at the same time looks younger. He's the same but not the same, it must be she who has gained weight, she can barely get her arms around him.

"Hey, little lady!" he says. "Whoa, there, I guess you really are glad to see me."

"When did you get here? Why didn't you call? How's Tahnee? I'm not quite finished packing."

"Now, uh, Murielle, it seems like there's been some changes. You see, in addition to my job as President and CEO of Bermese Pythion, I recently agreed to aid the Department of Homeland Environmental Security Issues and Regulations, and I am in charge of the Annual Survey – apparently this area is having a SloMoFly infestation, this could be a really bad situation."

"What? Darling, what are you talking about! What's wrong with you?"

"Just stopped by to check up on you and see how you are doing, special lady!" he says. "How's your…" He seems to be glancing at something in his hand. Notes? "How's your daddy, I know you've been concerned about him."

"Jesse, why are you acting so formal? Is everything okay? Have you met someone else?"

"Not exactly." Jesse struggles with his words. "Murielle, do you mind if we talk somewhere private?"

"Let's go inside, do you want some ice tea, or something stronger?"

"Whatever you're having."

She has never known A. Jesse to have anything alcoholic before. So this is it then, the breakup. Never again to lie in a steamy room, consumed with passion, the animal frenzy of sticky bliss. All that, for her, over. Finished. Never again to stumble into a room, a fan thumping softly overhead, desperate, wanting, pulling at clothes, a couple of frantic kids. And after, lying entwined, exhausted. Who else is there going to be for her? The whole thing has to be about something else, she has been conned, but why?

She whips up a couple of fiery Bloody Marys, trying to make some pleasant chitchat as she does so; maybe he will relax after a drink. "So, um, how's Tahnee doing?"

"That hot little chick? As far as I now, she's doing okay. My dad really seems to have taken to her."

"What?" She pours in half the bottle of Just-Like-Tabasco; she can't seem to stop shaking the canister of artificial red pepper juice. "I thought you told me your parents were dead?"

"Oh right. My, um, my step-dad."

"Murielle, is that you?" Her father is calling from upstairs. He wanders out to the top of the stairs, naked except for a plastic rabbit mask over his face and his glasses over that, only upside down. "Look what I found from Halloween –" He doesn't even see she has a visitor.

"Dad, what are you doing? Put some clothes on, you're stark naked! Where's Cliffort, anyway, isn't he supposed to be looking after you?" Dad doesn't move. Murielle rushes to get him back to his room. This is so embarrassing.

"I only came out to tell you goodbye. I met someone on the hologramovision. A lonely lady in van Hoek. I'm going to meet her – the Lady Juan Aishat – and we're going to help those poor, sad children who are enrolled at her day care center. They speak Dutch."

"Of course, Dad." She pushes him through the door "You can take the bunny mask with you." Jesse is fiddling with the drinks. "Sorry about that. My dad is –"

"I understand," Jesse says as he hands her a Bloody Mary drink. "Ah, Murielle, things have changed." He hoists the drink. "Here's to what once was."

She is horrified with herself but tears slide from her eyes. Hot crystal beads, she really should be saving them in a vial, there are all kinds of tests they can do based on tears arising from a traumatic event such as this, which it is, apparently; he is either out of his mind or just plain having a hard time breaking up with her.

She sits heavily and pours more vodka into her drink. How could she have been so stupid? She had been so happy, how could she have pinned her hopes on something she had only imagined, she had been tricked! Or, rather, she had tricked herself, once again.

"No, no no," says Jesse, sounding even more nervous. He sips the Bloody Mary and his nose begins to turn red. "You see, I wanted," he glances down at the papers in his hand. "I use paper and pencil rather than a Burberry-pod, because you know, anything you jot down onto one of those remains in cyberspace, somewhere, forever. At least with paper, you can shred it! Anyway, as I was saying what I am about to tell you you, must swear to me not to repeat to nobody. Alright?"

She nods. "Who would I tell, anyway, Jesse? It's not like I have any friends!"

"I can't bring you back with me just yet, Murielle, because the two of us have some work to do here. The government – my old friend from college, the President, has recruited me to become further involved in Environmental Security because apparently there's been a lot of 'leakage' from my laboratories. I can't figure out how this has happened honestly – I have top security men over there, former FBI agents and trained storm troopers; Wesley was ready to shut me down entirely, but I assured him it would be my responsibility to track down all the genetic material." Jesse sighs. "I really can't go into detail at this time... If this is inconvenient for you, though, would you mind just telling me... have you noticed any odd swellings on your person lately?"

"Odd what?" Murielle says listlessly. "Oh, Jesse, what happened to us? Just be honest."

"Oh, darling, how can you expect me to be honest? I'm one-fourth Scottish, one-fourth French, one-fourth German and a quarter Native American. My God, you have the most luscious, full lips! Talk about inviting!"

She blushes but she is also irritated. "I'm not doing so well here, Jesse. You've been so cold on the phone; now you've come back. To paraphrase

Roald Hoffman, Nobel Prize winner of the last century, who provided today's calendar quote, 'You're the same but not the same'."

It doesn't really matter, however, when he stares at her so stupidly.

On the other side of the lawn the two men have returned with a large metal case and seem to be removing various electronic devices and surgical-looking implements from the ground.

Nervously Jesse (B.!) glances at his notes. "We spoke on the phone the other day? Ah, I'm sorry about all this, but it had to happen. I don't know how much you people were told, following the plane crash, but at this point it's become pretty much containment and health-related safety issues. Again I am not supposed to talk about it, but it's related to the Partnership of Reference Policies."

"Terrorism? Health-related? Should I be alarmed?" Murielle can't control herself any longer, she bursts into tears.

"There there, don't cry, my special lady, I tell you what, let's keep in touch." He's strapping his heli-backpack on and twitching, no wonder, looks like he's over the weight limit as he starts up the motor; the blades can barely lift him off the ground. Appears he's about to hit the roof of the house, the heli-pack blades dip, hesitate, but finally with a mechanical stutter shift into gear. He is barely above the rooftops, his legs smash here and there, but slowly the damn thing lifts him and he disappears from view.

At least it is Sunday, her day off, she doesn't have to go to work. What is happening with Tahnee, anyway; she wishes she had asked him that! Julie's sitting at the kitchen table. "Oh Julie, I hate men," Murielle says. "Never have anything to do with them!" She opens the door to the refrigerator, there must be something; rummaging, she finds cold old Tripac EZ Mac, okay, maybe a little green at one side, just chuck that part.

Julie's vision goes in and out. Awake, briefly, she stumbles into the kitchen and watches in horror as her mother plops the coils of macaroni into her mouth leaving next to nothing for anyone else, not that anyone would want it, that stuff is gross! It's that darned Sue Ellen, Julie thinks before her sight fades once more.

"My head! My head!" Murielle suddenly screams.

"What?"

"My head! Get it off me! It's stuck."

"Oh, Ma it's supposed to be there. You're just like Miss Fletsum, she was always thinking somebody else took her stupid head. I kinda miss her, actually. Am I ever going to be well enough to go back to school?" Disgruntled, Julie wanders back to her room. Can't her mother ever think of someone beside herself?

Her head, Murielle thinks, what is it doing perched up there? She goes off to her room, maybe she can nap. The whole thing is too much, Jesse's weird behavior, so disappointing to say the least; fooled again, fooled again, you'd think by now she would have learned something, at her age it is worse. But what happens is never the same thing, exactly.

She will try to sleep. If she is going to have insomnia, why does she have to have it at night? Why can't she at least have it during the day, when she is so tired and always falling asleep on her feet?

So it's to be like this then, her life coming to an end with nothing to show for it but musically inclined glow-in-the-dark cockroaches and the shocking glimpse in the mirror. She looks down at herself in the bed and sees a floating belly, bloated like a cadaver, how the hell did that get there? Whose is it? Once, time had been slow, her childhood had lasted forever and she felt no identification with the old people – old, to her, might have been twenty-one! It seemed a country which she would never even visit. Now all of a sudden she is in the middle of it, transported, only she doesn't feel any different except when she sees her deterioration. Now when she talks to kids she thinks of herself as their age and keeps forgetting that when they look at her it is with that same sense of distance – distance and horror – that she had once had when she looked at adults.

The next day she is so miserable over Jesse she leaves work early. There, in front of her house, a line has formed; she can't understand what is going on. Some kind of yard sale nearby? An open house? Now she sees it is her house they are waiting to go into! Is Julie up to no good? "What the hell?" she says, and makes a dash up the front steps.

"Oh, um, Miz Antrobus –" It's some Indian guy.

"What's going on here? Who the hell are you?"

"Um, just a minute, I can explain –" He shouts out to the line. "People! That's all for today. Keep your number." He looks at Murielle and seems to give up, his voice weakens. "If you get here by seven in the morning you can keep your number and position in line, otherwise you have to start over! Coffee and donuts available until we run out. Allow me to introduce myself, madam, I am Khem Singh, a friend of the Patel family."

The crowd, disgruntled, shuffles off. "You tell the Boiling Girl I love her!" shouts one gimpy woman twisted with arthritis. "I brought her a teddy bear! You tell her!"

A man comes to the steps. "Hey listen, bud – how about five hundred bucks to get my wife in tonight? She's real sick – I'll pay the girl extra, too."

Khem Singh looks reluctant – he glances down guiltily, then quickly at Murielle... "Um... I don't know what you are talking about; in any event, Boiling Girl is very tired..."

"What is going on here? Who is 'the Boiling Girl'?" Murielle yelps.

"That's, ah, you know, that's what Julie Fockinoff's known as. Sorry, the Patels didn't think you would mind. We always ask the clients to park down the block and most of them arrive on foot, so I do not think it is going to cause trouble."

"But... what are they doing here?"

"Oh. They've come to see Julie, she is known as a diagnostician and perhaps more importantly, she can cure people by a simple laying on of hands to the person's aura..."

"Julie? But why?"

"Um, allow me to explain."

She doesn't wait for an explanation but bolts in. "Julie? Julie?"

"The Boiling Girl is busy right now," says a nurse in the hall.

"I don't care, that's my daughter!" She pushes past the nurse and shoves open the door. "Julie?" The room is dark. There is a man sitting in the armchair. The room smells stale and dusty.

"You have Derwent Chuff's Syndrome, Stage 1," Julie is saying from bed. Her eyes are bandaged and a strange buzzing, not audible, but something different, like electricity, emanates from the bed. "Ma, oh, Ma, what took you so long! Mama, I can't see, I mean, without the bandages, hardly at all, and it's getting worse."

"But tell me about me," the man says. "You can speak to your mother in a moment, what am I supposed to do? Is there any cure you can give me? You know, I have been to a dozen doctors."

"What are you doing here?" says Murielle to the man. "Who are you?"

"Don't worry, madam. I will make sure your daughter is well looked after. See those flowers?" He points to a lavish display on the windowsill; they must have cost a fortune. Beside it are boxes of chocolates from the most expensive confectioner's, pink, tied with gold bows; bottles of perfume, stacks of music disks – where could it all have come from? "Now will you please leave us alone for a minute; I can see she's distracted by your presence and it took me forever to get this appointment..."

Puzzled, Murielle goes out to wait in the hall.

Outside, one of the Patel boys is shouting through a megaphone, "There are inexpensive rooms available at the Patel Vastly Superior Inn, turn right on Kobe Bryant Drive, you must take the back roads, the highway is blocked." Another son is handing out maps. "If you want to be here first thing in the morning, Patel's is your best bet."

She spots Rima Patel. "Rima, what is going on here?"

To her surprise Rima does not immediately start screaming about dog shit, or Tahnee. Instead, she sounds utterly nice. "Murielle – you don't mind if I call you Murielle, do you, such a lovely name. Wouldn't you like to stay and have an onion bhaji? For you, no charge." Rima holds her by the wrist.

She pries loose. "I came home early to see my daughter."

"Yes, you caught us all off guard I am afraid." She laughs a tinkling-type laugh. "Perhaps for the best if you do not see Julie just yet, until I have prepared you."

"What are you doing to her?"

"You know, we have been so worried about your little girl! And one day my husband and I rang your bell, with some food. She told you this, I am certain."

"No, she didn't."

"What a remarkable child she is, Murielle!"

"You're talking about Julie?"

"I hope you are not minding, but after she spoke to my husband, she says the tremors are due not to Peplum's Scourge, which is what our doctor thought, initially, but a prostate complaint due to an environmental contaminant! Yes, here in our own back yard, can you believe it! And, as I had been saying to the doctor, surely it cannot be Peplum's. Yet with a simple remedy: fondling his aura, your daughter cured him! Then, I could not help myself, you see, I have a friend who is very ill and – the doctors do not know what is wrong with her!"

Murielle doesn't have a clue what the woman is going on about.

"I knew how worried you must be, there she lies in that dark room, alone all day, I promise you we will look after her while you are at your work. You see, we have almost lost our motel franchise, but it is thanks to Julie we are able to save it now, with the additional clients! Oh, it had been so terrible! As you know, they said we were not keeping up the standards and we said, 'Why do we need your name when you, the Superior Inn Franchise Corporation, simply take our money and offer no assistance at all, only to overcharge us for your required products?' So we left the corporation, and they forced us to change the name of the hotel, now we call ourselves the Vastly Superior Inn, but they are threatening to…"

"But what is going on here?"

"Have a lime soda. Isn't it wonderful!" says Rima, "So refreshing and delicious, I have made it myself from citric acid the flavor of kaffir limes – and you must try the onion bhaji, it is a kind of little fritter, I hope you do not find it too spicy."

She had not known what a talker Rima could be. "No, thanks."

"I am so glad we are friends now, I have longed to have someone to confide in. You see, it was the representatives from the Superior

Corporation who came in, secretly, a few times a year, to visit the various franchises, and discovered that we were not using the correct oil paintings and bed linens: hideous mustard-tone acrylic blankets and brown patterned bedspreads! But you must see, they charge a markup that is twelve hundred times as much as what these things are worth! And my husband, he has gotten so lazy – do you know, that scoundrel has completely lost his mind, he is smoking opium or some synthetic substitute? Yes, believe it or not, I found him in the linen closet, with sixteen customers waiting to check in and no one there! 'I will divorce you,' I told him. 'Have you lost your mind? You are such a dork!' I had just not known nor understood how isolated I would be in New Jersey. The scum next door, hanging out on their front lawn, the trashy girls, the drunken husband, the bad smells of roasting pork." She pauses, realizing this was not perhaps the right thing to say. "Now of course I know better! To think that all this time I might have thought the better of you. My family is not here, except for my younger ungrateful sons! Locu has gone, simply disappeared, I am distraught! And now, my husband has finally driven the Patels' hotel into the ground, adding chili powder and things that he knew were not supposed to be adding to the complimentary buffalo wings. 'These people want bagels,' I told him. 'They do not want spicy food, many of them are Orthodox Jews, go to the day-old store and get them some old bagels for the complimentary breakfast.' But does he listen?"

Obviously the woman is out of her mind, Murielle thinks, does she even realize how rude she is being to rant on and on like something has come unstuck? "I still don't understand what is happening here, the people lined up; my daughter." Murielle says.

"I am telling you, Murielle, although our relatives in India send us money each month, it is not enough, I wish my family had been allowed back to India The Homeland! But they said after three generations you cannot return, you are no longer Indian. India is so rich, this would not happen there! In India, even the poorest person has a lovely home, medical care. Here, for my son Locu all I can hope for is that he can obtain a position as a geisha to the rich in Nature's Caul."

She is never going to get an answer from this woman, Murielle thinks. At least the crowds have dispersed, the block for now is quiet. "Listen, you really have to go."

Grandpa is watching hologramovision.

"It appears that a few of you have been following the World Cup soccer," the President is saying. "And I know that some of you are curious as to why the US is not participating. For that, I have a good answer —" He glances quickly at the prompter. "Not only are very few Americans interested in soccer, it not being a particularly American game, but in addition Congress has stated they feel the US must preclude itself because we would undoubtedly win, and the other countries would be angry and even more jealous of us. So for those of you who have a warm and generous spot in their hearts, you should be happy that as always we are showing American kindness to —"

"Baboon-bottom breath." Grandpa spits in a paper napkin and turns to the advertisement channel.

Some nitwit broad takes a couple of steps forward, she's yammering away as she practically climbs into bed with him! "For a limited time you can have direct delivery, straight from the bubbling subterranean system of Brooklyn directly to your door! And because we use a special patent-pending method of purification, our water is so clean it's even better than the first time around. Because while water doesn't grow on trees... a tree grows in Brooklyn water."

Now what the heck is that supposed to mean, he thinks. There aren't any trees in Brooklyn. Besides, who wants someone else's recycled... On the other hand it is cheap and probably — by law — has to be okay. He decides to order the service, on line for only the next fifteen minutes act fast now! To his delight the blonde broad who has somehow gotten into his bedroom starts jumping up and down, now he realizes he can see through her shirt! She's shouting, squealing as she jumps up and down on his bed. "I can't believe it! This kind of thing never happens! It's unbelievable! Guess what: you've won a round-trip first-class trip to the destination of your choice." There are bells and whistles going off and other people outta that weird HGMTV machine have started crowding around him, it looks like they want to shake his hand but whenever he reaches out his hand goes right through theirs, like they're some kind of ghost? "Congratulations! Please say yes or no to one or more of the following offers – Almuncle Antrobus, would you like to have a degree in Criminology? A half-gallon of enzyme-enhanced peptides with sparkling oxygen crystals? Treat foot fungus! Fast and safe effective treatment in three easy payments. Learn more about brewing beer at home?"

"Well… maybe."

"Sweetie, in order to be eligible for the free first-class ticket to the destination of your choice, you are obliged to say yes to at least three of our valuable offers. Do you have one or more mortgages? What about applying for refinancing of your home?"

Four hours later Almuncle is still clicking off boxes when someone new cuts onto the screen.

"What? Who the heck is this?"

"It's me, Papi – Dyllis! I hear little Hulia is getting sicker, how is she doing?"

"Who?"

"Julie? Your granddaughter."

"Oh. Yes. That is what has been troubling me. Listen, I'm almost out the door, the taxi should be here any minute."

"Where you going, Papi?"

"I've won an all-expenses-paid first-class ticket to the destination of my choice! It's all been recorded and I've signed the necessary papers!"

"Why, Papi? Why you going?"

"That bitch Murielle won't put me in the nursing home! All I ever wanted was for her to sign me into that darn nursing home – they have a gym, a sauna, nightclubs! – but instead she's got me trapped in this cockaroach-infested hellhole with Frogboy and my granddaughter who's got a line of people around the block coming into the house. I don't know what she's doing in there, some kind of brothel?"

"Listen to me, I don't know what's going on, I will come over and try to help."

"That's fine with me," Grandpa says. "The taxi should be here any minute and I'm off to Amsterdam. First stop, the Red Light District; then on to van Hoek to meet my love, sweet Lady Juan Aishat! I was supposed to look after Julie while Froggy went out, but I ain't sticking around here!"

Though Julie is still barely able to walk, and bandaged over virtually every part of her body, she's managed to get out of bed to sit on a chair in front of the living room window. "Grampy – he's gone, Dyllis."

Dyllis pulls up a chair and sits down beside her. "I know, little mommy, he told me. That's why I come here, to see you, but I don't wanna leave you alone. Your granpappy, he tell you goodbye?"

"Yes, Dyllis. He gave me this to watch when I'm better."

It's an antique ZVD3, maybe a half century old, labeled *Death, Doom and Disaster, Or, How We Brought Destruction On Ourselves*. "Ju know, when I was a little girl," Dyllis says, "people always talked about how there used to be all kinda birds. Sparrows, pigeons, Mister Robin Redbreast, some leetle kinda of blackbirds, alla them die of the bird 'flu. They must have been pretty, right? Birds flying around in the trees, chirp chirp, picking up worms from the grass…

"It's probably good the birds all died," Julie says, "since there's no trees or grass any more either. The only birds I've seen around here are those seagull-vulture kind of things and most of them look pretty sick."

"I feel pretty sick too! And jour dog, did you have a look at heem? She's losing all her hairs, you got jourself a bald dog there."

It is true that Breakfast's fur has dropped off in huge patches and he looks quite miserable, pinkly gray, and constantly scratching. "He looks the way I feel," Julie says. "If I could just get these bandages off and scratch. I feel like I'm going out of my mind. What the hell's wrong with me, anyway? Why won't anybody tell me?"

"Nobody tell you? You got the boiling pox." Dyllis almost forgets she has a Spanish accent. "My gawd, Julie, I don't know why they didn't let you know, that's terrible. I've always believed in telling the truth. It's some kind of variation on smallpox, you know, a mutant strain or something: that's why the injections they gave you when they first took you in didn't work, or made it worse or something. They think there was a vial of the stuff in the plane crash, they're gonna level the whole area, turn it into a memorial. I mean, they don't normally do that for plane crash sites."

"But Tahnee and Cliffort were there and they didn't get sick..."

"Some kinda immunity, I guess... or maybe they never touched the stuff, you only get sick from direct proximity... Well, one good thing: you got yourself a boyfriend, didn't you?"

"You mean Cliffort? Oh Dyllis, I think so; I hope so, I love him so much but now look at me, how fat and ugly... Dyllis?"

"Jes?"

"I was responsible for that plane crash," Julie says miserably.

"What chu talking about? You had nothing to do with it."

"Yes, I did. Cliffort was teaching me how to shoot, you know he has some guns, and I wasn't paying attention and when the plane came in overhead, it was my shot that hit it."

"It was an accident. If it was anybody's fault it was Cliffort's – you're just a child. I think you should get rid of him."

"You're not really helping me."

"If you wanted to be punished, you've got your wish by getting smallpox or whatever it is you have. Why do you think all these doctors and scientists keep coming over?"

"I didn't know. Nobody even told me who they are or were."

"Come on. Eet a nice day. I help you outside, you get some fresh air." Dyllis puts her arms around Julie and carefully ushers her out the back door. Slawa had built a barbecue pit, years before, out of cinderblocks; it takes up half the yard, which had mostly been concreted over. The rest is dust. There is a metal table and chairs and Dyllis seats Julie in one of the chairs before unfurling the umbrella.

"I'm gonna go get you a hat; and I'm gonna get you something to drink, you gotta keep drinking liquids."

"I itch all over, Dyllis."

"That the pustules. Try not to scratch... Sh-sh-sh-sheet! I stepped in dog sheet!"

Breakfast at long last has managed to defecate and now prances around looking pleased with himself. In the corner of the yard a large insect, the size of an overgrown watermelon, emerges from under a pile of refuse.

"Breakfast!" yells Dyllis. "Get over here! Goddamn it, that look like one of the bugs escaped from the lab. I don't like that, that shouldn't happen, we don't know nothin' about what it can do. You got a rake or a shovel some place?"

"Maybe in the garage. What are you going to do? Don't hurt it!"

"You don't understand. If it's what I think it is, it have a stinger with, like, poison ivy kinda fluid, you be scratchin' something fierce!" The insect, with a large striped carapace, is unafraid. When Dyllis approaches it with a trowel, whitish fat squirts from the hole in its back. She hammers it and she keeps hammering at it until it topples over in a greasy heap, legs and antennae still twitching. "Lemme get a bucket soapy water, some lighter fluid maybe clean up this spot, I dunno… Okay, Julie, I gotta go. You wan' me to help you back inside?"

Julie's eyes are beginning to burn. She lets Dyllis help her up the back steps of the house and into bed; once she is tucked in Dyllis has to go home.

The hours pass in quiet exhaustion, each second carrying with it a tick of pointy pain. Her eyes are worse and she keeps the bandages on all the time; to remove them, even for an instant, is needles in her eyes.

She eagerly awaits her mother's return, but when Murielle arrives she says she has a migraine and goes right to bed. In the middle of the night the phone-screen starts to ring, she should have turned it off before going to sleep: it's that little disappointment, A. Jesse.

Why is he still pestering her? He has no business calling her this late. "What is it?" she says, though not without hope, perhaps after all he has snapped back to the old Jesse, or he has news about Tahnee.

"Actually it's more than just the SloMoFlies we're looking for," he says at last.

"What now?"

"Let me explain something to you. We have reason to believe your husband is a terrorist."

Was it possible? No, Slawa was too fat and feeble. The whole thing was ridiculous…

"Murielle."

"Oh, Jesse. What is it?"

"Murielle, I want you to leave. Get out. Now."

"Get out? What do you mean?"

"The place is going to be bulldozed and quite frankly, they don't care if you're inside or not. In fact, they hope you will be."

"They? Who is they?"

"Who is they? Murielle, you know how I feel about grammar. I'll let it go, for now. In any event, I can't reveal that."

"But how can they do that? Just bulldoze my house?"

"It's not just your house. It's all the houses in the area."

"But why?"

"It's going to be a memorial. They say this comes from the Federal Department of Homeland and Abroad Acme Construction, though it's actually because the contractors have such a powerful lobby: they control everything, kind of like the Masons. They need to enlarge the highway."

"But the highway is already twenty lanes wide, and the houses aren't anywhere near the road."

"They're going to say it's a contaminated zone. A danger area, slated to become a memorial site for the victims of the terrorist attack."

"What terrorist attack?"

"The plane crash, it was an act of terrorism."

"I just don't –"

"I didn't want to have to tell you but it's your daughter."

"My daughter? She's thirteen years old! You said it was my hus – my ex-husband."

"It's both. Murielle, don't argue with me. I'm giving you a warning. That's all, take it or leave it. Get out while you still can."

The guy is nuts; on the other hand, what if he is right? But how is she supposed to get out with her boiled daughter, still slowly cooking from the inside out. And the dog. And Dad. They can't drive, the main roads are permanently blocked by traffic, most people have either moved into their cars or long since abandoned them. It is all too absurd.

Hours have passed when Murielle wakes with a jolt. Her sleep has been so deep that for a moment she cannot remember where she is, opens her eyes: a lady's fan appears on the ceiling, folded white light, shuffling open wider and wider and then dreamily flicking shut: the reflection of a passing car's windshield. But it can't be a car, what the heck is it?

There is a tremendous noise going on outside, on the streets the neighbors are staggering this way and that; nobody seems to know what is going on, overhead the lights of a huge flock of helicopters whirr angrily as they come lower, lower, almost touching the roofs of the houses and then buzzing off again... What is happening? A secret celebrity wedding is her first thought, two famous and important people must have purchased a house in this dingy little development in order to hide from the press but then decided to have it leaked. There have been rumors that Stella and Colin are about to tie the knot. Also, Lottie and Russell were seen canoodling in New Hollywood's hippest nightclub. Brandy Crowe is pregnant, who could be the father? Alien invasion, spacecraft in the swamp? Another plane crash? Or, as had happened once before, a cell of terrorists renting a nearby house to manufacture bombs?

Anyway, here is Mrs Patel, squinting in the bright white stream, up to the window. "Have you heard from Tahnee? I call and call, they say Locu was with her! Where can he be?"

Murielle shakes her head. She knows with certainty something is about to go wrong or at least something is about to happen that is not going to be good. Luckily Breakfast is back, slurping from his water dish. "We've got to get out of here," she tells him.

"Les' go," the dog says. His words are slurred, she hopes he hasn't been lapping up that antifreeze again.

"I wish you'd try to enunciate more clearly! Oh, what am I saying? Julie! Julie! Dad! Grab your stuff, we're getting out of here." A sense of something like deja vu comes over her, or maybe this really has already happened?

"Ma? What's going on?"

"They're coming in tonight."

"Who?"

"I'm not sure, exactly, but what I do know is that they plan to wait until we're asleep and bulldoze the whole place down, and they're going to say later that they told us we had to be out, but we refused to leave – something like that. We've got to go – now. Where's Grandpa?"

"He said he was going to Amsterdam, something about rescuing Dutch children. A taxi picked him up a while ago."

"What? We'll have to go without him. And Cliffort?"

"Oh, Mom – we had a little fight and he's really not around most of the time any more, he just stops by once in a while but I think he must be living with someone else. He hates me!" There is a banging at the front door. Julie staggers to answer it and comes back shouting, "Mom, Mom, they've cordoned off the roads, I think we better get out of here, at least for the night, they are saying they're going to fumigate or something."

"How can we go, are they letting people out?"

"No, it's a road block, but we can go through the swamp."

"Take what you need in a knapsack!" At random she throws things into her canvas shopping bag, which reads on the side **Old Farm Security Homestead Organic Non-Engineered Heritage Food Produce**. A bottle of water? Some diet pop? A can of dog food? Mosquito repellant?

She doesn't know where they are going, nor for how long. Or even why, except that it's the sort of thing the sensible people do in the movies, escaping just as the rest of the village, town, city, culture, is getting wiped out, exterminated, sent to the camps, put on the long march, quarantined and left to die, decimated by fire, flood, famine, you hadda get out or perish! Let's go go go!

"Breakfast! Breakfast! Here, get in," Julie whispers to the dog and stuffs him in her bag, which barely has enough room, stuffed full as it is with **HoneyBumble's Pure Lip Balm; Maude Lauder #12 Extra Volume Taupe Mascara; Maybelline Daisy Fresh Centomax Face Wash** and a plethora of other items without which no thirteen-year-old can live without. "Come on, let's go," yells Murielle.

"Wait, wait!" Julie quickly runs to the basement to release the various fluffy, clawed pets, shoos them up the basement steps into the yard in the hopes that somehow they will survive. As they head out into the swamp Julie can't really believe that anything much is going to happen to them. They hear the explosion. The blast is so loud and bright the sky behind them is white.

For a moment they stop and turn to watch. It appears to have occurred right where their house was. And then Julie, followed by Murielle and Breakfast, continue out into deeper water.

20

Slawa is livid, he is so livid he can only hope Julie didn't see how upset he was; there is no use in getting her upset too. Cliffort. That damp-skinned… thing that came out from behind a toilet, who obviously had something to do with the plane crash and now may have very well impregnated his thirteen-year-old daughter. It is another barbed bandarilla from the mocking picador stinging his hide. He is more than enraged; he can't sleep, he spends the night in the cool darkness of his own private nightclub-lounge, listening as the subway cars pass by, first fairly often, then with greater lapses of time between trains as the night wears on.

It occurs to him Bocar has not uttered a word, and is clutching a box to his chest. "Are you all right?"

"I am not all right," Bocar says. "My box is empty."

"What's that?"

"I say, my box is emp-ty. In it CON-tained the fingernail clippings of my parents. It was be-ING all I had of them. All my life I have kept this. And al-WAYS I have sav-Ed to some day have my parents cloned. Yes, this can be done. It is fea-SIB-le. Never, I am thinking, will I have enough money; yet still it gives me hope and at night, I sleep beside my Mum and Father."

"I will help you save," says Slawa. "We can do it together."

"Now, it is too late. My uncle has found me with the box and thrown the con-TENTS away. Instead, he has put used clippings of himself and my aunt. All this time I have thought it was my parents, carried with me for so long. My uncle laughs, he had not planned to tell me. Only to see the event if I ever did win the lottery and get enough money, how surprised I would be to be given clones of my aunt and uncle, and not parents!"

Slawa doesn't want to ask, if this were to occur, how Bocar would be able to recognize two babies as not being his parents, how anyone could identify an infant as his uncle or aunt – but he doesn't say anything. He knows these clippings were the only things Bocar had on the planet. "I am going to leave the box here. If someday I do not return, in the box is something for you. Please remember! You know when I go home they will beat me, perhaps this time even kill me," Bocar says.

"I tell you what," Slawa says as they head out. "Let's get married, that way they can't touch you." The boy stares at his hand with amazement.

"You are doing this for me? But why? What do you wish in return?"

"No, I do not want nothing in return, you are my friend, this is friendship that is all, so now you will not need to return to your uncle. When later you are having green card, we can divorce. Meanwhile, two is stronger than one, you can help me in shop and with kitties."

They take the blood tests and apply for the license. Until the marriage takes place Bocar will hide out in the basement of the shoe repair store.

A couple of days later they go to City Hall. Slawa would give Bocar a ring but the only ring he had he gave, years ago, to Julie. Bocar is very nervous. His hands are ice cold, he will never be warm again in this country where it can snow in July. On the fifth floor he asks Slawa to find out where the men's room is – he is embarrassed: nobody except Slawa can understand him. Slawa approaches a young man. "He wants to know where the toilets is."

"He's the bride? Or groom."

Slawa shrugs. He hasn't thought things through that far. But then he remembers the expression, once a groom, never a bride and, after all, he has been a groom twice before. "He is bride, I guess."

"Two floors down," says the man – he seems to work in the building. "It's for him? Gosh, he's pretty. Tell him to be careful – a guy got raped in there last week."

Slawa can't help but wonder whether the rape victim was about to be married… Some poor virginal kid?

The Justice of the Peace – or whatever he is – a tubby mustached fellow, makes a complete mess of the whole speech. "Do youse, Slawa… Slawa Al-yo-ishus – Fockinoff… Wow, that's some name, huh? Take youse, Bocar Abdul bin Benin, to be your lawful wedded spouse…"

The whole time the J.P. stares out the window. Waiting behind them are couples, men and women, couples with four, five kids, people seem to be crowded into the waiting room as if today was the last day on the planet anyone might get married, in wedding gowns and tuxedos, Halloween costumes of vampires and warlocks.

After, they go for lunch nearby; they each have a glass of champagne. As a devout Muslim Bocar normally doesn't drink. He sips his shyly. Thank God it seems nothing has changed between the two of them, Slawa had no intention of consummating the relationship; he isn't gay, after all. But that evening when they are about to go to bed, before he has reached up to turn off the light he is doubled over in pain. His head, the wound, what can be the matter with him and he has no money to pay for some brain-scan let alone an operation…

"Here, I am mass-aging you," says Bocar, and while he is lying on his stomach he doesn't see that Bocar has removed his own clothing and… somehow it does not seem to matter when the massage continues into… something more…

Naked… shyly.

The kid is really magnificent, with his long hair, his nubile body, like a prepubescent girl, though narrow-hipped, long in the waists, totally flat-chested.

"My friend," says Slawa, who finds himself aroused, perhaps with nervousness and embarrassment as much as anything else. "You are very sweet, but there is no need to do that. As you know we are married only for the purpose of trying to rescue you from your aunt and uncle and get you out of military duty."

"But I want to," says Bocar simply, and pulling the blankets aside, he crawls beneath…

When Slawa can't see the body it hardly matters what sex it is. The experience is, for Slawa at least, of great beauty. Afterward when they lie together he asks Bocar if he has ever done that before. Bocar hesitates. "No, you can tell me. I want to know..."

It turns out the boy has been taken advantage of by various men since he was ten years old: there have been soldiers and others, on and on for years, most recently his uncle. "But you must understand, with you, this was the first time I wanted someone. You did not take advantage of me."

If that is true, Slawa thinks, it is pathetic. There he is with his big gut, his balding head. He resolves to get into shape. He feels such tenderness for the boy and at the same time something queasy, is it love? But of what sort? He still can't think of himself as gay; Bocar seems so much like a girl, or perhaps his son. He has never expected to have feelings of this sort and they are disturbing in every way. "My little friend," says Slawa, "I would like to do something for you, is there something I could do that would make you happy?"

Bocar says nothing but Slawa feels... There is something, unstated, though it is not until he grabs Bocar and begins to wrestle him that finally the boy blurts, "It will make me happy if you would convert to Islam."

It is damp. And then the rains come, day after day, everything is soaked, flooded, mildew sprouts on every surface, more chunks of the ice caps have melted and now the city streets are many feet deep in water. It is possible to get schistosomiasis, bilharzia, other invasive, non-indigenous vector-carried diseases. You need hip waders to get anywhere, even then one sudden slop, a sanitation truck churning up the muck as it passes by, stuff comes in over the tops; for a time there are fish that can bite, that seem to be some combination of piranha and Chinese something-or-other – anyway, they occasionally – okay, rarely, it is true – join up in a school and can go through the rubberized boots in a matter of minutes... All that time they rarely go out, it is cozy in the old Smoke-Easy; Bocar has made a little hole no one can see, to get onto the subway platform and he comes back with food and things for Slawa to study.

The process of converting is simple. Schedule an appointment with the Imam of a mosque. You will need a couple passport-size photos of yourself as well as two tax stamps (material), and some other documents. They'll give you a list. Go there, preferably dressed in Muslim garb, with a Koran if you have one. You will need to recite two things, which the Imam can help you with. One is "Bismillahi ar-Rahmani ar-Rahim'. Then there is a statement that says Allah is the only god and Mohammed is his prophet, 'Asyhadu anla ilaha illa Allah, wa asyhadu anna Muhammadan Rasulullah'.
— *website for men converting in order to marry Indonesian women*

The mosque is far uptown. On the day of his conversion he and Bocar cross the streets of skyscrapers – once this area was Central Park, now only a tiny dark patch is left, so dark real grass can't grow and it has long ago been replaced by artificial turf – in silence.

Before the ceremony they go shopping. Sheepishly Slawa tries on different types of Muslim wear. He is convinced he looks like an imposter, but to wear on this day at least he finds a decent enough bisht, and an Islamic cap, and for other days, perhaps he might wear a salwar kameez, or dishdash. He already has his Koran and a nice little prayer rug that Bocar found for him in the fabric district, quite by chance. Still, he is nervous at meeting the Imam, he is afraid he will make a mistake, even though Bocar has told him not to worry and he has practised what he is to say over and over again. He is having a bad day, his head hurts. Bocar now knows when Slawa is about to have one of his 'spells'; no amount of aspirin can help any longer, and only very occasionally the touch of Bocar's hand, on his temples, or the back of his neck, can somewhat diminish the agony.

He would have liked Julie to be his witness but she is too ill, though no one is quite certain what is wrong with her. As for Bocar's aunt and uncle, his cousins, he has not told any of them where he is, if they found out they would kidnap him and who knows what. Who will be witness to Slawa's conversion? The Imam finds another cleric – he can't seem to believe that neither of the men have friends, or family who will be there on this important occasion.

But the Imam has a huge following and finally some others are rounded up. The sacristan – if this is the man's title – is astonished at the number of flies that have suddenly entered the mosque. Bocar and Slawa are both nervous – they both want to laugh, it is hard for them to keep a straight face. They remove their pumps, which are placed on long shelves with a few others, for it is mid-day during the week, there are not many worshippers.

Slawa's so anxious, he's got the skeeves. "Do you know the five pillars of Islam?" asks the Imam, who exhorts him to follow the faith, to read the Koran and to do the things required as a Muslim. At the end of it they sign the two certificates, one for the Imam, one to keep, in the presence of crying witnesses; one fellow, Ali, gives Slawa prayer beads, a string of ninety-nine pink plastic beads. Now, through prayer, he will be able to determine what Mohammed would wish him to do. Anyway, it is very touching. They congratulate Slawa, reminding him to pray five times a day. "And now we must look for a nice Muslim girl for you to marry," he is told. He glances shyly at Bocar, the men laugh. Hassan gives Slawa a little box; inside is a plastic key chain with a picture of Al Kaaba Asaulash Anfa, and on the other side is aya 3 of Surat Attalq.

The Imam takes Bocar and Slawa to one side and talks about that trip to Mecca to make hajj at least once before they die. "That's it in a nutshell," says Bocar, too loudly when they get outside.

And though he has never touched the boy in public, never embraced him, it is not his style – not even after the wedding – he now takes the boy Bocar's hand in his own; it is dry and rough with such long sensitive spatulate fingers, the skin on the palm pink and on the back a color of milky espresso – I really must get some crème for his hands, he thinks, poor little chap, poor chapped dry hands – and hand in hand, they begin to walk north, slowly, both gasping for oxygen in air that seems to have been stripped of oxygen. The subways have broken or there is no power supply, at least today; a public bus costs hundreds of dollars, due to the price of gasoline, besides, they can walk faster than a bus moves in traffic.

The sour asphalt beneath their feet steams and heaves in the heat. "Take it easy," he says to the kid, "We don't have to be in a rush, the air is bad, and too hot; we just walk slowly, we get there some time."

There is a shop a few blocks away where Bocar buys Slawa some men's cologne, sandalwood, made without alcohol. Slawa hopes that this is just a present, not something given because he smells. At least, though, the scent seems to drive away the flies, which Bocar is always trying to swat. They still follow Slawa, but at a respectful distance. "Slawa," Bocar says, "If some day you do not find me, it is not I who left. They may take me. On-LY then, look in my box."

"Nonsense, they can't take you now, we are married, I will protect you, soon you will have Green Card, Resident Alien Card, Social Security Card, Driver's License, maybe we enroll you in school, obtain Work Visa, Student Visa –"

Slawa hopes the boy is reassured. Bocar smiles sadly but says nothing more.

It transpires that though they are married (not a Muslim marriage, of course, but civil!) Bocar still can't be saved from military duty unless the government is reimbursed… and the money – but who had gotten it, where has it all gone, nothing has been put aside for the kid – easily amounting to four hundred thousand, and interest is added to this amount each day.

Slawa had thought for a time that with his conversion, with prayers facing east five times a day, either in a mosque or simply in his shop, his endless counting of the prayer beads, he would be calm. He had thought with Bocar living there in the basement of the shoe repair shop, on his own mattress nearby, he would not be alone, there would be no time to sit and seethe, fluids building behind his eyes. But quite the opposite occurs. His rage builds and builds and finally he decides that it is up to him to show the world what has been done. And the boy will be the one to help. The boy will be the new Savior. Yet how or what he – they – are meant to do is not yet known to him.

Now he does not want to leave the planet, he loves the boy so much. During the day he rarely speaks to him, what is there, after all to say? But simply to be around him is enough. It is at night, beneath the cat-scented blankets, when they lie together that he is able to travel to this other place, where... things, like floating balls, bubbles on a sea... without knowing why, this sense of pleasure, and he is back as a boy.

The way on a hot summer day the little kiosk was cool and musty with a few products, a bottle of wodka and outdoors the scent of baked vegetation. Then he looks up and the boy is smiling down at him, lissome, his face open and mild, petals of a flower. Holding a mug of tea which Bocar hands to him. "Come, now, I must make the bed."

It is the boy's voice. The boy's voice, and he is back to being a boy. A certain pitch, resonance, high-pitched, slightly nasal, that connects directly with his dick and causes it to tremble. It has nothing to do with anything else; it is all about sound. But how much better this is, why has he never thought of it before, no more women's vaginas, those hairy holes in which he is supposed to thrash around... in the hot and slippery... how can he not be enjoying this time, he has been wasting it all in his rage and despair that they are coming to get Bocar, but for now at least Bocar is here and the kindness of the child, how can he not love him?

"If I can get coins enough for the pay phone, ever, I'll call my daughter and tell her we got married," he says.

The boy is quiet. "She will not mind?" he says after a while.

"Maybe. After all, I got remarried without telling her or inviting her but I can only hope she'll understand."

The boy's question has flattened, slightly, his newly realized joy. He drinks his mug of tea, Bocar has put in milk and sugar, just the way he likes it. He wants to ask Bocar certain questions: if the boy cares for him, if the boy had slipped into bed beside him because he wanted to or because he felt obliged, now that they were married... really, if that is the case, it need never have come to that.

But he keeps his mouth shut. Perhaps he doesn't really want to know. The boy is quick, neatly making up the beds, folding the blankets on the pallet. A mewing: his favorite cat, the red Persian, proudly drops a dead... mouse? He takes it away from him. It is maybe poisoned or sick, he has no faith in his cat's hunting skills.

"Thank you," he says to the cat. "What a day of presents, eh?" He has forgotten that with his back turned away the boy can't read his lips and he goes over and tenderly begins to massage the boy's shoulders; the boy leans back into him purring... Things must be okay for him, then.

Just as suddenly it is a new month and the water – and the fish and worms – disappear, now it snows; all records are broken! And the city has run out of money to keep plowing, salting – which is okay, because, just as abruptly, the snow stops and the temperature goes back up. August, mixed with snow, sleet, a tornado... each day has a different climate. It could just as easily be January or July with a hundred and twelve degree weather one day and below freezing the next, or sudden darkness in the middle of the day, or even light all night long.

Though he has managed to collect enough coins to make a call of perhaps thirty seconds, there is never any answer at his former home and finally he tells Bocar he will go home to tell Julie in person they are married. He travels by night, arrives twelve hours later.

His house – his former house – is in ruins.

Where is his daughter? In tears he half squats in the sour burnt stench, only to find something glinting. Kitchen knives, forks, and crooked white bone, a blackened ring with a cabochon stone that has crackled. What. What. What? Surely it can't be. It's the ring he gave Julie. It must be her fingers. He holds the carbonized ring, the burnt shriveled finger to his chest, bent over, sitting in that terrible mud of hardened ash. The remains of his driveway, still nicely re-tarred. At that moment from around the corner Cliffort lopes into view, his ridiculous hopping gait. One or two bounds, Cliffort is by his side. "What happened?" he says, looking up, "What happened? Where are they? Where is my Julie?"

"Gone." That wet-skinned creature is leering, chinless with his big Adam's apple. "Came back, found the place like this."

What's the freak doing, patting him on the back? Trying to comfort him? With a roar Slawa springs up in hot bliss, punching and kicking. This weak clown does not even strike back! Before he knows what he is doing Slawa has his knife in his hand, open blade, and slashes at that scrawny neck, the blade is so sharp he barely touches him. His knife peels an apple, only in reverse, first the creamy pale flesh and then the dart of red. Cliffort's blood. In horror Slawa flings down the knife, stumbles back across the destruction and flees. Later he will be sorry to have left it behind, the comfortable weight of it, the bone handle, the honed blade.

And when he gets back to the shoe repair shop, keys made, fifteen, twenty hours later, sneaking in through the underground passage, Bocar is no longer there.

"Bocar?" he calls. "Bocar?" But Bocar is gone.

21

It's another night for Murielle and Julie. The moon is up, with its crooked happy face. It would be a full moon, except there is a big chunk missing, from the era when the moon was used as a site to detonate old nuclear warheads, the idea of some former President who got elected on the Environmental Platform.

Helicopters are flying low over the swamp just as they emerge by the highway. "Mom, I think we're safe, if we stay under the overpass."

"Tomorrow, we'll go back to the swamp to head toward the city, maybe your dad can help us, I think he's living in the repair shop."

"Okay, that sounds sensible."

They unfold their sleeping bags on the gravel. "Do you want something to eat?" Her mother rummages in her pocketbook. "Let me tell you what I brought along: dried apricots, some sour balls, two tuna-fish sandwiches..."

"That's okay, Ma. I'm not hungry."

"Well, you should eat something, you'll sleep better."

"That's okay..."

Maybe her mother is right, she should eat something. She lies in her little mummy bag, the dog alongside her, but can't reach that place, the weird transparent place that comes between wakefulness and sleep; how can she make herself get there? Julie is fairly certain that Sue Ellen – if that is even her name – is accompanying them on the long march. For one thing the bag is clammy all night and in the morning when she gets out it is soaking wet, and it is definitely not her!

Bowel movement. If there is this ghost, why did it have to come with them? She is a practical person, yet inexplicably, while her mother opens two cans of Spicy D-8, Julie finds herself scrawling in the dirt with a stick: CAPITALIST ROADER! COW DEMON! and muttering aloud "Ghost demon! Huli!"

"What are you saying, Julie?" her mother asks.

"I dunno," says Julie. What the hell is it all supposed to mean, she is sure it didn't come from her and the only explanation is that Sue Ellen won't leave them alone.

Poor Sue Ellen. For her it is something similar to being trapped... in an L-shaped ashtray; only there are different staircases that led up to rooms crowded with furniture. The whole thing is a nasty business – there is no way to make any sense out of it. It all seems real enough, just... ugly. And half the time she felt as if she were waiting on line to use a toilet... an endless line to a women's room with toilets that never flushed or were out of loo paper... or there was no door to the stall, or the stall is so small there was no way to sit on the toilet without crushing her... knees. She knows it isn't the same as being alive, that somewhere she must have taken a wrong turn but now... What is she supposed to do, she can't figure out how to get back – or go ahead. And Damnit, they keep calling her by the wrong name! Stupid Landowners, she would never be able to re-educate them!

In the morning they head south, through the sludge and stickers of marsh grass and finally up onto the twenty-lane highway. Here and there people have moved into the abandoned cars, the cars and vans and trucks are bumper to bumper, long out of gas, batteries dead, though fully optioned with reclining leather seats, satellite connections, sunroofs...

The squatters have stitched up curtains, removed the front seats and turned the back into a bed... Around the cars on the tarmac the contents of the trunks have been scattered: extra tires, scrapers, shovels, coolers, salt and bags of sand for icy conditions, burnt-out flares, surfboards and tents.

A scrawny bird, furiously jumping up and down, hops into view. Are her eyes that bad? Julie can't believe it, she has never seen a ground bird before. "That a rooster?" she asks.

"Sick chicken," one of the men explains. "She having a seizure. Chicken fit."

The other men crowd around eagerly. "Chicken fit! Chicken fit!" They begin to lay bets on whether or not it will produce an egg.

An egg coming out of a bird? That is so bizarrely unnatural, Julie thinks, hobbling down the hot tarry highway as she inhales peppery acid wind from the burning garbage, carrying Breakfast, whose little paws are burning hot and sore.

Some miles down they come to Great Adventure World. It has been out of business for years since the newer, Better Greater Adventure World had been built. Now before them are fifty acres of roller coasters that no longer work, creaking rustily, a gondola ride that once went up in a tunnel to the top of a mountain with a fake Swiss Village; water slides long since drained of water. The whole place is surrounded by a heavy-duty electric fence, no longer receiving electricity, snipped in places with wire cutters... Someone has hooked up a generator and attached a boom box, from which loud Spanish music – merengue? The rumba? The cha-cha? – blares... The smell of marijuana and hot grease...

Julie is scared. "Ma, I think we better get going."

"Hey, look! There's Dyllis!" Her mother lets out a shrill taxi whistle and begins yelling. After a pause she hears the pounding of footsteps through gravel coming up to the fence.

"Oh! Vayo con dios! I can't believe ju found me!"

Dyllis is accompanied by a little lavender donkey with feathery wings, too small to be useful. Nevertheless, Dyllis had rescued it; she thinks she can make some money by giving little girls rides – that is, if she ever sees any little girls with any money. "My gosh, Dyllis, what are you doing here?" says Murielle.

"I lost my yob! That Jesse March Bishrop, he come in, he says, where the animals? Ju geev me them now. I say, 'Mister, I don't know nothing about no missing animals, ju crazy!' So he fire me. And after I invented, myself, the palm-sized lion! The man make millions from me, this is how I am treated!"

"Oh my gosh!" Julie bursts into tears, "I know it's my fault! I was the one who took the animals home!"

Dyllis doesn't respond. Finally she says, "Come on in, ju can meet my frien'. Ju remember Cliffort?"

Julie can't believe Dyllis is traveling with Cliffort. "Cliffort?"

There is a grunt. A croak. She knew all along he wouldn't want anything to do with her now that she is almost blind and boiled. But... wait just a minute, he is wrapping his long cool arms around her, and in her ear he erupts with a long, low, "Ribbit!"

"Oh, Cliffort, what's wrong?"

"Julie, I don' know how to tell you," says Dyllis, "I fin' him left for dead, he got his throat slit. He no die, but now he no can talk and he don't remember who do this thing to him. And something else. When he perspire, he sweat..."

"Is he sweating green?"

There is a grunt. He is looking into her eyes. Such strange round eyes, almost lidless, or at least so they appear, unblinking. But even though they are nearly expressionless she knows he still loves her. She cautiously reaches out her hand and he takes it in his.

Julie sighs with happiness and closes her eyes. "*Chromidrosis: in very rare instances the perspiration may be colored yellow, red, green or blue. In most of the observed cases the eyelids have been affected. The action of micro-organisms is suspected of causing the pigment to be formed.*"

"So Julie, what can he do? Ju know, he a proud jung man, a leetle bit vain, he so ashamed alla time to be sweatin' bright green."

Julie shakes her head. "Nothing's coming to me for a cure."

"So... he gonna be like this forever? The people, they see him, they laughing. They like to embarrass him to make him sweat, or make him hop around, ju know, to see the green come out all ovah hees body."

"Oh, poor Cliffort." He nuzzles her tenderly, his skin is so cool and soft; she is happy.

"So, Murielle, eet's a good thing you got outta your old neighborhood. I went by, a couple of days ago... They bulldozed the whole place, they gonna cover it over. Some kind of contamination, at least, that's what Rima Patel told me." Dyllis babbles on as they go through the rusted amusement park... it is almost empty apart from wispy creatures who occasionally flit here and there, children, perhaps, skittering out of the crumbling Haunted House of the Doomed, darting below decks of the Jolly Roger Pirate Ship.

They stay at the park for two nights. The dog keeps talking about sex, muttering, "Let's fock."

It always seems to happen just as Julie is dozing off, or is having a nice dream… It drives her nuts, that little weird voice, "Come on, leetle mommy, let's fock –" She grabs him by the scruff of his neck and says, "Breakfast, you've got to cut it out! What's wrong with you, you never used to be like this."

"I sorry," he says. "I sorry. I can't help. But everthing so… so… so nice, Julie. We in outside, so good for Breakfast! I loff! But Julie…" the little dog whines.

"What is it?"

"Now I hungry…"

"Me too." But there is nothing to eat and finally they give up and get into the sleeping bags, the little dog snoring softly in Julie's ear. All night long the strange sounds, wind in the creaky and rusting rides, between the bones of the roller coaster that had once spun screaming passengers upside down. But more than that, a kind of intestinal carping, the splitting of the globe's… skull?… the mysterious shriek of car wrecks, though the sounds had to be ghost sounds, no cars could get anywhere near here… almost the same groans as a sinking ocean liner or the sea itself drying up with a steamy hiss. But in any event, the sounds go on for so long, eventually they no longer notice. And so they sleep.

The men camping are from Mexico, Puerto Rico, the San Blas Islands, somehow they have made their way here by boat, hoping to find work but had been turned away; now they are in danger of being picked up by the police and conscripted into the military…

Dyllis explains it is almost impossible for them to survive, they have no credit cards, no cash, there is nothing for them to eat… The grilling meats are rats which they manage to catch, and the occasional giant eel-lugworm that was able to live in the polluted marsh-mud.

The men are kind to share the little they have. There is a kind of Northern alligator that can survive even in bitter cold, it was originally designed to feed on sewage and other waste… Once, the men say, they found one almost fifty feet long. They killed it and tried to eat it but it was absolutely inedible, no matter what they did to the meat: the taste of rotten garbage was too profound to cover up. Sometimes they collect snails, which they keep in a box for a few days until their systems are cleaned out. Fried in oil, the snails taste of peanuts. The only difficulty is in having to fry snails that make little squeaky sounds and have such big blue eyes with lashes! "Probably a bio-genetic engineer snail, right?" says Dyllis. "I remember there was another lab, they spliced a cetapod with a legume and something else. Maybe some escaped? At least Bermese Python wasn't the only one."

A hologramovision crew from the Humanitarian Poverty Channel stops by; at first everyone hides. Finally someone is coaxed out to speak to the camera after being promised voice and face will be disguised; it is to be a human interest story on the men's plight.

The crew decides to leave behind a half-eaten box of chocolates and some hard candy, hand sanitizer, a can of soda and a half-eaten canister of veggie bacon bits which one of the cameramen likes to have as a snack. "I'm so sorry we didn't bring any other food with us!" says the blond reporter who did the interview. "And clothing! And old magazines! But I'm sure after this airs, you'll be getting tons of help!"

"Help, yeah," mutters one man. "After eet air, they gonna come and close us down."

Her mother and Dyllis discuss the reporter with a mixture of envy and loathing: the blond hair with highlights in a perfect hue of ashen gold! The clean gray suit with the monogrammed pink silk shirt and neon-blue codpiece! The petit-point slippers in ecru echidna-skin! "I bet that's how Tahnee is living these days," says Murielle.

"If we can ever get in touch with her maybe she'll take us to live in Nature's Caul," says Dyllis. Both sigh dreamily; there are probably only a few hundred people on the planet who are able to live this way, with private jets and hairdressers.

The rest gives Breakfast's paws a chance to recover. He is so tired that at night he snuggles with Julie and Cliffort in her sleeping bag, murmuring and whimpering in his sleep. "Daddy... where are you?"

Julie also misses Slawa. She is worried about him. She hugs Breakfast and remembers how Slawa had been so gentle to the dog, teaching him how to speak. There had been a couple of times when in some sort of fit of pique Slawa had kicked him across the room. But that had only increased the dog's love for its master. Why would that be? She asks the dog, but Breakfast is unable to articulate and only mumbles. Eventually the dog's slow breathing becomes her own and she falls asleep.

In the morning everyone has emptied out of the camp, except for Murielle and Dyllis and Julie; Cliffort is off with the men on a hunting-and-gathering expedition. Even the dog is gone; he has found or begged some rat bones and is happily gnawing some distance away. It is a Perfect Beach Day, the hot wind and the sound of slapping flags or sails, the sky ice-blue and without a cloud. Soon it will be too hot to do anything.

When Julie goes off for a pee, squatting by the side of the muck, she is horrified to find a slushy mass of jelly sloshes out of her, somewhat firm, clear with tiny black dots in it. Is it her period? But she thought that was supposed to be blood. She shoves the pile into the water, covers it over with dead sticks and a rock before she goes back, oddly bereft and homesick.

The men return from the hunt. It is late in the afternoon, the sun is trembling into pale orange, the skies frosted with lavender and green pollution, when the choppers are heard. At first at a distance and then closer, until finally dirt begins to whirl around the camp, thick clouds containing human remains; heavy metals (including lead and arsenic); a small quantity of nuclear waste – all of which has been dumped here over the past hundred years.

Then through the dust come men on motorcycles, are they Hells Angels? More men, these on horseback, a cavalry galloping right into the people. There are men in jackboots, Panzer men, storm troopers, bovver boys, Cossacks. What the heck is going on, is a film being shot? Guys in camouflage, dressed as Vietnam War soldiers holding archaic Kalashnikovs. Maoris, naked except for loincloths, pound their chests, chanting the Haka. Somewhere someone has a sound system blasting ancient music: "All along the watchtower…" Gurkhas, guys in kilts with bellowing bagpipes, Algonquin, Delaware and Iroquois, fiercest of The Five Nations!

"Run! Run! It's the undercover cops! It's a round-up!"

"If we get separated, we'll meet up at Daddy's shoe store, the same as we planned," Murielle shouts. "You can find your way there, right, Julie?"

The men are scrambling to pack their few things, it is time to get out! Only now, for most of them, it is already too late. In the melee Cliffort grabs Julie by the arm and they run. But if they are headed in the right direction neither is sure.

22

If the top of Mt. Olympus is flat, Slawa thinks, then he is going to Mt. Vesuvius. At first he assumes Bocar's uncle and aunt have come and nabbed him, though when he checks their restaurant he finds it is boarded up, shut down, out of business. Is it because they have taken Bocar for resale? Or is it because the food was so inedible it was obvious the restaurant was never going to stay in business for long?

He wanders the streets. The whole city is crumbling, friable bricks and sandstone, quivering glass windows, rusted metal. The mentally ill and homeless have taken over the streets, and these people, they don't travel light! Shopping carts filled to the brim, shoeboxes, hair curlers and hula-hoops, squash racquets, dustpans and binoculars, there are more of these people and more of their stuff than ever before. Soon it will be as tall as the first story, swelling and expanding with the years until it reaches the highest roof.

Maybe Bocar is working someplace else.

He searches Hunt's Point Market at dawn. It is here all the fruit and meat and fish and vegetables are delivered into the city, not that these days they are more than laboratory-grown tissues molded and dyed to resemble oranges, or strawberries, or slabs of meat. Men are at work unwrapping the fish and spritzing them with fish smell. Though it is not far from where Bocar had said he lived with his relatives, there is no sign of him. How foolish to think he can wander the streets and somehow, by accident, find him. Especially if Bocar is being kept prisoner.

Groups of tourists and schoolchildren are now arriving, led on tours to show how food enters the city. Do they know the food isn't real? He knows, because the manufacturing laboratories were so near his home in Jersey. Once he had even tried to get a job there but it was the wrong time; there were cutbacks. There were always cutbacks. The less human contact there was with the food the less chance there was of the particularly destructive strain of z.coli that infected everything these days.

But surely the men in the quaint uniforms hoisting mottled legs of lamb tissue are spreading disease and contamination? Dirty hands unloading the chubby pigs, made in pig molds. Nearby fake butchers waited to cleave, slice and subdue the product into all the old familiar shapes – pork chops, loin, ribs, honeycombed tripe and crinkled brains. In fact it's all the same stuff, meat tissue.

A world in which so little yet so much was left. As had once been: a gray beach mottled with crab shells and strings of kelp. Only now what is left are the ancient, immutable remnants of an earlier age: strands of cassette tape, shiny brown, and foam coffee cups. And walls, posts, columns, covered with giant hologramovision screens.

He remembers Bocar telling him how when he had first gotten to New York and his uncle had been a bit nicer, he'd given him a bit of cash, and he spent five dollars on an apple, a huge red-and-yellow globe, but, what a disappointment! The hard waxy skin, and bite of mealy flesh, flavorless.

He knows he will not find Bocar but still he goes on, watching crates pried open, the shouting negotiations, all the chefs from restaurants of Manhattan! One fingers a dainty ladyfish; another leers at the silvery mackerel. Here's an artificially pink arctic char, here are moony green wedges of crescent bananas, wheels of golden parmesan; but it all comes from the same manufacturer.

The huckstering, boisterous market air is a complete fake. Of course, Bocar would not have been able to hear it anyway. Sound is only a ripple in the airwaves to him; his hearing, Bocar said, was getting worse and worse. Bullets had gone off next to his ears. The damage could never be repaired. How could he have been so stupid as to have forgotten to tell Bocar that most of the people in this country were deaf, only from plugs in their ears playing loud music all the time?

He hasn't been paying attention. Now something on one of the hologramovision screens makes him stop short. It's the President, President Wesley and Scott, standing on the tarmac as hundreds of young men and women are being escorted by military police on to a gigantic plane.

"You see, these are all mercenaries, hired by American citizens," the President is saying. "This has cost the American public a great deal, every single one of these folk has pocketed the money and then gone AWOL from the service, where they had signed papers agreeing to fight in place of the young person whose money they had so willingly absconded with. Of course there is no hope of getting any of that back, and for many of you it could have been used for retirement funds or medical purposes. We would have liked to charge these people for their guns and food supplies, the uniforms and fine boots we provide each of them with, which it would now appear they have traded for brand-name sneakers and fast-food coupons... Many of you will say to me, what is the good to send them back to their homeland? Scott, would you like to respond to that?"

The teenage soldiers, boys and girls, are crossing the airfield naked (in order that no one attempt to blow up the plane, though why any of these kids would do that now, on their way home, seems unlikely), no carry-on luggage except each is bearing a small cage of gerbils, which they have been given in order to repopulate the desert, where gerbils have long been extinct, so that the people can once again become self-sustaining.

In a year's time, Scott explains, each female gerbil can produce up to forty offspring who themselves will begin to reproduce, and not only can gerbils provide a tasty morsel of protein-rich food, their skins can be sewn together for warm clothing and their droppings are a rich fertilizer for crops.

"Boys in the front, girls in the back," says the flight attendant briskly, with a clap of the hands. "Those of you in the process of gender reassignment, middle four rows."

The nubile bodies troop across the tarmac and there, up toward the front of the line, Slawa is almost certain, is Bocar.

"Mr President, our feeling at the White House is, yes, it is a shame that many of these young people will not be tried in the Democratic system, but it is their own government's responsibility to punish them as they see fit, according to the rules of their lands... Naturally most of these countries are overseen by UN Peacekeeping Missions, and though where necessary we have placed our own Democratic leaders in place of a corrupt regime, we must allow these young Democracies to learn and grow unimpeded; we can observe, but it is not our responsibility, nor our duty, to take action."

The camera cuts to the anchor people. "After this commercial break," one is saying, "we're going to take a look at just what those kids were allowed to bring with them out of the country, and what kind of situation they can expect to return to in homelands they haven't seen in many years…"

"That's right, Bonwit," says the other newsperson, "we have Wolf Goebbels on the scene and I think he's going to be permitted by the militia to stop and chat with some of the kids boarding the plane. We'll be right back after this important announcement."

The announcement is a public service instructing Americans how to get a reward based on information leading to the capture of an absent-without-leave mercenary soldier.

His head, Slawa puts his hands on his head, that terrible tightness above the eyes, in the back, the head could be breached in so many manly ways! Up the nose, through the mouth, just above the eyes; there are tender spots, too, at the back of the neck and in all of them ice picks, he thinks, are being driven with great force. Why is a head so unprotected? Surely the head shouldn't harbor the soft, fleshy parts; wouldn't it make more sense? Evolutionary-wise the eyes should be on the back of the hands, ears on knees, and mouth near the stomach. That way the brain could stay safe, inside an impenetrable, virtually impenetrable, skull. But the Intelligent Designer must have known what he was doing, because when push comes to shove, one chooses another neural circuit. Or rather, one's head does it for one. And that is totally cool!

Oh, he almost forgot. Now he no longer believes in the Intelligent Designer unless his name is Allah, his name be praised! He touches the Koran in his pocket. Not sad, no, not even lonely. He has his cloud of friendly flies, after all, since Bocar is gone he no longer wears the sandalwood cologne. Something Bocar had said comes back to him. If Bocar disappears, Slawa can find the answer in Bocar's box. He goes back.

Inside the box is a note.

my friend, if you are opening this box it is because I am gone I am feeling it is enough for your country, if you agree with me I will ask you to do this in my name, as it is my tribute. by the time of this I am not here... in the phial is the substance if you can find method of disbursement if you are willing, must be air-borne, additionall, to firstly inject yourself with antidote vaccination for your safety, my friend. and to follow, is the recipe and instruction manual to manufacture the time bomb, if you will be willing to make this and place in subway beneath seat, as the subway moves so does the contents of the time bomb upon detonation make sure you are far away in another state or continent if possible. I love you my friend, praised be the name of Allah.

A vial of some kind of deadly powder and the instructions for how to make a time bomb. Poor kid, Slawa thinks, does he really think this stuff would work?

Bocar was right: there were boys like him all over the planet who were being bought and sold, cannon fodder for a war being fought in countries where people did not have the same beliefs – did not have any political beliefs, only religious ones – did not want a war, so that the nimble fat men with their sheen of expensive butters and pomades, the businessmen of the USA, would get rich. How many years have gone by, could these men not understand nor see how much they – and their country – is hated?

The pale pink tips of his fingers... the color of his skin. Slawa tries to recreate Bocar in his head, it is no use. The kid vanishes into time, swallowed up by the days.

All the things Bocar had told him, these things had never mattered to him, he had listened, sure, but not really paid attention and now he wished he had recorded them. Bocar's life.

There had been a time – but how long, three years? – when Bocar lived in a village with his mother and father, there were other children, brothers and sisters, his parents loved him. And there was the sand and the water hole and the tasty goat milk.

And then one day they were gone, all dead. They told Bocar, "It was the government," and others said, "It was the rebels," and then, later, they said it was merely gangster robbers, but one thing was certain, whoever had done it had guns, weapons, made by the US and sold by the US, and they knew that because that was where all three sides got their weapons. Finally he went with the rebels. They taught him how to make bombs: it was easy enough, they said, there were instructions on the computer and the ingredients: US plastics, US fertilizer, US switches – could be found everywhere, even when there was nothing to eat.

He had learned to make bombs as a kid – all types of arsenals – which was how he had gone deaf… Learned to understand English through reading but because he couldn't hear it he had appalling pronunciation… so bad because he put the emphasis on the wrong syllable. In other words, syllable was sil-LAB-ul.

Then the Rebels mysteriously became the Government.

But once the rebels were the government, they no longer seemed to care that he – and his friends, or all the other young people who were poor, desperately poor and without any real family – were put onto the slave planes. Some were going to be workers in Nature's Caul where the rich people lived, in order to make beds or iron underpants.

But mostly they were going off to serve as soldiers in the army, paid for by rich people who did not want their American sons to have to serve. He had read, over the years, some political theory. And the rebels had taught him that Communism was bad. But no one had said Capitalism was good. How much worse could Communism have been for him than Capitalism? He would have been screwed under any system.

Shouldn't Slawa do what Bocar had asked? At least in this fashion he would bring attention to Bocar's plight and that of so many others. He has to do what Bocar said, so that Bocar will never be forgotten.

He removes the hypodermic needle, takes off the cap of the tube marked antidote-vaccine, sucks most of it up through the needle and injects it near his hip, as suggested. This way he will have enough time to do his job; it will last as long as it takes, although he knows then he will be out of time. The stuff, oily, burns and stings as it enters, then he is hot and prickly, nothing matters to him much any more.

But how is he to spread the powder? It's supposed to be transmitted through air. What will disseminate the powder through the air? How can a powder become airborne?

His flies. Yes. A drop of honey added to the white stuff and he goes out, carrying the sandalwood cologne. Then on the street he opens the lid. The first fly joyfully leaves his shoulder to have a taste.

Poor fly, they all trust him, there is only room for one at a time. Now the first emerges, white powder on black oversized legs. Slawa gives the air a spritz of sandalwood and the fly angrily buzzes off, puzzled and betrayed. Thus the first fly flies away:

"Like a long-legged fly upon the water, he moves swiftly and is gone."
— William Butler Yeats

The others, though, are still on him. He walks quickly through the city. He stops in hospital lobbies, in movie theaters, in shops. Every few blocks lets another fly dip and feed and then, with feet nicely dusted he drives it away.

(9:11) His flies are dying like flies. As it is said, some die stuck to fly paper, some die under the swatter, some die happily feasting on garbage and - whoomph! - get sucked into sanitation truck and crushed, yet not before spreading and contaminating. For it had been decided, who shall live and who shall fly, and who shall die by hanging, poison or being snapped up by a dog all the days of THY life.

So it should be enough, he thinks, when all the powder and all the flies are gone. We shall see. Then on with the second part. At least, having taken the antidote, he is supposed to have enough time.

The results are so instantaneous and dramatic it is a shock. He has not even had time to contact the Press explaining the purpose of this; as he returns he can hear the ambulances and sees people doubled over on the sidewalks. More people, kind of... staggering, not many, no big deal but then as he walks he sees more and more: some have blood coming out of their eyes and mouths, some have fallen or sit with visible pustules beginning to bubble up on the faces and arms and legs, others now hunched in pools of excrement, bloodless, teeth chattering, some rip off clothing. A taxi veers out of control. The doors to buildings are being locked, some people trying to get in, others, out.

By evening reports are coming in on the hologramovision, though of course the hologramovision anchor-people do not wish to alarm the American people, the hospitals are filling with people, perhaps some sort of epidemic.

And by the following morning it is already too late. What the hell is the stuff? There are no more ambulances left – did the drivers become sick? But there are still sirens and overhead the roar of helicopters. A massive traffic jam, apparently people were trying to flee the city.

And already it is time for Part Two. He goes back to the Shoe Repair. Perhaps he can find at least one cat, to tell it goodbye. There are certain things there as well that he values, pictures and objects, he would like to smell and touch. But most of all there is the other thing Bocar has asked him to do.

The landlord has fixed a lock on the door: an eviction notice.

It doesn't matter, he knows the secret way to crawl in underground. He knows how to booby-trap the place. He bolts the door from the inside and piles up anything available against it.

Is that Bocar's hand holding his? He must be hallucinating, it is all so odd and he is getting more and more nervous; oh it is so wonderful to hold hands, no one could ever want more, or less; it is the same feeling he had when he put his forehead to Breakfast's, the dog would press his head against his and together they entered the yellow ring of light... He stands.

There is no Bocar. He is gone. He is dead or the equivalent. Perhaps there never was a Bocar, but he can't believe that. And yet he can't be certain. He had once told the boy, "Like you, one day I come home, my mother is gone. Father dead. By year two thousand and five, all old people in Moscow, they disappear. I don't know what happen. Once, a lot of old babushkas. My mother, after fifty-five, sixty, I never find her again. Who knows? But... that is my country." Everything has disappeared, is disappearing: mother, Julie, Bocar, Breakfast, even his own memory.

His cats are dying. Some are already dead. They have returned from their prowls to die at the letterbox. He knows there is nothing he can do. He is hardening, the shell of a newly molted crustacean becoming strong.

He stays up all night making the time bomb, which he wraps in plastic, ready to take along; he writes a note explaining that what will happen will be for Bocar. Not for anyone to read. But to leave behind.

It is odd to be so detached. He thinks of himself as a compassionate person who has been pushed to the very edge; it is the only way any changes can be made in the system. The system is designed for the rich to get richer. The system is designed to continue killing the poor and the meek. If there had been a way to target, say, those in government, those of the ruling class – those who ruled by virtue of having the most money! – he would have done so. There is no way, not one that he could see, other than what he had to do; is doing.

"Allah's will be done." He scribbles on the paper as he hears the banging upstairs. Probably he will be caught very soon. He would have liked to make hajj, at least once, before he dies or is sent to prison where he will die – but there is no way now.

"There is no god but Allah."

Upstairs the banging, the police? He grabs his stuff and the time bomb, goes out through the way he has come in, an underground passage through the nightclub into the subway tunnel. From there he picks his way, carefully, in the dark, staying far from the third rail. At the nearest station he pulls himself up onto the platform, just as a subway train is arriving. What luck; sometimes they don't come for an hour, even longer, and when they do the cars are packed, and so many on the platform there have been times when hundreds have been pushed by the others onto the tracks and were electrocuted.

How long will it take to walk home to what had once been his home? A day? Two days, sleeping somewhere on a roadside overnight? He has no food, no water – the air is sour, yeasty gray. He is weary now. After all, he was used to doing long enforced marches, he is from Russia, isn't he? Or... Anyway, he is used to long marches somewhere. Siberia? Siege of Leningrad? Does it matter?

In fifty billion years the sun will shrink to the size of a desk. The sun will be no bigger than a watch, then a thimble, a grain of rice. Then it will die. And on that grain of rice will be everything that ever was.

So much, he now sees, for which there had not been time. Yet he has done so very much! He has studied Gurdjieff; he has been a boxer, not pro, but without protection, no helmet, and, briefly, a pro wrestler. He has sold illegal vodka and he has for a year had his own cat circus. He has had a child. He has loved and been loved.

Slawa attaches the bomb with pink putty, far back under the subway seat. It looks and feels like an old wad of gum. Is that the whole device? Seems so little, something, some part, left off? He rummages in his pocket. Oh God, the fried finger stuck into the burnt ring. His daughter's finger, he is certain. Who else's could it be? He had given that ring to her. He thinks. From Russia. Once belonging to royalty. Let them be together, bomb and finger and time for eternity. He pushes the finger deep into the putty.

He is sure now that Bocar is dead. Bocar has told him, somehow. He has communicated from the Great Beyond. Bocar has told him the time bomb is so big it will have, as its ground zero, the subway car. Then will spread, slowly, out further and further. The timer is set to go off in forty-eight hours, to give him time, even though he knows there he can never really get away. He slaps the bomb in place, presses the starter and then at the next stop gets off the train.

23

When Julie wakes she has no clue where she is, or what has happened. For a moment she thinks she is back in her own bedroom, at home. It is only then that she realizes Sue Ellen is no longer with her. The moldering dampness is gone, yippee! She is so relieved, but where is Breakfast? Her mom?

Her mother is gone, and the dog, and Dyllis. They don't dare return to the campsite; Cliffort will be taken somewhere – it is against the law to be homeless; Julie will be hauled off to foster care. Julie wants her daddy.

"Cliffort," she says. "Do you think we're going the right way? I wish you could talk. I wish you could tell me who did this to you. Cliffort, I want to find my daddy."

He croaks something that sounds like, "Me, too," and nods, pointing to his throat. She thinks this means yes. They set out in silence, picking their way through rusted refrigerators, heaps of tires, past mounds of heavy-duty trash bags which had been tossed from cars or trucks, years ago, never collected… And with every minute, now that the moldering wet spot is gone, the boiling inside Julie grows worse. Now she goes on boiling, faster and faster, each cell exploding in turn, and she is in constant pain, not so awful but tiny, sharp and constant. But perhaps equally as terrible her skin is peeling in sheets, layer after layer, as it is being cooked, though no one could say where the heat was coming from except that in a sense her own body is burning itself up, as eventually so do all stars.

Dyllis is always so cheerful but now she is getting tired. And her lavender feather donkey grows weaker and weaker. Murielle has to keep removing their items from the panniers the donkey carries, but even that is no good, and emitting a sound that is a cross between a bray and a crow, it keels over – poor little thing, dead in the dirt, and the bright eyes of rats peep from dirt holes and pipes, only waiting politely for them to leave so they can begin a carrion feast.

Dyllis is also looking sickly; she darts behind refuse every few minutes to relieve herself. "You okay?" asks Murielle.

Dyllis shrugs. It is odd but she feels she is running out of words.

Both Murielle and Dyllis are thinking, is it cholera? Typhus or yellow fever? Whatever it is, Dyllis can't go on any more. She has only a few words to say. "I can't go on."

"But we must go on! Just a little further, we'll find somewhere to stop for the night." Murielle can't help her much, she has to carry Breakfast, it is too difficult for him to walk now on his tender, blistered pads.

"I'm sorry. Thank you, Mama. Where we going, Mama?"

"We're trying to get to your daddy's, poor doggy." In her fatigue, loveliness has come over her, she is kind, the dog wags its tail, how gently she carries him, cradling him in her arms.

"How far?" Breakfast asks.

"I don't know, I guess… it's gotta be, what, thirty miles away? We'll have to sleep somewhere, eventually, and keep walking in the morning, maybe we can go along the highway, don't worry, honey, Mama's in charge… Come, Dyllis, I think I see something."

In the darkness, ahead, is a fire, not too large… Rapists? Not too likely, there really aren't any men around capable of sex, let alone those who want to have it with a woman… Murderers? Perhaps, but then one speaks to her in such a polite tone, somehow… old-fashioned, courtly. "Ma'am?"

She coughs. "Hello… Mind if we join you?"

The people around the campfire shift where they squat or sit, looking nervous. "Ma'am? Any chance you got any work fer us?"

"Don't any of you have a job?"

The fire crackles gently. "Cain't find no work, nowhere, ma'am."

Derelicts, homeless people, crazies… who knows… they must look pretty terrible by now themselves. She takes Dyllis by the elbow, the others make room. "Sorry about the dirt, ma'am."

One has a guitar and is strumming a few unfamiliar notes. "'*I've been doing some hard travelin', this much I know...*'"

"My friend's sick and my dog needs some water. We're tired out and can't go on. The government bulldozed my home and they hunted us down." Murielle is weary, so weary, and though she hasn't eaten in what seems like days she has shown no signs of weight loss. Is it her metabolism, then? If only she could lose even five pounds, then she would be happy. Maybe she could exercise, do crunches, Pilates, yoga – but without any strength, how can she?

"I'm sure you're welcome to join us."

"It'd be a right pleasure, ma'am."

She sits next to Dyllis and is given a little dish and a bottle of Nature's Caul Morphew Valley Recycled Pure Export water. For a few minutes around the stinking rubber fire no one says anything. Then the man picks up his guitar again and another joins in, "'...Brother can you spare a dime?'"

"You know," says another man after a pause, "That little lady, she's got some kind of a ghost behind her, jes' a-floatin' there."

"Tha's right," says another, "mebbe we been out here too long, but I can see it too. Kinda... damp and gloomy, like."

Murielle knows nothing about any ghosts but at this remark a giant wet spot surrounds her and she is one with the wet spot.

It is so vivid, so real, that she begins to wipe herself off with her skirt, then rummages in her bag for one of the fancy towels she had bought on sale at the ZWiport Discount Outlet Mall and had the sense to take with her.

But the wet spot! It is scary. It is so sticky, so... gelatinous. It is as if she is far, far outside her body, up in the air, high above the planet, looking down at the stunted swirling seas and dusty continents, pink sand and black burning rubber tires. Or even higher, nothing but stars winking whitish blue phosphorescence in a sea of black emptiness. And someone screaming. What the heck, who is it? "Capitalist roader! Landowner. You no good. You eat and eat; I hungry all time."

"Oh no!" Murielle suddenly gets what Julie had always been blabbering about. "Now I've got to sleep on the wet spot!" She could have cried: the wet spot, she sees now, is the loneliest, meanest place in the world. "It's Sue Ellen!"

"You no even know my name, you calla me Sue Ellen, it Xie Yao Lin."

"Huh?"

"Yes, I Red Guard in Cultural Revolution, I turn in my neighbors, I turn in my teacher, I turn in my mother and when I find my father has used Little Red Book in toilet, I turn him in too! When I am student, twelve years of age, we go by train to Beijing, trip very long, train crowded, I no paying attention, I fall out window, hit head, die!" Xie Yao Lin's voice softens a bit. "Sometime I think, maybe I no fall, maybe I pushed, some girls, they maybe jealous, I am captain of squadron. But… anyway, it my own fault, my family not so good, I find Mother's Guoylin statues under floor, I smash and turn her in! These things of the corrupt past, we must move to future! Also she take extra food from place of work, she serving State Dinners, this wrong! I send her for re-education! 'Why, daughter, why?' Mother is crying, 'I only take food for you.' This not true, it wrong! Now your turn to learn. You know nothing! In China, first thing you say, 'Have you eaten?' You never ask *me* if I have eaten, you are land-owning family."

But, she's just a little girl! Xie Yao Lin, Murielle thinks, why are you bothering us?

"Hole through planet," Xie Yao Lin explains, "bad idea. Fell in. Little kids, we used to dig holes in ground and say, 'Let's dig all the way to USA!' Now I miss my mama, especially her dumplings."

Here and there as Cliffort and Julie walk hand-in-hand, bits of green are sprouting through the asphalt cracks. Rapid-growing weeds, maybe non-indigenous, or hybridized mutations. It is nice to see green things, however, even if the tendrils do claw at them, hooking into flesh, as they go by. As they get closer to the city, there are more and more homeless people at campfires. "We bin ta war with them torrorists for more n' eighty years now," says an old man.

"It's the darn President," says another. "He made an enemy of the country when he picked Robert Emmerling as GOP leader and Suki Fossing as Secretary of State."

"That's for sure," says the first. "And whaddaya think, the Mets going to make it to the finals this year?"

"Dyllis? Dyllis, are you okay?"

"I... I... I..." That is the last word Dyllis has left, and it is a short one. Then she dies.

It is too late to help. Murielle would like to bury her, but her arms are too weak to dig even if she had a shovel. She would like to cry, but her eyes have no tears in them. Dry eye syndrome. With the dog, Murielle departs, hoping to find help. So it goes. Who mourns Dyllis? It made no difference. Dyllis is dead. Dead as a doornail? Doorknob? Doorbell? Who knows.

Murielle forgets she wanted to find assistance in burying Dyllis. Murielle by now is miles away, at a different campfire, watching HDMTV. As always someone has one rigged up, somehow, to a generator or an engine. It occurs to Murielle that if she were alone, she could never make the slightest thing work; all of history, as far back as the Iron Age, even earlier, would be lost forever. No stainless steel, no cyclosporine, no telephone. There would be no hot and cold running fluids! Nor could she rub two sticks together to make a fire, nor repair an escalator, nor hunt with bow and arrow.

"Everything okay there, ma'am?"

Murielle shakes her head. She is being harangued once again by Xie Yao Lin, Little Miss-Know-It-All! Little Miss Red Guard is screaming at her, over and over, "You will be re-educated!" Her voice is the torment of a million flies. "You left your friend, she is dead! Now your beautiful decadent daughter is dying right this minute!"

"Who?" says Murielle.

"Number One daughter. You have no sons, you no good."

"What? Tahnee? What happened?"

"She dead, she no good. She go with men for money. She have baby in belly, no married. Had to be punished! You will be sent for re-education. You cow-demon!"

What is a cow-demon, anyway, Murielle wonders, watching the screen. A healthy blonde, fertile in appearance, announces in a superior tone, "Look around you. Doesn't this look so green? We are working to save the environment from Homeland ecO2-terrorism. We are working to keep it green. This is thanks to Bermese Pythion and Great Divide Petroleum Coconut edible jelly products. You can contribute by sending your money to PO Box 1128..."

"I don't know what this thing is but it sure is something," says one man.

"What are you talking about?" says Murielle.

"Ma'am? The big screen? We never seen nothing like it outside a motion pitcher house, and this one's got the craziest pitchers on it I ever did see."

She squints in disbelief. "Where are you fellows from, anyway?"

"Most of us... we lost our farms, dust bowl came and blew away our crops, an so the banks foreclosed –"

"What? Farms? Where?"

"Oklahoma, them parts."

"We thought we was heading for Californie," says another. "They say the oranges just fall from the trees."

"They say there's plenty of work out there," said the first. "But, I don't think this is the right place."

"What?" Murielle shakes her head. "You guys are nuts. California fell into the ocean years ago. You're in New Jersey."

"New Jersey! I don't understand. How'd we get in New Jersey?"

"That's east, ain't it?" says the first, taking out his guitar and beginning to strum. "We been traveling a long time. What year is it, anyway?"

"What year do you think it is?" says Murielle suspiciously.

"Nineteen hundred and thirty-three, thereabouts, I reckon," he says, and begins to sing while he plays, "'*This land is your land, this land is my land —*'"

The hologramovision blares in the background. "Looking at the five-day forecast, Monday there's a chance of snow, temperatures in the mid-twenties to low thirties, according to the Doppler radar. Tuesday, a beautiful day, folks, we're looking at ninety-degree temperatures, no humidity, get out your golf clubs and tennis racquets!"

Over the voice of the weatherman, the others join in, their voices cracking, out-of-practice, "'*From California, to the New York Island, from the Gulf Stream waters, to the redwood forest — this land was made for you and me.*'"

"Hey, ma'am, would you get your damn dawg offen me?" At the campfire the dog, normally very shy in public, begins to talk. Perhaps it is the fire, surrounded by glowing eyes; there is something left in him of the wild, after all. Who knows what genes have been incorporated in the lab to create him, there are still the genes of some distant ancestor who lurks just outside the outskirts of warmth, hoping for a bone or bit of fat and not a kick.

"Teecher. Bruther," he pleads with the man. "Please let me fock you. Please let me fock leg."

"Get away from me, peckerhound."

"Aw, Mike, let the little feller get some action."

"Aw, awwright. What the."

But it has taken all the dog's energy to produce such complex sentences and, feeling a possible bowel movement coming on, he goes off in the darkness to hunch.

He misses Slawa desperately, more than he would ever have guessed. It was Slawa who had the patience to train him to speak; he had tried for so hard and so long, when the girls first got him, but they laughed at his moans and dull squeals, it was Slawa who stroked his throat to show him how to push out air to form language, who placed a pencil in his mouth to press his tongue into place; it was because of Slawa's patience that when at last the first few words burst out they had a faint Russian accent. In Breakfast's head is a warm yellow circle. And though Breakfast thinks only in shapes, he knows that Slawa, eventually, will find him.

It seems days later that Julie and Cliffort arrive at the tunnel. They have to rent oxygen masks and canisters at one end, to be returned at the other – if they make it. The tunnel is lined with cars, moving so slowly it takes days to get through; the drivers bring along extra liters of sugaroline so they can refuel, the windows are cranked up and the air-conditioning is on, it is a passage only for the very wealthy; those traveling by foot will die if they can't move quickly enough, oxygen used up, but it is sometimes difficult to move at all, with the crush of other pedestrians attempting to squeeze by.

Strangely, the limited oxygen, the occasional blasts of carbonized caramel methane-monoxide gases, makes Julie feel healthier – maybe whatever organism inhabiting her is dying. She has to admit now, she has not been this well since Sue Ellen was around, if only because the ghost's mildewed wetness made the exploding cells within her, fat drops in a frying pan, burst less frequently.

In the city they find the nearest subway. Julie thinks she remembers the way, get off at 42nd Street, Times Square. Neither had realized they would wait so long for the uptown train to arrive.

A full day passes, waiting on the platform. This is how people in India used to live! The garbled announcements coming from overhead, "For your safety, let the people off the train! We are sorry for the unavoidable delay!" Mostly recordings, the occasional real voice saying, "Due to a police investigation..." or, an hour later, "Because of a fire earlier this morning –"

When the train does arrive the car they get onto is strangely empty. The odor is peculiar, perhaps that is why others have chosen, mostly, not to be on this car; the smell is familiar, Julie can't place it, until she realizes… it reminds her of her daddy. And the smell to her is curiously comforting.

Cliffort removes his chewing gum, his last piece of Terrific Exploding Cyclone Shock Strawberry Trouble Whammy Bubble Gum (a non-edible chewing product from Condé-Bertlesman!).

He has been chewing it for days, he sticks it under the seat, there is already a huge lump there, bumpy and hard. He sticks his piece on top; for some reason this strikes him as amusing. Gum on top of gum. Eventually the whole train will be a sticky rubber tomb.

"Watch the closing doors! If you see a suspicious object, report it! The next stop is…" There is a hissing noise, it sounds like it's coming from somewhere on their car.

Between stations, a woman in their car jumps up and yells. "No, no, no!" Then she runs to the doors between the cars and bolts. This is unusual, but only a little bit. The passengers shake their heads; another New York nut.

The train stops. The lights flicker, then go out. The pre-recorded announcement, "We apologize for the unavoidable delay," is followed by that of the conductor saying, "Folks, we have a sick passenger on the train –" The hissing becomes a shrill whine, similar to the sounds once made by cicadas, only nobody now knows that. The conductor speaks again. "Due to an ongoing police investigation –"

"So irritating!" Julie mutters.

Cliffort thinks it is coming from underneath the seat. He reaches down. No, it is only the big wad of gum, topped with that of his own. Strange, though, that the sound is so close. Still the train does not move, then, slowly the lights flicker on, they seem to be making progress. It lurches forward again.

Beneath the seat, the time bomb makes a sound like a heavily breathing man. Then a series of musical notes, the chord of D and then of G. The train is again moving! And in that time bomb is time, all the time in the world, all the time lost and wasted and the time that has been used. The time of a hot summer afternoon in 1898 in the Midwest when the green leaves snore on the tender branches and in a nearby office a young man looks out the window wishing he was at Lake Will O' The Woods. The children's laughter floats from the cool water, higher and higher into the atmosphere until it disappears but it is not gone. It is only somewhere else in time.

Time spins out of the canister in loopy curls, baked flat, a sheet cake topped with butter cream frosting and edible violets for Betty Smiekowski's twelfth birthday party in 1947. That takes forty minutes of time. 1969, three hours it takes two guys to walk two miles down the highway to Max Yasgur's farm; they had to leave the Karmen Gia behind when the road closed, bumper-to-bumper traffic, it's a slow walk, smoking a joint, talking to so many groovy chicks, digging the scene.

And the subway car fills with time, hanging in ropey coils, the time spent while four men in poplin raincoats and gray hats wait for the bus to Paddington Station in 1956. The time it takes in 1914 for the smell of orange blossoms to reach the nostrils of the last wild Carolina parakeet.

My gosh! Julie remembers Greg. She has been carrying him around all this time in that vintage matchbox. She slides open the top to give him a crumb and clean the place.

Greg's legs are sticking up. She touches him and he is a dry husk. Oh, no! "Greg? Greg?" She turns him over, he is dead, maybe it's not Greg? But there's that garnet chip of red on his back, as if someone has embedded a little chunk of apple. Is it that she forgot to feed and water him or was it simply the end of his natural life? She will never know.

It is time they are out of but time comes out in a ribbon of chalk. It takes time.

The length of time a bubble of air takes to be trapped in a cube of water turning to ice. And – aw, just look – the passengers smile, here is Ralph Waldo Emerson, standing at his cherry writing desk, so proud, a heron on one leg holding a quill pen. What a time we are having! We're all together now and the pollarded lime trees blossom at Yasnaya

Polyana, while – oh, oh! – here is the Minotaur sobbing and grunting in the back of his sour cave. It is the time it took – though no one knew who it is, or why it needs to take time. They are absorbed in time and then it is quiet.

Slowly it spreads, so slowly, so quickly, from the first subway car to the next, squeezing through a crack in a door or sliding through the molecules of the glass, and drifts across the platform, first one and then the next fall silent, and in time it floats up the stairs leading to the street, sometimes with an odor of mustard gas in the trenches, Ardennes, 1916, sometimes of fresh crushed rosemary in a garden in 1643 near Stratford-Upon-Avon. Or it might be the color one minute after the sun sets, when the sky changes from violet to bitter blue.

Breakfast sits pensively, alone now, at the edge of the fire, the flicking blades of light. "Pee-pul," says the dog in a mournful voice, "peepul, stay away from the brown acid. Stay away from the brown acid."

And the people on the subway car are still except for the occasional sigh or shuffle of shoes. One or two may have coughed; one says, in a small voice, "Mama?" but that is all.

The world is the same as always, only a little worse. Life as we know it is not the same, although it is pretty darn similar! Besides, who really knows how it was before? Nobody alive can remember.

They Is Us

With much gratitude, thanks and acknowledgement to:

Phyllis Janowitz for scraping my crumbs back together more often than is humanly possible; Tom Bell; Paige Powell; Ellen Salpeter; Susan (Miss Dingo Dog Girl Supreme) Ward; Dr. David Janowitz, you rule; Julian Janowitz; Dr. Laurie Goldstein; Dr. Larry Rosenthal xoxo; Dr. Fred Brandt, The Best Dermatologist in the World; Tim Hunt, my wonderful husband; Willow Hunt; David Meitus and Angela Westwater; Anthony and Anne d'Offay; Yuri Avvakumov and Alyona Kirtsova; Christian Wenaweser; Steven Greenberg for that swell party! Vivienne Tam with admiration; Diane Blell for her enthusiasm and kindness; Rob Wynn and Charles Ruas; Jane Kaplowitz Rosenblum; David Frank; Eames (ya hunk o' burnin' love) Yates; Nicole Miller; Luc and Marianne Coorevits; Betsy Lerner; Richard Weisman; Nic and Christa Iljine; Cristina Zilkha; Carlos Picon and Andrew Kepler; Susan Hunt; Rob Clark; Amy Snowdon; my wonderful Anne Sharkey and Philip Sharkey; thanks to Heather Smith; also thanks to Eric Newell and Glen Albin; Xian Yun; High Voltage; Dr. Steve Wexner; John Deyab; Paul Steele; John Reinholt; Brady Oman

And in Memory Of:
Ahmet Ertegun; Baird Jones; Muriel Guccione; Camilla McGrath; Ismail Merchant; Robert Rosenblum; Stephen Sprouse; Gregory Hines; Glyn Boyd-Harte; Dave Sharkey; Wallis Hunt; Ira Wexner;

And to all the one million who rejected me and this book but most of all with endless infinite gratitude to Nick Fox, Fay Weldon and Scott Pack. You magnificent genius thing, you.

Tama Janowitz

The Author and Publisher are extremely grateful for the kind permission to reproduce the following images:

Page 11 © Angelo Cavalli/ Getty Images
Page 38 © C Squared Studios/ Getty Images
Page 43 © Thomas Northcut/ Getty Images
Page 68 © Shoji Yoshida/ Getty Images
Page 86 and 198 © Joel Sartore/ Getty Images
Page 94 © Tom Brakefield/ Getty Images
Page 110 © John Foxx/ Getty Images
Page 116 (left image) © Diamond Sky Images/ Getty Images
Page 116 (right image) © John Foxx/ Getty Images
Page 146 © Nicholas Eveleigh/ Getty Images
Page 152 © Jonathan Kitchen/ Getty Images
Page 175 © C. Sherburne/PhotoLink/ Getty Images
Page 179 (left) © Livio Sinibaldi/ Getty Images
Page 179 (right) © Dorling Kindersley/ Getty Images
Page 195 © The Tennis Court Oath, 20th June 1789, 1791 (oil on canvas) After Jacques Louis David/ Getty Images
Page 246 © Pankaj & Insy Shah/ Getty Images
Page 273 © PHOTOGRAPH BY RORY DELL, CAMERA PRESS LONDON

Map on page 46 created by HL Studios (http://www.hlstudios.eu.com/)

Lonely Bob

by Willow Hunt

Bob lived alone, except for his dog.

After his dog died, Bob grew lonely.

Women came over.

They wanted to help.

Bob preferred

they not stay long.

They never did.

"Goodbye Bob. I'm going."

One day Bob had a thought.

He would get a new dog.

The dog grew large and rambunctious.

It knocked over objects.

His home became untidy.

It wasn't easy, but finally Bob got rid of him.

Bob was still lonely. But he realized things could always be worse.